Another Sky

JAYNE FROST

Editing: The Novel Fixer
&
ellie @ My Brother's Editor
Cover Design: Maria @ Steamy Designs, LLC
Proofing: Marla @ ProofingStyle
Inerior formating/Design: Champagne Book Design
Photographer: Lindee Robinson Photography
Models: Nick White/Alexis Susalla

For Victoria

To Linda –
Look up and find
your sky

xo Jorie Frost

Join my reader group on Facebook and become a VIP! You'll be the first to know about sales, giveaways, and Advance Reader Copies of the latest Jayne Frost books.

SIGN UP HERE: bit.ly/FrostFaves

Playlist

Preaching the End of the World—Chris Cornell

Black Hole Sun—Soundgarden

Alive—Pearl Jam

Say Hello 2 Heaven—Temple of the Dog

Four Rusted Horsed—Marilyn Manson

Bitches Broken Hearts—Billie Eilish

Blackbird—The Beatles

Let Her Go—Jasmine Thompson

The Crow and the Butterfly—Shinedown

Bulletproof Weeks—Matt Nathanson

Watch Over You—After Bridge

Live Forever—Oasis

Don't Let It Bring You Down—Annie Lennox

In My Life—The Beatles

Another Sky

Prologue

Miles

Six years ago—El Paso, Texas

PAIGE SHIFTED IN MY ARMS, AND I WAS INSTANTLY AWAKE. TIGHTENING MY grip on her waist, I held my breath.

One beat. Two. Five.

I didn't need to look at the glowing numbers on the clock to know it was close to dawn. Soon Paige would open her pretty green eyes, brush a kiss to my lips, and then disappear.

It was a pattern. *Our pattern.* For years we'd been doing it. Friends with benefits. Though, at this point, I couldn't really remember what the benefit was.

The sex, dumb fuck.

Not exactly true. Sex was the easy part. For both of us. The minute our band had signed our first contract, there was no shortage of ass. But by the time Damaged had reached superstar status, fucking strangers had lost its appeal. Paige was never that into it, anyway. And I was always into her.

What had started as a mutually satisfying arrangement now felt like some form of medieval torture.

For me at least.

There was a silver lining. Paige loved me. I never doubted it. But she made it clear—she wasn't interested in a relationship.

Relationships never work out. And it would kill me to lose you. I can't lose you, Miles.

It sounded good at the time. Until it didn't. Until the ache that settled within me when she left my bed far outweighed the pleasure of anything we did in the dark.

"Stay," I said as she brushed a kiss to the hard planes of my chest.

When she hesitated, I thought today might be the day. That

moment when the dark and the light finally met. Melting into the pillow, I fisted the back of her hair as her soft lips glided up my neck.

"I can't."

My heart stalled, her words slicing through me the way they did every time she said them. Swallowing my protest, I let the pain sink deep, all the way to my bones. And in that moment, it didn't matter that she was Paige Dawson and I was Miles Cooper. That we, together, were half of the hottest band in the country. Because this, whatever we had, was more important than Damaged.

Yeah, I'd made promises. Before we even began I'd vowed to never let anything jeopardize our friendship, and more importantly, the music. But all that flew out the window at the thought of facing another dawn without her.

Today might not be the day when light and dark reconciled, but Paige would give me some fucking answers.

Propping up on my elbow when she climbed to her feet, I flipped the switch next to the bed, flooding the suite with harsh light.

"Tell me why."

She sighed, tipping forward and snatching her jeans from the floor. "I already did."

Catching her wrist, I tugged her back down to the bed. "Not good enough. Things have changed. *We've* changed." My thumb skated over her pulse point, and I felt her racing heart. "I've known you since you were fourteen. I love you, Paige."

The truth had a beat of its own. A life. A cadence. I was *in love* with her. Always had been, if I were honest. And though I was relatively certain that she wasn't looking for something else—something better—the door was open. Either we closed it for good and committed to each other once and for all or we moved on.

A deep crease formed between her brows as she searched my face. "I love you too."

The desolation threading her tone was enough to break me. And for a minute we just sat there and let it press in on us. Instead of letting her go when she twisted free of my hold and stood up, I followed.

"I'm not your daddy, Paige." I loomed over her, willing her to look at me. "You're not going to wake up one day and find me gone."

She swayed as if I'd slapped her, then sank into the overstuffed chair where I'd been waiting for her when she'd slipped into the room last night. Her fingers skated over the cushion as if she remembered all the things we'd done in that very spot. "I'm not worried you're like my father, Miles." Lifting her chin, she met my gaze with sad eyes. "But that *I* am."

The air punched from my lungs, and I took a step back. Then another. And all the while she watched me with an inscrutable expression.

Paige was nothing if not honest. And I wondered how many times it had crossed her mind, this distant future where she left me behind for another man.

But hey, we could still be friends, right?

I eased onto the side of the bed. "So I guess this is it, huh, sunshine?"

She didn't say anything, just dressed while I stared at the patterns on the carpet.

I thought she might simply leave. That was her way.

But then she was in front of me, lithe fingers tangling in my hair. I willed myself not to lean into her touch.

After a moment, she whispered, "Have I ever told you the story about the sun?" I shook my head, and she inhaled a slow, controlled breath. "They say the sun loves the moon so much, she dies every night just so he can shine." As she smiled down at me, a tear rolled off the end of her nose. "You're my moon."

My stomach cratered, and my arms encircled her waist. She let me hold her for a moment, then pressed a kiss to the top of my head and spun for the door. "I'll see you at sound check, okay?"

Pausing in the foyer with her hand on the brass knob, she waited for my reply. My assurance.

"Sure thing."

As she slipped out the door, shafts of morning light spilled onto the plush carpet. We'd finally met the dawn together. But in the end, Paige was right. I was the moon, and she was the sun. And we were never meant to share the same sky.

xiv | JAYNE FROST

The door to the bus opened with a loud hiss, and I groaned. I'd managed to avoid Paige all day, even ducking out of the post-show festivities early. All I wanted to do was nurse my bottle of Jack in peace and lick my wounds. Alone. But I guess that was too much to ask.

"Miles…Are you in here?"

Paige's voice floated to my bunk, her words slow and maybe a bit slurred. She'd been drinking too. Which was rare. Maybe she regretted our last conversation as much as I did. More likely though, she was just celebrating.

Pressing my lips together, I hoped she'd get the hint and go away. Because even if we ended up tangled in the sheets, the euphoria would be short-lived.

Tonight was our final show of the tour. And tomorrow we'd be home.

On the road, we could pretend. But whatever we had and whatever we were, it didn't exist in Austin. It never had.

Footfalls echoed off the metal walls, and then I felt her on the other side of the flimsy curtain. "Miles?"

Flipping onto my back, I stared at the ceiling. "Yeah?"

"Do you want some company?"

Anger flashed red hot, boiling my blood, and I ripped the curtain back. Meeting Paige's wide eyes with a stone-cold stare, I waited a beat before sliding my attention to the front of the bus. "Why? Did you bring someone who's looking for a good time?"

It took a second for her to catch on. Then the column of her throat bobbed, and she swallowed hard. "You're mad."

I was. So fucking mad I could barely look at her. But I did anyway. And she was so beautiful. Hair all mussed and dark makeup smudging her eyes. My gaze fell to her mouth, stained crimson to match her hair.

Suddenly, she was sixteen again, standing outside her mama's house with tears rolling down her cheeks because the douchebag who'd swiped her cherry hadn't even bothered to show up to take her to our junior prom.

I was there, though. Ready to stand in. To stand up. To fill the space. Because that's what friends did.

And the next day, I broke my hand when I beat the shit out of the guy who should have been there.

For you R. S. who pinned on a badge

And gave of your life, no, taken away

Your never faltered, nor swayed

You failed not, your courage not skewed

So others could live the day anew

The cold we did brave, bitter and frost

We wanted to try, no matter the cost

For we wanted you here and try we did do

The sacrifice of blood, spilled and given

The tears have been shed, all for you

Thank you dear Robert, for all you did do

James R. Howell

(For all those who were there,
I dedicate this poem and this story)

Evening and morning and at noon
I utter my complaint and moan,
and he hears my voice.
He redeems my soul in safety
from the battle that I wage,
for many are arrayed against me.

Psalm 55:17, 18

To view pictures / crime scene photos visit
"Echoes of Shannon Street"
on
Facebook and YouTube.

Table of Contents

Prologue

In many ways, this is a story of colors. Black, white and blue. It is a story that remains controversial, and one that has been examined through many different prisms, with many different conclusions.

The characters are real. They are men, who walked on both sides of the law, yet they hold a common frailty in this event - they were people drawn into a violent situation over which they had little or no control, and no personal power - whether internal or external - to stop.

Sadly, and without making excuses for him, that includes the harbinger of the event, a man once considered a kind and eccentric neighbor, but who on January 11, 1983, instigated a vicious execution of a police officer.

Despite the fact that during the sixties and seventies Memphis saw far less racial violence than other larger cities such as Detroit and New York, it has long suffered the stain of perceived racial oppression, with the assassination of Martin Luther King Jr. on the terrace of the Lorraine Motel often set down as a cornerstone of proof.

But the city's history, in terms of both race relations and police-community relations is a long and sometimes violent one.

During the Civil War, a battle fought just north of Memphis, at Fort Pillow, saw black Union troops defeated or massacred, depending on whose book you read, by Confederate soldiers.

The Confederate commander, General Nathan Bedford Forrest, a Memphis native, would later make history as the founder of the Klu Klux Klan.

One of the more famous race riots, in the history of the United States, which was known simply as the Memphis Riot, occurred just after the Civil War. In 1866, white mobs marched through Memphis targeting blacks and black owned property. The incident that allegedly sparked the riot was the attempted arrest of a black soldier by white policemen which resulted in one policeman being killed. The riot started soon after and lasted for three days and left several whites and over forty blacks dead.

In March of 1968, the city sanitation workers in Memphis went out on strike and Martin Luther King Jr. came to Memphis to support the workers. On the 28th of March, King led a march that began at the Clayborn Temple and was to end at City Hall. The march quickly turned into a small riot when black radicals, known as the Invaders, began fighting police. Police responded with night-sticks and tear gas. One person was killed, sixty were injured and two hundred and eighty people were arrested.

Four thousand National Guard troops moved into the city and a 7:00pm curfew was put into place. The following day, three hundred marchers left Clayborn Temple for City Hall, escorted by armored personnel carriers and jeeps. By April 1st, the curfew had been lifted and the troops left the city the following day.

King returned to Memphis, in hopes of leading a more peaceful march, to show his support for the sanitation workers. On the evening of April 4th, 1968 King was shot and killed by a white man, James Earl Ray, as King stood on the balcony of the Lorraine Motel.

Radical groups like the Invaders and Black Panthers pointed to the King killing as proof that non violent protest did not work. In 1969 the Invaders changed their name to the National

Committee to Combat Fascism and claimed a large membership in Memphis. A house the group was using as a party headquarters was destroyed by a bomb. The group blamed the Counter Intelligence Unit of the Memphis Police Department.

In January of 1971, the group moved several families into vacant apartments of the Texas Court Apartments located in south Memphis. The apartments were government housing managed by the Memphis Housing Authority. A tense confrontation between the armed group and Memphis Police ended with the members surrendering to police.

The Invaders soon became a full Black Panther Party chapter. Memphis, in fact, became the headquarters for the state chapter of the Black Panther Party.

By 1983, the streets were quieter, and the city had made the adjustment to an integrated government with many prominent black elected officials.

Beale Street, in downtown Memphis, was about to come into its own through a massive redevelopment plan that would light up the abandoned blues club area, bringing renewed interest in the music of W. C. Handy, Rufus Thomas and B.B. King.

Sun Studios would gain new prominence, and six years after his death, the Elvis Presley family would continue to receive millions of tourists into his Graceland home. Other celebrities from the city would emerge: Kathy Bates, Tim McCarver, Cybill Shepard, Shelby Foote, Morgan Freeman, and a reverend named Al Green

Memphis would boast of having the largest artesian well water system in the world and home to the biggest distribution center with the Fed Ex complex. It would also take pride in the fact that its zoo had once housed Volney, the roaring lion at the beginning of all the old MGM movies.

But even with the budding revitalization, things still continued to be seen in black and white, sometimes even black versus, white. City wide arguments would continue over such things as the statue of Nathan Bedford Forrest and a small memorial patch of green on the bluff called Confederate Park. The very history of Memphis was threatened by this us and them mentality.

Racial tensions remained just under the surface throughout most of the city, but in some places, it began to simmer.

At the forefront stood the Memphis Police Department. And for many, it did not matter if the police officer was black or white - he was simply blue, and represented the status quo establishment.

Some areas of Memphis were actually considered anti-police. In other neighborhoods, it was only one or two families that seemed to have it in for the police or vice versa.

Police officers in every precinct knew who needed watching, who was stealing, or who would back-shoot you, if given the chance. The bad guys came in all shapes, sizes and colors. Each knew the rules when it came to dealing with the police. If you fought the police, the police would fight back. If you pulled a knife or fired a gun at the police, then you could expect to get shot.

In the 1970's, a fairly large group of motorcycle gang members from Hell's Angels or Outlaws, (depending on which police officer told you the story), rode into town and started trouble at a bar. A few officers made the scene and were promptly assaulted and thrown out of the bar. The police returned shortly, much better prepared the second time, and mopped up the bar with the gang members.

After the cyclists got out of the hospital, they left Memphis never to return in any sizable number. Those that did seemed to have conducted themselves in a manner that could only be described as angelic.

For a cop, it was a tough city and you had to be tough to work it.

In January 1983, as the city was awakening to a new year, some citizens reading through blood shot eyes, learned of the events of the past few days and nights. The Commercial Appeal, one of two newspapers in Memphis, carried the following stories.

In West Memphis, Arkansas Incumbent Mayor Joyce Ferguson had lost her bid for another term in office. Ferguson had been the first elected female to hold the office of Mayor in West Memphis.

In sports, the University of Tennessee was beaten by Iowa in the Peach Bowl, Vandy lost to the Air Force Academy in the Hall of Fame Game, and Arkansas beat Florida down in Houston.

In the coming days the local newspapers would tell of the grand opening of Gold's Gym at the East Gate Shopping Center set for the 14th of January.

Scott Appliance was advertising 19 inch color T.V.'s for $289.00 and large capacity microwaves for $249.99.

Money rates were 11% to 11 ½% for prime.

Fox Gate Lincoln Mercury was advertising a 1983, Grand Marquis, at $10,887.

The Memphis State cheerleaders and pom-pom squads both took first place in national competition.

Ironically, the January 11th edition of the *Commercial Appeal* carried an editorial about the dual community in Memphis. The writer spoke of a split along racial lines. Within hours the split would be far larger than anyone could imagine.

A press conference held by newly elected Mayor Richard "Dick" Hackett and newly appointed Police Director John Holt was featured. It was announced that the department would begin hiring more officers in an attempt to increase the size of the departments complement, which currently stood at 1,225 sworn officers. Of this 1,225 man force, 568 were in uniform patrol, assigned to four precincts.

The previous year had been one of loss for the Memphis Police Department. On January 14th, 1982 Officer Larry Childress was ambushed and shot to death on a snow covered lawn at an upscale house in East Memphis after having recently transferred to the East from the North Precinct. An officer, who worked with him, at the North Precinct, would later relate a conversation he had with Childress on the day before Childress took up his new assignment. They briefly commiserated about their time together and when asked why he was leaving, Childress replied, that he wanted "to go out East where it was quieter".

On December 31st, 1982, twenty-two year old North Precinct officer John Wesley Sykes and his training partner, Charlotte Creasy, had been shooting radar on Austin Peay Highway. Seeing a car driving erratically, they attempted to stop it. When the car failed to stop a chase ensued. The pursuit went into darkened, John F. Kennedy Park. A single, one in a million gunshot fired from the speeding suspect car found its mark striking Sykes in the neck. He would die hours later. Sykes had been a police officer for just nine days.

The shock of Sykes' death and the grief of his funeral would still be fresh on every officer's mind when the sun rose on January 11th, 1983.

That day started like any other winter's day, the routine of just another frigid day in Memphis. As the hours of day dissolved into the shadows of a moonlit night, the quiet of the city only reinforced feelings of normalcy.

At 9:00 p.m. two police officers were called to a little, darkened street in north Memphis to investigate a routine complaint.

At 9:10 p.m., everything came to a standstill. For the next thirty hours, officers of the Memphis Police Department would hold their collective breath.

When it ended, eight men would be dead, one of them a police officer.

Twenty-five years later, the memory of the event has not faded. Few officers will speak of it and those that do speak in hushed tones. The memory is one filled with the echoes of screams, fitful cries for help that would go unanswered. The echoes come most often when they sit in the dark, with their minds clouded in drink.

It would be a tragic event, one still not equaled in this country, an incident that would see the greatest number of suspects to ever die in a non-riotous, local police action.

The name of the little darkened street was Shannon.

The police officer's name was Robert Sterling Hester.

CHAPTER 1
Legend of the Greasy Man

Fall, 1982 - Hyde Park Community / North Memphis
Flash point?-Legend of the Greasy Man

Her steps were slow, if not slightly unsteady, as she maneuvered around and over the numerous cracks in the sidewalk. Her left arm was wrapped tightly around a grocery bag while her right shoulder balanced the strap of her purse. The weight of the bag seemed to grow heavier with each step and she almost regretted not calling her son to pick her up at Wong's Grocery. Oh well, I have carried far heavier burdens, she thought, as she shifted the weight of the bag to her right arm.

She was approaching sixty and the first tint of gray had just begun to appear in her jet black hair. Everyone who met her for the first time always mistook her for a much younger woman. It was a mistake that she never minded people making. Her husband had been dead now six years, struck down by diabetes, but not before losing a leg and his eye sight. He had died a hard death but it had been no different from the harsh life he had endured. He had served his country in a segregated army during World War II and lost a brother to the Klan in 1948.

They had raised eight kids and not one had ever gotten into a lick of trouble. Her youngest son lived two houses down from her and one of her eldest daughters lived in one of the new subdivisions in Raleigh, just a fifteen minute drive from her house. The other children had moved from Memphis. Her son and his wife had been such a help to her, especially after the lost of her husband, but the void from his passing was one that none of her kids could ever fill.

She was supposed to fix dinner for her son and his family tonight as she ran through the dinner preparations in her mind. In the distance her porch light beckoned her home as she sighed with relief.

It waited in the shadows of a nearby alley. The large, elongated face of the beast was covered in long, dark brown, matted hair. Four inch simian incisors protruded from its mouth. The hair covered hands bore fingers that were thick and much longer than any human. It watched the woman pass by on the sidewalk. Its eyes blinked once as its head turned slowly scanning the empty street. It stepped out slowly and began to move silently from the safety of the darkness as it stalked the female from behind. It leered in anticipation as its long silent strides brought it closer and closer to the small figure shuffling slowly along the sidewalk. It began to flex its fingers as it broke into a hurried trot.

She half turned her head to the sound of the rapid footsteps behind her. Her aging eyes picked up the outline of the large figure as it descended with arms straining to reach her. She screamed loudly as she stumbled backwards. Her heel caught the uneven edge of the sidewalk as she lost her grip on the bag. The groceries scattered across the walk and into the road as she

Come near Paige again, and I'll end you.

Totally worth it.

My irritation fled along with the memory, and I swung my legs over the side of the bunk. Molding my hands to her hips, I pulled her between my knees and looked into her pale green eyes. "What am I going to do with you?"

Dragging her fingers through my hair, she smiled. "Love me."

I *did* love her. I'd always loved her. Didn't she know that?

Cupping her ass, I dipped my head and pressed a kiss to the exposed skin below her belly button. She tasted so good. Like fine whiskey. Smooth and warm, with just the right amount of burn.

Despite being a little drunk, I managed to slide her zipper down with my teeth. Hooking my thumbs in her belt loops for leverage, I gave the denim a tug, but got nowhere. "Do you paint these on, or what?"

Before I could pull her into the bunk and finish the job, her fingers closed around mine, halting my progress. "Someone's coming."

Muffled voices drifted through the open window. Tori's and Rhenn's. Our best friends. Bandmates. The two people we shouldn't have to hide from.

Tightening my grip, I held her gaze. "So?"

A beat of silence, and then she gave me a nudge, stumbling out of my hold a second before Tori topped the stairs, Rhenn close on her heels.

"There y'all are," Tori said brightly. "We were looking for you."

Scowling at the happy couple, I grumbled, "Well, I guess you found us."

Rhenn cocked his head, brown eyes darting from Paige to me. "What's going on?"

"Nothing," Paige answered, a little too quickly.

I could see the wheels turning in Rhenn's head, but before he could comment, Rusty, our driver, lumbered up the stairs.

Scratching his thinning mop of orange hair, he shifted his feet. "We're all set," he announced. "Y'all ready to roll?"

Rhenn clapped Rusty on the back, exuberant at the prospect of heading home. "Absolutely. Let's get out of here."

While the two men put their heads together to discuss the route, Tori foraged around in the small cupboard where she kept her secret stash of sweets. "I'll make the sundaes," she chirped.

Once everyone was occupied, Paige shifted her focus back to me and smiled softly. "I'm sorry. I thought we'd have more time."

But we didn't. All we had were stolen moments. And that wasn't enough anymore. Retreating to my bunk, I picked up my pint of Jack and unscrewed the lid.

"I can come see you after we get on the road," Paige whispered, worrying her bottom lip. "After everyone's asleep."

A consolation prize. Awesome.

I took a long pull from the bottle. "I think you'd better stay in your own bunk tonight, sunshine."

Holding my breath, I waited for Paige to protest. To fight for me. For us. But she didn't. Instead, she tipped forward and brushed a lock of hair out of my eyes. "Okay. I'll see you in the morning."

It came out like a question, and I snorted, because, where was I going to go?

Hurt flashed across her features, and she made to pull away. At the last second, I caught her wrist and pressed a kiss to her palm. "Sleep tight, sunshine."

And then I rolled over, letting her hand slip from mine. For a long time, Paige didn't move...just stood there, her reflection framed in the moonlight pouring in from the small window in my bunk.

You're my moon.

The knot in my stomach unwound.

Paige may not have been able to give it all to me right now. But someday she would. We were bound together. Through music. And life. And love.

Her lips curved into a smile, as if she knew what I was thinking. That we'd be all right. Because this was bigger than us. Written in the stars. And there was no hurry. We had all the time in the world.

BREAKING NEWS

DAMAGED FRONT MAN, RHENN GRAYSON, AND LEAD GUITARIST, PAIGE DAWSON, PERISH IN FIERY BUS CRASH OUTSIDE FREDRICKSBURG, TEXAS.

Stonewall, Texas—Sources at the Gillespie County Sherriff's Department confirmed that an early morning crash on Highway 290 just outside of Fredericksburg claimed the lives of Damaged front man Rhenn Grayson, and lead guitarist Paige Dawson when a semi-truck crossed the median and hit the band's tour bus at a high rate of speed. Lead singer Tori Grayson and drummer Miles Cooper were airlifted to Brackenridge Hospital where they remain in critical condition.

Story Developing...

Chapter One

Miles

GRAVEL CRUNCHED UNDER THE TIRES AS MY TRUCK COASTED TO A STOP ON the shoulder of the two-lane highway. Cutting the engine, I sank against the leather upholstery and looked out at the open field.

And for a moment, the thin veil separating then and now slipped away, and it was six years ago.

On my back beneath the smoke-filled sky, I'd waited for death to claim me. To put an end to the pain.

I was sure it would.

But then I heard the voices. First Rhenn's—so faint it was nothing more than a whisper. And then Tori's.

But not Paige.

Never Paige.

Shifting my gaze to the passenger seat, I almost expected to find her there. But the space was empty. Except for the sealed bottle of Maker's Mark. Rich, amber liquid whispering promises of peace. Of oblivion.

Lies. All lies.

Because no matter what I drank or smoked or swallowed, peace eluded me. Tranquility had died in this field all those years ago. Crushed under the weight of twisted metal and drowned in the pouring rain.

Grimacing, I dug my fingers into the muscle on my thigh, right over the area where the bone had come through the skin. My leg had suffered the worst of the trauma. Broken femur. Dislocated knee cap. A spiral fracture to my tibia.

Maybe if I weren't a drummer, it wouldn't have mattered. But the injuries had silenced my beat. Sadly, there was no grave to mark its passing. No monument to the lost rhythm. Just this empty field.

I guess that's why I always ended up here. In the place where the music died. Right alongside my best friend and my best girl.

Blowing out a breath, I stashed the bottle in the inner pocket of my leather jacket. Two stints in the psychiatric ward at Millwood, and I knew better than to dance this close to the fire. But I didn't care. I wasn't planning on drinking it.

Throwing open the heavy door, I braced a hand on the steering wheel and slid off the seat, making sure to land on my good leg. I didn't bother with my cane. There was no need for pretense.

Not here.

As I waded into the dried brush, "Blackbird" blared from my phone's speaker. Tori. I'd lost track of how many times she'd called.

And yeah, I got it. She was concerned.

Less than twenty-four hours ago, we'd been on stage at Zilker Park, capping off the biggest rock festival Austin had ever seen. A Damaged reunion. One last hurrah for the fans. And closure for Tori and me.

Finally.

Except…nothing felt closed.

And as much as I wanted to, I couldn't talk to Tori about it. Not now.

She'd finally moved on from her grief. Fallen in love again. And in some strange way, that had brought us back together.

After the accident, we'd drifted apart. And that was a good thing. Something we'd needed to do. Because when we had been together, sharing the same space, it was like the sum of our losses was too big. All-consuming.

Knowing that Tori was out there in the world with a heart as heavy as mine had made my own burden a little easier to bear.

But now I felt the weight of it more acutely than I had in years. A fact I was determined to hide. So, I'd been avoiding her calls.

Reaching the far end of the field, I eased onto the soft ground beneath the burned-out shell of the elm tree where I'd found Rhenn and lost him minutes later.

"Hey, buddy. Guess you know about that gig last night." My voice fell to a whisper, and I looked down. "Of course you do." Squeezing my eyes shut, I blew out a staggered breath and pulled the whiskey from my pocket. "It was weird, you know, not having y'all there to celebrate. So I thought I'd bring the celebration to you."

Twisting off the cap with shaky fingers, I fought the urge to bring the bottle to my lips.

One drink. What could it hurt?

As I pondered throwing away years of sobriety, a gust of wind blew across the field, kicking up topsoil and dust.

Chuckling, I rubbed the sand out of my eyes. "Message received. You don't have to get all testy about it."

I wasn't an alcoholic. Or a drug addict. But booze was still a slippery slope. A year after the crash, I'd landed in rehab from an "accidental" overdose that wasn't an accident at all. It only took the counselor a week to get to the root of my real problem. Soul-crushing depression—the clinical kind.

They'd fixed me up with medication that kept the dark clouds at bay. Mostly. But I never told anyone about my diagnosis. Somehow it was easier to let people believe I was a drunk.

With a sigh, I turned the bottle upside down. "Miss you, bro." After the last drop of liquor soaked into the hallowed ground, I hauled to my feet. "See you on the other side."

Taking a last look around, I stopped breathing when I spotted a little patch of wildflowers some twenty yards away. Most of the blossoms had wilted on the stems. But a few buds remained.

Red, like Paige's hair.

After all this time, I'd found her.

My feet moved swiftly with little protest from my bad leg. Brushing a hand over the velvety soft petals, tears spilled onto my cheeks, surprising me. Because I'd never cried for Paige. She didn't visit me in my dreams. And I couldn't see her face when I closed my eyes.

That was my penance. The price I'd paid for rejecting her that final night.

But she was here with me now. Her scent on the breeze, and her warmth on my skin. And she gave me the one thing I'd been searching for, even if I didn't deserve it.

Forgiveness.

Chapter Two

Miles

I WOKE WITH A GROAN, LIGHT DANCING BEHIND MY LIDS AND A THIN SHEEN of sweat covering my body. Everything hurt. Not the dull, aching pain I was used to. This felt like someone put my leg in a vise and cranked the damn thing to the limit.

Rolling onto my side, my thigh brushed warm, soft skin. And when I opened my eyes, ribbons of dark hair fanned the pillow, spilling over slender shoulders like an ebony river.

Trinity.

I scrubbed a hand down my face, searching my memory for any clues about last night. Thanks to the pill I'd taken after I'd gotten home from the crash site, I was pretty far gone by the time I'd gotten out of the shower.

Is that when she'd shown up?

Peeking under the covers, I blew out a relieved breath. I was still wearing the same T-shirt and sweatpants I'd thrown on after my shower. Given my condition last night, I was relatively certain there had been no sex. But the clothes were an added reassurance.

I gave up trying to piece things together and swung my legs over the side of the bed. Trinity was here because she was supposed to be here. We had an arrangement. But it was never meant to include sleepovers.

I'd met her a year ago when I'd needed a plus one to accompany me to a charity event. Scaring up a woman was about as easy as walking into a bar on Sixth and snapping my fingers, but I'd given up on doing that after a fangirl went on to describe her "wild night with Miles Cooper" in great detail to a tabloid. Or ten.

It took a little digging, but I found an escort service—completely above board—with non-disclosure agreements and iron-clad contracts.

Sex was not part of the deal. And Trinity made sure to reiterate that when I called to make the arrangements for our date.

"*I don't sleep with my clients.*"

I'd replied with a snort because I had no interest in sleeping with the girl. Until she'd climbed onto my lap in the limo after the fundraiser.

Our one date turned into a standing Friday night arrangement.

It wasn't just about the sex. Sometimes we shared a meal. Or watched a movie. I didn't mind spending time with Trinity as long as she was gone before morning. There was a kind of peace that went with knowing I didn't have to play games and pretend we were something we weren't.

So much for that.

Irked, I reached for the bottle of Advil on the nightstand. After swallowing four of the pills, I hauled to my feet and hobbled to the desk. Rifling through the drawer, I found my rarely used checkbook. A kernel of doubt tickled the inside of my brain, drawing my attention to the bed. One glimpse of Trinity's contented smile and I finished filling in the blanks.

Her eyes fluttered open when I laid the envelope on the nightstand. "Morning," she said dreamily as she stretched her arms over her head. "What time is it?"

Late. Too late.

"Around six."

A beat of silence and she frowned, her focus drifting to my leg. "What's wrong?" She slowly rose to her elbows. "Are you in pain?"

Gold threaded her chestnut locks, and I wondered why I'd never noticed it before. Tucking a fallen strand behind her ear, I let my fingers dwell on her soft skin. "Not too much." Dropping my hand, I forced a smile. "I'm going to grab a shower. You should go."

I started for the bathroom but only made it a few steps before her voice rose up behind me. "What is this, Miles? My payoff?"

Her voice trembled. In anger. Or hurt. I wasn't sure.

Schooling my features, I turned to face her. Tears pooled in her eyes as she held the check with a shaky hand.

"You can keep your twenty grand. I don't want your money."

She searched my face with sad brown eyes. Like maybe if she looked hard enough, she'd find something else. Something more.

"Money's all I got, Trin. I thought you knew that."

Dashing a tear from her cheek, she climbed to her feet. "Then why did you ask me to stay?"

It came back to me then. The words I'd whispered before I drifted off. Words that were never meant for her.

Stay with me, sunshine.

"I didn't."

I braced myself, expecting her to argue the point. Instead, she sank onto the side of the bed and just blinked at me. "It was never about the money," she said softly. "I just wanted to be with you."

Guilt coiled around my heart. Heavy and familiar. But I pushed it away. Because I wasn't a prince. Or a savior. Or whatever the hell Trinity saw when she looked at me. I was just a guy who paid to make sure she was gone before the sun came up.

"I know, darlin'. That's why you need to go."

An hour later, I finally managed to make it downstairs. Clenching my teeth against the pain searing down my leg, I headed straight for my salvation—the built-in coffee machine.

"Rough night?" Emily asked as I poured a cup.

Jumping out of my skin, I spilled some of the steaming brew on the floor. "Fucking hell, Em," I growled, my gaze snapping to the window seat where she was perched. "What are you doing over there?"

Her teasing smile faded as she looked me over. "What is it? Are you in pain?"

I didn't bother to hide my discomfort. It wouldn't have mattered anyway. This was Emily. She'd been working as my assistant for three years, running my errands and making my doctor appointments.

"A little." Shrugging off the confession, I stirred sugar into my cup. "I'm sure it's nothing."

Ignoring my weak attempt to downplay the situation, she eased to her feet. "Bullshit. How bad is it? Scale of one to ten."

I took a sip of coffee, hiding my grimace. "About a seven."

Really, I was at an eight. Fast approaching a nine. But even more concerning was the edginess. Normally, things didn't faze me. My meds made sure of that. But right now, I was keyed up. Wound tighter than a guitar string. It was like the world was too bright. Too loud all of a sudden.

Emily shook her head as she swiped through the contacts on her phone. "I'm calling Dr. Reber."

In a flash, the edginess escalated to full-blown anger, and I made a grab for her cell. "Did I ask for your help?"

She jumped, shock painting her features. "Whoa, Miles. What's up with you?"

Her attention slid from my face to the veins cording my neck, and I could see the wheels turning.

Blowing out a frustrated breath, I dropped onto a barstool. "Sorry. It's just…Trinity was here this morning when I woke up. She spent the night."

If Emily had looked shocked before, it was nothing compared to her surprise now. She glanced over at the archway as if she expected Trinity to materialize at any moment.

"I told her to leave," I said, staring into my cup. "She won't be coming back."

The regret I should've felt an hour ago swamped me. Not because I'd broken it off. That needed to happen. But did I have to be so cold about it?

Another stabbing pain, and I looked down, only to find my fingers digging into my thigh with a vengeance.

Self-harm. Lovely.

Bracing my elbows on the bar, I dropped my head into my hands. "I guess it wouldn't hurt to give Reber a call."

Emily jerked a nod, the phone already pressed to her ear. She spoke in a hushed tone as she wandered to the other room. But there was no need. I couldn't concentrate on what she was saying if I tried. My mind was everywhere.

Easing back into my seat, I finished my coffee, hoping the caffeine would help me center myself.

Five minutes later she reappeared, a satisfied smile curving her lips. "You've got an appointment in an hour." Reading my surprise, she lifted a slender shoulder in a half shrug. "He's squeezing you in."

Tamping down my irritation, I stalked to the coffee maker for another dose. "Jesus, Em. I hope you didn't make it sound like I was dying or something." She didn't respond, her focus on the window. "What are you looking at?"

I tapped my spoon on the edge of the cup to get her attention, and she jerked. Maybe I wasn't as astute at reading her as she was at reading me, but I knew when something was up.

"Considering my mood," I said in a measured tone, "I'd think twice about keeping something from me."

Digging into her pocket, she pulled out a business card and slid it onto the marble countertop.

Daryl Creston. Private Security.

Emily's hands flew up when I lifted my murderous gaze. "It wasn't me. I swear. He was waiting by the front door when I got here. I tried to ask him some questions, and he clammed up and gave me that card."

At the height of my fame, bodyguards were essential. Ridding myself of the constant intrusion was one of the only perks of slipping into obscurity.

"Well, he didn't hire himself," I grumbled, flipping the card over in search of clues.

And that's when I saw it. A small logo with two hearts wrapped in barbed wire. Twin Souls.

Emily inched closer. "Isn't that Tori's company?"

And Taryn's. But I kept that to myself. Like maybe if I didn't say her name out loud, all the things I'd pushed down would stay buried. But it was there. A huge ball of guilt and remorse and shame in the pit of my gut with Taryn's name on it.

Taryn had been Damaged's manager. And Paige's best friend. She was also the first person I saw when I woke up in the hospital after the accident. And the only person I allowed to stick with me through my recovery. And stick, she did. Even after I told her I didn't need her anymore, she came by my house every day. To drop off food I didn't eat. And hold my hand when there were no words.

A year later, it was Taryn who found me on the floor of my bathroom, barely breathing, with enough booze and pills in my stomach to bring down a horse. She'd saved me. But at the time I hadn't wanted to be saved. A fact I'd made abundantly clear when I'd come to in my bed in the psych ward with her in the chair beside me.

"Don't you know how pathetic you are, Taryn? Always trying to help. Always hanging around. Even when you're not wanted. Paige thought so too. She was just too nice to say it."

All the while, Taryn had just sat there, a single tear dancing on the tip of her lashes. I'd hated that tear. Because it meant she cared. That she'd mourn me if I died. And that's the reason I'd agreed to check myself into Millwood. Taryn and that single tear.

My leg throbbed in earnest now, and I welcomed it. The trade of one kind of pain for another. That was my life. A series of compromises and lesser evils.

Tossing Emily a grim smile, I shoved the card in my pocket. "I'll worry about it later. I need to get to my appointment."

On my fourth try, Tori finally answered the phone, issuing a sleepy, "Morning, Miles" in her lazy drawl. I guess love agreed with her. Because there was a peace in her voice I hadn't heard in years. But since I was hanging by a thread, I didn't bother with any pleasantries.

"Call him off," I growled as I jerked to a stop in the parking space in front of Reber's office. "Tell him to go the fuck home or wherever he came from."

Adjusting the rearview mirror, I glared at the dude climbing out of the Jeep. He was dressed all in black from his T-shirt to his boots. A pair of mirrored aviators hid his eyes, but I knew he was looking right at me.

Tori's chuckle raced across the line. "You must be talking about Daryl."

I sneered at his reflection. And he smiled. Fucker. "The dude is a creeper. Jumped out from behind a pillar in my garage when I was getting into my truck. I don't even know how he got in there! I told him I wasn't interested in his services. But he won't get a fucking clue."

"He doesn't work for you," Tori said, the smile in her tone evident. "So I doubt he'll be taking any orders, no matter how loud you bellow. Besides, Daryl's all right. He did a great job for me. That's why Twin Souls put him on the payroll."

I stifled a frustrated groan. "If he's such a cool dude then why isn't he with you?" When she didn't answer straightaway, I cast a suspicious glance at my phone. "Please tell me you have security."

A deep rumbling laugh I recognized as Logan Cage's bled through the speaker. "She doesn't need security. She's got me."

Images of Tori in Paris a couple of months ago flashed in my head. The swarm of paparazzi. Tori on her knees, shielding her face from the cameras. And of course, the now infamous photo of Logan being dragged away in handcuffs while she dissolved into a puddle of tears.

If that was Cage's idea of protecting her, he had a lot to learn.

My already frayed nerves unwound a little more, and I snapped. "This is a private conversation, bud. So back off. I'm talking to your girl."

His girl. The words left a sour taste in my mouth. Because they were true. Tori was Logan's girl now. Not Rhenn's.

All the fight left me, and I let my head fall back, digging my fingers into my eyes while Cage squawked in the background. I couldn't make out exactly what he was saying. Which led me to believe something was muffling the speaker.

And then things got quiet. Just Tori's breath on the other end of the line. In all the years we'd been estranged, I'd never felt such distance.

"Miles? Are you still there?"

"Yeah."

Tori sighed. "Logan didn't mean anything. He would never let anything happen to me. You know that, right?"

Anything I said would likely lead to a fight, so I settled for a grunt.

"Anyway," she went on, forcing cheer into her tone. "It's you I'm worried about. I've been watching the news coverage since the concert. Sixth Street is a zoo."

I snorted. "You think I've been out clubbing?"

"I don't know. Maybe? You're not at the house. That's a good sign."

My gaze wandered to the empty lot adjacent to the cluster of medical offices. To the spot where Brackenridge Medical had once stood. The city demolished the hospital over a year ago, but I could still see it clearly. Aging white facade. Rows of windows. And the roof with the helipad.

"Listen, Miles," Tori said, dragging me out of the past. "I have to go. But if you really have a problem with Daryl, give Taryn a call. She's the one who assigned him. But try not to hurt her feelings. She went through a lot of trouble shuffling things around to make sure his schedule was clear for you."

"Taryn?"

Why in the hell would Taryn care if I had security? She hadn't spoken more than a handful of words to me in years. Even after I'd apologized, she'd kept her distance. And I gave her that. Owed it to her.

Oblivious to my turmoil, Tori snorted a little laugh. "Of course, Taryn. She handles all the security. But when it comes to you—your fan mail, your schedule, your safety—she'd take someone's head off for trying to intervene. Even mine. And you damn well know it. Anyway… gotta run. Love you."

Dazed, I tried to form a question, but she was already gone.

As far as I knew, my schedule, fan mail, and all the other mundane shit I didn't want to deal with was handled by some junior nobody.

Snatching my phone from the cup holder, I scrolled to my contacts and found the main number for Twin Souls.

I cleared my throat when the receptionist answered. "Yeah, this is Todd with the…uh…Houston Review Daily Gazette."

I squeezed my eyes shut, shaking my head

Really, dude?

"How may I help you?" she replied sweetly, like I hadn't just totally combined at least three newspapers from different cities.

"I'd like to schedule an interview with Miles Cooper for our publication." When she didn't say anything, I added weakly, "From Damaged."

"Yes, of course." Her tone turned decidedly brusque. "All inquiries for Mr. Cooper are handled directly by his manager."

"And who would that be?"

"Taryn Ayers. She's unavailable, but I can patch you through to her assistant."

My stomach sank "No…Uh…Thanks anyway."

Ending the call, I felt the air leeching from my lungs, and I tipped forward, resting my forehead against the steering wheel.

How did I not know this?

A minute or an hour later, traffic from the busy street filtered into the cab of the truck, and I remembered why I was here. My leg throbbed, keeping time with my heart as I eased to my feet. Daryl pushed off the bumper of his black Jeep, and I threw him a glare when he fell into step behind me. "Keep your distance, bro," I warned. "I ain't in the mood."

Chapter Three

Gelsey

STANDING AT THE FRONT DESK AT AUSTIN ORTHOPEDIC CENTER, I GAVE Cassidy a tight smile as she swiped my bank card through the reader.

Please.

Holding my breath, I silently prayed there was enough money in my account to cover the co-pay. I didn't want to take advantage of Dr. Reber's generous nature any more than I already had. Half the time, he didn't charge me for the cortisone shots he administered to treat my bad back. Or the electric stimulation he used when my tendonitis flared up. He'd even given me a portable TENs unit I could use at home.

While Cassidy fumbled with the numbers on the keypad, I looked around for my best friend. Shannon was one of the kinesiologists on staff, and I was hoping she'd be the one to check me out. But she was stuck in a consult with one of the orthopedists.

I jerked when the machine spit out my receipt.

Thank you, God.

Cassidy tore off the slip and slid it across the counter with a smile. "Just need your John Hancock."

I picked up the pen with the flower attached to the top and quickly signed my name. My stomach had just started to unwind when Cassidy hummed. "It looks like Dr. Reber has requested an MRI. Where do you want to have that done?"

I blinked at her. An MRI? I couldn't afford an MRI. My attention slid to the medical release that Dr. Reber had signed, sitting next to Cassidy's can of Dr. Pepper. Without it, Ivan wouldn't let me dance. Nobody in our company was allowed on the floor without a yearly certificate of fitness.

Swallowing my nerves, I licked my dry lips. "Um...Did he say why? I mean, he signed my release."

Cursing the tremble in my voice, I clenched my fingers into fists at my sides and tried to look nonchalant while Cassidy opened my file to investigate. "Looks like it's just a precaution. He wants to have the bump on your knee scanned." She offered an apologetic smile. "Better safe than sorry."

The bump on my knee was tendonitis. I'd stake my life on it. But apparently, Dr. Reber wasn't willing to take that bet. And I got it. Eleven years ago, I'd stood right in his office with my mother when she'd come in to have a lump on her shin examined.

"I'm sure it's just an old injury from my performance days flaring up. It goes down a little when I ice it. But it always comes back."

Because cancer was funny that way.

Insidious.

Stealthy.

Dr. Reber had ordered an MRI then too. Or maybe it was a CAT scan. Not that it had mattered. The bone cancer had already spread. And Mama died eleven months later.

Of course, Cassidy knew that. Everyone did. Living in the shadow of Katya Orlov was hard enough. But living in the shadow of her death was even worse.

Shannon slipped through a side door, and when our gazes collided, her steps faltered. But she quickly recovered, pinning on a smile for her coworker.

"Hey, Cass. Mr. Mendoza is in exam room four. He needs some samples of that new medication the Pfizer rep dropped off. It's all in his chart. Why don't you take care of that and I'll finish with Gelsey. We have lunch plans anyway."

I nodded a little too enthusiastically, grateful I'd have my best friend to help me find a solution to this dilemma.

Cassidy popped out of her chair, pulling a ten spot from the pocket of her scrubs. "If y'all are going downstairs, can you get me a chef's salad with ranch dressing?"

Shannon rolled her eyes as she took the cash. "That's not a real salad. You know that, right? You might as well eat a cheeseburger."

"Life's too short to not sample all the things," Cassidy said as she waltzed off, calling over her shoulder, "Pick up a Snickers bar while you're at it."

Shaking her head, Shannon sank into the chair. "You look a little green. What's going on?"

Before I could open my mouth, she flipped open my chart and started reading Dr. Reber's notes.

"Why are you doing that?" I hissed. "You didn't even let me answer."

She arched a brow, and I mimicked the gesture. Maybe I'd been evasive in the past. But that was when we were kids. Shannon was three years older, but given my advanced skill as a dancer, we were always in the same classes at the academy. Competing for the same roles. Which hadn't inspired me to open up about my injuries. Even at eight or nine, I was practiced in the art of keeping quiet. But I was twenty-two now.

Shannon relented with a sigh, easing back in her seat and folding her hands in her lap. "Proceed."

So dramatic.

Rolling my eyes, I tipped forward and lowered my voice. "Dr. Reber wants me to have an MRI on my knee." Shannon's brow lined with worry and I shook my head. "Just as a precaution. He already told me it's tendonitis. But I need my certificate of fitness for Ivan."

"So do the MRI." I cringed, and she nodded her understanding. "You can't afford it, right?"

I offered a weak shrug. "Not right now."

Shannon thought about it for a moment, thumbing the corner of my certificate. Even if she offered it to me, I wouldn't accept. It wasn't worth risking her job.

"I got it," she said, her eyes lighting up. "My buddy Trina works over at Central Texas Imaging. She's the office manager. You can get it done there."

"But—"

She waved a hand. "I'll get her to eat the co-pay or let you make payments."

As if the matter were settled, Shannon slid the release in front of me.

My hands flew up, and I took a step back as if the paper had teeth. "No. I don't want you to get in trouble."

"Reber didn't say you *had* to have the MRI to get the release. He wouldn't have signed it if he didn't think you were fit. He's just being cautious. Because…well, you know…"

In all the years since my mom's death, Shannon had never once mentioned the illness that took her life. It was almost like she was afraid that if she spoke that truth then maybe I'd suffer the same fate. But she didn't have to worry. According to the doctors, my chances of inheriting the disease were slim to none.

"Thank you," I said as I tucked the release in my bag.

She winked and picked up the phone. "Don't mention it. Give me a minute and I'll work my magic."

Since I didn't want to eavesdrop, I popped in my earbuds and proceeded to scroll through my playlist. The fist around my heart loosened when "Here Comes the Sun" bled through the tiny speakers. I thought of my mother, and all the times she'd danced around the converted studio in our house without a care for anything but the beat. No pirouettes or leaps. No complicated positions. Just her natural grace. And the Beatles.

Jerking when I felt a tap on my shoulder, I looked up and met cold brown eyes, a chin carved from granite, and the most incredible full lips I'd ever seen. I fumbled to take out one of my earbuds. "Yes?" I croaked.

"Do you mind, darlin'? You're kind of in my way." When I didn't immediately jump to do as he asked, his nostrils flared in irritation. "If you're done gawking, I'd really appreciate it if you'd move your ass."

Stunned, I blinked at him. *Move my ass?* Gorgeous or not, the guy was way out of line.

Lifting my chin, I gave him a bland stare. "I'll move when I'm finished. Wait your turn."

Shaking my head at his nerve, I shifted my focus back to my best friend, ready for her to excoriate the douchebag for his lack of manners. But she wasn't paying attention to me. Her eyes were locked on the giant breathing down my neck. And her mouth. I'd never seen it hang open in that particular way.

The hulk followed my gaze to Shannon who still hadn't found her voice.

"Catatonic," he muttered, raking a hand through his hair as he looked around. "That's just perfect."

His jaw set when he spotted Dr. Reber outside an exam room.

"Wait!" Shannon wheezed, jumping up when he spun in that direction. "You can't just…"

Apparently, he could, because he didn't spare Shannon a glance as he stalked away.

It was then I noticed the slight limp. And the stiff set of his shoulders. The taut muscles in his back, evident through his form-fitting T-shirt.

Pain.

I could read it a mile away.

Dr. Reber stopped what he was doing and welcomed the guy with a smile before ushering him farther down the hall to his private office.

"I guess rude works for some people," I mused, my attention back on Shannon.

Her mouth was closed now, but her eyes had yet to return to their normal size. "You don't know who that was?" she asked, incredulous.

"Not a clue." My stomach let out a rumble. "Ready to go to lunch?"

Snorting, she plucked a compact mirror from Cassidy's top drawer. "That was Miles Cooper. Drummer for Damaged. And I'm not leaving until I see whether they need a kinesiologist to confer on his case."

Shrugging, I picked through the jar full of lollipops on the counter, snagging two yellow ones from the bottom. "Well, he's an asshole. But it seems like he's hurt. His leg, I think. Or his back. So maybe that's the reason for the attitude."

My hand froze on the cellophane wrapper when I noted Shannon's look of shock.

"You really don't know who Damaged is…er, was?" My flaming cheeks must've given me away because she shook her head. "Sheltered little ballerina. You should look them up. Their music was everything."

She went back to gazing at her reflection while I fiddled with the wrapper on my lollipop. At times like this, I was painfully aware of how different I was from most women my age. I'd never had a serious boyfriend. Or stepped foot inside a classroom. I knew nothing about pop culture. And the only band I listened to had broken up thirty years before I was born.

"I think I'm going to head home," I said, hoisting my bag a little higher on my shoulder.

Shannon stopped primping. "I probably won't be but a minute. We can grab something to eat when I'm finished."

"Nah." I shifted my feet. "I'm a little nervous about tomorrow. I want to make a good impression."

Silence swelled between us, and I could almost read her thoughts. *Don't get your hopes up.* Instead of voicing her concern, she smiled. "You'll do great, Gels."

"Thanks."

As I turned to leave, she said, "I'm adding a new Burdenko class to the schedule starting on Wednesday. I could really use your help. Twenty bucks a session."

I squeezed my eyes shut. *Charity.* That's what I'd been reduced to. Shannon didn't really need an assistant. She was an expert in aquatic rehabilitation. But I was in no position to turn down twenty bucks, so I flashed her a smile over my shoulder. "Sure. Sounds great. I'll see you then."

Miles

Digging my fingers into my thigh, I watched the clock on the wall in Reber's office. And I waited. At least I had some privacy. Away from the gawkers. And Daryl. I'd barely managed to slip into the private reception area without him following. And that's only because he had been a good ten paces behind, and I'd ducked in behind a nurse.

So now he was stuck in the waiting room. Served him right. Maybe they'd call the cops on his creepy ass when they realized he wasn't a patient.

The door swung open, solid wood dragging over thick carpet. "Sorry to keep you waiting, Miles." Reber scooted behind his desk and took a seat in the ergonomic chair, steaming mug in his hand. "What's got you so worked up today?"

He posed the question like we were shooting the breeze. A couple of old pals sharing a cup of coffee. Only, we weren't friends. And I was anything but relaxed.

I tossed two prescription bottles on his desk blotter. Pain relievers and antidepressants. "There's something wrong with my meds. They're not working."

He watched me over the rim of his cup for a long moment before tipping forward to inspect a plate of cookies. "Why would you say that?"

Because I want to rip your arm off and beat you with it.

Only the reminder that there were dozens of people on the other side of the closed door kept me from doing it.

"I don't know. I'm just…off. I can feel it. And my leg hurts like a bitch."

Another pause as he took a large bite. "So you're in pain. What else do you feel?"

He seemed more interested in wiping the crumbs from his tie than my answer.

"Unsettled."

He tore himself away from his snack long enough to grab a pen. Relieved, my stomach uncoiled. The peace was short-lived, though. Because instead of reaching for the prescription pad he kept in the silver holder, he opted for a leather-bound notebook. "Unsettled, you say?" He met my gaze. "Tell me about that."

If Reber had suddenly taken an interest in psychology, I wasn't going to be his guinea pig. I had a shrink. He knew that. The two of them had worked together since the beginning.

Clinging to the last piece of whatever was keeping me from crawling across the desk and choking him out, I forced a smile. The kind that said, "Nothing to see here. I'm right as rain. Ignore the bulging vein on my forehead."

"There's nothing to tell. I just need you to switch up the pain meds and up the dosage on my anti-depressants."

Contemplating, he tapped the pen against his lips. "So you're depressed?"

"No," I bit out. "I'm fucking pissed and I'm in pain."

The declaration flew out of my mouth with zero thought. But it was true. I was pissed. Mad as hell and I didn't know why.

Switching gears, he folded his hands in front of him. "Tell me about the concert. How did the leg hold up?"

"Fine. Not a twinge. It didn't start hurting until after the concert. But it's not just that. I feel like I'm crawling out of my fucking skin. I've been trying to do everything right. And now—"

He held up a finger, and I paused. Was I talking too fast? Racing mind. Jumbled thoughts. I remembered that from before the overdose.

"Miles?"

From the look on Reber's face, I'd missed something. A question, maybe. I dug my fingers into my thigh again, the shooting pain forcing me to focus. "Sorry, I didn't catch that?"

"What's everything?"

For a minute, I wished he'd go back to the cookie and stop trying to analyze me.

I blew out a breath. "All the pre-show interviews. The press. I wanted to make sure the show was a success. And it was. But now my leg is fucked. And my head is fucked. So if you can just switch my pills, or up my dosage or whatever, so I can…"

My tongue tied into a knot as I tried to finish the thought. But I really didn't know what came next.

"Miles…" Reber shook his head. "There are no magic pills. You're angry. I get that. You have a good support system at Millwood, and I encourage you to keep pushing forward with Dr. Sheppard. We've conferred on your case a great deal throughout the years. But I can tell you with a relative degree of certainty that depression isn't the issue."

Instead of storming out, which I really wanted to do, I sat back. "Explain."

His lip twitched into a half-smile like I'd made his fucking day. "After the accident you *were* depressed. And because of the depression, you withdrew. From your family. Your friends. From life. You didn't participate in any form of rehabilitation. Almost as if you didn't care about getting better. That was a choice." He shrugged. "This is also a choice."

"Yeah, right." I scoffed. "You think I'd choose to be angry?"

"Anger is a part of life. The life you decided you didn't want five years ago." I bristled at his not so veiled reference to my overdose, but he pushed on, despite my warning glare. "You weren't ready to join the fight back then. You didn't care about your leg. Or the pain. You were content to live with it. But now you're not. The problem is, you just can't *decide* you want your life back and expect everything to fall into place." He chuckled good-naturedly. "Did you really think you could bang on your drums for two hours, with zero preparation, and not suffer any consequences?"

The weight of his stare forced me to look away.

"I think that's really why you're angry," he continued. "You made this effort to move on, finally, and your body won't cooperate. But now that you're ready, there are things we can do about that."

We. There was no "we." There was only me. Because Reber was right about one thing: I'd pushed everyone else away. Tori. Taryn. All my other friends. Even my mama. Not that she'd minded.

I had Emily, whom I paid. Which meant I could dismiss her anytime I wanted. Same for Trinity.

Shit.

I looked up to find Reber studying me carefully. But not in the way he used to, like I might break if he applied enough pressure. I hated that look. But this one wasn't much better. *Expectations.* That's what I saw in his eyes. How long had it been since anyone expected anything from me?

Releasing a tremulous breath, I eased back in my seat. "I'm listening."

Chapter Four

Gelsey

I SAT PERFECTLY STILL AS DOUG, THE TRAINER AT VOLKOV REPERTORY palpitated my knee. I'd spent the last eighteen hours on my couch with a bag of frozen peas on the injury, and the swelling was practically gone.

"I told you I was fine." I flicked my gaze to his face to gauge his reaction, but he didn't look up.

"When do you go for the MRI?"

"Next week. It's just a precaution. Reber says it's tendonitis. And it's almost gone now. See?" I flexed my foot, smiling. "No pain." He dug his thumb into the little knot, and I winced. "Unless you aggravate it."

Oblivious to my scowl, Doug's fingers moved to my calf, then my ankle, and even my toes. Satisfied when I didn't flinch at any of his probing, he let go of my leg. "I tend to agree with Reber. But make sure you get that MRI. And remember to ice. Twenty minutes on and twenty minutes off. You don't want to take any chances."

Nodding like I hadn't heard the spiel a million times, I eased to my feet. "So, I'm good then?"

Doug added a couple of reminders about rest and elevation as he pulled a roll of KT tape from his smock.

I took a step back when he motioned for me to get on the table. "You know I can't."

There was no such thing as "modified" practice at Ivan Volkov's dance company. You had to be one hundred percent or nothing. And today of all days, I couldn't risk being excluded.

We stared at each other for a long moment, only breaking eye contact when music floated in from the studio. Doug shifted his focus to the door, and I held my breath. He had the authority to sideline me with only a word. I prayed he wouldn't exercise that power.

"Promise me you'll stop if you feel anything," he finally said, resignation written all over his face. "It's not worth risking a permanent injury. I mean it, Gels."

Normally, I'd agree with him. But it wasn't every day that Ivan invited guests from other dance companies into his kingdom. The scouts were here for Sydney, his latest prodigy. So my chances of getting noticed were slim to none. But still, I had to try.

"I promise."

Doug jerked his chin to the door. "Go."

Beaming, I grabbed my bag and rushed out of the room before he changed his mind.

The music stopped, and I slowly let my arms fall to my sides, my weight shifting from my toes to the balls of my feet, and finally, my heels. Careful not to slouch, my attention ping-ponged between Ivan and Sydney.

Technically, she'd executed every move flawlessly. But something was off. There was no sparkle. No excitement. And even now, she couldn't be bothered to hold her stance. Toeing the floor with her pointe shoe, she crossed her arms over her chest...and *sighed*.

My mouth dropped open.

At twenty-two, I might risk the small rebellion if Ivan pissed me off enough. *Maybe*. But at eighteen, Sydney's age, I would've cut my foot off before disrespecting him like that.

The woman at Ivan's side, a scout from the New York City Ballet, cringed and dropped her gaze to the floor.

You could've heard a pin drop as Ivan stalked toward Sydney. Mouth set in a grim line and murder in his eyes, he leaned forward into her space. "Are we keeping you from something, *malysh?*"

Expecting Sydney to buckle under the weight of his formidable stare, I was shocked when she lifted her chin. "I have a date."

A murmur rose in the studio. Quickly silenced when Ivan's lips parted. Wincing, I braced for the fallout, certain he was going to blow the roof off the place. Instead, his steely blue glare shifted to the group, assessing us one by one, before falling on me. And he smiled.

"Gelsey, come here, please." He pointed to a spot beside Micha, who looked ready to swallow his tongue. As the male lead for our company, Micha's fate was inexplicably tied to Sydney's. Just as it once had been tied to mine.

As far as anyone knew, we'd merely been partners. But our relationship had run much deeper. Micha was my first kiss. My first love. My first *everything*. And because I had as much to lose as he did if anyone ever found out, I'd suffered in silence when he'd dumped me.

After a moment's hesitation, I swallowed my pride, taking my spot in front of Micha.

"Places everyone," Ivan bellowed.

In my periphery, I caught a glimpse of Sydney, eyes wide and full of shock. I had no illusions. Tomorrow or the next day or the next week, she'd earn back Ivan's favor. But for now, she was on the outside looking in. Where I'd been so many times. She stumbled backward with the rest of the crowd, looking like she was ready to cry.

And for a moment, I felt bad for her. Until I sensed Ivan at my back. Palms molding my hips, he adjusted my stance as the first strains of Tchaikovsky's *Sleeping Beauty Waltz* filled the air. A second before my cue, he dipped his head and smiled against the shell of my ear. "Make me proud, *dorogaya moya.*"

Precious one.

Ivan hadn't called me that in years. And the fact that he probably didn't mean it now, that he was only using me to prove a point, didn't matter. I was ten years old again, dancing for the very first time on the big stage. Before the injuries. Or the expectations. Or the failures.

And I just wanted the moment to last.

Of course, it didn't, and before I knew it, the song ended, and Micha was holding me above his head in our final pose. It took a second for my brain to engage. And then, as gracefully as possible, I slid down his body, landing on the tips of my toes.

Perfection.

I could feel it. Apparently, I wasn't alone, because applause rang out from someone in the crowd. Loud, enthusiastic applause. I cringed inwardly. Because Ivan's rules were quite clear on the subject of praise inside the studio.

Would you clap for the man who serves your food or bags your groceries? This is your job. Nothing more.

My focus shifted to the rule-breaker, who I assumed was one of the visitors. But it was Ivan himself, standing straight, a small smile pinned to his lips. My heart squeezed painfully, and on instinct, I dropped into a deep curtsey, my chin falling to my chest. Also forbidden. But I didn't care. Ivan was my teacher, my mentor, and he deserved the respect.

Linking my fingers with Micha's when he didn't move, I gave his hand a sharp tug. "Bow," I hissed, and for once he did as he was told.

We held our positions—only breaking character when Ivan turned back to his guests. Curving a hand around my elbow, Micha pulled me to my feet. Instead of the scowl I expected to find for telling him what to do, he smiled down at me the way he used to. Only now, the blinders were off, and I saw him for what he was. An opportunist. A user. And a liar.

Micha's palm skimmed higher, coming to rest on my nape. "Damn, Gels. That was awesome. Have you been practicing?"

Fire ignited in my blood. Because I hadn't missed a rehearsal in months. Which only proved I didn't exist in Micha's world. Not as a dancer. Or a person.

"Every day."

Out of the corner of my eye, I noticed the three scouts heading our way. Micha saw them too, and his arm fell to his side. Walking backward with a stupid grin spreading across his face, he said, "You were great today, Gels. Thanks for helping out." He glanced me over with renewed interest. "We should have dinner sometime."

Before I could tell him I'd rather eat dirt, he turned on his heel and sauntered toward the scouts. Burying my disappointment when not one of them looked my way, I held my chin high and turned for the door. By the time I got to the dressing room, the adrenaline rush had faded, leaving only shaky hands and wobbly legs.

Dropping onto the bench in front of my locker, I rubbed my knee, fighting back tears.

"Is everything all right?"

Whipping my gaze to the door, I blinked at the woman from the New York City Ballet.

"Uh...yeah. I'm fine." Hauling to my feet, I forced a smile. "Can I help you find something?"

"No." She glanced me over, astute blue eyes lingering on my knee. "You are injured?"

She spoke with the same Russian accent as Ivan, and I straightened, despite myself. "Just a little tendonitis."

Stepping closer, she took in every inch of the dressing room. "Katya had weak knees as well."

Surprised by the familiarity in her tone, I blurted, "You knew my mom?"

Smiling, she glided over to me with a dancer's grace, her four-inch heels barely skimming the tile. "*Da.*" She motioned for me to sit, then eased down beside me. "I'm Tatiana. Katya and I danced together. Well, mostly I watched. She was the star."

"You trained at the Joffrey?"

Wistful brown eyes swept the room once again. "No. I trained in St. Petersburg. With Ivan. In a studio very much like this one." She brushed perfectly manicured fingertips over one of the lockers before turning back to me. "*Ty govorish' po-russki?*"

"Oh, no." I shook my head. "I mean, *nyet.* I don't speak Russian."

"Neither did Katya. She butchered the language, actually. I just thought, with all the time you've spent with Ivan..." She patted my leg. "Never mind. Now tell me about your troubles."

"My what?"

"Your knee. How bad is it?"

My gaze slid to the door to see if Ivan was lurking in the hallway. But who was I kidding? Ivan didn't lurk.

"Why do you want to know about my injuries?" When I realized what I'd just admitted, my throat tightened. "Not that I have any."

She laughed. "Nonsense. We all have injuries. I just want to know the severity of yours. Do you have your medical records?"

"Wait...what?" I shook my head. "I'm sorry, Tatiana. I don't mean to be rude. But why would I possibly share that information with you?"

She folded her hands in her lap, all traces of humor gone. "I thought you understood—that Ivan told you—I'm here on behalf of the New York City Ballet. Before I can recommend you for an apprentice position in the company, I need to know exactly what we are dealing with."

If her face weren't so serious, I'd think she was joking. She had to be.

"But...I'm twenty-two," I sputtered.

Past my prime. Not a has-been. A never-was. And that was worse.

She tilted her head. *"Da. So?"*

The hope blooming in my chest shrank against the harsh light of the truth. *My* truth. Because once I answered her question, she wouldn't be smiling anymore.

As if she could sense my inner turmoil, Tatiana took my hand. "In Russia, we have a saying. I do not really know how to translate. But basically, it means we do not feed our devils." When my brows drew together, she sighed. "It's more like a superstition. We do not talk about the things that can hurt us. We do not...give them life. Perhaps you are more Russian than you think?"

Curling my free hand around the edge of the bench, I dug my nails into the wood. Should I tell her? Trust her with my secret?

"My knee is not the problem," I began hesitantly. "It's my back. I was born with a... defect. In my lower spine. It's a stress fracture that will never heal." Expecting her to wish me luck and walk out, I was surprised when she merely nodded. "It's permanent," I added, in case I wasn't clear. "Forever."

She contemplated for a moment. "Have you sought treatment?"

Recalling every hour I'd spent on the exam table or with the strength coach or in the pool, I nodded. "Extensively. This is as good as it gets."

"Well, it never held Katya back. So I think it will not be a problem." My mouth fell open and she gave me the oddest look. "You did not know your mother suffered from the same ailment?" I shook my head, and it was Tatiana's turn to sigh. "Katya was very guarded about her secret, so I am not surprised. Very few people knew."

Bits and pieces of my mother's most notable performances lit the corners of my mind. The Black Swan in *Swan Lake*. Aurora in *Sleeping Beauty*. Clara in the *Nutcracker Suite*. I'd seen the footage a thousand times on YouTube. The way her body bent, so effortlessly.

"Of course, you will have to take more precautions, the way your mama did," Tatiana continued as she pushed to her feet. "Listen to your body. Rest is essential. But I see no reason I should withhold my recommendation. Unless..." Her shrewd gaze raked me over once more. "What is it you are not telling me?"

I felt the flush rise from my chest. "I don't...I mean...I haven't..." *Just say it.* Lifting my chin, I looked her in the eyes. "I don't have any money. So I don't think New York will be an option for me."

She waved a dismissive hand like she was swatting away a fly. "The company will put you up in an apartment. Shared, of course. And you would earn a small wage. Should you land a bigger role, your salary would increase. All you need is spending money for a time. After that, the patrons will follow."

Patrons...

When I was young, I had a few donors who saw the potential in my dancing. Maybe because I was Katya's daughter, they considered me a good bet to fill her shoes. But they all disappeared as my injuries piled up. Leaving only Ivan. He covered the cost of my essentials. Shoes and clothes and any trips.

"What about Ivan?" I asked. "Is he aware...I mean, does he know... about this?"

"Do you think your mentor a stupid man?"

Amusement flashed in Tatiana's eyes, and I smiled in response. "No."

"Out of all the young women out there, he chose you."

"But, Sydney—"

"Is a willful child," she interjected. "Spoiled. And Ivan knows this. He was not surprised by today's outcome." Straightening to her full height—no more than five foot four without the sky-high heels—she looked down at me. "Have you ever played chess with Ivan?" I shook my head. "You should. Then you will realize he never makes a move without knowing what his next one will be. Money aside, are you interested in coming to New York?"

I glanced over the framed photos lining the walls. Fonteyn and Pavlova and Baryshnikov. Ivan. My mother. "It's all I've ever wanted," I said softly.

As if the matter were settled, Tatiana took my hands and gave my fingers a squeeze. "Good. Then I will make the arrangements. All you need to do is prepare your solo piece. Ivan will help." With that, she headed to the door. "See you soon, Gelsey."

Chapter Five

Miles

THE YMCA. SERIOUSLY? THIS WAS WHERE MY MIRACULOUS RECOVERY was supposed to take place? At the Y?

Peeking out the window of the swinging door in the men's dressing room, I scanned the pool area. I'd done the whole physical therapy thing before. Briefly. Blue-haired old ladies with bad hips in orthopedic shoes. And one dude who was older than my granddaddy.

But this was not that.

This crowd was comprised of mostly twenty- to thirty-somethings. Fit. Tanned.

My gaze lingered on a woman in a red one-piece, gathering equipment from a bin by the metal bleachers. Long blond hair and barely there curves. She looked more like a high school student than a therapist. Hell, maybe she *was* in high school.

Stop staring at her then, you perv.

But something about her was familiar, and I couldn't look away. She turned, and the light pouring in from the glass ceiling shone directly on her face.

Fuck. My. Life.

It was the angry little mouse I'd sparred with in Reber's office. Her golden locks cascaded down her back, landing just short of her ass. She was so small. Slender to the point I could see a hint of her ribs.

This is who Reber tasked with teaching me the miracle moves to restore my range of motion and get me out of pain?

I banged my forehead against the glass insert in the door, groaning.

Behind me, Daryl cleared his throat. And I wanted to punch him. "You got a cold or something, bud?" Scowling, I met his gaze in the reflection of the glass. "And just so you know—you look like a douche wearing sunglasses inside."

A smile curled his lip. Not the self-deprecating kind. Dude was smirking. At me. My desire to punch him intensified.

"Maybe so," he said blandly. "But I figure I got about three minutes before you bolt. So I'm good."

I whipped my head around. "What makes you think I'm going to bolt?"

He shrugged, pushing off the wall, and I had to wonder if he was the one with the bad leg. Fucker was always leaning against something.

Sidling up next to me, he surveyed the pool area over the top of his aviators. "There's a lot of people out there."

I side-eyed him, snorting. "You think I'm afraid of people?"

As if to answer my own question, my hand crept to my thigh. My loose-fitting board shorts covered the worst of the devastation. But I could feel every peak. And every valley. Every scar that stretched over my skin like a roadmap.

Another shrug. "I don't know."

"What *do* you know, then?"

It was meant to be a put-down. A way to shut him up. But Daryl slowly turned to me, unflinching. "You've been hiding behind this door for ten minutes. Either you're afraid or you don't want to put in the work."

You never really tried.

Reber's accusation from a couple of days ago filtered through the static in my brain. I'd take it from him. But not this douchebag.

"You don't fucking know me, dude." Shoving my gym bag at his chest, I smiled when he let out a little *omph*. Daryl was the size of a small mountain, with thickly muscled arms and tree trunks for legs. But I was no slouch. And at six five, I was the one looking down at him. Just barely. But it was enough. "Stay in your lane."

Before he could respond, I pushed through the swinging door. Chlorine hung thickly in the air, burning my throat as I marched toward Blondie.

Startled, her big blue eyes jumped from me to Daryl, then back again. "Can I help you?"

Probably not.

"I'm Miles Cooper. I'm here for your class. Where do you want me?"

Gelsey

Stunned, I took a step back, heat exploding in my cheeks as I blinked up at the scowling giant I recognized from our encounter in Reber's office. Miles Cooper.

Annoyance flashed across his features, and he closed his eyes, a muscle in his jaw ticking under a layer of dark stubble. "Focus, sweetheart. I'm here for your class. You can check me out later."

And there was that attitude again.

Now that I knew who he was, it didn't surprise me.

I'd taken Shannon's advice and looked him up. But only because I didn't have anything better to do when I was confined to my couch, icing my knee.

Rock God. Hermit. Survivor.

Those were just a few of the terms the press threw around. And of course, they mentioned his looks. The cheekbones. And the toffee-colored eyes. Those full lips.

His photos didn't begin to do him justice. But tall, dark, and brooding didn't do it for me. And the arrogance was straight out of Ivan's playbook. Making him far less attractive in my eyes.

Infusing steel into my spine, I crossed my arms over my chest. "Don't call me sweetheart. And I'm not the instructor." Hitching a thumb over my shoulder, I smiled sweetly. "That would be Shannon. The catatonic one in the blue bathing suit."

His gaze flickered to my best friend, and he blanched. For a second, I thought I saw something else—regret?—and I waited for the apology. But then he brushed past me like I wasn't there.

"Asshole," I muttered to his back.

Shaking my head, I popped in my waterproof earbuds. "Penny Lane" blasted from the tiny speakers as I eased into the water, intent on getting a few laps in while Shannon went over the rules.

I'd just completed my second lap when I noticed how empty the pool was. Breaking the surface, I blinked the chlorine out of my eyes.

What the hell?

I dog-paddled toward the shallow end where everyone was congregating on the deck. Not just people from our class. It looked like everyone in the place was here.

I spotted Miles in the thick of the crowd. He didn't look particularly surprised by the commotion. More like resigned.

A collective groan echoed off the tiled wall when the guy who'd shadowed Miles into the pool area barked out a warning for everyone to move along. A couple of staff members appeared, herding the interlopers out the door.

Shannon shouldered her way through the wall of bodies and headed straight for me, eyes even wider than they were the other day at Reber's office.

"Can I speak to you?" she asked through a clenched smile.

I parked my hands on my hips and waited for her to descend the stairs.

"Remember that guy—" she began.

"Miles Cooper. Yeah, I know." I made a rolling motion with my hand to get her to move on. People were staring. And her star client looked royally pissed. "What do you need?"

Looping her arm through mine, she spoke close to my ear. "Miles needs to be in the back so he won't disrupt the class. But I can't really see him if I'm in the front. So I need you back there, checking his form and guiding him through the moves."

Was she serious? Apparently so, if her death grip was any indication.

"The man hates me." I glanced in Miles's direction, and he scowled. "You'd better find someone else."

Shannon's nails dug into my skin. "There is no one else. Come *on*. It's only this once. He'll catch on after that."

Considering she added new moves to every session, I had my doubts. But that wasn't my problem. "Fine. Just this once."

She practically squealed. Grabbing her arm when she started to glide away, I asked, "What are his injuries?"

I'd avoided any of the articles on the net that went into detail about the accident. It felt like an invasion of his privacy.

"Leg, hip, and back. The full enchilada."

She knew more, but now wasn't the time. And it didn't matter. Miles would need to get acclimated to the routine before adding any moves specific to his injuries. I'd be long gone by then.

Trying not to look interested, I watched out of the corner of my eyes as my best friend motioned for Mr. Personality to get in the pool. Reluctantly, he joined her by the steps, out of earshot. After a brief exchange, she pointed at me, and he shook his head.

As far as I was concerned, that was that. Relieved and a little insulted, I dunked under the water and smoothed my long hair away from my face.

When I popped up, Miles was right in front of me.

"Oh...hey," I said, quickly securing my long tresses in a high ponytail. "I'm Gelsey."

He looked anywhere but at me. "Shouldn't you be in school or something?'

"School?"

His eyes found mine, slowly falling to my chest. "You know...high school? Or middle school? What are you...like, twelve?"

I felt the flush rise on my skin. A little girl, that's what he saw.

"Fifteen, actually," I said brightly, grinning when his eyes bugged.

A beat of silence turned into two. Then four. All the while, Miles kept his focus pinned to my face, like he was afraid to investigate my non-existent curves for confirmation.

Shannon's voice boomed from the deck as she introduced herself to the class. Miles snapped out of his haze and took his place at my side, leaving three feet of space between us.

When I was sure he'd suffered enough, I leaned toward him and whispered, "I was kidding about my age. I'm twenty-two."

His gaze cut mine, and for the first time, he allowed his eyes to wander. Seemingly unimpressed, he turned back to Shannon, raising both arms over his head to mimic her stretch. "Good to know."

When my hand slid to his hip to adjust his posture, he nearly jumped out of his skin. Ignoring his discomfort, I asked, "How old are you?"

He raised an eyebrow. "How old do I look?"

Tilting my head, I searched his face. His skin was smooth. No wrinkles. But his eyes—they looked tired. And not from lack of sleep. "Fifty? Wait…no…" I bit my lip. "Fifty-five?" His mouth dropped open, and for a minute I thought he actually believed me. I laughed. "Kidding." Taking his wrist, I gave it a tug. But he didn't budge. "Stop fighting me. You have to stretch your obliques."

"Oh."

To my surprise, he bent with ease. Whatever the issue with his back, it wasn't too bad.

"Sorry to disappoint," Miles said, slipping back behind his mask of indifference. "I just turned thirty."

Close. I would've pegged him a couple of years younger.

His eyes narrowed when I scooted in front of him to check the alignment of his shoulders. "Why are you here? I mean…what's wrong with you?"

I thought *I* was bad. But this guy took socially awkward to another level. Either that or he didn't give a shit. "Shannon's my best friend. I'm just helping out." I smiled reassuringly. "Don't worry. I know what I'm doing. I've taken the classes before."

My attempt at casual conversation came to a screeching halt when he looked away. For the rest of the class, Miles kept his eyes trained forward, and he didn't say another word.

After what felt like a million years, Shannon blew her whistle. I turned to Miles to wish him luck, but he was already trudging toward the steps.

"You're welcome," I muttered and shifted my pointed gaze to Shannon.

She shrugged, mouthing "sorry," but I just shook it off. Miles Cooper was a puppy dog compared to Ivan. And I'd been dealing with his brand of assholery since I'd learned to walk.

I helped gather the equipment, then took a quick shower and headed out to the parking lot, "All You Need Is Love" spilling softly from my earbuds as I trudged across the pavement.

Halfway to my car, I noticed Miles sitting on the open tailgate of a red Ford truck, his bodyguard a few feet away.

"Can I talk to you?" he asked, easing to his feet when I jerked open the door to my old Honda Civic.

"Sorry. I'm running late." Miles looked so confused I almost laughed. "Not used to being told no, are you?"

He rubbed the back of his neck. "Actually…"

I flashed him a wry smile as I tossed my gym bag into the back seat. "That was a rhetorical question. But it doesn't surprise me."

He grabbed the door as I slid behind the wheel. "I want to hire you. To help me with the training."

From the look of distaste, you'd never know he was asking me for a favor.

"I'm not a therapist. You should talk to Shannon."

"I did," he bit out. "She told me I should ask you."

"Again…not a therapist." I made a little shooing motion with my hand. "Good luck."

"I can pay you," he said flatly.

Inclining my head, I looked up at him. "Do you even remember what my name is?" That granite jaw of his ticked. "Didn't think so."

His eyes darkened. "A thousand a week."

Everything has a price.

My *babulya* told me that when she related the story of selling her favorite gold necklace to pay for my mom's first pair of pointe shoes.

Did that apply to people too? Obviously, Miles thought so.

"You can't buy me."

The words slipped out in a whisper. More for myself than Miles. Because I wanted to be that girl. I wanted her strength. And her principles. But I *needed* the money. And need trumps want every day of the week.

A retraction coiled around my tongue. Miles must've seen it, my internal struggle and my imminent surrender, because a smile ghosted his lips.

I couldn't abide it, that smile. Not for a thousand dollars. Or ten thousand.

"Thanks anyway," I said, offering a smile of my own as I yanked the door out of his hand. "I'm not interested."

Chapter Six

Gelsey

Olga smiled when I walked through the door of Ivan's office later that afternoon.

It felt weird to be here in my street clothes. "Hey. I got a message to meet Ivan?"

"He's with Micha in the studio," she said. "While you're here, I've got some papers for you to sign. And…" her grin widened, "look at *this!*"

She flipped her catalog around and slid it in my direction. I scanned the page. Item after item from the New York City Ballet. Suitcases. Warm-up gear. Socks? All with exorbitant price tags.

"What's this for?" I asked, turning the page to find even more stuff.

Olga bounced in her seat. "It's for you! You have to order your gear! Isn't it exciting?"

I felt the blood drain from my face. "What gear?"

She tore out a form from the back of the booklet. When she saw my expression, she patted my hand. "Don't worry. You only need the things that are highlighted."

I forced a smile. "Just those, huh?" I did a quick calculation, my brain shutting down when I reached eight hundred dollars. "When do I have to place the order?"

Tapping her finger to her lips, she scanned the fine print. "It says 'allow eight weeks for delivery' so I'd say a month or so?"

A month. Before I could recover from the initial trauma, Olga said, "You need your passport now, though. They want to see proof of your application within a week."

Swallowing hard, I wiped my sweaty palm on the front of my jeans. "How much is that?"

"A couple hundred dollars, I think. I'm not really sure."

Panic rose as she shoved all the paperwork into a huge envelope.

"Here you go. We're so proud of you, Gels. I can't wait to see you decked out in your tracksuit." Her smile turned sheepish. "It's on page fifteen. I think I'm going to order one for myself."

Nodding weakly, I tucked the ticking time bomb under my arm.

I needed two hundred dollars in less than a week, and who knew how much more a month later? I had to sit down.

"Thank you. I'm going to wait in Ivan's office."

Olga tossed me a wink, and I tried to look enthusiastic, even with my stomach tied in knots.

Once inside Ivan's office, I took a seat in one of the chairs and buried my head in my hands.

Think, Gelsey.

But the only thing that kept running through my mind was Miles Cooper and his stupid offer. And then my father's voice, laced with irritation.

More pride than sense.

That's what he'd told me when I'd refused to pose for some pictures for a yoga company to use on their website. Five hundred dollars to wear a leotard *thong.* Imagining the day I'd have to explain my naked ass on the Internet to Ivan, I'd immediately refused their offer.

Angry voices knocked me out of my stupor. Micha burst through the door first, face beet red and green eyes lit with fury.

I barely spared him a glance, my attention fixed on my teacher, following a step behind. Ivan's features were schooled into a mask. Unreadable. But his cornflower blue orbs were pools of ice.

"Did you know about this?" Micha hissed, dropping into the seat beside me.

"I don't—"

"Enough, Micha," said Ivan, easing into the chair behind his desk. "You are trying my patience."

Though every fiber in my being demanded answers, I snapped my mouth closed as well.

Ivan's focus shifted from Micha to me. "We were just discussing the piece you will be performing in New York for your placement in the company."

Micha shifted, and I could feel the anger vibrating off his body. The meaning was clear. He didn't want to be my partner.

"I know the dance," I blurted, turning my body toward Micha. "The one you've been working on with Sydney? I can be ready. I can—"

"Quiet, *dorogaya moya,*" Ivan interjected. "That is not the right piece for you."

In a flash, Micha was out of his chair. "This is bullshit," he seethed, pacing in a tight circle. "I'm not going to New York with a ballet *you* choreographed to accommodate a weaker dancer." Pulling a crumpled sheet of paper from his back pocket, he tossed it on Ivan's desk. "I'll take my chances with a solo piece."

Micha started for the door, and Ivan leaned back in his chair, looking more amused than put out. "In this particular instance, *you* are the weaker dancer." Micha spun around, daggers shooting from his eyes. Ivan shrugged. "That is not my judgment. The scout was not impressed with your form. So a solo dance is not an option for you."

Micha remained silent for only a second before shaking his head. "No. No. No. This is not my fault. I'm only as good as my partner. Isn't that what you always say? *You* paired me with Sydney. *You*—"

Ivan's cool facade finally cracked, and he slowly pushed to his feet. "This was not Sydney's audition, it was yours," he growled. "Sydney is young. Undisciplined. And therefore, it was your job to take the lead. To guide. As you have been taught. You failed to do so. And when you were paired with a stronger dancer, she overshadowed you." Ivan laid his palm flat on the sheet of paper that Micha had tossed on the desk. "This ballet was created for Gelsey. And since you are riding her coattails, I would suggest you shut your mouth, and *learn* it. Or your offer to go to New York could very well be rescinded."

The standoff between the two dragged on for several tension-filled moments before Micha ceded his ground and stormed out.

I blinked at the door, too stunned to speak.

"Micha will come around," Ivan said confidently as he rounded his desk.

I took the sheet of paper he held out, a little gasp tumbling from my lips as I read the title at the top of the page.

The Dance of the Flower by Ivan Volkov.

"This is for me?"

I knew it was. My name quite literally translated to Jasmine or flower. Still, I couldn't believe it. My bottom lip quivered as I traced the title with numb fingers.

"That is your ballet." Ivan tipped my chin with his knuckle, and a tear slid down my cheek. "I've been working on it since you were a child. Since the first time you danced en pointe. We will begin rehearsals in two days."

There was so much I wanted to say, to ask, but I couldn't force anything past the lump in my throat. "Thank you, *uchitel'*."

Teacher.

The only one I'd ever had. Everything I was, or would be, I owed to him.

Popping out of my chair, I threw my arms around Ivan's neck. He stiffened at first, then returned the embrace.

"Come," he said, pulling away. "Dry your tears. I have something to show you."

I followed without question, offering Olga a watery smile as we passed her desk. Down the hall we went, to the little accounting office next to the changing rooms.

When Ivan flipped on the lights, the air squeezed from my lungs. The utilitarian desk in the corner was gone, replaced by a small vanity with a lighted mirror. And the walls were no longer white, but the palest pink. Photos from my recitals decorated the space, along with a poster from my mother's guest performance at the Royal Ballet in London.

A dressing room. For me.

Gratitude and love and so much more bubbled up. But when I turned, Ivan was already gone, the door whispering closed behind him.

"Thank you," I said softly.

Maybe he didn't need to hear it. But I needed to say it. Even though he already knew.

Pawn shops had to be the most depressing places in the world. People milled about, some buying. Some selling. Everyone looking grim.

Melting into the shadows by the wall of instruments, I ran a hand over one of the guitars like I was window shopping. Funny, since I didn't have two nickels to rub together.

A stocky man in his mid-fifties approached with a wide smile. Something I wasn't expecting. But then, he wasn't the one who needed money.

"Can I help you find something?"

Shifting my feet, I forced myself to meet his gaze as I pulled the title for my Civic out of my back pocket.

"I need to see about a title loan."

To my surprise, his expression didn't change. He just nodded, took my registration, and motioned to the counter. "Step over here, and we'll see what we can do."

I pretended to check out the jewelry in the case while he busied himself punching data into his computer. Wedding rings, gold lockets, and other trinkets glinted under the harsh lights. I felt like an intruder, glancing over someone else's memories. And their misfortunes.

Abandoning the pursuit, I turned to a woman a couple of feet away with a baby propped on her hip. Her voice was strong as she haggled with another employee over the best price for the ring she intended to purchase.

But no. She wasn't buying. She was selling.

They finally agreed on a number, and she kept that stoic look in place until he turned for the register. Only then did I see defeat marring her features. Our eyes met, and she gave me a little shrug.

"Miss Howard." Shifting my focus back to the clerk, my heart did a nervous somersault. No longer smiling, he sized me up with narrowed eyes. "We can't make a loan on your vehicle since there's already an outstanding debt."

I glanced down at my registration, then up to his face. "I don't understand. That's my car. It's paid off."

Maybe it was the tremble in my tone. Or the way my hand started to shake. But his features softened. "The debt is with us," he said quietly as he slid another paper in front of me. "It's right here."

He pointed to the date. Six months ago.

"H-How? It's my car. And I have the title."

Shrugging, he tipped his chin to a sign above the register.

Get money today! Keep your title! Easy terms!

"The loan was made to a Christopher Howard. He's on the title." His voice lost the rough edge. "Is he your...?"

Silence swelled. But I couldn't bring myself to admit Christopher was my father. It felt like a betrayal. Or proof he didn't care about me.

I cleared my throat. "Yeah...Sorry. I must've forgotten about that."

Cocking his head, he rested his forearms on the glass. "If you've got something else, I'll try to make you a deal."

I had nothing. The notion hit me like a ton of bricks, and my shoulders sagged. Twenty-two and I had nothing of value to bargain with. His eyes fell to my right hand—to the ruby and diamond ring that never left my finger.

No.

I took a step back. "I can't sell this. It's my mother's."

Was my mother's.

"A loan then? You've got three months to pay it back."

I darted a gaze to the jewelry case full of other people's abandoned mementos. And I wondered if the owners had willing parted with them, or just ran out of time.

Don't do it.

But I was already sliding the band off my finger. I felt naked without it. Stripped bare.

Dropping the bauble into his waiting palm, I said, "Just a loan."

He nodded with no conviction. "Sure. Sure."

My skin crawled as the clerk took out a loop and examined the ring for flaws. There weren't any. To me, it was perfect. But I kept my mouth shut.

"How much do you need?" he finally asked.

In my periphery, the woman with the baby watched our exchange. Recalling her determination, I infused steel into my spine and lifted my chin.

"I won't go less than five hundred."

Scrubbing the tears from my eyes, I ran out of the pawn shop and slid behind the wheel of my mortgaged car.

For all my determination, I'd ended up with only three hundred dollars. The flash of courage did me no favors when it came to negotiations. Not that there were any.

"Three hundred. Take it or leave it, sweetheart."

Worse yet, I still didn't have all the money for my passport, my whole reason for pawning the ring in the first place.

Seems there was an interest payment coming due on the title loan. And since my dad had been suspiciously absent lately and not returning my calls, I didn't trust him to take care of it. That wiped out one hundred and ten dollars.

I drove through town in a daze, my thumb sliding back and forth over the indentation on my finger.

Was this really how life was supposed to be? Did crushing defeats always follow triumphs?

As if to answer my own question, I turned onto the quiet street and coasted to a stop under a tree in front of the house where I'd once lived with my parents. Before things turned bad. Before my mom died and my dad lost himself to booze and gambling. When he could still look me in the eyes, because now he saw his dead wife's face.

Pulling out my phone, I checked Dad's whereabouts on the tracker he'd installed. A red blip in New Orleans, Louisiana. The dot hadn't moved since last night. And since my dad was a truck driver, I surmised that he was holed up in the Crescent City. Lured by twenty-four-hour booze and gambling. I couldn't compete with that.

Sniffling, I swiped my finger over his name. Straight to voice mail.

Instead of telling him I knew about my car or berating him for spending the two days he was off a month getting lit and blowing our money one state away, I forced a smile he couldn't see.

"Hi, Daddy. I was expecting you last night. I guess you got tied up." Cursing the tremble in my voice, I pressed my lips together. "Anyway. I've got some good news. Give me a call, okay?"

I ended the call before another plea slipped over my tongue. He didn't deserve it.

My gaze lingered on the white house my mama had purchased

with the last of the money she'd made from her endorsements. All gone. Along with the proceeds from her life insurance policy.

All that was left was the ring.

Digging my thumbnail into the vacant spot on my finger, I leaned on the gas and sped away. Leaving the memories of my better life behind.

Chapter Seven

Miles

WHAT HAS YOUR LIFE BECOME?

Normally, when that kind of shit floated through my head, it was time to call my shrink. Because esoteric questions about the meaning of life usually foreshadowed some type of breakdown.

But not today.

Today, as I stared out the window of my truck at Daryl, looking ridiculous in his faded blue T-shirt, board shorts, and flip-flops, I really wanted to know what the hell had gone wrong in my world that this dude was my only ride and die.

"Fuck my life," I muttered as I grabbed my gym bag.

Daryl fell into step beside me as I headed for the entrance to the Y. Because he did that now. Not in front of me. Or behind me. Right beside me like we were BFFs.

Jesus.

Cutting in front of him to pull the door open, I gave a pointed look to the floral print board shorts as he passed. "Flowers, dude? Really?"

He didn't bother to respond, just pushed his sunglasses on top of his head and did a slow perusal of our surroundings. Doing my best to hide my annoyance, I flashed my membership card to the kid at the counter. He had that deer in the headlights look.

"How's it going, bud?" I asked as I shoved my wallet back into my gym bag.

The column of his throat bobbed. "Fine," he squeaked. "Good, I mean. Really good."

"Awesome." I rapped my knuckles against the desk and then headed for the locker room, passing a smirking Daryl.

"I hear there's an aerobics class for seniors," I said, hitching a thumb at one of the workout rooms. *"Sweating to The Oldies* or something like that. Feel free to join. I got this covered."

My shit-eating grin froze when we rounded the corner and came face-to-face with a small mob. Mob might be overstating it, but the narrow hallway was packed with bodies.

At first, I thought someone might have keeled over in one of the classes. But then I felt the electricity as several sets of eyes turned my way. The hackles on the back of my neck stood up in response. Not that I thought I was in imminent danger. But the power balance was definitely not in my favor.

Before I could get my bearings and plow through the crowd, Daryl stepped in front of me. "Stay or go?" he asked, shooting me a serious look over his shoulder.

I rolled my eyes and made to pass him. "Don't be so overdramatic. It's just a bunch of soccer moms."

One of Daryl's meaty paws wrapped around my bicep. *For fuck's sake.* Rather than start a fight, I let him do his thing.

"Excuse me, ladies," he said gruffly as he waded in with me in tow. "Coming through."

Grimacing, I put my head down. "Take it easy, dude."

I'd had bodyguards in the past who were a bit overzealous. Daryl didn't seem like the type, but I didn't want to give him a reason to go all Rambo.

Parting the crowd with relative ease, he delivered me safely inside the locker room.

Unlike the last time I was here, the place was deserted. Except for Shannon, who spun to face me, eyes wide and skin pale.

"Oh, thank God." She rushed forward, and I instinctively retreated. "Sorry. Sorry. I tried to call, but there's no phone number for you in our system."

I chuckled, motioning to the door and the fans on the other side. "You think?" I dropped my bag in front of an empty locker. "Ask me sometime about the girl who worked at my dry cleaners. She posted my cell number on her Facebook account. Along with my address. Fun times."

Back then, it had really pissed me off. But now, I wasn't sure how I'd react. How much longer would fans bother with me, anyway?

Shaking off the feeling of being a has-been at thirty, I yanked my T-shirt over my head.

"What are you doing?" Shannon asked, panic glazing her tone. "Put that back on."

Damn, this chick is high-strung.

I offered a patient smile. "It's just a few fans. No big deal. I'll sign a couple of autographs…" I sighed. "Why are you shaking your head?"

"Steven is really freaked out. It's more than a few fans. The bleachers around the pool are overflowing."

Meeting Daryl's stony gaze, I jerked my chin to the pool area so he could check it out. He nodded, then marched away, while I turned my attention back to Shannon. "Who's Steven?"

"The facilities manager. He's afraid someone's going to crack their head open on the deck. Or drown. Or…I don't know."

Biting her bottom lip so hard it lost color, she wrung her hands.

I pushed to my feet. "Well, then. Let me talk to him. I'll set his mind at ease."

It struck me then, how much I wanted to be here. Out in the world. I'd known it since the morning after my talk with Dr. Reber. Takeout food and one night a week with a woman I paid just wasn't enough anymore.

Daryl sauntered back in, slashing a finger over his throat and shaking his head.

Fucking perfect.

"Look, I get it," I said to Shannon, my tone taking on a harder edge than I intended. "But my leg is fucked. I need the therapy. So we gotta come to some type of terms."

She contemplated for a second. "I suppose I could try talking to Gelsey again." When I gave her a blank stare, she shook her head, exasperated. "Gelsey Howard. The woman you talked to after the last class."

The angry little mouse with the fucking attitude.

"She's not interested," I said. "Turned down a grand a week and told me to get bent. I guess she's got another gig."

Shannon's brows shot up. "You must've really rubbed her the wrong way. And she doesn't have another job. Or she wouldn't be here filling out an application for a janitor position."

"She's here?" My gaze swiveled to the door as if she might appear out of nowhere. "Like, now?"

Shannon's eyes widened. "Well, yes. But—"

Hopping to my feet, I tossed my gym bag over my shoulder. "What are we waiting for, then? Let's go talk to her."

Gelsey's angry glare slid over Shannon's shoulder and landed squarely on me.

I made a sweeping gesture around the messy room.

That's right, little mouse. All of this could be yours.

Sweaty rubber mats. Overflowing hamper filled with dirty towels. And the trashcan looked especially ripe.

Surely, spending a few hours at my place was preferable to cleaning up this pigsty.

Or maybe not. Her scrunched up brow and pursed lips told me she was a minute away from turning down the deal. Again.

"I wouldn't do that," said Daryl when I pushed out of my chair.

"Well, you ain't me," I shot back. "Just keep propping up the wall and mind your business, leaner."

Gelsey straightened when she saw me coming. Which maybe added a half inch to her height. Making her eye level with my Adam's apple.

"Twelve hundred," I growled as I skidded to a stop beside Shannon. "And I'll send a car for you."

The angry little mouse glanced me over with eyes the color of blueberry jelly beans. I hated blueberry jelly beans. Usually. Almost always.

"I have a car," she said, crossing her arms over her chest.

"But you don't have a damn job. At least not one that pays thirteen hundred bucks a week."

Her lips parted slightly, and I bit down a satisfied grin. If everyone had a number, this was hers.

But instead of agreeing, she flicked her gaze to Daryl. "Boyfriend?"

I felt my lips twitch. *Good one.* But not good enough. "Husband. We're deliriously happy. Are you going to take the job, or what?"

Shannon inched out of our semi-circle. Away from the line of fire. "Y'all have got this covered. So I'll just…"

Waving her off, I kept my eyes glued to Gelsey, who'd yet to say yes.

"Fourteen hundred," she countered.

I was about to agree when I noticed her fingers, balled into fists at her side. She wanted the job. But she also wanted to win. But then, so did I.

"Thirteen-fifty."

"And you'll send a car?"

"An Uber."

The smallest one I could find. No air-conditioning? Super.

Gelsey peered up at me through her lashes. It wasn't a sexy look. More like she was ready to flay my balls. "I'll take the job if you can answer one question. What's my name, Miles?"

Angry mouse.

"Gelsey Howard. Now, do we have a deal?"

She jerked a nod. "Yes."

"Good. You can start in the morning. I'll leave my contact information with Shannon."

I'd just about made it to the door when Gelsey called my name.

I spun to face her, wondering what the hell else she was going to ask for. "Yeah?"

"I would've done it for a thousand," she said, a smile tugging her lips.

Chapter Eight

Gelsey

I LOOKED UP FROM MY DINNER WHEN SHANNON SLID INTO THE SEAT across from me on the patio at the Moonshine Grill.

"You really must be upset," she mused, eyeing my plate of chicken-fried steak, baked macaroni and cheese, and garlic mashers. "Keep eating like that, and Micha won't be able to lift you."

She was right, of course. And I rarely indulged in comfort food. But at the moment, I was too busy being terrified to worry about it.

"Why didn't you tell me?" I hissed as she picked up her menu.

"Tell you what?" She looked around, presumably for a server. "I need a drink. Do you want a drink?"

I rolled my eyes. "You know I don't drink."

"You also don't eat complex carbohydrates. Yet, here we are."

She had a point. Maybe I could use a drink. Maybe if I got drunk enough, I'd forget about the fool I made of myself this morning. Or the rock god I'd agreed to work for. At his mansion no less. No, no…his *estate*. That's what Architectural Digest had called it. Was an estate bigger than a mansion? Probably.

Shannon finally noticed my distress and put down the menu. "Jeez, honey. I was just kidding. What are you so worked up about?"

Before I could answer, the server appeared. Shannon quickly ordered a raspberry Cosmo, whatever the hell that was, then turned her attention back to me. "Well?"

"He gave me his address. I looked it up. It's…been in *magazines*. Multiple."

Austin was teeming with musicians. You couldn't drive down Sixth Street without seeing a bunch of guys who looked exactly like Miles with drumsticks hanging out of their pockets or guitar cases slung across their backs. But I had no idea that most of them were actually trying to *be* Miles.

I rubbed my forehead with the heel of my palm, willing away the headache attacking my frontal lobe.

"He's paying you thirteen fifty a week," Shannon said, unable to hide the amusement in her tone. "That didn't clue you in?"

When she put it like that, it made me feel even more foolish.

Straightening in my chair, I crossed my arms over my chest. "Yeah, well. I'm not going to do it. I'll just call and tell him he has to get someone else. End of story."

"Gelsey—"

"Don't even try to talk me into it. I'm not going to be responsible for breaking a national treasure at the largest estate in Austin."

She snorted. "You're not going to break him. It's water rehab, the same thing you've been doing since you were twelve. If it makes you feel any better, I told Dr. Reber I recommended you and he thought it was a great idea."

"He did?"

She smiled at the server who dropped off her Cosmo, then slid the cocktail my way. "Of course, he did. Now take a drink and relax."

Reluctantly, I picked up the martini glass and sniffed the purplish liquid. The last time I'd sampled one of Shannon's drinks, I'd nearly spit it out.

"Bottoms up, I guess."

To my surprise, the berry flavored liquid went down smoothly, with just a hint of warmth. Smacking my lips, I evaded Shannon's grabby hands when she tried to reclaim her glass.

"Easy with that," she warned. "It may taste like candy but there's still quite a bit of vodka in there."

Nodding, I took another small sip and my nerves started to abate.

"All those articles about Miles on the net," I said, running my finger over the rim of the glass. "None of them mention how badly he was hurt. It's all just speculation. Why do you think that is?"

Shannon sighed. "Probably because he disappeared after the accident. Tori, the other survivor, she kind of reinvented herself. She's a band manager now. And she's dating Logan Cage."

I stared into the drink, frowning. "I have no idea who that is."

For the next hour, Shannon ran down the list of notable bands from Austin that were tied to Damaged in some way. Groups that rose to prominence in the wake of the tragedy.

"So Miles doesn't play anymore?" I asked after Shannon had finished her story.

"Nope." She dipped a bite of my chicken fried steak into the garlic mashers. "He just kinda faded away after the accident. Until the reunion concert. There were reports he went to rehab a couple of years ago, but it's all hush-hush."

I slid the plate in front of her when she reached across for another morsel. "I still don't know if I can help him. I'm not even sure where to begin since he won't talk about his injuries."

"Why don't you just ask him?" I gave her a you-can't-be-serious kind of look. "It's not prying. You need to know what you're dealing with in order to help him. Jot down some questions, the same kind the therapist asks you when you go in for treatment. Speaking of, how's your knee?"

I flexed my foot out of habit. No pain. But then, I hadn't danced since I got my offer from Tatiana. "It's good. I'll see how it holds up in rehearsal."

"Are you going to tell the mad Russian about your new job?"

I snorted. "Do I look crazy to you? Ivan's been really nice to me lately. The last thing I need is for him to pull his support."

"Yeah, right," she scoffed. "Like that would ever happen. You're his little star. His dragonmoya."

"*Dorogaya moya,*" I said softly.

"Whatever. He adores you."

Of course, Shannon thought that. And I'd never bothered to correct her. I wouldn't do it now, either.

A lie by omission.

Shannon had already left the company when my back had flared up the last time. She didn't know about the four weeks of rehearsal I'd missed. And she wasn't there when Ivan brought Sydney in to replace me.

I shouldn't blame him. But I did. Deep inside, in a place that would never see the light, I condemned him for abandoning me. And a pretty pink dressing room wouldn't change that.

I drained the last of the Cosmo, the trace of liquor strengthening my resolve. "I'm not taking any chances. I've got three months to get my ducks in a row. Now help me with these questions for Miles. Because there's no way I'm going to New York with no money."

Miles

Sixteen steps down the narrow staircase to the basement and I was there. At the door to my studio.

After the accident, Taryn had converted one of the rooms on the first floor so I wouldn't have to come down here to make music. She hadn't asked. When I'd arrived home from the hospital, it was just there. Shiny, clean, and new. A sterile room with white walls and no memories. And no life.

Tori and I had practiced in that space before the reunion show.

She had a studio at her place—more elaborate and three times the size—but it had a ghost of its own.

My little room on the main floor was neutral ground.

Switzerland.

But down here, I could practically hear the wail of Paige's guitar and the timbre of Rhenn's silky smooth voice.

Hovering at the threshold, I flipped on the light and looked around. Against the wall sat a couch with an indent that hadn't been there six years ago. The hollow told the story of the many nights I'd spent here. Always when it rained. Because in this room there were no windows. And no sound. No way to hear the thunder or see the lightning or feel the storm.

But tonight the skies were clear. So there was no reason for me to be here. Except for the pull. I felt it in my chest. A tugging at my heartstrings.

Stepping inside would be a surrender. So I didn't give in. Not completely. Instead, I eased onto the carpet, resting my back against the doorframe. One foot in this world and one in the past.

And that's where I stayed until morning light crept down the stairs, and the invisible string unwound.

Chapter Nine

Gelsey

S HAKING OUT MY HANDS, I MADE THE LONG TREK FROM THE CIRCULAR driveway to the door of Miles's three-story Spanish style mansion. Needing a moment to center myself before ringing the bell, I closed my eyes and let my head fall forward, concentrating on the soft music floating through my earbuds. And I breathed—in for three counts, out for three counts. In for three counts…

"What are you doing?"

Gasping, I jumped back a foot, my hand flying to my chest. "Jesus!"

Miles leaned a shoulder against the doorframe, eyeing me curiously. "Were you like, meditating or something?"

When I gaped at him, he raised a brow like I was the weird one.

"No, I wasn't meditating!" I wheezed, yanking off my headphones. "How did you know I was out here?"

A smile ticked up one corner of his lips. "You tripped the motion sensors when you stepped onto the porch. There are also at least a dozen cameras in the yard. Wanna tell me why you've been pacing around behind the fountain for the last twenty minutes?"

I glanced over my shoulder at the granite sculpture in the center of the driveway. "You have cameras? Out *there*?"

I shifted my attention back to Miles, who was already heading in the other direction. "Yep. If you're finished casing the joint, the pool's in the back."

Slipping inside, I glanced around as I toed off my ballet flats. The house was enormous. And elegant. With white marble floors and high ceilings. Venturing a little farther, I passed room after room filled with expensive furnishings and exotic knickknacks.

"Miles!" I called and skidded to a stop when I stumbled upon a room that looked different from all the others. Instead of fancy art, the walls were covered with posters. And records inside glass cases. A drum kit sat in the corner, next to a piano and a stand that held three guitars. Wandering in to get a closer look, I paused in front of the first poster.

DAMAGED—SIXTH STREET REVIVAL TOUR 2012

There had to be at least fifty cities in a dozen countries.

"What are you doing?"

I whipped my head to Miles, hovering in the archway. "There you are. This place is huge. I kind of got lost." I glanced back to the poster. "You really went to all these places?"

At that moment, I realized I'd never seen Miles angry. *This* was angry. No ranting. Or smart-ass comments. Just deadly calm. And a dark gaze.

"Let's go," he roughed out.

"I'm sorry. I got lost, like I said."

"This way." I thought he was going to show me to the door. But instead, we ended up in the kitchen.

"Stay here and don't move," he ordered before storming out of the room.

Since I couldn't find the front door without a roadmap, I buttoned my lip and wandered over to the bay window. The entire city was laid out in the distance. Tall buildings painted against a cloudless sky.

My heart sank as I heard feet pounding against the stairs, followed by a door slamming. Because I knew there was no dealing with Miles Cooper. And this would end badly.

Burying my disappointment, I slid a hip onto the barstool and waited.

By the time Miles returned, I had my phone out, the Uber app lighting my screen.

Slamming a paper onto the marble in front of me, he spat, "Sign this. It's an NDA. In case you get it in your head that you want to sell a story to the tabloids, this is ironclad. And I will sue your ass if you violate it."

Tipping my head all the way back, I searched his face for any sign of warmth and, finding none, I eased to my feet. "I don't think this is going to work out. Can you point me to the door?" Miles narrowed his eyes. "The door?" I repeated, more forcefully this time. "I want to leave now."

The words finally penetrated his thick skull, and he snorted like he was the aggrieved party. "Yeah. Sure thing."

He led me back through the house, feet slapping against the marble like he had a vendetta. Against me or the stone, I wasn't sure.

As soon as I spotted the foyer, I scooted around him. "Thanks. I can take it from here."

In the time it took me to shove my feet into my shoes, Miles closed the distance between us. "Why won't you sign it?" he challenged, glaring down at me like he expected me to crack under the weight of his stare.

Arrogant prick.

"Because you didn't ask," I hissed, yanking the door open.

The sun warmed my face as I stepped onto the porch. With a shaky hand, I pulled out my phone and summoned the Uber. Eight minutes. Enough time to make it to the end of Miles's long ass driveway. I'd just pulled my earbuds from my bag when my phone buzzed with a message.

Your payment method has been declined.

Sinking onto the first step, I tried again with the same result. My dad still hadn't put any money in my account. And since all I had was the cash from the pawn shop, a taxi was my only option. An expensive option, but well worth it to get me out of crazy town.

The door creaked open, and I hopped up like I was on springs, scampering to the bottom of the steps.

"Gelsey."

Bracing myself, I turned and faced Miles, framed in his massive doorway. "Don't worry. I'm leaving."

I only made it three steps before a bellow sliced through the morning air. "Stop!"

And I did. Not because Miles commanded me to. But because I was pissed.

Spinning around, I parked a hand on my hip. "Is that how you talk to everyone? If it is, it's no wonder you stay locked up in your house. Because I'm sure you don't have any friends."

My smile chased the shock right off his face, and he slowly meandered down the steps. "Is that what you heard? That I don't have any friends?" He chuckled. And it wasn't dry and brittle for a change. "What else do you think you know about me?"

As much as I wanted to tell him about the site I'd found that went into great detail describing his assholery, I held my tongue. By all accounts, he was kind to his fans. It was the press he had a problem with.

And me.

"Nothing," I said truthfully. "I didn't even know who you were until Shannon told me. I'd never heard your music, and I couldn't pick you out of a crowd. But just so you know, I'd never sell a story to a tabloid. And I wasn't snooping. I just got lost."

He crossed his arms over his chest, contemplative. "If you didn't know who I was, then why did you agree to help me?"

I thought about all my injuries. My constant struggle to stay fit so I could dance. And the pain etched on Miles's features the day we met.

"Because you offered me a lot of money."

He laughed, rubbing the back of his neck. "At least you're honest."

The genuine smile I'd glimpsed yesterday when we were sparring appeared out of nowhere. Full lips and sexy stubble. Straight white teeth. And a dimple. He looked so different when he smiled. Younger.

"Good luck, Miles," I said sincerely.

His hand came down on my arm when I turned to leave. The touch was barely there, but I felt it sizzle all the way to my marrow.

"Listen...maybe I overreacted," he said. "I'm not used to having people in my personal space. But I'm in a shit ton of pain, and I could really use your help."

His index finger traced a circle over my skin. Once. Twice.

Walk away, Gelsey.

"On one condition." A little suspicion crept back into his gaze, but he nodded anyway. "You've got to trust me. Not with anything personal. But if you question my motives every time I open my mouth, this will never work."

Miles sucked in a deep breath and looked around. Anywhere but at me. "Yeah. I can do that."

I had my doubts, but I didn't voice them, and he took my silence as agreement. Sliding my gym bag off my shoulder and onto his, he placed his free hand on the small of my back, urging me toward the house like I might change my mind.

When we reached the door he looked down at me with a furrowed brow. "You've really never heard my music?"

I thought about the playlist of Damaged songs I'd added to my Spotify account after my Google stalking. And I smiled. "Nope."

Chapter Ten

Miles

G ELSEY STOOD IN FRONT OF ME, STUDYING MY POSTURE WHILE I STUDIED her. She looked so determined. To do what, I wasn't sure. So far, the only thing she'd done since we got in the pool was adjust my stance.

I twitched when her hand slid over my hip, and she shot me a worried look. "What's the matter? Are you in pain?"

Since I was on my best behavior, I resisted the urge to roll my eyes. "No, I'm fine."

Relief flashed across her features. "Good. Just tell me if I hurt you." I nodded, like I'd done the past three times she'd reminded me. Another series of minor tweaks and she smiled. "You're doing great."

I raised a brow. I couldn't help it. And then I was smiling too. "Well, we've established that I know how to stand. But you can't take credit for that. I've been doing it successfully for twenty-nine years."

Biting down a grin, she went back to work. "It's not about standing. It's about engaging your core." She laid her palm flat on my six-pack. "You're not having any difficulty yet because these muscles right here are solid." Her hand drifted a tad lower, her pinky grazing the waistband of my board shorts. "These muscles though, they need some work."

I snorted. Couldn't help that either. Before the accident, full body workouts were my thing. But now, the only muscle groups I worked consistently were my abs and my arms.

"We're going to have to agree to disagree on that. My abs are a work of art."

A dainty snort parted her lips. "I can prove my theory if you'd like."
"Oh yeah?"
She shrugged, so confident. "Once we get out of the pool, I'll lay

you down and show you how much work you need to do on the lower abs."

A visual popped into my head sending all the blood racing to my dick. Something in my eyes must've given away my dirty thoughts, because Gelsey shook her head, panicked.

"No, no. I didn't mean…If you were thinking I meant…" Groaning, she hid her face behind her hand. "Of course, you weren't thinking that."

I dipped my head to catch her eyes. "And you're a mind reader now?"

She chuffed out a little breath, then dropped her voice to something that approximated a baritone. *"Aren't you supposed to be in school? You know, high school?"* Her shoulders sagged. "I don't have to read your mind since you made yourself clear."

I thought back to the day at the Y, and the way I'd spoken to her. *Dick*, my inner voice chided.

"It was a joke."

Gelsey dismissed the comment with a shrug. "Can you turn around, please?" Peering up at me when I didn't move, she added, "I need to check your back."

Welding my teeth together to keep from saying something to make it worse, I did as she asked.

After a moment, she said softly, "My body is pretty typical for a ballet dancer." Her hands traveled casually up my spine, feeling every vertebra. "Long neck. No boobs. Skinny as a rail. So I can't blame you for thinking that."

I twisted to look at her, and she gave an admonishing little glare, which I ignored. "I was just being a dick. I'm good at that. But I didn't mean it." It wasn't the apology she deserved, but I was out of practice. She offered a shaky nod, and adjusted my shoulders, forcing me to face forward.

"So you're a ballet dancer?"

"Yes," she replied, the smile in her tone evident. "I've been invited to dance at the New York City Ballet Company. I'm leaving in a couple of months."

I didn't know shit about ballet, but that sounded impressive. "Congratulations."

"Thanks. I just have to make sure I don't get injured between now and then."

A hint of anxiety threaded her tone. Barely there. But I heard it.

"Is that a problem for you? Injuries?"

I felt the warmth against my back when she sighed. "Yes. I have something called a spondylolisthesis. It's why I have so much experience with water therapy." Her touch traveled over my shoulders and down my arms. "Good. You can turn around now."

I faced her, and she crouched to adjust my hips. Lifting her gaze, she smiled. "Eyes forward. You're slouching."

My back went board straight, mostly because her hand returned to my stomach. Forcing my thoughts away from what it would feel like if her fingers skimmed lower, I picked a spot in the distance to focus on. "So…this spondylo thing. What is it and how do you treat it?"

"There is no real treatment. I have what's known as a bilateral pars defect. It's a stress fracture in my spine that allows the vertebra to slip back and forth." She popped to standing and stepped beside me. "Arms out in front of you."

I shifted my attention her way without moving my head. "You can't have surgery or something?"

Turning my palms upward, she pursed her lips. "No, it's inoperable. I just have to make the best of it. Unfortunately, dancing makes it worse."

"Then why would you—?" Our gazes collided, stealing the question from my lips. Dancing wasn't a choice for Gelsey. I could see it in her eyes. The same glow I used to have when I talked about music. Like it was air. And I'd suffocate without it. "Is it going to get worse over time?"

"Not if I keep up with my core training."

I got the feeling she was speaking in half-truths. Or maybe it was wishful thinking.

She put some distance between us. "I think we're done for today."

I nodded, and she made a beeline for the steps. The way she moved, she didn't look injured. Just the opposite. She was thin, no doubt, but every square inch of her was toned. And her ass. It was shaped like a perfect heart.

I joined her on the deck and she wrapped a towel around her waist, obstructing my view.

No fair, little mouse.

Plopping onto the chaise lounge, I reached for my pack of smokes. I was about to light up when I noticed Gelsey's expression. It was somewhere between mild distaste and oh-my-God-you're-fucking-disgusting. I used to feel the same way. When it mattered.

Tossing the cigarette on the table, I leaned back and tilted my face toward the sun. In my periphery, I caught sight of Gelsey pulling the band out of her hair. Golden locks spilled over her shoulders, landing just short of the towel cinched around her waist.

Since I didn't like blondes, I closed my eyes. They popped open a minute later, seemingly of their own accord.

"I thought you were going to prove me wrong," I said, rising on one elbow.

Gelsey continued to rifle through her bag. "You've already had a day. We'll do it next time."

I went back to gazing at the clouds. "Yeah, I get it. I wouldn't challenge me either."

Biting down a smile when wet feet padded against the deck, I settled deeper into the lounger.

"It wouldn't be a challenge."

I squinted up at her. "I guess we'll never know."

Deep blue eyes roamed over my face. "Scale of one to ten, what's your pain level?"

"Three. And before you say anything, that's as good as it gets."

Chewing her lip, she contemplated for a couple beats. "Okay. Flat on your back."

Any hope I had that the test would involve Gelsey climbing on top of me flew out the window when she moved to the end of the lounger. "Raise your legs to a ninety-degree angle and hold them there. Don't let me push them down."

Lifting my head to see if she was serious, I raised a brow. She countered with a dramatic eye roll.

"Fine," I said, getting comfortable. "This shouldn't take—"

Before I could finish the thought, my calves hit the back of the lounger with a thud.

What the actual fuck?

"I wasn't ready," I ground out.

Her hands flew up in mock surrender. "No problem. You want to try again?"

"You're damned right." This time when I lay back, I focused. And lasted all of two seconds.

Three more attempts and I jerked myself to sitting. "What was that? Some kind of trick."

"Nope." She eased down onto the lounger next to mine. "My turn."

"Yeah, right." I scoffed. "I outweigh you by a hundred pounds."

"Yet you toppled like the Roman Empire under my mighty touch." She wagged a finger at me. "No using your bodyweight, though. Just your arm. Lay it flat on my shins and push."

This was more than confidence. Or a trick. And I knew then how it would turn out. Still, I dropped to my knees at the end of her lounger to take my medicine.

In the back of my head, I still expected it to be hard for her. And maybe it was. But she made it look easy.

"Well, that was embarrassing," I said, dropping onto my butt on the deck when the demonstration was over.

"Don't feel bad. Nobody ever uses those muscles unless they need to." She patted her legs, then popped to her feet with a smile. "I'm going to get going."

I skimmed her petite frame as she wandered over to the table. My dick twitched in protest when she shimmied into a pair of sweats and a faded tee.

After hoisting her bag onto her shoulder, she turned to me. "So…I'll see you day after tomorrow."

It wasn't really a question, but still, she hesitated, like she was waiting for a response.

Reclaiming my spot on the lounger, I closed my eyes. "I'll be here."

Chapter Eleven

Gelsey

I CRASHED TO THE GROUND, MY ASS MEETING THE FLOOR WITH AN unceremonious thump. Micha's hands flew up, like it was my fault he'd dropped me.

"*Pridurok,*" I hissed as I rubbed the sting out of my hip.

Our first day of rehearsal, and I was already resorting to name calling.

Micha paused with the water bottle halfway to his lips. "What did you say?"

He'd spent as many years in this company as I had. How he'd never picked up a word of Russian, I'd never know.

Before I could reply, Ivan stepped between us and offered me his hand.

"She called you an idiot," he said, hauling me to my feet. "And I tend to agree with her."

Micha shifted his focus to our teacher. Which showed me where I rated in this conversation.

"It's not my fault she has weak ankles. I never had this problem with Sydney."

My gaze immediately fell to the floor. Because maybe he was right. My ankles were weak. Along with my knees and my back. He was a dick for pointing it out, though.

"Perhaps you should spend a day in her pointe shoes," Ivan said mildly. "Or a month. Or years. And then we will see how your body holds up. Let us take it again from the top. And this time," he looked right at Micha, his tone dripping with sarcasm, "try not to drop her like a sack of potatoes."

Warmth bloomed in my chest, spreading to my sore muscles. In all my years of study, I'd never heard Ivan defend one of his ballerinas. He was old-school. More than a little sexist. And I wasn't sure if he even re-alized the disparity between the male and female dancers. Sure, the men leaped higher and were just as graceful. But they didn't have to balance on the tips of their toes. Or worry about being dropped from six feet in the air.

I didn't dare to acknowledge the comment, for fear I'd be treated to an equally scathing remark. But when the music started up again, my spine straightened out of habit.

"So this is how it's going to be?" Micha asked glaring holes in Ivan's back. "You two against me."

For the first time, I noted something besides utter confidence in his stance. And though I loved seeing him brought down a couple of pegs, I needed his head in the game, and not on Ivan. Less chance I'd end up on the floor that way.

"I'm not against you," I said. "We're in this together. Shake it off."

He shimmied his shoulders, something he always did to loosen up. "I'm good."

But he wasn't. I caught him stealing glances at Ivan as we began our first side-by-side sequence. And the moment he hoisted me in the air, I knew something wasn't right. The position of his hands was off. Not a lot. But enough to throw me out of balance. He lost his grip, and I went sailing to the ground for the third time.

Before another insult passed my lips, he caught my wrist and pulled me to my feet. "I'm sorry," he whispered. "Are you all right?"

The fingers of his free hand trailed up my back before slowly gliding down to settle at the curve of my waist. A couple of years ago, the gesture would've melted me on the spot. Now I couldn't get away quick enough.

Micha's eyes flashed with anger at the rebuff. "I wouldn't drop you if you'd just stay still."

His tone was resolute, and I wondered if he'd always been able to bend the truth with such ease.

I love you, Gels.

Obviously so.

"I *didn't* move," I bit out. "Not a muscle."

Micha dismissed me with an eye roll, his focus on Ivan. "She isn't used to working with a partner anymore. Maybe she should improve her balance before we move on to choreography. I'm not going to take the blame if she gets hurt."

Snatching his towel and his water bottle, Micha strode out of the studio.

"I held my position," I said, as much for myself as the man watching me carefully from across the room.

Ivan shrugged as he eased to his feet. "We will make sure to tell the doctors that when they are stitching up your face."

Despite the harsh words, his tone was as placid as I'd ever heard. Which gave me the courage to speak up. "How is this my fault, Ivan? I'm doing the best I can."

He thought about it for a moment. "It is not your fault. But unfortunately, Micha has the power. He is the horse, and you are merely the rider."

My shoulders sagged. "So what do I do?"

"Get better so you are not bucked off."

Anger bubbled in my veins at the injustice of it all. "So *I* have to improve to make up for Micha's shortfalls. That's not fair."

Ivan tossed a couple of mats on the floor next to the balance beam. "Life is not always fair, *malysh.*"

And I knew he wasn't speaking about me.

Once upon a time, Ivan was set to become the next great Russian dancer. He had it all—grace, athleticism, and the rare ability to transcend the medium. But during a guest performance at the Bolshoi in Moscow, he ruptured his Achilles tendon, cutting short his career.

It ended where it began. In Russia. And I have no regrets. It was my privilege to dance for you.

That's what he'd said in the last interview he'd ever given before he retired. But sometimes, like now, I wondered if he believed it.

Music vibrated from the speakers, pulling me out of my thoughts.

"Come," Ivan called, tapping the beam. "Let us see if we can find a way to keep Micha from dropping you on your head."

On my way home from rehearsal, I picked up some equipment from Shannon to use in my session with Miles the next day. Along with some samples of prescription strength anti-inflammatories, and a gluten-free tuna casserole she'd made especially for me.

Everything ached, and I couldn't wait to crawl into bed and let the pain relievers and the ice work their magic.

As I pulled into the carport, my heart sank a little when I noticed my dad's rig wasn't parked anywhere around. He'd sent me a text with a promise to swing by after picking up a load in New Mexico. And foolish me, I'd believed him.

With a sigh, I grabbed my tuna casserole and trudged up the concrete steps, inwardly cursing Micha for the pain radiating from the baseball-sized bruise on my leg.

He had one job—*don't drop your partner*—and he couldn't even get that right.

The thought floated away when I stepped onto the landing and spied the red notice pinned to my door. Clutching the Pyrex dish a little closer to my chest, I scanned the document.

Three Day Notice to Vacate

My heart stalled when I shoved the key into the lock and it wouldn't turn.

"Please."

I tried again, ramming the flimsy wood with my shoulder. Daphne, my neighbor, popped her head out.

"Gelsey. What's the matter, love-bug?"

The smile slid off her face when I turned with what I could imagine was panic in my eyes. "I can't get into my apartment! They said I had three days!"

Her gaze shifted to the notice in my hand, and her features softened. "It's okay." She approached slowly, like one might a skittish cat. "May I?"

When I didn't answer, she slid the paper out of my hand. After scanning the document, she grabbed the doorknob and turned the key.

"These old locks are a little tricky," she said, like I hadn't lived here for almost five years. "Sometimes you gotta give 'em what for."

"Th-Thank you," I said, as she pressed the eviction notice into my hand.

"No problem." She gave my fingers a squeeze. "Let me know if you need anything."

Pulling myself together, I jerked a nod. And then I stepped inside my apartment so I could figure out what the hell I was going to do next.

Chapter Twelve

Miles

SHIFTING IN THE UNCOMFORTABLE-AS-FUCK FOLDING CHAIR, I SIPPED MY coffee and stared out the window at the gunmetal gray clouds.

The storm had rolled in sometime after midnight, electric fingers stretching across the inky sky and lighting my bedroom from corner to corner. Then came the thunder. So loud it shook the walls. After that, there was no sleeping. Just hours of tossing and turning and fighting the urge to hide out in the basement.

At the first hint of daylight, I'd hauled myself out of bed and headed here—to Millwood. Not that I was in the mood to pour my heart out. But the hospital, with its schedule of meetings that started at the ass crack of dawn and took place hourly, was the perfect place to blend in. Here, I wouldn't have to deal with Emily's looks of concern. Or her questions over my bloodshot eyes. I could tuck into a corner, drink my coffee, and thumb through the ancient copy of Rolling Stone I'd found without arousing suspicion.

The air punched from my lungs when I came across a large photo of Paige, number nineteen on their list of the greatest guitarists of all time. Words jumped out, full of praise for her insurmountable talent, and sorrow for a life cut short.

When I couldn't take it anymore, I tore the article from the binding and quickly folded the paper into the shape of a bird. It was a sad little ritual. Crazy, really. But I didn't want pieces of Paige in the world floating around aimlessly. So I collected any I found.

"Miles?"

Tucking the bird into my pocket, I shifted my attention to Dr. Sheppard, both brows raised. He'd seen the look before. But instead of heeding my silent warning, he propped his ass against the side of the desk, folding his hands in front of him. "Do you have anything you'd like to share with the group?"

In the few times I'd been here, I'd never spoken. He knew that. But by addressing me, he gave everyone in the room an invitation into my neurosis. Sometimes I wondered if that was the point.

Recognize that guy in the corner? Yep—it's Miles Cooper. And he's as fucked up as you are. Feel better about yourselves now?

I couldn't even call him on it. Doing so would only add *paranoid narcissist* to whatever notes he kept on me in his file.

Ignoring the stares from the group, I glared at the doc. "I'm good."

We continued our standoff until a snort from a kid slumped in his chair in the front row broke the stalemate. Early twenties, if I had to guess. Long, stringy hair. Mad at the world.

"You too good to talk to us?" The kid sneered. "Or maybe you know you ain't got any real problems. Unless your supermodel girlfriend left you."

The dig sank in deep, hitting some buried target, and Paige's image peeked from the corner of my mind. Red hair. Bright smile. Petal soft skin that tasted like vanilla pudding.

My silence only spurred the little fucker on.

"Is that it?" he taunted. "No more morning blowies for the rock star?"

I didn't realize I was on my feet until Dr. Sheppard stepped in front of me. "Miles," he warned, both hands on my chest now. "Sit down, please."

Given the doc's stature—five nine or so to my six five—I could easily look right over his head and into the kid's spiteful brown gaze.

"You don't know me, son," I growled. "So you better shut your mouth. Unless you'd like me to shut it for you."

Sheppard tensed, his fingers digging into my pecs. But I didn't spare him a glance. I was too busy watching junior's eyes light up like I'd just made his fucking day.

Shoving the sleeves of his hoodie up to his elbows, he took a step back. But not to retreat. More like an invitation. "Come on and get some then," he spat.

I smiled, more than willing to take him up on his offer. Until

I noticed his arms. Scars marred his pale skin. Some faded. Others so fresh, the scabs had barely healed. But it was the wound that ran from his wrist to the crook of his elbow that made my stomach flip.

The kid was no poser. He was all in with the pain. And that's why he was taunting me. He couldn't exactly pull out a blade and carve a nice little notch into his skin right here in front of everyone. No. He wanted me to bring the relief. A fist to his face. Or a blow to his ribs. Anything to mute the voices inside his head. And I got it. I really did.

"Come on!" he hollered, his face contorting with rage.

My anger slid away, pooling on the ground at my feet like thick sludge. "Some other time."

I dropped into my seat, and his smile faded, leaving nothing but anguish. The kid was an open wound.

"Chickenshit," he spat before stomping for the door.

Sheppard made a valiant attempt to regain control of the group. But it was no use, and he dismissed everyone a moment later.

Instead of heading for the exit, I sank back in my chair.

"That was Blake," the doc said with a sigh as he removed his glasses. "He's a good kid."

"I can tell." I scoffed, immediately regretting the comment when I thought of the kid's arms. "What's his problem, anyway?"

I wasn't sure why I asked. It's not like I didn't have enough trouble of my own. Or else I wouldn't have come here in the first place. To a psych hospital. Because I couldn't handle a fucking rainstorm.

"He was in a boating accident a couple of years ago. He was going too fast and took a turn too sharply. His younger brother fell over the side. He didn't notice right away and, Tanner—that was the kid's name—he drowned."

My gut loosened enough to send bile racing to the back of my throat. "How? I mean…"

"He hit his head." The doc rubbed his eyes and sighed again. "He was a strong swimmer, so he didn't have a life jacket on. But he was only nine, and the wake pulled him under. Terrible tragedy."

Taking a sip of lukewarm coffee, I dug my fingers into my thigh. My own little exercise in self-harm. Because I knew how the kid felt.

I blamed myself every day for Paige's death. I didn't admit to it.

Mostly because I couldn't stand it when people tried to absolve me of the burden. It was mine. All I had left of her.

"You know," Sheppard mused. "Blake is a musician too. At least he was before all this happened. Maybe you could talk to him?"

A bitter laugh scraped my throat. Because he had to be joking. "Why the hell do you think he'd want to talk to me?"

He took a quick look around to make sure no one was watching, then said in a tone close to a whisper, "Well, he shelled out five hundred bucks to go to your concert. We talked about it during one of our sessions. But that stays between us." Fairly certain he'd at least *bent* the rules on client confidentiality if not broken them completely, I nodded. Satisfied with my promise, he stood up. "Think about it."

And I did.

Finishing my coffee, I stared out the window, weighing the pros and cons while Sheppard buzzed around, collecting paper cups, napkins, and half-eaten donuts.

When a couple of people wandered in for the next session, I pushed to my feet. I'd only made it to the end of the aisle when something told me to stop. That voice in my head that sounded so much like Rhenn's.

Do something.

Sheppard paused when he noticed I hadn't moved. "Is there something else, Miles?"

"No. I mean yes." I rubbed the back of my neck. "Is the kid a resident?"

The doc nodded, a hopeful smile curving his lips. My eyes immediately drifted to the ceiling. *Stay out of it.* That was all me. My own voice warning me not to get involved. Which made it easier to ignore.

"Have him in your office for my next session," I called over my shoulder on my way to the door. "Better tell him to check his attitude, though. 'Cause if he mouths off to me again, I'm putting him on his ass."

Chapter Thirteen

Gelsey

"Where are you now?" Shannon's tone held a hint of anxiety. "Can you turn around?"

I wiped the fog off the inside of the windshield with the sleeve of my hoodie. "No. I'll be at Miles's house in ten minutes."

Maybe. *Hopefully.* I wasn't sure exactly where I was.

After staying up all night trying to get a hold of my dad, my brain was a little hazy. He hadn't answered my calls, and after my fourth message, he'd turned off the tracker app off on his phone.

Nobody was going to save me.

Strangely enough, that was the push I'd needed to pull myself together and formulate a plan. Which I'd then shared with Shannon, since it involved couch surfing at her place. Thankfully, my best friend was an early riser, and by six a.m. she'd given me her blessing.

An hour later, I had all my clothes in plastic garbage bags.

It wasn't until I'd dragged the first load out to the car that I'd realized a storm had rolled through in the middle of the night. Since the rain had slowed to a trickle, I'd decided to keep my appointment with Miles. I needed to ask him about the money, anyway.

Casting a glance at the ominous clouds, I said, "I'll wait until the storm breaks and then head your way."

I didn't want to tell Shannon that my windshield wipers were on the fritz. She'd only worry.

"Okay," she said wearily. "I left the key under the frog on the porch. Please be careful."

"I will. Thank you for everything."

"It's no problem." After a beat of silence, she sighed. "I'm so sorry about your dad, Gels."

"Me too."

I took my eye off the road long enough to end the call, and when I looked up, the entrance for Rob Roy Estates was right in front of me. I jerked the wheel to the right, and my worn tires lost traction on the rain-slicked road. After the longest two seconds of my life, I regained control. But not before adrenaline flooded my system. By the time I reached the gate guarding Miles's long driveway, tears stained my cheeks. I managed to punch the numbers into the keypad before the sobs broke free.

I didn't even try to hold back. Or pretend the universe wasn't playing a cosmic joke on me, giving with one hand and taking with the other. After ten minutes or so, I pulled myself together and, easing off the brake, I started down the long driveway.

My heart stalled when I spotted Miles pacing by the fountain.

Before I'd even come to a complete stop, he yanked the door open. Crouching at my side, he grabbed my hand. "What happened?"

"N-nothing. I just…" A fresh torrent of tears spilled onto my cheeks, and I looked down. "Sorry."

"Don't apologize." Lacing our fingers, he stood up. "Come on. Let's go."

"Go where?"

"Inside." His grip was like iron, but also comforting in a strange way, so I let him help me to my feet.

"Wait," I said. "I need my tote."

He reached around me and pulled the back door open. A garbage bag full of my clothes tumbled out, landing on the wet pavement with a splat. Without missing a beat, he tossed the bag back onto the seat and then grabbed my faded canvas carryall.

"This?"

I nodded, wondering if there was a limit to how much embarrassment a person could endure. Surely this should count as double.

It was then I noticed his bare feet.

"What are you doing out here without shoes on?" I asked as he hustled me up the walk.

"I saw you on the camera, sitting in front of the gate." He glanced over his shoulder at me. "I thought you might've had an accident."

I looked down. "No."

Daryl was waiting inside the foyer when we ducked inside. "Miss Gelsey," he said to me before shifting his focus to Miles. "Anything I can do?"

My cheeks flamed when Miles turned to me. "What's wrong with your car?"

"I-I... Nothing. It's just old."

"Why don't the windshield wipers work?" he pressed.

Was he really that observant? And how long had he been watching me? My stomach sank as I pictured the ugly crying. And let's not forget wiping my snot on the shoulder of my hoodie. He squeezed my fingers. "Gelsey."

"Oh...there's a short in the electrical system. The wipers work, but only on the intermittent setting."

"What else?" he asked. I blinked at him. "What else is wrong with your car?"

I shifted my feet. "The blinkers on the driver side don't...uh...blink."

Miles closed his eyes, the muscle in his jaw ticking furiously. "Don't you know how dangerous that is?" His tone was quiet but lethal. "What if someone had slammed into you in the rain? Never mind. Give me your keys."

"M-My—"

"Daryl's going to take a look." Miles's dismissed me for the moment, addressing his bodyguard. "Didn't you say you used to work on cars?"

"Planes," Daryl replied smoothly, holding out his open palm. "Same principle."

A nervous chuckle tripped from my lips. "You don't have to. I'm leaving as soon as it stops raining and..." The big man took a step forward, wiggling his fingers. And Miles had yet to let go of my hand. It was like being sandwiched between two large mountains. I pulled the key fob from my pocket. "Here you go."

"Fix it," Miles said to Daryl. "And if you can't fix it, find someone who can. We'll be in the den."

Holding my ground when Miles started to walk in the opposite direction, I smiled at Daryl. "Thank you. I really appreciate it."

Miles turned, made eye contact with his bodyguard, and mumbled, "Yeah, thanks."

A smile curved Daryl's lips. More like a smirk. "Don't mention it." Tossing the keys in the air, he sauntered toward the door.

Miles waited until he was outside to say, "Fucking leaner. It's about time he earned his keep."

"What's a leaner?" I asked, falling into step behind him.

"Just a nickname. He's always leaning on something."

"Do you assign all your employees nicknames?" He shrugged, which was as good as a yes. "Do *I* have a nickname?" The muscles in his back bunched up, and I dragged my feet in response. "Tell me."

When I stopped altogether, he ground to a halt as well. It was either that or let go of my hand.

"Angry mouse," he said.

My mouth fell open. "Angry *mouse?*"

He smiled, and it changed his whole face into something...*extra.* "You look like a little mouse with your fur all hacked up when you get mad. It's cute."

He was cute.

And why hadn't I noticed it before? Handsome, yes. Devastatingly so. But not cute. Cute was for puppies. And Miles was more like a bear. A teddy bear.

"Come on," he said, giving my arm a gentle tug. "Let's eat some lunch and you can tell me why you have bags of clothes in your back seat."

Miles

"I want to meet her," Emily said, her eyes fixed on the door.

I grabbed two bottles of water from the open case on the island. "You can meet her later."

Emily pulled a face but didn't ask any more questions. Which was a good thing since I didn't have any answers. There was no good reason my assistant shouldn't meet Gelsey.

Fishing a Post-it Note from my front pocket, I dropped it on the counter. "Can you place an order for lunch? All the information is there. And get something for yourself." My gaze slid to the back door, and I felt my lip twitch. "And get something for what's his name too."

"Daryl." Em propped a hip against the counter and perused the order, wrinkling her nose. "What kind of restaurant is this? And what the hell is bone broth?"

I shrugged, because I had no idea. I'd told Gelsey to pick anything she wanted. And the girl went way off the reservation. No burgers. No fries. Just a variety of organic meats and steamed vegetables. And bone broth.

"It's healthy," I said. "Nothing wrong with that."

Em strode to the fridge, grabbed a Dr. Pepper, and defiantly popped open the top. Her eyes rolled back in her head as she took a sip. "Yum." Smiling wide, she tapped her can to my bottle. "Here's to your boring meal. I'll be ordering a pizza. Nice and cheesy. You know when the grease soaks right through the cardboard box? Yeah, that."

"Funny." I headed for the door. "Let me know when the food arrives. And steer clear of the den."

Cursing my slip of the tongue, I cringed and kept walking. Maybe Em wouldn't notice. No such luck.

"She's in the *den?* Nobody's allowed in the den," she called after me. "*I'm* not allowed in the den!"

"Yeah. Yeah," I muttered. Em was right. And I still couldn't figure out why I'd marched Gelsey there. Back to the scene of the crime. The room I'd almost eviscerated her for daring to enter days ago.

But inside, I knew.

Gelsey was all about the quid pro quo. The only way to earn her trust was by revealing something about myself. I wouldn't be doing that. But she could get a pretty good feel for who I was by wandering around my den. It was all there. A cabinet full of my favorite 80s movies on DVD. Posters from my tours and platinum albums. My drums. All the remnants of the me I once was.

Maybe if she saw all that, she'd feel inclined to answer a couple of questions. Like why the hell she was rolling around town with all her belongings in the back seat of her death trap.

I tapped out a text to Daryl. *Any news on Gelsey's car?*

He responded seconds later. *It's a piece of shit.*

Smiling, I replied: *That's not news.*

Slipping my phone into my pocket, I rounded the corner, my steps faltering when I heard the music.

I stepped into the room, and Gelsey beamed at me. "You have the entire Beatles catalog. On vinyl."

Sidling up behind her, I glanced at one of my classic albums on the turntable. "You ever used one of those things?"

"Yep," she quipped, taking the bottle of water out of my hand. Sinking to her knees, she started flipping through the albums. "Oh my God. You've even got one of the UK editions of *Please, Please Me.*" She ran her fingers over the cover, biting down a smile. "Of course, you do."

I eased down beside her, amused. "How is it you've never heard of Damaged, but you know the difference between the UK and the US edition of a group who broke up twenty-five years before you were born?"

Tilting her head, she pulled out another LP, opening the cover with the care of someone handling a Fabergé egg. "Twenty-seven years."

"Huh?"

Cutting her gaze to me, she smiled. "I was born in ninety-seven. The Beatles broke up in seventy. Well, technically sixty-nine, since that's when John Lennon announced he was leaving the group. But it wasn't official until April the following year. So that's twenty-seven years."

Even the most hardcore music fan couldn't pull dates like that out of their ass. "You didn't answer my question."

She crisscrossed her legs and took a sip of her water. "The Beatles are the only thing I listen to besides classical. They were my mom's favorite band."

Which also made no sense. "But your mama's what, late-forties? Fifty?"

Gelsey looked down, and even with the blond hair curtaining her face, I could see the sadness. "She would've been forty-three this year. She died when I was eleven. Bone cancer."

Before I could offer even a word of comfort, she climbed to her feet. "I need to make a call. I'm supposed to be moving today."

Which explained the bags in her car. But not the way everything was thrown in the back seat like she'd fled a burning building.

None of your business.

"Sure."

She wandered over to the window while I pretended to check my phone. But other than putting a little distance between us, she made no effort to conceal her conversation. Since it was my house, and there were a dozen other rooms, I should've given her some privacy.

Shoulda. Coulda. Woulda. *Didn't.*

"Hey," she said and paused for a beat. "No, I'm still over at Miles's. How's the weather over there?" Silence, and then a groan. "Really? How bad?" Stealing a glance, I found her chewing her bottom lip. "Okay, well, Miles is having someone check my car. The windshield wipers aren't working." Letting her head fall back, she closed her eyes. "I didn't tell you because of what you're doing right now," she finally said. "Please don't worry so much. I'm a big girl. This is just a minor bump in the road." She laughed, and for some reason, my shoulders relaxed at the sound. Just when I thought her conversation had taken a turn for the better, she sighed. "Nope. I haven't heard from him. What's he going to say? 'Sorry you're homeless. My bad.' He'll wait for the dust to settle and then he'll make contact." She pressed her forehead to the glass, and I could see her bottom lip wobble in the reflection. "I know he's messed up. But I love him."

Welding my teeth together, I digested that little nugget. At least I knew Gelsey wasn't in any danger. She was just in love with a douchebag. Good on her.

Shoving to my feet, I busied myself putting the album back in the sleeve.

When she appeared at my side a moment later, I tossed her a curt smile. "Lunch should be here anytime. Let's go find Daryl and check on your car so you can be on your way."

Chapter Fourteen

Gelsey

I followed Miles through the house, a little confused by his latest mood swing. But why should I be? The guy was a walking, talking contradiction.

Two days ago, he'd nearly taken my head off for setting foot in the room where he'd deposited me after bringing me in from the rain. And for an hour, while we'd discussed lunch and music and other nonsensical things, he'd been relaxed. I'd let my guard down too and made the mistake of talking about my mom. And that's when everything had changed.

Obviously, his little sanctuary was filled with too many ghosts to accommodate mine. My ounce of sadness combined with his ocean of misery disrupted the balance. And now he wanted me gone.

At least I'd get lunch out of the deal. And that would give Miles time to settle down enough so I could ask about my pay.

I wasn't at all familiar with the layout of the house, but I thought the garage was off the kitchen. But instead of heading in that direction, Miles pushed open a door and we stepped into a gym that rivaled the one at the dance company. Top of the line Nautilus equipment all around the room. Along with an elliptical, two treadmills, and a stationary bike.

I'd barely had time to take in my surroundings when he marched me through another door and onto the patio in the backyard. We were on the far side of the pool now, next to a breezeway that connected the house to the garage. We entered through the first bay and passed four cars that looked like they'd just been driven off the showroom floor before coming upon the truck he always drove. It was a nice truck but looked out of place in comparison to the other sleeker and more expensive vehicles.

My mouth dropped open when I spotted my little Civic, her hood up and her guts strewn out on a tarp.

"Your electrical system is shot," Daryl said as he wiped his greasy hands on a shop towel. "You're lucky the whole thing didn't catch fire. I'm not sure it's worth fixing."

Panicked, I glanced over all the parts. "Can you put it back? I mean, I don't need the wipers or the blinkers. I just…" My chest caved in when the first tear spilled onto my cheek. Stupid tear. I swiped it away with a determined hand. "I need my car."

In a flash, the other Miles appeared. The one with the kind eyes and the easy smile. He wasn't smiling now, though.

"Did you hear what he said?" He stepped in front of me, blocking my view of anything but him. "Your car isn't safe. I don't trust that it will ever be safe. I think the best thing to do is to give Daryl the title so he can sell it for scrap."

Whatever animosity I thought I felt for my father doubled in size, taking up all the space in my body.

"I don't have a title…my dad…"

I couldn't finish the thought. A tiny piece of me would always protect my father. Or at the very least, not betray him.

While I stood there, gasping for breath, Daryl scooted by, patting Miles on the back on his way to the door. Miles didn't acknowledge him, his eyes locked on mine. And I held on. Even as the waves threatened to drag me down, I didn't let go. And then his hand found mine, and I could breathe.

"Come on. You need to sit down."

I squeezed his fingers, afraid he might let go. But he only walked us a few feet to the rear bumper of his truck. With his free hand he released the liftgate.

"Up you go." Banding an arm around my waist, he hoisted me onto the cool metal. "Now what about your dad?"

When I didn't say anything, he lifted my chin. And it was like he'd broken the seal. Everything poured out in a rush. Things I hadn't even told Shannon yet. And the whole time, Miles nodded, his thumb sweeping back and forth over mine.

When I finished, I looked over at my broken-down car, everything I owned crammed into the back seat.

"It's really pathetic," I whispered. "This is all I have to show for my life."

"So far," Miles corrected, and I blinked up at him. He smiled, tucking a strand of hair behind my ear. "This is all you have to show for your life *so far*."

He hopped beside me on the liftgate, still holding my hand. "How about we do this? Daryl can work on your car a few hours a day. Lord knows, he needs something to do. And you can stay in the pool house and drive one of my cars until he's finished."

His grip tightened when I tried to pull away. "Miles… No. I can't do that. You don't even know me."

He sighed. "Your name is Gelsey Howard. You're a ballet dancer with good taste in music. Sort of. You weigh about…" he looked down his nose at me, "a hundred pounds. You're really strong for a tiny thing. You've got blue eyes. And you look like an angry mouse when you get mad. Am I missing anything?"

"You're missing *everything*."

"Name one thing."

For the life of me, I couldn't. Besides the fact that he didn't know me, like at all. Which I'd already mentioned.

"Come on," he said, bumping shoulders with me. "It's not a big deal. The pool house is completely self-contained. You won't even have to see me if you don't want to. And I know for a fact it's really close to your new job."

I rubbed my forehead, trying to think of one good reason I shouldn't do this. *Think.* There had to be at least a hundred.

"Just until my car's fixed," I said, peering up at him. "And I want to pay you rent."

Shrugging, he helped me to my feet. "Fine by me."

"Wait…how much rent?"

He threw his head back, laughing. "I don't know. And I don't care. I'm starving. Let's go get something to eat."

Miles

The son-of-a-bitch was going to make me say it. I didn't think for one minute that Daryl didn't understand exactly what I was trying *not* to put into words. He was just torturing me. And it was working.

Hip propped against the workbench in my garage, he treated me to one of his bland stares.

Heaving a sigh, I rubbed the back of my neck. "All I'm saying is that it wouldn't be a tragedy if you couldn't fix the damn thing."

Swinging my gaze to Gelsey's Civic, I glowered at the piece of shit.

"*So,*" Daryl drew the word out slowly, "you just want me to *act* like I'm trying to fix it? But you don't want me to actually fix it?"

I got the urge to pat the fucker down and see if he was wearing a wire. Because, yeah, it sounded all kinds of shady; me telling him not to repair the damn car since Gelsey had agreed to live here until it was fixed. But honestly, I'd only thrown in the suggestion that she should move into the pool house on a whim. Picturing her sleeping on the couch at her friend's place didn't sit well with me. Not when I had a seven thousand square foot house.

"Yes," I bit out. "She's leaving for New York in a few months. I'd like to see her make it there in one piece."

That much was true. I knew better than most that Fate was a fickle bitch with bad timing. And tempting her never turned out well for any-one involved.

Daryl surveyed me for a moment. "I can do that."

"Thanks."

I paused on my way to the door. "You know that title loan place off Guadeloupe? Ez Pawn?" He nodded, and I turned around. "What do you think they give for a car like this? Loan wise?"

I had no clue, but it seemed like Daryl was a man who knew a little about a lot of things.

He shrugged. "No more than a few hundred."

Dipping into my pocket, I pulled out a wad of cash, chuckling to myself. Apparently, I had more money than sense. A given, since I was worth about a half a billion dollars. Peeling off eight one-hundred-dollar bills, I said, "If you happen to run by there, can you pay off the title loan?"

His brow arched as he took the cash. "Sure. The loan's in her name?"

Shit.

The look on Gelsey's face when she'd told me about her father left no doubt that she loved the man. And that she'd protect him. So she probably wouldn't appreciate me outing him to my bodyguard.

"No. It's under Christopher Howard," I said offhandedly. "But she'll need a clear title to haul the car to the junkyard. I don't want this thing in my garage for any longer than it has to be. She can pay me back whatever they give her for scrap."

A smile ticked up one corner of Daryl's lips. We both knew I was full of shit, and I'd never take a dime from Gelsey. It wasn't about money, though. If Gelsey ever had reason to call the pawn shop, she'd think her prick father paid off the loan. And I was fine with that if it led her to believe that he actually cared a tiny bit.

I took a giant step away from my partner in crime when Gelsey walked in.

Her baby blues jumped from Daryl to me, and she frowned. Shit. She'd probably heard something.

"I'm sorry to interrupt," she said hesitantly. "I was just going to get some of my clothes out of the car. And see if you have a key for the pool house. I asked your assistant. But she told me to ask you. She seemed a little…put off."

I glanced at the house and found Emily peering out the window with a scowl. Shooting her an "I'll-deal-with-you-later" glare, I shoved my hands into my pockets. "There's a code on the door. Grab your stuff and I'll let you in."

Daryl pushed off his spot. "See y'all in the morning."

Gelsey watched him go, then pulled open the back door to the death trap. "Does he live with you?"

I barked out a laugh. "Please, God, don't even joke like that. He's only staying here until Tori gets back."

"Who's that?" Her gaze shot to mine, and she smiled tightly. "Sorry. Is that too personal?"

Amazed, I looked down at the polished concrete and shook my head. "Tori Grayson is probably one of the most well-known celebrities in the world. The fact that you live in the same town and don't recognize her name…that's just weird."

"Oh, right. Tori was your bandmate. But don't most people call her Belle?"

"Yep."

My one-word answer did the trick, and she dropped the subject and went back to sorting through her stuff.

A second later when she crawled out of the back seat with only a handful of items clutched to her chest, I said, "You're going to be here at least a week. Don't you need more than that?"

She frowned. "I guess I was in a hurry this morning. My stuff is spread over all those bags. I'll come out here and sort through it tomorrow."

I scratched the back of my head. "Why not just take them all into the pool house and sort through them there?"

"I thought it might freak you out if I took everything I own inside your house."

"Pool house," I corrected brushing past her. "And I don't get freaked out." Emerging from her back seat with four bags, I inclined my head toward the other two. "Grab those, will you?"

For once she didn't give me a weird-ass look and did as she was told. After showing her how to work the lock, I pushed the door open to the pool house.

"Okay, so you got your kitchen over there," I said, walking toward the bedroom. "The fireplace works, though I don't think you'll need it. Oh, and the shower doesn't have knobs. Just set the temperature on the control panel and it does what it does. Some kind of water conservation deal." I dropped the bags next to the king-sized bed, then retraced my steps. "I'm not sure where all the remotes are for the televisions, but I'm sure you can find them."

Frozen in her spot, Gelsey looked around.

"What is it?" I asked.

"Miles…" She blinked up at me. "I don't know if I can stay here. It's too much." Letting the bags fall to the floor, she dropped onto the couch. "I feel like I'm taking advantage. I don't even know how to thank you."

I raked a hand through my hair, watching her as she looked around again. Easing down next to her, I left an adequate amount of space between us. An explanation coiled around my tongue, but I trapped it behind tight lips. Until she brought her gaze to mine.

Taking a deep breath, I said, "Before the accident, I was rich. After the first three albums, I had enough money to live comfortably for the rest of my life." My hand slid to my thigh, and my fingers dug in. "But the thing is, we sold even more albums because of the tragedy. There were bigger licensing agreements. And then…"

Scooting a little closer, she dipped her head to catch my eyes. "Then?"

I'd already told her more than most people knew. But I pushed on.

"The company the band used to modify our bus cut corners. One of the two gas tanks was in the wrong place. The rivets were faulty. And the metal they used was substandard. Even the windows weren't the right kind of glass. Their insurance company paid an astronomical settlement. And because of that, I now have more money than I could spend in several lifetimes. But here's the thing. I'd give it all away if I could go back in time and get what I lost that day. The two people who aren't here anymore. So this," I waved my hand around, "all of this…it means nothing to me."

Gelsey's eyes were like fingers on my skin, too personal. Too probing. So I shoved to my feet.

"It's just a room, Gelsey. Use it or don't." I headed for the door. "But there's no reason to thank me. And I'd prefer if you didn't."

Chapter Fifteen

Gelsey

"WHAT ARE YOU DOING?"

I spun toward Miles's voice, eyes wide like he'd caught me with my hand in the cookie jar.

Looking me over like he had a bad case of buyer's remorse, he sauntered toward me, bare feet soundless on the polished concrete floor.

I inched toward my car. Or what was left of her. Yes, she was old. But more importantly, she was the only thing on these grounds that was all mine. Not that I could beat a hasty retreat with her parts spread all over the tarp.

"You're up early," I said brightly.

I'd seen Miles shirtless on several occasions now. But something about his tousled hair and low riding sweatpants made my cheeks heat. He really was a beautiful man. But apparently, he wasn't a morning person, because my cheery greeting did nothing to wipe the frown from his face.

"What's in your hand?" he asked, serious brown eyes glancing me over with suspicion.

"Oh…" I looked down at the key fob with the Ford logo. "You told me I could drive one of your cars. But…no worries. I can get an Uber." He stepped toward me, and my mouth went dry. "Or a cab."

Gaze locked on mine, he gently pried the key from my hand. "Not the truck." He seemed to relax once he had the fob in his possession. "You can drive anything here, but never the truck."

Lack of sleep and nerves about this morning's MRI conspired, and the filter between my brain and mouth didn't engage. "Why not the truck?"

The minute the question slipped over my tongue, I regretted it. Miles blinked at me, then stowed the key in his pocket. "No reason."

In the short time I'd known him, I'd never seen him drive anything but the Ford Lightning. Which seemed odd now that I'd seen his fleet. But I had bigger things to worry about than my new landlord's eccentricities. Like how I was ever going to drive any of the vehicles in this garage. Glancing over the exotic sports cars, I swallowed hard.

"I think I'll just get an Uber."

He smiled then, and as usual, it changed his whole face. "Why would you do that?"

Recalling what he'd said last night about his wealth, I didn't want to bring up the fact that most of his cars probably cost more than I'd make in five years.

"I don't know how to drive a stick shift."

I was reaching. Playing the odds. Miles seemed like a purist. The kind of guy who wouldn't settle for an automatic.

He brushed past me and plucked a key fob from the pegboard.

"Problem solved," he said, pressing a Mercedes key in my hand.

I chewed my bottom lip. "Which one is this for?"

"The SL 600." When I blinked at him with what must have been a deer in the headlights expression, he treated me to another easy smile. And this time his dimple made an appearance. "Come on. I'll show you."

Lacing our fingers like it was the most natural thing in the world, he ushered me to the third bay, and tipped his chin to a beautiful cherry red two-seater.

"It's a hard-top convertible," he said, his lips turning down at the corners. "It's really safer if you keep the top up. At least in the city. Around here it's fine. Let me show you how it works."

He took a step, then looked down at our joined hands when I held my ground.

"You don't need to show me." A nervous laugh tripped from my lips. "Are you sure you wouldn't be more comfortable if I took the truck? I'm an excellent driver, and I have insurance." I looked over at the Lightning. "It would cover the cost of that. But not any of these."

Miles dropped his gaze, tension lines forming around his mouth.

"I'm sorry," I rushed to say. "I didn't mean to push."

"It belonged to Rhenn." He smiled softly, and it looked so out of place. "My bandmate. You know…the one who…"

The thought stalled on his lips, and his brow pinched. I knew that expression. Had seen it on my own face. Sometimes when I spoke about my mom, the finality of it would hit me. She was gone. I'd never see her again. My thumb found the vacant spot on my finger where her ring had been. My touchstone. That's what the truck was for Miles. Just a lot bigger.

"I understand," I said, and he looked at me like maybe I did. Like I was part of the club and this was a secret we shared.

Sighing, I glanced over the convertible, dipping my head to look in the window. "I guess you'd better show me how to work this thing so I can get out of here."

I stepped out of the small bathroom wearing the requisite blue paper dress, my clothes in a ball under my arm.

The smell of antiseptic lingered in the air, and my stomach turned. It was in a place exactly like this that my whole life had changed. Dreams were re-aligned. Expectations lowered. And it all started with the faint smell of antiseptic.

The nurse looked up from my chart and smiled. "You're a tiny little thing. That gown is four sizes too big."

I nodded, too nervous to respond.

She didn't seem to notice. Or more likely, she chose to ignore my pale skin and wide eyes. Because there was no reason for it. I was getting an MRI, not having a kidney transplant.

"Ah, well," she said, her tone light. "Good things come in small packages. Hop up on the table and we'll get you fixed up. It should only take a few minutes to scan the knee and then I'll be along to start your IV."

I froze, one foot on the plastic step stool. "IV? I thought you were only scanning my knee. Why would I need an IV?"

She glanced down at the chart. "Your doctor ordered a contrast MRI of the lower spine. To check your spondylolisthesis. You weren't aware of that?"

Goose bumps rose on my arms. "No."

When I didn't move, she tucked the pen behind her ear. "Let me check the order. Maybe there was a mistake."

She slipped out the door, and I took a seat on a plastic chair as far away from the hulking machine as I could get. I'd always been superstitious about my condition. No news was good news. Why would Dr. Reber order another scan?

When the nurse returned long moments later with Shannon on her heels, I sucked in a breath. My best friend was only supposed to be here so we could grab some lunch after my scan.

"What is it?" I asked, my gaze jumping back and forth between the two.

Shannon gave me a smile as she eased into the seat beside me. "Maxine asked me to call the office to see why Reber ordered the additional test. They faxed this over."

Request for supplemental medical records. New York City Ballet Company

"I don't understand."

Shannon pointed to the small print at the bottom of the page.

All records, including diagnostic tests for previous conditions, must be current.

"Your last contrast MRI was five years ago," Shannon explained. "So, not current."

"But I'm fine," I said, my voice shaky and reed thin.

"You can always refuse," the nurse piped up, eyeing me over the top of her glasses.

But I couldn't. These were the terms of the offer.

"No. I'll go ahead and do it." I shrugged at my best friend. "What choice do I have, right?"

I wanted her to tell me there was another option. That we could fix this. But she only nodded in agreement.

While I sat there, hoping the ground would swallow me whole, the nurse rifled through some more paperwork. "It says here the doctor ordered a push of Benadryl. It'll keep you from getting hives in case you're sensitive to the contrast agent." She flicked her gaze to Shannon. "Will you be driving her home?"

"No," I interjected. "I have a car."

The two exchanged a knowing look.

"It's going to make you really sleepy," Shannon said, patting my hand. "Don't worry about it. I'll drive you. But I need to get to the office, since this is going to take longer than I thought." Leaning in, she pressed a swift kiss to my cheek. "You got this, right?"

"Sure. I'm good."

She pushed to her feet, giving me a little nod of encouragement on her way out.

My shoulders sagged, and I forced a grim smile for the nurse. "Let's get this over with."

Chapter Sixteen

Miles

ROCKING BACK ON MY HEELS, I STARED AT THE SCREEN IN SHEPPARD'S OFFICE. "You know this makes my skin crawl, right?" I cut my gaze his way without moving my head.

The doc sat back in his chair, a troubled look on his face. Like he'd been caught. But then it was gone, and his professional mask slipped back into place.

"Come on, Miles. You're not that naïve. This is a psychiatric hospital. Having no surveillance in the common areas wouldn't be prudent."

He was probably right. But that didn't mean I had to like it.

Ignoring the monitor, and Blake, the kid I was here to talk to, I flopped onto the chair in front of Sheppard's desk. "What about privacy?"

"There is no expectation of privacy in common areas." I felt the scowl pull down my lips, and he pointed a finger at me. "Before you start judging, it's no different from traffic cams, or the eye in the sky at the grocery store."

He shifted, averting his eyes, and I wondered how much he would reveal. Not about any particular patient. But just the standard procedures.

"There are no cameras in the patients' rooms," he said with a sigh. "Or in the area where we hold group therapy. But I suspect you know that."

I did. And for that reason, in the two months I'd spent here, I'd never taken a meal in the dining hall. Or hung around in the rec room. And though it was against policy, Sheppard had allowed it. It was the only victory I'd ever claimed over him. And from the look on his face, he was still a little salty about it.

"Yeah, I knew," I conceded. "But I gather since Blake isn't in his room or up here, you want me to meet with him out there." I pointed to the monitor, and when the doc nodded, I scrubbed a hand over my face.

"Just at the beginning," Sheppard was quick to add. "Blake is volatile, Miles. But I don't think he's a danger to anyone but himself. That being said, I'm not taking any chances. So far, Blake hasn't done anything bad enough to ruin his life. Which gives me a little hope."

"Why?"

"Because, despite whatever darkness he's wrestling with, he still thinks he has one." Resting his forearms on his desk, he tipped forward and looked me in the eyes. "I know this could be a deal breaker for you. Going out there. Exposing yourself."

Tilting my head, I lifted a brow. "I won't be exposing myself, doc. I gotta draw the line somewhere."

A relieved smile curved his lips at my joke. "Point taken. So you'll talk to him?"

Glancing over my shoulder, I spied Daryl through the glass insert in Sheppard's door. "Yeah, I'm fine with it. But the big guy might take some convincing."

Blowing out a breath, I meandered over to Blake's table in the back of the rec room. Daryl's gaze followed me from his perch inside the glass bubble in the corner that served as a nurses' station. It was as close as he was allowed to get. And he wasn't happy about it.

Glancing over my shoulder, I tossed him a wink before dropping into a chair across from Blake.

The kid looked up, confusion lining his brow. But he quickly masked it and continued strumming his guitar.

"So…you're back, huh?"

I didn't want to start off with a lie. But keeping it simple was probably my best shot at getting him to accept me.

"It would appear so."

A bitter smile curved his lips. "And we all…fall…*down*…" he sang, brown eyes flickering with the same rage I'd detected in group therapy.

Ignoring the jab, I sank back in my chair and listened for a while.

The kid was good. Smooth. And I could tell right away who he was emulating. Maybe he was doing it for my benefit. To mock me. Or maybe Paige had influenced him because she was just that fucking good.

I closed my eyes, and I could see her sitting on the floor of my childhood bedroom, hunched over her Fender.

Listen to this, Miles. I think I wrote a song.

Shaking off the memory, I leaned in to get the kid's attention.

"You're fumbling over that transition in the middle," I said, my focus on his fingers gliding across the frets. "Use a modified F and pick up the pace."

Blake didn't acknowledge me, but when the melody circled back around, he took my advice.

A smile ghosted his lips, like he couldn't believe my trick actually worked. "Do you play? Guitar, I mean?"

"Yeah."

I was actually pretty good. But my skill level had never risen to that of Paige or even Rhenn. But those confessions were best saved for another day, so I didn't elaborate.

Reaching into my back pocket, I pulled out my drumsticks.

Blake lost track of the chords when I began to tap out an eight-beat riff on the edge of the table. I kept going, and eventually, he caught up.

"What are you doing here, man?" he finally asked. "Did you relapse or something?"

"Nope."

"Then why?"

Changing the tempo, I added a little flourish when he reached the end of the sequence. "Just play, dude. There's time for all that later."

The kid nodded, and after a moment, he stopped to jot something in a notebook. Lyrics. He really was a musician.

An hour later, an announcement came over the loudspeaker directing everyone to the cafeteria for lunch. Blake's lips fell into a frown when I stowed my sticks.

"You're not really back, are you?" he asked.

I might lose him, but I couldn't keep avoiding the question. "No."

Disappointment flashed across his features. But he masked it and quickly averted his gaze. "That's a good thing, I guess. Prove 'em all wrong."

"Who?"

He smiled again, and it wasn't bitter. More conspiratorial. "The bloggers. Some are laying odds on how long it will take for you to fall off the wagon and end up back in rehab."

Shifting in my seat, I picked at a loose piece of laminate on the side of the table. You'd think for what they charged they could afford better furniture.

Inhaling deeply, I clasped my hands to keep from destroying any more property. "I was never on the wagon."

"You're still partying, then?"

Chuckling, I shook my head. "Nah. Booze and pills were never my problem. I wasn't here for that."

I saw the recognition flicker in his eyes as his focus strayed to my wrists. But he'd find nothing there. No proof. And he *wanted* proof. "What were you here for?"

"I chased a bottle of pills with a bottle of booze."

Blake's head tilted to the side. "But you're not an addict?"

"Nope."

"So...?"

He pressed his lips together when the nurse strolled up, slumping back in his chair with the same defiant posture. But this time it wasn't directed at me.

"Miss lunch and you don't eat," she warned, tapping the watch on her wrist. "This isn't a country club, Blake."

Shooting me an exaggerated grin, he pushed out of his chair and handed the nurse his guitar. "Guess that means we should cancel our tee time, eh, bruh?"

"Looks like." I stretched, then casually hauled to my feet. "You know...I could come back next week. Bring my guitar. If you want to jam again."

Blake scratched his arm, looking anywhere but at me as he mulled it over. "I wouldn't mind," he finally said, then added a little more eagerly, "What day?"

Shit. It wasn't a trick question, but for some reason the hint of excitement in his tone threw me.

"Uh…" I rubbed my forehead. "Tuesday?"

His smile was genuine, with a hint of something else. Relief?

"Cool."

And then, as if I might change my mind, Blake spun on his heel and headed out the door.

"You got your hands full with that one," the nurse remarked as she turned toward a locked cage in the corner with games, other instruments, and even some athletic equipment.

"I thought that was Blake's guitar?"

"It is," she replied, pulling out a set of keys for the padlock.

Ambling over, I shoved my hands in my pockets. "He really shouldn't keep his guitar in there. It needs to be in a case. Preferably in his room with a humidifier. I can bring—"

She faced me with a stern expression. "He can't keep this in his room."

I glanced down to where her finger moved back and forth over the frets. And then I pictured what the kid could do with the steel string in the privacy of his room.

"Yeah," I roughed out, my throat dry and tight as hell. "Got it."

Suddenly the room felt too small. And my lungs felt too tight. The tattoo on my chest, Paige's flying guitar, pulsed with every beat of my heart.

Daryl eyed me as I stepped into the hallway. But I didn't break my stride. I needed out of this place. Into the world where razors were for shaving, and guitar strings were for plucking.

"You all right?" he asked.

Nodding, I pulled my phone out of my pocket when it rang. Unknown. I hit ignore. A second later when a text came in, I made a mental note to tell Emily to change my number. But then I saw the preview of the message. Swiping a finger over the screen, I scanned the rest of the text as I slid behind the wheel of the truck.

"I need to pick up something on the way home," I said to my shadow as he folded himself into the seat beside me.

"Lunch?" he asked hopefully.

I chuckled, the tightness in my chest diminishing. "No, Gelsey."

Chapter Seventeen

Gelsey

"GELSEY."

I was dreaming. I had to be. Because why would Miles be here? At the imaging center? But even with my eyes closed, I recognized his voice. And his soft touch caressing my cheek.

Definitely dreaming.

I leaned into it anyway.

"Wake up." His thumb skated over my bottom lip. "It's time to go home, little mouse."

"I don't...I don't have a home."

The thought made me sad. And I just wanted to sleep some more.

"Are you sure she's all right?" Dream Miles asked, his voice gruffer now.

Since I didn't think he was talking to me, I didn't answer. Nurse Maxine did though. She was here too.

"She's fine. She had a slight reaction to the contrast dye. We gave her a dose of anti-nausea meds, in addition to some Benadryl. It knocked her out pretty good."

I wanted to tell her I wasn't asleep. But obviously, I was. So I kept quiet.

The voices faded, and I was cocooned in strong arms, my cheek against soft cotton. And the smell. Citrus soap and something else. Miles. I could hear his heart beat against my ear.

But how?

Because you're dreaming.

Then sun was on my face then, light seeping through my lids. I wanted to ask where he was taking me. So I did.

"Where are we going?"

Miles didn't answer. Just held me tighter, his chin pressed to the top of my head. And since I was dreaming, it didn't seem to matter.

My eyes flew open when I landed on something cool and soft. But not as soft as the cotton. Leather. I was in a car. And Miles was leaning over me, fastening my safety belt.

I touched his cheek. Because I could.

He stopped what he was doing, lifting his gaze to mine.

"Why…why are you here?" I asked.

And I wasn't sure if I meant in my dream, or in my life.

The dimple winked from under his stubble when he smiled, and I traced it with my thumb.

"I don't know."

Since that seemed as good an answer as any, I smiled back and let my eyes drift closed, allowing the dream to take me wherever it wanted to go.

Miles

Two hours. That's all it took for the first photo of me carrying Gelsey out of the imaging center to hit the Internet. A blog. Not a major one like Perez Hilton. Some obscure little nothing site. Where it probably would've stayed if there wasn't video attached. A twenty-second clip of me telling the nurse in charge that she was an idiot for leaving Gelsey alone in a room. Passed out. In the dark.

How could I not think that someone would whip out a cell phone and capture that moment on tape?

Pure fucking gold, since the mainstream media had picked it up.

And now the speculation had begun.

Since the imaging center was in a three-story medical building with doctors who specialized in everything from bunion removal to severe mental issues, the headlines accompanying the video were off the chain.

Twins on the way! Miles Cooper carries pregnant girlfriend out of doctor's office.

Miles Cooper and girlfriend treated for substance abuse. Troubled drummer caught leaving hush hush clinic in Austin with mystery woman in tow.

Miles Cooper's heartache! Drummer's new love reportedly suffering from anorexia! Inside his private battle to save her.

And on it went.

The stories had one common thread—Gelsey was my girlfriend. My "new love." Some articles even claimed we were married. Ridiculous, since they didn't even know her fucking name.

Parked on a lounge chair in front of the pool house, I watched the alerts pour in. Each one more outlandish than the last.

A cloud of smoke hung over my head, courtesy of the twenty or so cigarettes I'd sucked down while waiting for Gelsey to wake up so I could explain. And what would that even look like?

Sorry I freaked out when you were having a routine exam. The video's gone viral. My bad.

My actions were stupid and irresponsible. I knew fucking better. But seeing Gelsey curled up on that metal table in a tiny room with no one around, like she was nothing, I couldn't help myself.

Daryl flopped onto the chair beside me, scrubbing a hand over his face. For once, I wasn't thoroughly put off by having the leaner around. He'd mobilized a small security force—five or six burly dudes who were now stationed at different locations around the property. I'd thought it was overkill until I'd noticed a contingent of press on the video monitor gathering outside the gate.

I knew the drill. In a few days it would die down. But for now, we'd have to ride it out.

We.

My gaze slipped over my shoulder to the pool house. The door was open, and I could see straight through to the bedroom. It was still dark. No surprise since the aftercare instructions the nurse had shoved into my hand while trying to hustle me out the door clearly stated that Gelsey might sleep through the night.

Plucking a cigarette from my pack, Daryl stretched his legs, looking weary.

I passed him my lighter. "I didn't know you smoked."

He took a long drag, shoulders relaxing as he rolled the smoke around in his mouth. "I don't."

Stubbing out my latest butt, I chuckled. "Yeah. Me neither."

After he finished his smoke, he sat forward, bracing his elbows on his knees. I'd seen him serious before. Usually when he'd had enough of my smart-ass commentary.

"Spit it out, dude," I said. "The suspense is killing me."

He didn't crack a smile. "I'm having some additional cameras set up tomorrow. But for now, you should go inside and stay out of view."

"Additional cameras for what?" I scoffed. "This place is a fortress."

I gazed out at the vast nothingness beyond the lighted patio. Trees lined the property all the way to the cliff that overlooked Austin Lake. Unless someone planned on boating in and then scaling a fifty-foot crag, they weren't getting up here.

Daryl frowned, seemingly unconvinced. "The property is secure by 2013 standards. But you're a high-value target for the paps again."

I sat back, unsure of what stung worse. The fact that my security was out of date, or that I'd only just regained my status as a high-value target.

"Look, Miles," he said, his tone softer but no less firm. "The surveillance you have is good, if all you were covering was the ground. But we need something in the air. For drones."

I barked out a laugh. I couldn't help it. *"Drones?* Are you fucking kidding me?"

My smile faded when his resolve didn't waver. Not even a fraction. He was serious.

I scratched at my scruff, my skin feeling too tight all of a sudden. *Drones.* What the fuck?

"I'm not trying to freak you out," he continued. "The house itself is secure. But you don't even have window alarms on the pool house. That's the reason I put the extra men in place. If someone managed to get in the backyard…"

Biting his lip, he let the threat dangle. But I had a pretty good idea of where he was going. Gelsey was in the pool house. And as of a few hours ago, she was a "high-value target" as well.

"How long will it take?"

Daryl blew out a breath, scratching his head. "A day...maybe two. I'd like to work at night so nobody knows exactly what we're doing."

He shifted his feet, clearly holding something back.

"What else?" I muttered, my patience gone. "Just give it to me straight. All of it."

"Two things. I think it's a good idea to move Gelsey into the main house until we secure the building. And also...have you thought about who's going to shadow her until this dies down?"

I let my head fall back with a laugh. "Dude. She's a nobody."

I'd been toying with the idea of putting Gelsey up at the Four Seasons or some place equally secure. As soon as she was out of my orbit, the press would lose interest.

"Don't look at me like that," I snapped when Daryl's gaze turned suspicious. "I'm not just going to abandon the girl. But it's probably better if I didn't move her into my house. Drive her where ever she needs to go in the morning. Stay with her. And I'll figure out something after that."

He pushed to his feet. "Whatever you say."

Daryl frowned, eyeing the pool house as he walked away.

Whatever.

Grabbing my phone, I scrolled to my contacts and, before I could think better of it, I swiped my finger across Taryn's name. She answered on the second ring but remained silent. Maybe this wasn't such a good idea.

"I can hear you breathing, T-Rex," I finally said, digging my fingers into my eyes.

"Hey, Miles." Instead of the strain I expected to hear, her tone was soft, almost wistful. "How are you?"

Shame and guilt flooded my insides. Because even after everything, I knew she wasn't talking about the press. Or the video. She wanted to know about me. My life.

"I'm good," I replied, voice a little shaky. "Look, T-Rex, I got no right to ask. But I could really use your help. You've seen what's going on, right?"

"Yeah. Of course. But I'm in Dallas right now with my...um... Chase. The guy you met at the concert. He's got a thing."

And because she was still her, and I was still me, and we shared a friendship that spanned decades, I couldn't help myself. "Jeez, Taryn. I hope he's got a thing. I'm sure I would've heard if you changed teams. But if you did, I'd like details."

Her laughed raced across the line, bridging more than the distance between us. "God, I've missed you, Miles."

My heart squeezed, and I couldn't find the words. And maybe she knew that too, because as soon as her laughter died down, she said, "I'm flying home in the morning. How about if I drop by and you can tell me what I can do to help."

I cleared the lump of emotion from my throat. "Yeah. Sounds good."

"Okay...see you then."

Before she could end the call, I blurted, "Taryn!"

"Yeah?"

"I...um..."

She chuckled, and I pictured the smile dancing on her lips.

"I know," she said lightly. "Me too. See you tomorrow."

Chapter Eighteen

Gelsey

TEARS STUNG THE BACKS OF MY EYES AS I STALKED TO THE WALK-IN closet. Balling my hands into fists, I looked around the vast space. *Stupid girl.*

After my talk with Miles last night, I'd felt comfortable enough to hang my clothes. I knew I'd only be here a week, maybe less. But claiming that little spot in the corner of the closet for my few belongings made me feel like a guest and not a charity case.

But I wasn't a guest. Not to Miles. Hell, I didn't even exist.

She's a nobody.

That's what he'd said to Daryl.

At first, I'd thought I was still dreaming. Things were a little fuzzy. I didn't exactly know how I'd gotten here but figured it out pretty quickly. Miles had picked me up. And now he was laughing about it.

She's a nobody.

I wasn't sure what precipitated the comment. And I didn't stick around to find out what other gems he'd regale his bodyguard with.

Spinning around, a garbage bag in one hand and an armful of clothes in the other, I screeched when I found Miles hovering by the door of the closet.

His gaze bounced from the garments to my face. "What are you doing?"

"Leaving."

He didn't seem all that surprised, but he also didn't move. So I dropped the items on the floor and turned to grab another handful.

I tensed when I felt his warm breath skate across the back of my neck. The heat from his chest scorched me through my peasant blouse, and I closed my eyes. Didn't the man own a T-shirt?

"I know you're probably pissed," he said. "And I don't blame you. But can we talk about this?"

If I turned around, it would be worse, so I took my time peeling each item off the satin hangers. "Why would I be pissed? I'm a nobody, right?"

"Why would you say that?"

His tone held a note of shock. And that was enough for me to forget all about the heat. Or his stupid citrus scent.

Whirling around, I came face-to-face with his rock hard pecs. "*I didn't say it! You did!*"

He cocked his head. "What…When?"

Instead of owning his comment, maybe throwing in a half-assed apology, he stood his ground like I was the crazy one.

"Have you looked at your phone?" he asked calmly, crossing his arms over his chest.

There were only three people who'd have an occasion to call me. Shannon was on my shit list for asking Miles to pick me up in the first place. My dad was MIA. And I didn't even want to think about what it would take to get Ivan to pick up the phone.

She's a nobody.

Miles was right. But I'd never admit it. And why was he changing the subject?

"What does my phone have to do with anything?"

Whizzing past me like a man on a mission, he buzzed around the bedroom for a minute before returning with the crossover bag I'd worn to the imaging center. He shoved the purse at me. "Check your phone."

Lifting my chin, I took the bag and dug around inside. Nothing on the screen except an apology from Shannon. Good. Maybe she'd feel bad enough to pick me up, so I wouldn't have to stuff all my shit in an Uber.

"What?" I waved the phone at him. "There's nothing here."

Closing his eyes like he was praying for strength, he muttered, "Your browser. Check your browser."

My cheeks went up in flames and I dropped my arm to my side. "I don't have a data plan."

Not exactly the truth. I'd just exceeded my usage on my pay as you go plan. But I wasn't in the mood to share.

Miles's mouth dropped open. "You don't have a...?" He shook his head, like the idea was unfathomable. "How do you get on the Internet?"

"I use a Wi-Fi connection," I said quietly. "It's not a big deal."

But it was. For someone like Miles. He probably had every piece of technology known to man, while I had a five-year-old iPhone and a first generation Kindle.

"My laptop is from the stone age as well," I added, sarcasm dripping from my tone. "Would you like to look at that too?"

He shook his head, then commenced to rub his neck like he was trying to remove a layer of skin.

"I need to pack," I said, dropping to my knees in front of my clothes. "It's your house, so I can't exactly tell you to leave. But I wish you would."

Wrestling his phone from his pocket, he shoved the device under my nose. "Not until you see this." I rolled my eyes and kept on folding. "Take it, Gelsey. Please."

Blowing out a frustrated breath, I did as he asked.

"Hit the first link," he said as he eased down beside me. I gave him the side-eye. "Just do it."

Reluctantly, I hit the link, and the TMZ logo flashed. A familiar voice bled from the speaker, but I couldn't place it. Not until the camera focused in on Nurse Maxine, jogging after...*Miles?*

"Mr. Cooper! Please!"

It was Miles, all right. He had a woman in his arms, swaddled in a blanket and burrowed against his chest. All I could see was a mass of blond hair. And ballet flats.

"That's me," I croaked.

Miles nodded grimly. "Watch."

I returned my attention to the screen in time to see Miles whirl on Nurse Maxine. "What possible excuse do you have for leaving her passed out in a dark room? For who knows how long? What if she fell off the table and cracked her skull?" He snorted derisively when the nurse lifted her chin. "Yeah, you don't have an answer for that, do you?"

"This isn't a hospital," she spluttered. "We don't have adequate staff to watch every—"

"Save it," Miles spat.

The camera stayed on Nurse Maxine as he marched away. Once he was a safe distance, she called, "If you feel that strongly, then perhaps you should've been here sooner!"

The camera swung to Miles who replied with an expletive that was drowned out by a loud beep. Daryl was now in the frame, holding the door open to the SL600. They exchanged a couple of words, then Miles gently eased me onto the seat.

The camera zoomed in as he buckled my safety belt. From the angle of the lens, I noticed a hand on his face. *My hand.* He smiled and said something the microphone couldn't pick up, then pushed to his feet, striding confidently to the driver's side.

The TMZ logo flashed again, and the screen went black.

"You were there," I said quietly, my eyes still glued to the phone. "I...I thought I was dreaming. Why were you so mad?"

When I chanced a peek, he was frowning. "The nurse took me to a dark room in the back. I guess that's where you had your test. The door was closed, and you were curled up on a metal table. Passed out from some meds they gave you." He shook his head. "Maybe I overreacted."

The warm feeling in my chest evaporated, a thousand questions pinging around in my brain. But none found their way to my lips.

Miles took my hand, scooting a little closer. "When you heard me talking to Daryl, I said you were a nobody because you're not famous. He wants to put a bodyguard on you until this blows over."

"But...no one saw my face, right?" He nodded, and I closed my eyes. "Thank God."

"That doesn't mean you can just waltz out of here." He tugged a fallen strand of my hair. "One look at this mane and everyone will know who you are."

"How?"

He took the phone and, after scrolling around a bit, he turned it back in my direction. I recognized the gate in front of Miles's house. Only people were there now. With cameras.

"Reporters?" I asked, zooming in on one of the faces.

"Paparazzi. They're sniffing around for a follow up to the story."

"What story? I don't understand."

He reclined on his palm. "Well, I did carry you out of a medical building. So the prevailing theory is, you're my girlfriend. And you're either on drugs or you're pregnant. Maybe both." He ran a hand through his hair. "My publicist is coming over tomorrow. She'll know how to spin this. Who knows? It could all blow over by then." A small, unconvincing smile touched his lips. "Don't worry. I'll handle it."

I looked down at my hands. "I'm sorry, Miles."

He sat up, dipping his head to catch my gaze. "Why would you be sorry?"

I sighed. "If you hadn't gone to pick me up, none of this would've happened. I guess it would be better if I just went to Shannon's. Does Daryl have any idea how I could...I don't know...sneak out of here without anyone noticing?"

I chewed the hell out of my lip while he contemplated.

"You can't go to Shannon's," he finally said. "Not right away."

"But—"

"There's a chance that whoever took that video is going to come forward. Even if that doesn't happen, someone is going to recognize nurse what's her name."

"Maxine."

"And when they do," he went on, "they'll start throwing money around to find out who you are. It may not work. There are laws, and I have excellent lawyers. But if it does, I can't protect you at Shannon's. It's better if you stay here."

My stomach flipped as the gravity of the situation sank in.

"I have to tell my coach," I blurted. "He can't find out from some gossip site." I buried my head in my hands as the panic took hold. "He's going to kill me."

"Gelsey—"

"You don't understand! Even if it's not true, I'll have to tell him the whole story. That I accepted a job with you. *Shit.*"

My breathing came faster, and Miles ran a hand up my back. "And he'd have a problem with that? Because of who I am?"

My gaze shot to his. "No. It's just...I'm not allowed to work outside of dance. It's a rule. Ivan has lots of rules. And I still have to rehearse."

The oddest look flashed across Miles's features. And I got it. To someone outside the dance world I probably sounded crazy. But to his credit, he didn't ask any more questions, just continued to stroke my back.

"Let's see what kind of solution my publicist comes up with in the morning," he finally said, squeezing my shoulder. "She's a genius at this stuff. You may not need to say anything."

"Okay." I blew out another breath, corralling my wayward thoughts. "Tomorrow, then."

Miles hopped to his feet, and I scrambled up as well. "I hate to ask," I said with a sheepish smile. "But I didn't go shopping. Do you have some peanut butter at your place I can borrow?"

He laughed. "Borrow? Like you're going to give it back?" Flashing me a heart-stopping grin he tipped forward and grabbed a handful of my clothes. "I'm sure we can do better than that."

My hand shot out to grab the items. I felt so stupid for jumping to conclusions; I was eager to stow the evidence. "Let me get these."

But Miles didn't let go. Instead, his grin widened, the dimple carving out a little nook in his cheek.

"Didn't I tell you?" he said, his index finger brushing over mine. "You're moving up in the world."

"Up?"

"To the main house." When my eyes widened, his smile slipped. "It's not safe out here, Gels."

Not safe.

I thought of the reporters at the gate. And the video. And all the sites dedicated to his fame. Miles was probably right. So I let my hand fall and nodded, wondering how I'd ended up here in the first place.

Miles

Gelsey held tight to a fistful of her clothes, clutching them to her chest like a security blanket. "I don't understand. Why can't I just stay out here? If no one knows who I am…"

I could see the wheels turning, and for a moment I actually considered tossing her over my shoulder and ending the discussion.

That's kidnapping, the voice of reason in my head not so gently reminded.

Technicalities.

Still, I took a step back to keep from following through with the plan.

"It was Daryl's idea," I said with a shrug, hoping that invoking the name of the bodyguard might set her at ease. "This place isn't secure. The windows and the door aren't hardwired into the security system. I'm taking care of that tomorrow."

Gelsey rubbed her forehead with the heel of her palm. She looked a little unsteady on her feet, so I inched forward, ceding the ground I'd surrendered five seconds ago.

Jesus. Why couldn't I stay away from this girl?

"You okay?" I asked, my hands buried in the armload of clothes I'd grabbed. Thank God. It was the only thing keeping me from touching her.

Peering up through her lashes, she studied my face. "Are you sure you don't mind?"

I bit down a smile. Literally sank my teeth into my bottom lip to keep from grinning. "I'm sure."

Her shoulders curved in resignation. "Okay." Parking her hands on her hips, she glanced around at the mess on the floor. "Give me a few minutes to tidy up."

"No need. I can get someone to—"

Leveling a serious glare, her lips flatlined. "If you tell me you have a maid or a butler, I'm sleeping in the Civic."

I rubbed the back of my neck, wondering how in the hell I was going to keep Cora the housekeeper hidden.

Gelsey barked out a laugh. "You do have a maid, don't you?"

"She's more like …" *Think, you idiot.* "A house manager."

Who cleans. And does my laundry. Cooks occasionally. I kept that part to myself.

Gelsey shook her head as she stuffed items into the Hefty bag. "Well, you do have one hell of a house. So I won't hold it against you."

Crouching down to help, I steered clear of the lacy thongs, boy shorts, and bras.

"What about Emily?" Gelsey asked, her attention fixed on her task. "What does she do?"

Something more than idle curiosity threaded her tone. Or maybe that was wishful thinking.

"She's my personal assistant."

Her gaze flicked to mine. "How personal?"

Pausing with a fistful of her T-shirts in my hand, I kept my eyes trained on hers. But she didn't look away.

"Pretty personal. She handles my appointments and keeps me on track." I shoved the last of her clothing into the garbage bag. "Never seen her naked, though. If that's what you're asking."

I expected Gelsey to turn red. Maybe stutter a little. Instead, she pushed to her feet and smiled. "Good to know."

Was she flirting with me? My dick answered with a hopeful "yes," and all the blood rushed south. But my brain wasn't as easily convinced. Gelsey was eight years my junior with an innocence that couldn't be denied.

Not my type at all.

If I were smart, I'd toss all her stuff into Daryl's Jeep and have him drive her to the Four Seasons. Because I didn't need these kinds of complications in my life.

You don't have a life.

I wanted to argue the point. But since it was Rhenn's voice, I kept quiet.

He was the one who didn't have a life. Not anymore. And maybe that's why a piece of him remained, floating around the cosmos. Imparting his dime store wisdom. To remind me that I was still here. Still breathing. Still alive. And maybe it was time for me to move on.

Whatever that meant.

Chapter Nineteen

Gelsey

DARYL'S HEAVY BOOTS ECHOED BEHIND ME LIKE SMALL CLAPS OF THUNDER. It was an odd sound, since these hallways were usually inhabited by dancers in soft soled shoes.

I paused at the door to Ivan's office and turned to the bodyguard with a tight smile.

"Would you mind waiting out here?"

Daryl took a second to think about it, and that unnerved me. I'd heard the warning Miles had issued from behind his closed bedroom door before we left the house. *Don't let her out of your sight.* Obviously, Daryl had taken the order seriously.

But I couldn't worry about that right now.

The short text from Ivan, summoning me to the dance company, left no doubt that he knew something. How I wasn't sure. My name hadn't been leaked in the press. Yet.

"There's no one here," I added to set Daryl's mind at ease. "Just my teacher."

It was true. The place was empty for the moment. Which was a good thing. I didn't want the entire company to hear Ivan lay into me. Or worse. It was the worse that had my skin prickling and my palms sweating.

Daryl jerked a nod but didn't look happy about it.

Straightening my spine, I blew out a breath before slipping into the lion's den. The room was eerily quiet, morning light filtering in from the window behind Olga's desk.

Ivan lifted his gaze when he sensed me at the door to the inner office. Easing back in his chair, icy blue eyes looked me over.

"Come in, *malysh*," he said, his tone measured.

As I took a seat in front of his desk, he turned his laptop in my direction. I blinked at the frozen image on the screen. A YouTube video of Miles and me outside the imaging center.

639,427 views.

My gulp was audible. A dead giveaway. "How did you know it was me?"

A shadow crossed his features. He looked…insulted. And just as quickly it disappeared. "Never mind that." He tipped his chin to the screen. "Explain."

And I did. I told him everything. From my original visit to Dr. Reber, to my first meeting with Miles, to the eviction. And finally, my appointment at the imaging center.

The weight of his intense stare forced my gaze to my hands. "I'm sorry."

For a long moment, Ivan said nothing. I cringed when the springs of his chair squeaked. And then he was in front of me, a hip resting against the desk.

"For what?" he asked, and when I looked up, he smiled. "Getting caught?"

Classic Ivan. I smiled back. "Partly."

But there was more. His was the only opinion that mattered. And not just about my dancing.

"Why did you feel you could not tell me?"

I kept my features schooled despite my shock. "You've always said that—"

"Whatever I have said does not apply to you," he interrupted, the edge in his tone making my stomach churn. Silence swelled between us, followed by Ivan's heavy sigh. "But I suppose you did not know. And that is my fault."

Breaking eye contact—something he rarely did—Ivan shifted his focus to the wall. To something beyond our conversation.

"Before your mama died…I promised her I would take care of you," he said quietly. "I fear I have not always done a good job."

At the mention of my mother, the air grew still. Quiet. Just the sound of my beating heart in my ears. "I don't understand. Why would Mama ask you to take care of me?"

The corners of his lips ticked up slightly. "Because I loved her." My mouth dropped open, and he shrugged. A helpless gesture from such a strong man. "We cannot help who we fall in love with, *malysh*. But in a different world…" He took me in from head to toe, his gaze lingering on my worn shoes. "The money Katya left you from the insurance. It is gone?" he asked cautiously, as if he knew the answer.

The screw in my chest tightened. "For a long time now."

Ivan's lids closed, the muscle in his jaw ticking. The movement wasn't exaggerated. But since he rarely showed emotion, it seemed monumental. "And you did not come to me?"

Defeat marred his tone, and I shifted uncomfortably.

"I…"

The outer door creaked, and we turned in unison. Expecting Daryl to lumber in, the breath caught in my throat. But it was Micha who appeared, looking perplexed.

"Who's the scary guy in the hallway?" He glanced between Ivan and me, and an explanation coiled around my tongue.

"Never mind that," Ivan said brusquely. His eyes found mine as he reclaimed his seat behind the desk, and I pressed my lips into a firm line. He didn't want me telling Micha about Miles. That much was clear.

Micha shrugged off his curiosity, flopping onto the chair beside me. His foot brushed against mine, and I gave him the side-eye, discreetly shifting away from him. The muscle in his neck jumped, but he kept his attention on our teacher.

"Tatiana called yesterday to extend an invitation to the opening of their production of *Swan Lake*," Ivan said casually. "You will be able to meet your new roommates and acquaint yourselves with the city."

Micha and I both sat forward.

"When?" I asked, barely able to contain the excitement in my tone.

New York. It was really happening.

"One month," Ivan replied before releasing a measured breath. "But it is not all fun and games. You will be expected to demonstrate your skills for the Company."

"Demonstrate?" Micha asked. "Like, the piece we're working on?"

"A portion, yes. You will also need to put in extra time to make sure that every move is on point. Every pirouette. Every leap. This first impression will be crucial. You must practice together, and also individually. Will that be a problem?"

I shook my head. "No problem."

Micha clapped his hands, then rubbed them together maniacally. "When do we start?"

Ivan's gaze snagged mine. It had been a long time since he'd spoken to me with just his eyes. It was a language we'd perfected when I was young. When the answer to every question was yes. More practice. More lessons. More time in the studio.

I promised your mama I would always take care of you.

And he had.

Despite the ache in my joints from yesterday's ordeal, I smiled. "I'm ready whenever y'all are."

Chapter Twenty

Miles

TARYN WANDERED AROUND THE DEN, HER FINGERS SKIMMING LOVINGLY over picture frames and knickknacks. I sat on the couch, letting her take her time. God, I'd missed her. And yet, seeing her like this, relaxed and completely at ease, was painful in a way I couldn't describe.

In public, Taryn was the face of one of the most prestigious management companies in the music industry. But here, she was the girl I'd met in junior high. Paige's best friend. They shared the same mannerisms. The same inflection in their speech. Was I the only one who noticed it? And was this ache the reason I'd pushed Taryn away five years ago?

I froze when she snatched the origami bird I'd made out of Paige's Rolling Stone article from the table. I hadn't had the chance to put it with the others.

"I forgot you did this," she said, facing me with a smile. "What's it called?"

"Origami."

"Yes!" She flopped down beside me, plucking one of the wings on the bird with her thumb. "You made me one, remember?"

My head dropped back, and I laughed. "A dinosaur. I remember, T-Rex."

Her features softened as her nickname slipped over my tongue. She'd earned the moniker because despite her small stature, Taryn roared like a prehistoric creature when she was angry.

Breathing deeply, she looked around, like she was inhaling the memories. They were thick in this room.

"So, tell me about the girl," she finally said, easing into the corner of the sectional. Her stormy eyes held a million questions. But as usual, she waited for the confession instead of prying it out with a crowbar.

And I realized that's what she'd always done. No judgment. Only love.

I was a bastard for pushing her away. And a bigger bastard for calling her now, when I needed help.

I took her hand, the one not holding the bird, and skimmed my thumb over the diamond-encrusted band on her ring finger. "First tell me about this."

Happiness flashed across her features, but just as quickly she bit down the smile. My hackles went up, and it was as if no time had passed.

If someone had hurt her…

"What is it?" I asked.

A soft smile curved her lips, her shoulder lifting in a half shrug. "Nothing, really. It just occurred to me how much everything has changed. Chase…he makes me so happy. And I'm sad that you don't know him. That Paige will never know him."

She sat up straighter, and a sinking feeling washed over me. Taryn had on her apology face. But why?

"Listen, Miles—"

"I'm sorry," I blurted, beating her to the punch. "So fucking sorry, Taryn."

She shook her head and then went on as if she hadn't heard me. "I knew how much pain you were in." Her gaze dipped to my leg, and she winced. "I was so busy trying to organize things, I didn't think about getting a nurse to monitor your meds. I picked up your prescriptions. Read the warning labels on the inserts they stapled to the bags about interactions with alcohol. But I didn't think…"

Shock stole my breath as her apology floated between us. All this time, I thought she knew. That she was keeping my secret. And that was bad enough. But all these years she'd been mired in guilt over something I'd never even considered.

"I know you're going to tell me it wasn't my fault," she said dully. "And logically, you're probably right. But I had only one job after the accident. Being there for you and Tori. I took it on willingly. Maybe if I wasn't so busy trying to manage everything I would've seen the signs of addiction and—"

"I'm not an addict, Taryn."

She blinked at me, and if it were possible, her eyes grew even more troubled. "You can't say things like that, Miles. It's dangerous." Her tone was soft. Cajoling. "I know because Chase is an addict."

Her fingers found her lips as if she hadn't meant to reveal that fact. But I already knew. From Tori.

"He was clean for eleven years," she went on after a long moment. "But he started thinking he had it beat. And you can't do that. Because the minute you let yourself forget, it can sneak up on you."

A shudder rolled through her. And I didn't know if it had something to do with Chase, or if she was picturing me on the bathroom floor the night I'd tried to end it.

Shame washed over me, and the explanation stalled on my lips. Until our eyes met. One look at the torment twisting her brow, and I set aside my embarrassment.

"The overdose—it wasn't an accident."

She cocked her head. "Not an accident? I don't understand."

Slipping the bird from Taryn's hand, I slowly unfolded the intricate design. The column of her throat bobbed as I smoothed a finger over the crease on Paige's face.

"You were right about the pain. But it wasn't my leg. Paige and I... we were together. For a long time. I loved her, T-Rex."

"No." She hopped to her feet, shaking her head. "I would've known. I was her best friend. She would've told me."

Moments passed as she searched my face. When her bottom lip wobbled, I took her hand again.

"There's more," I said, urging her down next to me. "The night of the accident, we had a fight. I wanted to bring things out in the open, and Paige wasn't ready. But she offered to come to my bunk. Just to sleep. We used to do that a lot." I forced out a breath. "But I said no."

I steeled myself for Taryn's reaction. The moment when she'd put the pieces together and realize what I'd done. What my pride had cost. She'd leave. And this time she probably wouldn't come back.

She melted against my side. Maybe from the shock. I looked down at her, prepared to meet the accusation in her eyes.

Tears shimmered in the blue depths, but no blame.

Threading her arm through mine, she rested her chin on my shoulder. "It wasn't your fault."

I should've felt relief. But I didn't.

You want to be punished.

Sheppard had told me that. And until I saw the acceptance in Taryn's eyes, I didn't believe it was true.

When I shook my head, it only strengthened her resolve.

"It was an accident," she insisted, her tone resolute. "A terrible tragedy. You don't get to own it or use it as an excuse."

Her touch was too soft for my liking. More than I deserved. "I'm not."

"You are." She held me tighter, fingers digging into my flesh. "You don't get to die, Miles," she croaked when I finally broke free. "Not when the rest of us have to keep on living."

I bristled at her use of the present tense. "I'm not trying to off myself. I'm right here. Alive."

She looked around. "This isn't living. It's existing. There's a difference."

A part of me believed that too. Or else Taryn wouldn't be here. I scrubbed a hand down my face. "That's why I hired the girl...er, Gelsey. The one on the video. To help me."

Taryn didn't say anything for a long moment. She wanted more information. And hell, she probably deserved it. But I couldn't. Not yet. And maybe she knew that too, because a resigned sigh parted her lips.

"Tell me about her," she said, tugging my T-shirt sleeve. "And we'll figure out what to do to get you out of this mess."

Chapter Twenty-One

Gelsey

DARYL REACHED INTO THE BACK SEAT AND PULLED THE BLANKET OFF ME. "Sorry about that."

Smiling weakly, I attempted to lift myself off the floorboard where I'd been hiding from the paparazzi at the gate.

"Not yet." His big hand came down gently on my shoulder. "Wait until we get into the garage."

Words were beyond me, so I sagged into my former position, resting my forehead against my knee. Now that my muscles had cooled from the five-hour rehearsal, the pain was everywhere. And I was so tired, I could barely keep my eyes open.

I felt a tap on my shoulder, and my head snapped up to investigate. Daryl was next to my open door, offering his hand. He wore the same concerned expression I'd noted all day long when our eyes would connect after I'd taken a tumble or slipped out of Micha's hold and landed on the ground.

"Thanks," I said, sliding my palm against his.

I bit down a grimace when he gave my arm a gentle tug. But he noticed, and his grip went slack.

"Maybe I should carry you."

I laughed softly. "No, I'm fine. Just a little stiff. This is normal."

"Nothing about what I saw today was normal."

Before I could comment, he banded an arm around my waist, and hauled me to my feet.

"You good?" he asked. When I nodded, he ducked inside the car and grabbed my gym bag. I reached for it, but he shook his head, slipping the strap over his shoulder. "Are you sure you can walk?"

"Positive." He matched my slow pace as I hobbled toward the side door.

"I thought you worked with performers." I peered up at him as we stepped into the breezeway. "This can't be all that different."

His hand curved around my elbow, guiding me around some uneven bricks on the stone path. "I haven't seen anything like this since the military." I chuckled to myself, picturing Ivan as a drill sergeant. But Daryl remained stoic. "You do this every day?"

I tried to shrug, but it hurt too much. "It's not usually this intense. We're learning a new routine."

My shoulders sagged in relief when we entered the kitchen. Until I saw Miles rise from his seat at the breakfast bar.

"What happened?"

He directed the question at Daryl, but his eyes remained on me. The intensity of his stare made my stomach flip as he closed the distance between us.

"Nothing," I replied, flustered by his proximity. "Just a rough day at the office."

Miles was dressed in board shorts and a T-shirt, reminding me of why I was here to begin with. I wasn't a houseguest. Or a friend.

Cementing on a smile, I straightened my spine. "You ready for your session?"

His brows dove together as he looked me over. "Yeah. That's not going to happen. Let's get you upstairs."

"Miles…"

Ignoring my sigh, he took my gym bag from Daryl. "I think I can manage to stretch all by myself. You can supervise if you want. After you get something to eat. What are you hungry for?"

A protest danced on the tip of my tongue. He didn't need to feed me. But my stomach betrayed me and let out a little rumble.

Daryl chuckled. "I'll whip something up if Emily's not around."

Miles frowned. "No thanks, dude. I've seen what you eat."

But the big guy was already heading for the fridge. I was secretly relieved when he slapped a couple of rib-eyes on the bar, along with fresh broccoli and sweet potatoes. From what I'd gathered, Miles existed on fast food, and he probably considered veggie pizza a nutritionally balanced meal.

"How do you like your steak?" Daryl asked me, ignoring Miles for the moment. When I hesitated, he added, "It's organic. And you need the protein."

I couldn't argue. "Medium rare."

Daryl went back to his preparation, and Miles let out an irritated snort. "Medium well for me. Thanks for asking."

Daryl's lip twitched in response, the only outward acknowledgment. Miles glared at him, but I saw the affection behind his narrowed gaze. He liked Daryl, whether he wanted to admit it or not.

"Emily's apron is in the pantry. Feel free to use it," Miles quipped as he grabbed my hand.

My skin tingled, a warm glow spreading from the place we were joined. It had been so long since anyone had taken care of me besides Ivan. And he wasn't exactly demonstrative.

I froze when we reached the stairs, keenly aware of my aching back. Miles slipped an arm around my waist, like he sensed my trepidation. "Lean on me. I won't let you fall."

I blinked up at him, recalling the same promise from Micha.

Trust me, Gels. I won't let you fall.

Why my mind went there, I couldn't say. Exhaustion. Or maybe it was all the bruises marring my skin. Because that's what happened when you trusted someone. It left a mark. On your skin or on your soul.

Breaking our connection, I made a valiant attempt to stand on my own two feet. But my legs were so heavy, I tripped on the third step.

Miles was right there, his strong chest against my back, and his lips next to my ear. I could feel his heartbeat. "I got you, little mouse."

And this time, I didn't fight.

Miles

Emily popped out of her chair when I walked into the kitchen.

"I didn't know you were still here," I said, setting the tray with

Gelsey's leftovers on the island next to a cooling rack with chocolate chip cookies on top. "You make these?"

Em scooted around me to collect the dirty dishes. "Daryl did. But I don't think they were meant for you."

"I hope not." I nudged her with my shoulder, chuckling. "I wouldn't be able to sleep at night if I knew he was down here making me desserts. Know what I mean?"

She shrugged without cracking a smile.

"What's up?" I asked, hoisting myself onto the island. "You look bummed."

She turned the water off, then braced her hands on the edge of the counter. "I got an email from Taryn Ayers a little while ago. Do you know anything about that?"

I should've known that Taryn wouldn't waste any time putting a plan into motion.

"Yeah." I cleared my throat, setting the cookie back on the cooling rack. "I meant to talk to you about that, but—"

Emily whirled around, pinning me in place with her glare. "You forgot? Kind of like you forgot to tell me that you moved your trainer into the house and loaned her one of your cars."

On a roll now, she tapped her finger against her lips. "Speaking of that—if the pool bunny was tooling around in one of your rides, how is it that we're now under siege by the paparazzi because you got videoed carrying her out of a medical building? I'm assuming that's the reason you need me to..." Pulling out her phone, she glanced at the screen. *"Accompany Miles to the Alamo Drafthouse to see a movie."* She shoved the phone in my direction without breaking eye contact. "Is Taryn running a dating service now? Because this sounds suspiciously like the emails I used to get from Match.com."

Reclining on my palms, I settled in for what was likely to be a lengthy conversation. Emily didn't thrive on drama. Going to this extreme to prove a point wasn't like her.

"Come on, Em. You didn't really have a membership to Match. com." I smiled wide enough to show off my dimple. "Did you?"

Her arm fell to her side, and she huffed out a frustrated breath. "Don't do that!"

"Do what?"

"Make me laugh when I'm mad at you."

She refused to look at me, so I eased to my feet and took a step. And then another. Soon I was blocking everything but the ceiling, and she had no choice but to meet my gaze.

"I should've told you about the email from Taryn." Vindicated, she lifted her chin. But her lips stayed sealed, so I wasn't out of the woods yet. *Fine.* I rubbed the back of my neck. "And about Gelsey. You want to sit down so we can talk about it? Or are you gonna keep pouting?"

She narrowed her eyes. "I'm not pouting. And what's there to talk about?"

Since she'd decided to hold her ground, I reclaimed my seat on the island.

"We eat there, you know," she said, propping a hand on her hip.

I shrugged. "No worries. This'll be Daryl's spot from now on."

Em looked away again, but only because she was having a hard time keeping her smile in check. When her attention returned to mine, a little growl escaped. "Fine. What do you want me to know?"

"Everything."

I gave her all the facts. Omitting the details that didn't matter. Like how my heart had pounded a little harder when I'd spotted Gelsey on the table in the imaging center. And how I hadn't been able to stop thinking about her since.

I'm sure there was some psychological reason for it. Something to do with seeing her wrecked and wanting to fix her.

"So Taryn thinks that if you and I go to a movie, the press will leave you alone?" Emily asked when I'd finished my explanation.

"No. It will only shift the focus. Taryn has a contact at the Statesman who'll plant the story along with a photo of us. I'll answer a couple of questions. The paparazzi will do some digging. Find out you work for me. They may follow you around a little. But since you spend your days here—"

"We get to control the narrative." Emily sighed. "I know. It was in the email. I guess it makes sense."

"I'm glad you think so because I'm not so sure." I hopped off the counter. "I'm beat and you need to get home. We can talk about it some more tomorrow. Sorry I didn't tell you earlier." Brushing a kiss to the top of her head, I whispered. "I won't hold it against you if you say no."

I winked down at her before snagging a couple of cookies and heading for the door.

"Miles?" I turned with a mouthful of chocolate chip, and she smiled, shaking her head. "I'll be happy to go to the movies with you. Just tell me when."

Chapter Twenty-Two

Miles

LIKE SHE WAS REACHING FOR THE MORNING SUN, GELSEY STOOD IN THE shallow end of the pool, arms high over her head in an arc.

From the deck, she looked as still as a statue on the balls of her feet; her lashes caressing her cheeks. Almost as if she'd become part of the water. Or the water had become part of her.

I eased onto the first step, trying not to disturb her.

Gelsey must've felt the ripple, though, because her eyes slowly opened. "Morning," she said, smiling brightly.

"Hey." I moved toward her. "Did you sleep well?"

"Wonderful."

As if to prove the point, she tipped forward, her back leg arcing up and out of the water, toes pointed at the sky. But her eyes stayed on me.

"What is that?" I asked.

"It's a dance position. *En haut.* It means 'high up.'"

She stayed on tiptoe, fingertips skimming the water.

"How do you hold it like that?"

"Balance, baby." Grinning, she dropped onto her heels and squinted up at me. "You ready to start?"

The girl could barely move last night without wincing. So I searched her face for signs of distress. And she frowned. "What is it?"

A little laugh bubbled from her lips. "Nothing. You're just really tall. It's hard explaining all this stuff when I'm not looking you in the eyes."

Without thinking, I sank to my knees. She was taller than me now. If she wanted me at eye level, I'd have to scoop her up and let her lock those smooth, toned legs around my waist.

Well, fuck.

I ran a wet hand through my hair. "Better?"

It came out grittier than I expected. Because I really wanted to explore the other option, where she had those thighs pressed against my ribs.

Gelsey nodded, oblivious. "Yes, thank you." She took a step forward, and her foot brushed against my knee. My cock twitched at the contact, but I kept my eyes locked on her face. On her porcelain skin. And the small freckle above her right brow.

"Let's start with your posture." Curving her hands around my shoulders, she nudged me into place. "You need to be stiff as a board."

Jesus Christ. No worries there.

"Got it."

Her lips continued to move, along with her hand. Lower, to my upper abdominals. Over to my obliques. Then down to my lower abs. But I couldn't hear a fucking thing over the static between my ears.

Somehow, I managed to follow her commands. At times she demonstrated the poses, and I got to ogle her unabashedly. Because... therapy.

I realized quickly if I didn't get the moves right, Gelsey would use those magic hands to correct me. Needless to say, she probably thought I had a learning disability by the time we were finished. But I must've done something right, because at the end of the hour, my leg was throbbing, and my abs were burning as I climbed out of the water.

"You should really take a soak," Gelsey said, tipping her chin to the built-in hot tub as she rearranged her hair into a topknot. "It'll help loosen your muscles."

I took a seat across from her to air dry, bunching my towel in my lap so she wouldn't see my semi. "What about your muscles?"

The gravel in my tone made it sound more like an indecent proposal than a genuine offer. Before I could start backpedaling, Gelsey rose from her chair and wandered over to the edge of the bubbling water.

"Are you coming in?" she asked, peering over her shoulder at me.

No.

That should've been my answer.

I'd just talked to Taryn this morning and agreed to her plan.

My "date" with Emily was just the tip of the iceberg. The press would get all the Miles Cooper they could handle over the next couple of weeks. Two radio interviews. An outing at the Parish Bar, the live music venue that Chase owned. Some well-placed photos in *People Magazine*.

"You said you wanted to start living," Taryn had said. "You can't do it if you never leave the house."

But right now, the house was looking pretty good. Because Gelsey was here. Gazing at me as if she carried the promise of another sky in her big blue eyes. One with no clouds threatening on the horizon.

You're imagining things.

Probably, I answered back to the voice in my head. But still, I was out of my chair. And a second later I was sinking into the water beside her.

"Shit." I groaned. "That feels good."

Gelsey eased down a little farther, her leg lightly pressing against mine. But I felt it everywhere, that touch. And when she hummed her agreement, it echoed through me like a warm buzz. And in the quiet, I imagined that same sound spilling from her lips when I was buried deep inside her.

"What kind of name is Gelsey?" I asked, flexing my fingers to keep my hands from wandering. "I've never heard it before."

Her head rolled to the side, and she smiled up at me. "It's Persian, I think. It means flower."

"I thought your family was Russian."

"They are. It's not a family name. You don't follow ballet, so you wouldn't know this, but there was a really famous ballerina in the eighties. Gelsey Kirkland. That's who I was named after." Her brows turned inward, and she frowned. "My mom didn't think that one through, I guess."

Shifting sideways to face her, I draped my arm over the decorative trim on the tub above her head. "Why is that?"

"Gelsey Kirkland was super talented. But she was also kind of a mess. Drugs. Men." Her eyes closed, and she inhaled a long breath. "Which goes to prove a name is just a name. Since I've never done drugs. Or men."

Her idle musings landed with the weight of an atomic bomb, stealing all the air.

No men.

"So, you're a…lesbian?"

My lizard brain couldn't help but slide straight to the porn stash in my head and cue up an all-girl scene where Gelsey was the star. I lost myself for a moment in the thought, and when I came out of the fog she was looking at me with wide eyes. "No. I'm not a lesbian."

"Bi?" I could barely choke the word out without inserting myself into the scene playing in my head. "Not that there's anything wrong with that."

Color bloomed on Gelsey's cheeks, but she didn't look away. If anything, her gaze was more intense. A richer blue. But still the same sky.

"No, that's not it either," she said, her tone low like she was sharing a secret. "I guess you can say…I'm inexperienced."

Inexperienced.

Apparently, lizard brain came with a side of muteness. Because I couldn't find any words to fill the awkward silence.

An exaggerated smile broke on her lips, and she patted my leg under the water. "Gotta go."

"Go?" I caught her hand as she scrambled to her feet. "Where?" *Form. A. Sentence.* "Where are you going?" I managed to croak.

"Rehearsal."

My focus drifted to the bruise on her hip, and I couldn't help myself. I ran my fingertips over the angry contusion. Her hand covered mine, but she didn't push me away.

"We don't practice lifts two days in a row," she said. "But I have to run through my movements, and then I'll probably hit the gym while I'm there."

"I have a gym. In case you didn't want to make the trek downtown with Daryl."

God. I sounded desperate. And I guess I was. Desperate to find out what she meant by inexperienced. And eager to volunteer to help with her learning curve.

She frowned. "Do you really think I need Daryl? I could just grab an Uber and—"

All the playfulness seeped from my tone. "No. Daryl goes. Things should be square in a couple of days. But for now, you can't leave the house without him."

Nodding, she dropped her gaze to her feet.

"Hey." I looped our index fingers and gave her hand a shake. "It's almost over."

I wasn't sure if that were true, but it was worth the white lie to see her brighten.

"Okay. I just hate to be a bother. I would stay here, but you don't have the right kind of floor for me to run through my movements. As soon as I get those finished, I'll bring him right back."

I shrugged, because where was I going to go?

No sooner had the thought crossed my mind, then I realized I needed Daryl to accompany me on my date. Maybe I should tell Emily to forget about it altogether and I'd just hit the town with the leaner and start a different kind of rumor.

No, if I were into dudes, I could do better than him.

"Can you be back by six?" I asked. "I've got a…thing."

Her face went blank, and then the exaggerated smile was back. "Oh…yeah. For sure." She nodded like a bobble-head doll as she backed away, practically hopping onto the step and then the deck. "I'm going to run, then."

She forced a tight smile before turning on her heel and dashing for the house.

Smooth.

Shaking my damn head at my own stupidity, I hauled to my feet and, after toweling off, I headed inside. Daryl was sitting at the island eating breakfast about a foot from where my ass had been planted the night before.

My eyes lit up, and I looked at Emily. She smirked, and pointed to the bucket of cleaning supplies, then to Cora, dusting off the plantation shutters.

Nothing was going my way today.

Emily shook her head at my dour expression before retreating with a cup of coffee and a book.

I poured a mug for myself, then turned to Daryl. "Those guys retrofitting the windows—do they do any other kind of construction?"

He popped his last bite of wheat toast into his mouth and chewed. "Yeah. They're full service. What did you have in mind?"

Good question.

I picked up a packet from the counter next to the sugar bowl.

Stevia. 100% natural.

A resigned smile tugged at my lips as I stirred three packets into my cup.

"I need to have the floor redone in the gym." I took a sip and tried not to blanch at the aftertaste. "The sooner the better."

Chapter Twenty-Three

Gelsey

I WAS A CHILD. OR MAYBE CHILDISH WAS A BETTER TERM. AND ungrateful. Also, passive-aggressive. That one stung. But it was true as well.

I continued to ruminate over my shortcomings until the Jeep rolled to a stop in the garage. Daryl yanked off the blanket and I peered up at him.

"I'm running late," he said. "Do you need a hand with this stuff?" His eyes stayed on me, never drifting to the packages on the floorboard. The evidence of my immaturity.

I gave him a weak smile as I pushed myself onto the seat. "No. I'm fine. You go ahead."

I thought he might say something. And I deserved it.

But he just nodded and jumped out of the car.

A tiny bit of relief washed over me when I noticed the time on the dashboard clock. Technically, we weren't late. I'd told Miles I'd have Daryl back by six and I made it with four minutes to spare.

He could still make it to his *thing* with no problem.

I knew it was a date. I could see it in his guilty gaze when he'd told me about it. The way his shifty eyes had darted around. And I didn't care. Not a bit.

Except that I did. Obviously, I did.

I glanced over the packages, rubbing my forehead. Retail therapy my ass. There was nothing therapeutic about spending money I didn't have.

Technically, that wasn't true either.

Miles had left me an envelope on the kitchen counter with my pay for the week. Money I had earmarked for New York. And car repairs.

And buying back my mama's ring. Not for panties and bras from Victoria's Secret that nobody would ever see. And costume jewelry from Claire's.

My stomach twisted as my thumb skated over the empty place on my finger where my mom's ring had once sat.

Why hadn't I gone to the pawn shop instead?

I would. Tomorrow. Even if I had to call an Uber. And I'd move in with Shannon. As soon as I was sure I wouldn't lead the paparazzi to her door, that's what I'd do.

With a plan in place, I grabbed my borrowed loot and headed for the house. I tried the door to the gym first, but it was locked. Everything was locked. Except the kitchen door. As long as Emily or Miles was here, that door stayed open. Much to Daryl's annoyance.

Slipping inside like a thief, I tiptoed for the stairs. I almost made it, too. But I froze when I heard my name.

Turning with a forced smile, my stomach churned when I saw what Miles was wearing. Faded jeans with holes in both knees. And a black button-down shirt with the sleeves rolled up to the elbows.

It was the first time I'd seen him dressed in anything but board shorts or sweats.

He hadn't bothered to shave. But why would he? The stubble was sexy as hell.

Like you would know.

Rocked by my inner dialogue, I held on tighter to the bags. "Oh, hey," I said, like I was surprised to run into him in the living room of his own house.

His gaze flicked to the packages. "You were at the mall?"

My spine straightened defensively even though I knew I was wrong. "Yeah. I had to pick up a few things."

Mentally, I patted myself on the back for my casual response. Butter wouldn't melt in my mouth. Because I didn't care about Miles or his *thing*.

I'd just about convinced myself when Emily rounded the corner. I did a double take since I'd never seen her in anything but yoga pants and a T-shirt, her hair in a high ponytail. But it was her, all right. In a little black dress that molded her body like a second skin. Not formal. More like something you'd pick up at Forever 21. Gauzy, with spaghetti straps and a high slit that showed off her long legs.

"Miles. We're going to be late if we don't—"

She froze, her eyes bouncing between Miles and me. She was his *thing*. Emily. His assistant.

I managed a little wave. And she smiled back. Which made it worse, since she'd never smiled at me before.

"Give me a minute, Em," Miles said, his eyes never leaving my face.

She nodded, backing out of the room like she was on eggshells while I tried to melt into the marble floor.

Suddenly, I felt small. Like a child who'd tried to play with the grown-ups and failed miserably. The bags were too heavy in my hands, and my finger too light without Mama's ring. Proof that I'd had a someone too. Once.

"I'm sorry," I blurted. "I lost track of time."

"Gelsey…"

I waited for him to say something else. To tell me I was an ungrateful brat. Impossibly rude. But he didn't. He just stood there rubbing the back of his neck.

Voices floated from somewhere else. Daryl's first, then Emily's. Then nothing.

"You'd better go," I said, my face about to crack from the pressure of maintaining my smile.

Miles hesitated for a moment before nodding jerkily. "Have a good night, Gelsey."

He turned on his heel, and he was gone.

I pulled my knees to my chest as I turned my new phone over and over in my hand. It was the only smart purchase I'd made during my ill-fated trip to the mall. With the discounts, I'd only spent thirty bucks. And now I had my own data plan with unlimited talk and text.

And a new number. One that no one would recognize if I called.

I scrolled to my contact information, my thumb hovering over my dad's picture. He was probably screening his calls, so I was stressing over nothing. If he answered, though, it would mean he was only screening me. *My* calls.

Did I really want to go there?

Biting my lip hard, I hit the button, then slowly lifted the phone to my ear.

My dad answered on the second ring.

"This is Chris."

Surprise stole the breath from my lungs. And not the good kind. But then, when was the last time a surprise had been good?

"Dad," I croaked.

Silence. Deafening silence. I'd never known the meaning of the words until they threatened to shatter my eardrums.

"It's Gelsey," I added stupidly. Like it would make a difference. And he'd remember he had a daughter. Because in that moment, that's all I wanted.

A sigh rumbled across the line. And there was so much defeat in that tiny exhalation, I could feel it all the way to my bones.

"Gelsey. I've been meaning to call you," he said, his tone resigned, like he'd been caught. "I just...I didn't know what to say."

Anger flared, a million responses coiling around my tongue. But I held them all back. If I could be small, unobtrusive, *forgiving*...maybe he wouldn't hang up.

"That's fine," I rushed to say. "It's okay. Really."

The absolution left a bitter taste in my mouth. He didn't deserve it. But it wasn't about him. It was about me. For a few minutes, I needed to know he was there. Listening.

"I'm staying with a friend," I continued brightly. "Not really a friend, but..."

Watching the clock on the dresser, I babbled on, trying to pack every detail of the last days into a few sentences. At the two-minute mark I paused to take a breath, my head spinning from the lack of oxygen.

There was no response from the other side, just the hum of the engine. Had he put the phone down?

I swallowed hard. "Daddy? Are you there?"

"Yeah, sure. Listen…" Tears pooled as my dad struggled to find the words. He cleared his throat, and I knew I'd lost him. "Everything sounds really good, Gelsey. Really good. But I have to go."

Smothering a protest, I nodded. "Okay, Daddy. I love—" The line went dead, and the numbers on the clock inched forward. Three minutes. "—you."

And I did. As much as it pained me to admit it. Pressing my forehead to my knees, I let the phone slip out of my hand, wondering why it was so hard for him to love me back.

Chapter Twenty-Four

Miles

Daryl coasted to a stop in front of the gate. Flashbulbs lit up the interior of the car as he rolled his window down and took his time with the keypad, so the freelancers could get the money shot—Emily and me in the back seat. Close but not too close.

Slumping against the door, I let it happen. It was too late now, anyway. Taryn's contact at the Statesman had already taken our picture as we exited the Alamo Drafthouse. By tomorrow, *People Magazine* would pick up the non-item, and the press would shift their focus to Emily and me.

And next week when Emily attended Taryn's birthday bash at the Parish Bar with her boyfriend, our story would die a swift death, since I'd be there too.

The perfect bait and switch with a twist.

"I thought the whole idea of us going out was to be seen," Emily mused as we started down the long driveway.

"What do you mean?" I asked.

She shrugged. "That was the shortest date in the history of dates. I barely got to finish my popcorn."

Daryl met my gaze in the rearview mirror, and I narrowed my eyes with a mind-your-own-damn-business warning glare. Whatever he thought he knew, he was wrong. I hated crowds. Despised publicity stunts. That was it. Nothing more.

"It did the job," I muttered, digging into the muscles of my thigh when we jerked to a stop inside the garage.

My terse reply earned me a glower from Emily, who grabbed my arm as I reached for the door handle. "What's wrong? Did I do something?"

I blinked at her, surprised. "Of course not. I just…"

What?

My sour mood went beyond having to endure a few photos. Maybe I wasn't used to the attention anymore. But it was like riding a bicycle. In public. In my underwear.

"I'm sorry, Em. Didn't mean to be a dick. I'm just tired."

It was a piss-poor excuse. Because, what did I have to be tired from? I didn't *do* anything.

Emily searched my face, and whatever she found there was enough to satisfy her concern, so she let me go.

Taking her hand, I helped her out of the car. For the first time all night, I really looked at her. Dark hair fell in loose ribbons past her shoulders, the tips a deep shade of purple that matched her eyes.

"You look pretty, Emmie," I said with as much enthusiasm as I could muster.

Her lips twisted into a smirk. "I didn't say anything when you started calling me Em. But I draw the line at Emmie. It sounds like one of the gold statues they give the soap opera stars."

"Fair enough."

Popping up on her tiptoes, she kissed my cheek and whispered, "Thanks for the date. Let's never do it again."

I laughed. "It wasn't that bad."

"It felt like I was on a date with my brother." She brushed off the front of my shirt, then patted my chest. "Also, I'm expecting a big bonus at Christmas time. Cash works."

Frowning, she eyed the beefy security guard conversing with Daryl next to the rented Town Car. "I don't suppose you'd let me—"

"Nope," I replied, anticipating her request. "He's going with you." I rolled my eyes when she continued to pout. "I'm giving you a week's vacation, all expenses paid, at a five-star resort in Galveston. *With your sister.* And you're looking at me like I ran over your cat."

"I know." She toed the concrete like a petulant child. "But why does he have to come with us? I don't even know him."

If Emily had worked for me during the height of my fame, she wouldn't ask. And I was too tired to explain. "Because I said so." Taking her by the shoulders, I spun her toward the car. "Now, stop giving me grief and go. Have a good time. Don't get sunburned. I'll see you at the party next week."

She let out a sigh, dragging her feet as she trudged toward the Lincoln.

I made eye contact with the bodyguard as she ducked inside, my stone-cold gaze resolute.

Anything happens to her, and I'll kill you.

He must've gotten the point, because he tipped his chin at me before sliding behind the wheel.

I watched the taillights fade into the night, then headed inside while Daryl did his usual grounds check.

Pausing in front of Gelsey's door when I heard music, I raised a hand to knock. But for what? It was ten o'clock at night. Anything I needed to tell her about Emily could wait until morning.

As I turned to leave, a little sniffle drifted from inside the room. And another. And then a sob.

"Gelsey." I rapped lightly. The music stopped, but she didn't answer, so I knocked louder. *"Gelsey!"*

Light spilled into the hallway as she peeked from a small slit in the door. Only one eye was visible, puffy and red-rimmed. And her cheek was blotchy.

"I didn't know you were home," she said, shifting her feet. "Was the music too loud?"

I laughed, despite the band tightening around my chest. "I'm a drummer. There's no such thing."

A weak smile ghosted her lips. "Okay, then. Did you want to talk to me about something? Or…"

Or held so much promise.

An invitation to taste her lips. Or run my fingers through her tangled locks. Or kiss away the tears staining her cheeks and ask her why they were there.

She opened the door a little wider, looking bewildered and so damn sad. In another life, I wouldn't have noticed. Hell, in another life, I wouldn't have cared.

My gaze flicked to the bed, then back to her face.

"No," I said, taking her hand. "But I do have something to show you."

Gelsey

I let Miles lead me through the dark house. I hadn't forgotten about Emily or their *thing*.

But I was an adult. And we were friends. I could push any silly little crush I had aside.

Real friends were rare. Something to be cherished. I should know, since I only had one.

At the bottom of the stairs, I cut right, toward the den. But Miles went in the other direction, and since our fingers were twined, I had no choice but to follow.

"You want to work out?" I asked with a laugh when we got to the gym.

He pulled me through the door, and I stumbled, colliding with his chest. His crisp citrus scent enveloped me. And he smiled that damn smile. Even in the sparse light, I could see the dimple.

Miles reached around me and flipped the switch on the wall.

"Maybe later."

Blinking against the sudden brightness, my hand flew up to cover my eyes. As my vision adjusted, the breath left my body in a rush.

The distressed hardwood was gone, replaced with the gray vinyl we used at the dance company. Mirrors surrounded me on all sides, a waist level barre attached to the longest expanse. The Nautilus equipment was still here, but closer together, inhabiting roughly one-quarter of the area.

It looked like…a ballet studio.

Miles slipped behind me, dipping his head to speak in my ear. "Do you like it?" Dark eyes locked onto mine in the reflection. "I mean, is it right?"

Right? It was perfect.

"Yes," I breathed. "But how?"

"The construction guys were already here tricking out the pool house." He walked around, bouncing on the balls of his feet to test the resistance. "I figured this was probably better for my leg anyway, right?"

"Right."

I discreetly wiped a tear on the shoulder of my sleep shirt. *Don't make more of this than it is,* the little voice inside my head warned. But it was too late. Because this was more. This was everything.

"But, why?" I asked.

Stuffing his hands in his pockets, Miles gazed around at this thing he'd done. This grand gesture. And then he smiled down at me. "Because you needed it."

It sounded so simple. And maybe for him, it was. But still, it had taken some thought. A phone call. Or a tiny bit of planning. And he'd done it all *for me.*

I rubbed my forehead, my knees weak. "It's so much."

Too much. But it's not like I could tell him to take it back.

Lacing our fingers, he dragged me over to the barre.

"Try it out," he said, sliding behind me again, his palms molding lightly to my hips.

My hand coiled around the wood, and my heart swelled. "It's real," I whispered. Maybe to myself. But Miles answered with a laugh.

"Of course, it's real. Now show me something."

He stood back and crossed his arms over his chest, gnawing on his bottom lip. Anticipation shone in his eyes, like he was waiting to witness something spectacular.

But I wasn't spectacular. Not this kind of spectacular. I was just me.

"Wait," I said, slowly releasing the barre. "Just...give me two minutes."

Miles wouldn't know a plie from a pirouette, but still, I wanted to give him my best dance. Something beautiful that he'd always remember. So I raced up the stairs to get my bag.

When I got back, Miles was on the floor, reclining on one elbow. I took a seat in front of the mirror and quickly slipped on my pointe shoes. Miles watched with rapt attention as I went through a brief warmup.

"I need some music," I said when I finished. "Do you have your phone?"

He wrangled the device from his pocket with a raised brow. "Sure. But I don't have any classical."

"What about 'Blackbird'? Do you have that?"

Surprise painted his features. And that's just what I wanted. To surprise him with a dance of my own creation. If I did it right, he'd remember it forever. The feeling. The flying. And the hope. And if I did it wrong, well, he wouldn't know the difference.

"Yeah," he said, sitting up straighter. "I'll put it on the sound system."

While Miles scrolled through his playlist, I moved into first position, my breath choppy under a current of nervous energy.

Closing my eyes, I waited for the music. And when the opening note drifted from high above, it lifted me onto my toes. Usually, it was just me when I danced. My partner, and even the other dancers, were just props. But I felt Miles in every movement. His eyes on my body as I told the story of a little bird who learned to fly on broken wings. Fast and slow, and high in the air, I wove the tale. Spinning into a series of pirouettes, I ended the dance with four revolutions, then sank to the floor with my head bowed.

I stayed still, wringing the last bit of magic out of the moment. When I heard Miles push to his feet, I waited for him to break the spell. With a word, or a gesture.

Instead, he eased down behind me.

His arm circled my waist, and my heart sped up, then fell into time with his. And just like that, he was part of it. The heaven between where the dance ended, and reality began.

Miles

Long moments passed with nothing but the feel of Gelsey in my arms. The smell of her hair, and the rise and fall of her chest. I feared she might fly away if I released her. Because she could. I'd seen her. And I knew I'd never separate the girl from the dance again. Not after tonight.

So I sat quietly the way I used to after a show. When the stage lights had dimmed and it was just me behind my kit. On top of the world. Only Gelsey was there now. And *here*, too.

"Tell me something no one else knows about you," she said, her voice a soft whisper.

I thought of all the things I kept hidden. Dark thoughts. And darker intentions. The lure of nothingness. And the fear that one day the clouds would return and block the sun forever.

Tightening my grip, I let her warmth seep through me. "I like ballet."

Chapter Twenty-Five

Gelsey

SHANNON WAITED UNTIL THE WAITRESS BROUGHT OUR FOOD TO TOSS THE issue of *People* on the table. The magazine slid toward me, a glossy photo of Miles and Emily in the bottom right corner of the cover.

Crossing her arms over her chest, she pointed to it. No words. Just a raised brow.

When I couldn't take any more of her scrutiny, I broke eye contact and dug into my salad. "We're just friends."

It came out quieter than I expected, and I recalled what Ivan always said about lies and whispers and how they went hand in hand.

Miles and I *were* friends.

The morning after I'd danced for him, he'd explained about Emily. The plan his publicist had thrown together. It had worked, too. Four days later and the photographers barely noticed my comings and goings. They were too interested in trying to catch a glimpse of Emily. Ironic, since she was hundreds of miles away, soaking up the sun in Galveston.

"Why do I get the feeling there's more to it?" Shannon asked as she unfolded her napkin.

"Because you have a dirty mind." Smiling, I batted my eyelashes playfully.

"And your mind isn't dirty enough." She pointed her fork at me, lettuce hanging off the tines. "Miles Cooper is fuck hot. Tall, dark and oh so handsome. Plus, he's got that brooding thing going on. Bet he's great in bed."

My cheeks flamed because I wouldn't know. I'd never know.

Friends.

Miles and I had spent a lot of time together over the past few days.

Movies and meals and late night dips in the Jacuzzi. But he'd never tried anything. Our touching was confined to the pool where I made so many adjustments during our sessions, just to feel his skin under my fingers, that he probably thought I was crazy.

He doesn't like you like that.

My stomach churned at the thought, and I chewed my lettuce slowly to keep from swallowing so I wouldn't have to reply to Shannon's comment.

"Don't tell me you haven't thought about it," she chided. When I shrugged noncommittally, she rolled her eyes. "And here I thought he'd be the one to swipe your V-card."

I choked, bits of cucumber flying out of my mouth.

"Will you shut up about my fucking V-card," I hissed, glancing around to see if anyone had noticed us. "And don't look at me like that. You've heard me swear."

I reached for my water, glaring at her over the rim as I took a drink. Discussions about my virginity were off limits. Not because I was a prude. But because I was twenty-two, and with each passing year, I felt more like a loser. If I were saving myself for something or someone, that would be a different story. But I wasn't. And Shannon knew it.

"Okay. Okay." She raised her hands in surrender. "Don't get worked up. I'm just saying."

Sufficiently chastised, she picked at her food, and the conversation dwindled to nothing.

"He's not into me," I admitted when the silence was too much to bear. Shannon tilted her head, her gaze troubled, and I shrugged. "He's not."

"But you are?" she asked softly. "Into him?"

I could lie. Shannon wouldn't call me on it. But I wanted her to know. Because it made it real, these feelings. I *knew* Miles. The person, not the rock star. I wasn't some fangirl.

"Yeah."

She flicked her attention to the magazine, consigned to a corner of the table under the bread basket. "And he's with his assistant?"

Lifting my chin, I shook my head. "No. That was a publicity stunt." Confusion lined her brow, and I tried not to squirm. "He didn't want the media to think…I mean, it was really sweet, but…" I swallowed hard. "He didn't want anyone to think we were together."

It stung just as badly now as it had when Miles had explained it. But I didn't show it. Not to him. He'd built me a dance studio, for Christ's sake. And offered me a place to stay until I moved to New York.

"It's his loss," Shannon said seriously, dipping her head to catch my eyes when I went back to my lunch. "You know that, right?"

Lifting a shoulder in a half shrug, I forced a smile. "Of course. I'm a catch."

She eyed me over her glass as she took a drink of mineral water. "What are you doing tonight?"

I thought of the Red Box movie I'd picked up for Miles and me to watch. "Nothing."

"Good. We're going out."

A piece of lettuce caught in my throat and I shook my head. Since I'd turned twenty-one I'd managed to successfully avoid the bar scene. "I don't think—"

"You don't have to think. Just leave everything to me."

Miles

Going to a club with Shannon. I'll probably stay at her apartment tonight. See you tomorrow!

I read Gelsey's message for the third time, and still couldn't figure out how to reply.

Ordering her to come back to my place didn't seem like the way to go. Especially since I'd spent four days trying to re-establish our boundaries.

If I were honest, my motives weren't purely altruistic when I'd built her the dance studio.

I wanted her. Up against the wall. In the shower. In my bed. But that was the extent of it. And she deserved more.

Biting back my jealousy, I tapped out a reply.

Have fun.

I continued to stare at the screen until Blake let out an irritated sigh. The kid had spent the majority of the last two hours acting like I didn't exist, and *now* he wanted my attention?

Slowly easing back in my chair, I crossed my arms over my chest. "Run through it again."

He flicked an accusatory glare at my phone. "Why? So you can ignore me some more?"

I rolled my eyes. "I can multitask, dude. You missed the transition. The B chord. Play it lower on the fretboard."

He thought about it for a moment before taking it from the top. But this time, he skipped the adjustment altogether, slowly dragging his thumb over the strings to make sure I knew it.

"You know what they say. Those who can—*do*. Those who can't—sit around and give orders." He launched into the opening riff of an old Damaged tune. "Now if Paige were here…" Shaking his head, he continued to strum. "Fuck hot and all that talent. I'd definitely take her advice."

I sprang out of my chair, fist balled and ready to fly before the last syllable slipped over his tongue.

"Don't you *ever* say her name again," I growled. "I don't care if you're in pain. We're all in fucking pain. Do you fucking feel me?"

Blake swallowed hard, the mask slipping just enough to see the flash of regret. "Yeah. I get it."

Sheppard strolled up clapping a hand on the kid's shoulder. "Time for afternoon group."

Blake pushed out of his chair, compliant for once. Lingering at the end of the table, his gaze found mine over his shoulder. "Are you coming back?"

No.

That's what I wanted to say until I noticed him tugging on his sleeves to hide his scars. Fucking hell.

He waited for my jerky nod and then headed for the door.

I was about to do the same when Sheppard sat down. "Let's talk for a minute, Miles."

I cleared my throat. "No…I…I have to go."

"It won't take long."

Ripping a hand through my hair, I reclaimed my spot.

"How are things going with Blake?" he asked as he pulled a bag of pistachios from his smock.

"He's a little fucker. Thanks for introducing us."

Smiling, he dumped a few nuts on the table. "And how are you?"

"Peachy. Can I go now?"

"What just happened between you two?" he asked, his focus on the pile of pistachios, not on me.

I dug my fingers into my eyes. "He mentioned Paige. And we agreed he wouldn't do it anymore."

"So that upset you?" He sat back. "Being reminded of her?"

"I don't have to be reminded," I spat. "She's always with me." I tapped my forehead so he'd know I meant metaphorically. We were in a psych hospital, after all. "In here."

He smiled, and I wanted to smack it off his face.

"And that's what started the argument?"

Crossing my arms, I lifted my chin to the camera. "You tell me, since I'm assuming you saw the whole thing."

Sheppard cracked one of the shells and popped a nut in his mouth, chewing slowly. "You didn't answer my question."

"Yeah. The kid's got a mouth on him."

"Did you argue a lot with Rhenn?" A snort ripped from my chest, and I rolled my eyes, disgusted with his lame segue. "How about Paige?"

Welding my back teeth together, I shifted my focus to the window. To the pale gray sky. And the storm on the horizon.

You should sleep in your own bunk tonight, sunshine.

"No."

His gaze shifted to my fingers, working fitfully on the muscle of my thigh. The nerves crackled, coming to life under my touch.

"Why are you doing that, Miles?"

"Because I'm in pain."

His brows turned inward. "Then stop."

Stop...

A lump rose in my throat, filled with all the grief and guilt I couldn't set free. But this I had. A meager payment for the debt I could never repay. "I can't."

He tipped forward, looking me in the eyes. "Try."

My hand stopped its feverish clenching, and the pain ebbed like the tide rolling out to sea.

Sheppard pushed the pile of pistachios my way, motioning for me to try them. I picked one up just to have something to do.

"So," he began, taking one for himself. "Tell me what's different in your life lately."

Chapter Twenty-Six

Miles

I WOKE WITH A START, BATHED IN SWEAT, FISTS CLUTCHED TIGHTLY IN the sheets. My leg ached, the humid air seeping through my skin and settling into my bones. I threw an arm over my face, willing sleep to come again.

But it was too late. The drops of rain on the window told me that. I knew what was coming. And how it would end. Smoke filled my lungs before the first bolt of lightning turned everything white.

Gripping my thigh, I squeezed hard enough to see sparks behind my clenched lids. Embers from a burning sky.

Blood pounding in my ears, I hauled to my feet, the couch in my studio my only goal.

I kept my head down, avoiding windows as I moved toward the stairs.

"Miles…"

My gaze snapped over my shoulder. To Gelsey. To the present. But my voice was still locked in the past. And maybe she was there too. In my nightmare.

Stranger things and all that.

Go.

But I held my ground as she closed the gap between us, reserving judgment on the whole "is she or isn't she a figment of my imagination" question.

"What's wrong, Miles?" She cupped my cheek, and my scattered thoughts coalesced.

She was real. And she was here.

Some of the feeling returned to my limbs, and my heart slowed. "I-I can't…I…"

Lightning flashed, and the fist around my throat tightened.

Gelsey's hand slid to the back of my neck, guiding my forehead to hers. "You're okay." Her lips brushed mine, breathing life into the declaration.

My fingers tangled in her hair, and I nodded.

You're okay.

I don't know how long we stayed like that. Minutes or hours. But every time the lightning came, or the thunder roared, her lips found mine, and she repeated her promise.

You're okay.

By silent agreement, I let her lead me back to my room. A wave of panic crested as she smoothed the tangled sheets. Would she leave now? Let me ride out the storm alone?

My gaze slid to the door. I could still find peace in the studio.

"Miles?"

I latched onto Gelsey's voice, my attention back on serene blue eyes. Easing onto the pillow, she held out her hand.

Past the point of pride, I took it.

Rolling onto her side, she banded my arm around her waist, our entwined digits resting on her stomach.

"Tell me something no one else knows," she whispered.

Breathing in her lavender scent, I buried my face in a soft pool of spun gold and searched my addled brain for some piece of trivia.

"Sour Patch Kids are my favorite candy."

She laughed, and I held her closer, the vibration calming me. And when I closed my eyes, there were no voices. And no burning skies. Just her.

Gelsey

Miles stirred, mumbling something unintelligible. His hand tightened over mine, and he whimpered into my hair, hot tears falling onto my back.

This had been going on for an hour now. Ever since we'd laid down. And my heart broke a little more each time.

I pried his fingers away and, after a couple of maneuvers, I was able to turn in his arms.

My eyes adjusted to the sparse light, and I smoothed my thumb over his crinkled brow.

"Shh."

My touch traveled to his lips. Eight times I'd kissed away his demons.

I wish I would've met you sooner.

I tucked the silly thought away. Chalked it up to exhaustion.

Thunder growled in the distance as the storm moved past us. Miles clenched his eyes tightly, and I framed his face with my palms, pressing my lips to his.

"You're okay."

Nine kisses. Nine whispered vows. Nine tiny pieces of my heart that were now his forever.

I rolled over and sank back into the well of his arms.

Knowing Miles Cooper would be worth the effort.

If only I had the time.

Chapter Twenty-Seven

Miles

I woke in my bed, memories of last night pressing in on me. The storm. Gelsey. Soft lips and whispered words.

You're okay.

Swinging my legs over the side of the mattress, I gazed out at billowy white clouds. Maybe I'd imagined the whole thing. My finger skated over the verse inked on my ribs.

All that we see or seem

Is but a dream within a dream

"Is that Poe?"

Gelsey hovered in the doorway, two steaming mugs in her hand. Long hair fell in golden waves to her waist and dark makeup smudged her eyes. Skimming her body, I lingered on her short black dress. I must've been really out of it if I didn't notice that last night.

"Yep. Poe."

She closed the distance between us, and I took the cup she offered. Coffee.

"I'm not really sure if I made this right," she said with a dubious look into her own mug.

Forcing down a small sip, I let the warm liquid soothe my throat. But the taste. Fucking awful.

"It's perfect," I said as she took a seat on the couch in front of the window.

Tension thrummed between us, punctuated by several seconds of awkward silence.

"So you came home last night, huh?" I frowned into another sip of the worst coffee on the planet. "Obviously."

"Yeah," she sighed, setting her drink on the table. Her eyes bounced around the room like she was afraid to look at me.

"So, what happened?" I asked as I eased back against the headboard. She cocked her head at me, and I tipped my chin to her ensemble. "With your big night out? I thought you were staying at Shannon's."

She smoothed a hand over the wrinkled fabric. "Yeah. The bar scene really isn't my thing. Shannon set me up with one of her friends, and I ducked out early so he wouldn't get the wrong impression."

I eyed her over the top of my mug. "So it was a date, then?"

"A set up," she corrected. "With one of her clients. A pro tennis player." Her shoulders sagged. "But there were too many bodies. And it was so loud in the club. And Jimmy, that was the guy, he kept wanting to dance, and do shots and…"

Steel replaced the bones in my spine. "Did he do something to you?"

"What?… *No*." She waved a dismissive hand. "Jimmy was okay. Just…"

Fidgeting, she chewed the corner of her lip while I ambled over to take a seat beside her.

"Just what?"

"I don't know. I wasn't attracted to him. But maybe he thought I was. So I decided to come home since the group was going back to Shannon's boyfriend's house afterward to spend the night."

My head tilted to the side with so much force I thought it might snap off and roll onto the floor.

"Oh, no," she rushed out. "There were like eight of us."

And further still. Whiplash was now a distinct possibility.

Gelsey covered her face with her hand.

"I'm screwing this all up," she said from between her fingers. "And it's your fault, because you have a dirty mind. Shannon's boyfriend is a gamer. They have this league or coven or whatever it's called. And they stay up all night and play video games."

I relaxed against the cushion, more relieved than I should've been. "One—I'm pretty sure it's not a coven, unless they're summoning the Dark Lord to win World of Warcraft. Two—the guy was definitely attracted to you. So good call." I took another sip of coffee, the bitter brew easier to swallow now that my heart wasn't in my throat. "And three—you have no idea how dirty my mind is."

Gelsey blinked at me, and I smiled. Flirting. She'd opened that door last night, and I was stepping inside.

Tearing her gaze away from my face, she picked up her drink. "So what about you? What happened last night?"

She studied me out of the corner of her eye as she took a sip. I couldn't lie. She'd seen it all. Probably. I still wasn't sure.

"I have nightmares every now and then," I finally said. "Sometimes when I'm awake. Sometimes not even at night."

"Because of the rain?"

I dug my fingers into my thigh. "No. Because of what happened in the rain."

I couldn't fully read her expression, but I imagined mine was shut down and as bitter as the coffee from the way she pressed her lips together.

Easing back, she tucked her leg under her bottom. "You want to talk about it?"

No.

"Maybe later. I thought you weren't interested in dating?"

I cursed my inability to control what popped out of my mouth. Usually a sign I was obsessing. A precursor to a bout of depression.

You're not depressed. You're horny.

At least I kept that part to myself.

"I'm interested," she began cautiously. "This could be my last chance for a very long time."

"You're going to New York, not Mars. There are actually more people there. You know that, right?"

Picking at a thread on her dress, she frowned. "The shelf life for a ballerina is short. It's really hard on the body. But for me, with my back, it's even shorter. The first year at an elite company is the time most dancers find themselves. Bend the rules a little before getting down to business."

Our eyes met, and she tried for a smile. "I can't do that, though. I don't know if I have two years or five. But I want to spend them on stage before it gets taken away."

Time.

It dogged Gelsey with the same relentless persistence that it had stalked Rhenn and Paige.

At least it wouldn't end in tragedy. And maybe this was my chance to right the wrong I'd inflicted.

"You know," I began, coiling a golden lock around my finger. "Back in the day, I was an expert at seizing the moment. So I can probably help you out."

Gelsey leaned a little closer, clearly intrigued. "How?"

"That's up to you." I tipped her chin and gazed into clear, blue skies. "What do you say? Wanna waste a couple of months with me?"

Her features softened. "And what do you get out of it?"

I brushed my lips to hers, swallowing her little gasp. "I'm sure I'll think of something."

Chapter Twenty-Eight

Gelsey

MILES PAUSED, TEASPOON HOVERING OVER HIS CUP AND GAZE LOCKED ON the garbage bag full of clothes in my arms.

I tried to play off my nerves as I headed for the back door. "Can I get a cup of coffee too?" I asked, tossing a smile over my shoulder.

I knew what he thought—that I'd changed my mind about our deal. Our two-month plan.

I hadn't.

But after thinking about it for the last twenty-four hours, I'd decided to move back into the pool house to avoid any weirdness.

Who was I kidding? The whole arrangement was weird. But I could take small measures to protect my heart.

When I returned a moment later, Miles wasn't there. Grabbing the mug he'd left on the counter, I set off to find him. Halfway up the stairs, I heard music, and reversed my course.

Miles stood in front of the turntable in the den, focused on the spinning disc. "Going somewhere, little mouse?"

I took a seat on the sofa. "Just to the pool house."

His shoulders relaxed slightly, but he didn't turn around. "Why?"

I took a sip of my coffee. Much better than what I'd made the day before. But then, I was no connoisseur.

When the silence got too heavy, Miles chanced a peek over his shoulder.

"Why?" he repeated.

I stared into my mug. "Have you thought about what it would be like—having me in a room across the hall—if you brought someone home?" I flicked my gaze to his. "Because I have."

"You think I'd do that?"

His tone was sharp enough to slice through my meager defenses, and I shrank against the soft leather. "I don't know. I just thought…"

Hands on his hips, he let his head fall back, and glared at the ceiling. "I haven't dated anyone in a long time. I had an arrangement with a woman who used to come by once a week. But I broke it off."

The tic in his jaw told me I didn't want to know, but I had to ask. "What kind of arrangement?"

"The kind where money was exchanged."

"You paid for sex?"

It was more accusation than question and Miles flinched. "I paid her to leave when the sex was over. I don't do girlfriends, Gelsey. Trinity and I…" Our eyes met, and he swallowed hard. "Let's just say our arrangement worked for me at the time."

Their *arrangement*.

I took another sip of coffee, the too hot liquid scalding my lips "So, Trinity was a…"

"An escort. She didn't sleep with her clients." He sighed. "Except—"

"You."

Suddenly it became clear. Miles was already paying me. Albeit not for sex. And I was leaving in two months. No chance for entanglement. I was his new Trinity.

I wobbled to my feet. "I should get ready. I have rehearsal."

Not exactly the truth. But I needed to get away.

"Gelsey!"

Ignoring the thundering footsteps behind me, I picked up my pace, fingers coiled around the package of Sour Patch Kids in the pocket of my hoodie. The evidence of my naivety.

Tell me something no one else knows.

I guess I got my wish, because I couldn't imagine Miles revealed this particular secret to just anyone. No, he saved that little bombshell for me, so I'd know exactly what his proposal was all about.

I made a wrong turn and ended up in front of the gym. My studio. When I spun around Miles was right there, remorse written all over his face.

"Gelsey—"

"Why did you have to tell me?" I cried, backing away from him. "I get it. *This*, whatever it is, it's nothing special. Couldn't you just…"

Pretend.

That's what I was doing.

His fingers coiled around my arm, and when I jerked, the candy fell out of my pocket and landed at his feet. Crouching to retrieve it, his shoulders curved inward as he ran his thumb over the wrapper.

"You're special, Gelsey." He looked up and those eyes. Sincere and stripped as bare as they were the night of the storm.

Catching my hand, he placed a kiss on my palm. "I'm sorry. Can we just forget I said anything?"

Could I?

A resigned sigh parted my lips. "On one condition. While I'm here, can it be just us?"

Just me.

Miles climbed to his feet and pulled me against him. "Yes. Just us."

He pressed a chaste kiss to my lips that made me think stupid thoughts. And want stupid things.

Grinning like he'd just won a prize, Miles tossed the candy in the air as we strolled back to the den. "My turn," he said as we took a seat. "Tell me something no one else knows."

You're going to break my heart.

Tucking the secret way down deep, I looked around. A photo on the wall caught my eye. Miles on a sandy beach. All smiles.

"I've never been swimming in the ocean."

Chapter Twenty-Nine

Miles

Standing in front of the window in Rhenn's studio on the third floor of Tori's mansion, I watched the breeze blowing over the water of Lake Travis.

Check it out, bro. I'm going to wake up every day to this sick view. Tell me I'm not a lucky motherfucker.

"Miles?"

Rhenn's voice faded, replaced by the low hum of the party as Taryn peeked her head in the door. Her features softened when her eyes landed on mine in the reflection of the glass.

"What are you doing in here?" she asked quietly as she stepped inside.

"Do you remember when Rhenn bought this piece of land?"

Frowning, she rubbed her hands over her arms like she'd caught a chill. "Of course."

I sank into the chair in front of the soundboard, fingertips skating over the dials. "How does Tori live here with all these memories?"

Ambling over, Taryn rested her chin on the top of my head. "I don't know. For a long time, I think she lived in the past. But now that she's moved on, I don't think it hurts her as much anymore to be here. Did you see her tonight with Logan?"

I nodded, guilt swamping me when a tiny pebble of resentment lodged in my throat for my best friend. Taryn must've picked up my vibe because she tipped back and looked down at me.

"I didn't want to like Logan at first either," she admitted. "But I had this dream. Rhenn and I were sitting at the edge of the bluff, looking out at the water." Her attention shifted to the window and her eyes filled with tears. "He told me he could finally rest, knowing that Tori'd found someone. He'd want her to be happy, you know?"

"I want that too. It's just—"

"Hard. I get it."

She rested her butt against the table while I looked down at my hands.

"What about you?" She nudged my foot with the tip of her high heel shoe. "Paige would want you to be happy too." My head snapped up, and she gave me a watery smile. "I found her journal when I was going through her satchel. The one she used to carry with all her trinkets."

"J-Journal?" The band around my chest tightened, stealing all my air. "I don't understand. It didn't…burn?"

"No. I guess it was thrown clear."

Bracing my elbows on my knees, I bowed my head, willing myself to breathe. Taryn's arms tightened around me.

"Was there anything in there…about…"

Us. The secret was so deeply ingrained, I couldn't push the word past my lips.

"I was shocked when you told me. Even though…I think I always knew," she whispered into my hair. "The way she used to look at you. But reading about it. She loved you so much, Miles."

Not enough. Never enough.

Clearing my throat, I sat up straight, gently extracting myself from Taryn's hold. I didn't deserve to be comforted. Not about this.

"I loved her too." I scrubbed a hand over my face, effectively ending the conversation. "We should probably get back."

Taryn sighed, dipping into her clutch for a tube of lipstick. "I went through a lot of trouble making sure the press would get some juicy photos of you and Clarissa."

"Who's Clarissa?"

"Your girlfriend for the week. She was waiting for you by the rope line when you got here, and you blew her off."

I rubbed the back of my neck, and Taryn stopped primping. *"Miles."* Concern colored her tone. "What don't I know?"

"Probably a lot of things," I joked. "I mean, it's impossible to know everything, right?"

She propped a hand on her hip, not buying what I was selling.

"Fine," I growled. "I'm kind of seeing someone." I raised a finger in warning. "Before you ask, it's not serious. She's leaving for New York in a couple of months, and—"

"The ballerina!" Taryn clapped her hands. "The one who's staying at your house? Oh, my God! She's so cute!" I cocked my head, and she shrugged meekly. "Daryl might have sent a photo. And don't get mad. It's his job."

"Not anymore." I grinned. "Tori's back. She can take custody. No visitation required."

"Never mind about that. What about the ballerina?"

"Her name is Gelsey. I'm surprised you haven't done a background check." I slowly rose from my chair when she averted her gaze. "You did a background check?"

Taryn finally looked me in the eyes, somehow managing to appear formidable and humble at the same time. "Of course, I did a background check. You think I'm going to let some chick move into your house without checking her out."

She shifted her feet, and my back stiffened in defense. *"Well?* Is she a serial killer or something?"

"No," she huffed. "She's just…really young." Shaking my head, I made to scoot past her, and she grabbed my arm. "Hear me out. I know she's twenty-one."

I crossed my arms. "Twenty-two."

"Twenty-two. But she's a very young twenty-two. And—"

"Taryn…" I bit down my exasperation. "I told you it wasn't serious. We're just having a few laughs before she leaves for New York."

I could tell there was more she wanted to say, but she pressed her lips together and nodded. Slinging my arm around her shoulder, I steered us toward the door. "Let's get back to the party before your boyfriend sends a search party. I need to take off soon, anyway."

"What's the rush?" She assessed me with narrowed eyes. "Does it have anything to do with that favor you asked me for?"

Fuck

I shrugged noncommittally, ushering her into the hallway.

Hand poised on the light switch, I took a last look around, my gaze lingering on a photo of Paige.

Goodbye, sunshine.

"Miles," Taryn growled, revisiting her interrogation when I closed the door. "What's on Padre Island?"

Smiling, I looped my arm around her waist and planted a kiss on the top of her head. "Just the ocean, sweetheart."

Chapter Thirty

Gelsey

"EXCUSE ME," I SAID TO THE DRIVER, CRANING MY NECK TO GET HIS ATTENTION. "Can you please tell me where we're going?"

He spared me a glance in the rearview mirror. The first one since I'd climbed into his car.

"No, ma'am."

Melting into the seat, I pulled the phone out of the pocket of my hoodie and re-read the text from Miles.

Car service picking you up in thirty. Bring a bathing suit. We're going swimming.

Glancing over my shoulder at the city lights growing fainter behind me, I muttered under my breath, "Swimming where? San Antonio?"

My heart leaped into my throat, and I sat up. "It's not San Antonio, is it?"

"No, ma'am."

"New Braunfels?"

The driver shot me a glare, and I shrank against the upholstery.

"Never mind," I squeaked.

Asshole.

I understood the need for privacy, but this was ridiculous.

Pouting, I scratched at an itch by my hairline. Squishy. I wrinkled my nose when I noticed green clay under my fingernail. I was already in bed with a pore refining mask on when I got the message from Miles. Wherever we were going, I hoped no one would see me.

Not that there was much chance of that happening since we were in the middle of nowhere now.

A sinking feeling hit my stomach when we took the exit for Austin Bergstrom Airport. Instead of following the signs to the terminal, we took a right and stopped at a small building outside a wire fence.

The security guard took a card from the driver, then flashed a light into the back seat before waving us through.

My eyes widened when we coasted to a stop inside a hanger next to Miles's truck.

And a plane.

I pressed my nose to the glass trying to get a better look, but it was too big. Not quite the size of a commercial airliner. But almost.

Miles hopped off the lift gate of the F150, slung a small duffel bag over his shoulder, and headed my way with a smile.

He peeked his head in the door. "Ready, little mouse?"

Dumbfounded, I took his hand and let him pull me to my feet. Blinking up at him, I swallowed hard. "You said…you said we were going swimming."

Looping his arms around my waist, he pressed a kiss to my mouth. "We are." He smiled against my lips. "In South Padre."

Chapter Thirty-One

Miles

Gelsey stood motionless in the tiny bedroom, palm pressed to the window overlooking the beach. The light at the end of the walkway illuminated the shore, but I wasn't sure how much she could see.

I slipped my arms around her waist, resting my chin on the top of her head. "Not what you were expecting?"

After my declaration at the airport, I'm sure she thought we'd end up behind the gates of one of the opulent mansions lining the shore instead of the small two-bedroom cottage.

Twelve hundred square feet. Less than the size of my bedroom in Austin.

"It's perfect." She spun around, her cheeks glowing. "It's like the house in Hansel and Gretel. The gingerbread house."

I laughed, eyes rolling up to the ceiling, which I could touch with the aid of a step stool. "You haven't seen it in the light."

But then, neither had I. Not in seven years.

She stepped out of my embrace, and I followed her the dozen feet to the small living room. "It's lovely," she said, rising up on her tiptoes to examine the knickknacks on the mantle above the fireplace. "Whose is it?"

Crossing my arms, I rocked back on my heels. "Mine. I bought it years ago. We used to come out here to go surf fishing."

Sinking onto the old couch, she tucked her leg under her bottom. "We? Like your family?"

Cursing my careless slip of the tongue, I forced a smile. "Nah. Just my friends."

She cocked her head, and I could practically see the questions forming on her lips.

Ducking around the breakfast bar, I pulled open the compact fridge. Which, thanks to Taryn, was fully stocked.

I killed a good forty seconds staring at nothing before emerging with a couple of waters.

If I thought Gelsey would fall for my lame attempt to change lanes, I was wrong.

"Do your parents live in Austin?" she asked, taking the bottle as I eased down next to her.

"Nope."

It came out harsher than I expected. Dismissive. And when I lifted my gaze, I could see the confusion furrowing her brow.

"My mama lives in Florida," I said on a sigh. "My dad…he's gone."

The invisible rope tightened around my throat. My warning to stop. But then Gelsey took my hand, and I could breathe. Maybe it was the rush of oxygen, or her fingers coiled around mine. Or maybe I just wanted her to know.

"He killed himself when I was fourteen."

Shame that wasn't mine accompanied the confession. And for a moment, I thought she could read it on my face. The history buried deep in Sheppard's file. The mitigating factor that earned me three months in Millwood.

Family history of depression and suicide.

I braced myself for the onslaught of questions, canned responses on the tip of my tongue.

No, I didn't see it coming.

No, he didn't leave a note.

No, blood doesn't wash out of carpets. They have to be replaced.

A minute passed before Gelsey climbed into my lap. And another before I could look her in the eyes.

She didn't say anything. Because she didn't have to.

You're okay.

It was right there between us. Her whispered words from the night of the storm.

Her fingers trailed through my hair. And my arms circled her waist. She pressed her lips to mine, and it wasn't comfort she offered. But permission. And I took it.

Chapter Thirty-Two

Gelsey

I DON'T KNOW WHAT I EXPECTED. A MAD FRENZY. CLOTHES RIPPING AND lace flying. But this *was not* that.

Miles eased us onto the mattress, slowly deepening the kiss we'd started on our way to the bedroom.

His mouth moved to my neck and my collarbone, lavishing attention on all the exposed skin. But he went no further. Not with his kisses or his touch. His hands stayed locked with mine, one above my head, and one at my side, our fingers entwined.

Clenching my eyes shut, I waited for him to tire of the leisurely seduction and move things to the next level. But he didn't. And after a few moments, I finally started to relax. Taking control of the kiss, I sucked gently on his tongue.

A soft chuckle, and I felt his mouth curve against mine.

"What?" I whispered, my lids fluttering open.

He let go of the hand anchored to my hip and squinted to look at me in the dim light. "I was waiting for you to join the party." His thumb swept over my swollen lips. "You were so stiff. I thought for a minute there you might break into a million pieces."

My cheeks ignited, burning all the way to my hairline. "I'm a little nervous."

He propped up on his forearm. "Nothing happens until you're ready. You want to fool around all night, I'm good with that."

Maybe if I were sixteen, Miles's speech would be endearing. But at my age, all I felt was the sharp pang of embarrassment. Inhaling a deep breath, I turned my face into the pillow to avoid further humiliation.

Miles huffed and rolled onto his back, taking me along for the ride like I weighed nothing. I was now on my stomach, draped over him like a human shawl.

"That's better." Pinning an arm around my waist, he gazed at me with a stern expression. "This," he motioned between us with his free hand, "doesn't work unless you trust me. I gotta know what's going on in that brain of yours."

Dropping my forehead to his chest, I groaned. "Because I've never had sex, right?"

I cringed inwardly admitting it, but Miles only chuckled.

"No, baby. Because I want it to be good for you. I want you to tell me what you like, and if you don't know, I want you to tell me what you don't like."

He stroked a hand down my back and waited patiently until I chanced a peek at his face.

"I'm twenty-two. We shouldn't be having this conversation. If I were normal—"

"Hey." His brows drew together. "You're special. I've never seen anyone dance like you. If it took missing out on a few sweaty romps in the back of a fucking car with some douchebag you wouldn't recognize on the street today, that's a small price to pay for greatness. I know because I've seen greatness. Real genius. And it came with sacrifice."

He flopped back, throwing an arm over his face.

Grasping the one thing that gave me some confidence, I asked, "You like the way I dance?"

He peered down at me while I traced the logo on his T-shirt. "You couldn't tell?"

"Not really. I mean, I hope people like what they see, since dancing is the only thing I've ever been good at."

"I'm sure that's not true."

I inched up until we were sharing the same pillow. "Maybe. But it's the only thing I was allowed to explore. Did you do other things besides music when you were in school?"

He thought about it for a moment, then smiled. "I played soccer in grade school. And baseball in junior high."

"Do you play anything besides the drums?"

"Guitar. Some keyboards. A little flute." My brow went up, and he grinned. "You're gonna be happy about that later. I can do some wicked things with my tongue." He shifted onto his side. "What about you?"

I batted my eyelashes. "I don't play the flute."

"Smart-ass." Pulling me closer, he slotted his leg between my knees. "You said you don't do anything but dance. There's got to be something else. You can't dance all the time."

Reaching up, he gently pried my bottom lip free from my teeth with his thumb as I pondered.

"I write poetry." I skimmed my fingers over his side where I remembered seeing the verse. "Not as good as Poe."

"Poetry? Will you let me read it sometime?"

A nervous laugh bubbled free. "Let's not get crazy. It's only a hobby."

His fingers sank into my hair, and he tipped my chin so I couldn't escape his gaze. "Lyrics are just poems that haven't grown up yet. Maybe we can write a song together. You can be the words and I can be the music."

"You don't write lyrics?"

The light in his eyes dimmed. "Rhenn wrote most of the songs. He was the genius I was talking about. I'm just...average."

I brushed a stray lock off his forehead. "I doubt that."

I don't know whether Miles initiated the kiss, or if it was me. But as soon as our mouths connected, it was like we caught fire. I couldn't get close enough. Even after he peeled our clothes off and we were skin to skin.

"Don't hold back," I breathed, my fingers sliding to the nape of his neck to hold him tighter. "Please."

"You sure?"

Summoning my new-found bravery, I reached between us and took him in my hand. He was thick. And hard. Pulsing in my fingers.

"*Fuck,*" he hissed, gripping the back of my hair.

Emboldened, I stroked the silken flesh as we fell into another searing kiss. I had nothing to compare it to, but I did worry about his size, and my size, and how everything was going to work.

"You're going to make me come," he whispered, a smile curving his lips when I pulled away. Large hands framed my face, and he touched his forehead to mine. "Coming is kind of the point, but you first."

"M-Me first?"

Nodding, he guided me onto my back with a kiss. My lids fluttered closed as he worked his way to my breasts. I'd just gotten used to the sensations zinging through my body when his hand dipped between my legs. I jerked and blinked down at him, but his eyes were already locked on mine. He continued to watch as he flicked his tongue over my nipple, and then...

"Oh, my God."

I gripped the sheets as he parted my folds, sliding one finger inside me.

"Fuck, baby, you're tight. And so fucking wet."

Wait...what?

He stilled when my head came off the pillow. "How wet?"

Grinning, he moved back up to my side. "Just right...now lie back." He punctuated the request with another kiss, and I complied.

This time, when his fingers sought the warmth between my thighs, his thumb grazed my clit. *"Miles..."*

He was inside me again, and with the added stimulation, I felt a heaviness in my belly that grew and grew.

"Ride my hand, baby," he growled into my hair. "I want to see you come."

The pressure built, and I started to move, my fingers clawing at his to hold him in place.

Squeezing my eyes shut, I gave in to the pleasure, my heartbeat a drum I could feel in my fingers and my toes. I turned my face into his chest and the smell of him. Crisp with a hint of something else. *Me.* I was all over him.

Stars exploded behind my lids, and his name was written on every one.

I was so lost in the euphoric haze, I didn't notice that Miles had shimmied down my body until I felt warm breath between my thighs.

"Miles?"

I looked down to find hooded eyes. "I've gotta taste you."

It's not that I'd never imagined Miles doing that to me. I just didn't think it would be so soon. Nodding slowly, I pressed the back of my head into the pillow, both fists coiled in the sheets now.

What if he doesn't like it?

What if I don't like it?

What if...?

"Fuck... fuck... fuck..."

A whimper accompanied my chant as his mouth closed over my sensitive bud. My hand shot down to grip his hair, because...nothing, *nothing*, had ever felt this good. His tongue was everywhere, and I wanted to kiss the person who'd taught him to play the flute. And maybe I said that too, because I was only vaguely aware of the words spilling from my lips.

Sensations took over, and the world went white as I splintered into a million pieces.

Miles was back at my side, both arms encasing me, but my lids were too heavy to stay open.

Through the fog, I heard him say, "Sleep, baby."

And I did.

Chapter Thirty-Three

Miles

Gelsey stirred in my arms, a moan parting her lips. Admonishing myself for being a prick—she could've been in pain for all I knew—I squeezed my semi-hard shaft.

I'd jerked off in the shower immediately after our almost-sex last night. Not that it had helped much. The minute I'd slid back under the covers and tucked Gelsey's body against mine, my hard-on had returned with a vengeance. A few more hours and my dick and I would no longer be on speaking terms.

I chanced a peek under the comforter. "Calm the fuck down, you little asshole," I hissed under my breath.

Jolting when Gelsey cleared her throat, I looked over to find her smiling, sex-tousled hair begging for my touch. "Are you talking to your... thing?"

Rolling onto my side so she'd feel exactly what I was dealing with, I said, "Dick, cock, penis...if you must. It's not a 'thing.'" I ground my hard length against her thigh. "You're going to offend him. And sometime soon you might want to have him on your side."

She glanced down to where we were skin on skin. "He's already on my side."

Her lip wobbled as she tried to keep a straight face, and I bit down a smile of my own.

"Don't make him angry," I warned. "You wouldn't like him when he's angry." One pale brow went up, and my jaw dropped. "The Incredible Hulk?" I croaked, and she shook her head. "Marvel?" A shrug. *"Comic books?"*

"Oh...sorry. I've never read one."

Her cheeks pinked, which was adorable. But still. Never read a comic book?

You're thirty, dude. Why are you still reading comic books?

Ignoring the stupid question, I twirled a golden lock around my finger. "We'll have to fix that. I've got a shit ton at the house. You kind of remind me of Susan Storm. Invisible Woman from the Fantastic Four."

Gelsey painted on an indulgent smile. "I'll read your comics if you come and watch a rehearsal at the dance company." Pale lashes caressed her cheeks when she lowered her gaze. "I mean, if you want to."

I did.

And that's what surprised me the most.

Gelsey had helped me deal with the storm and my fucked-up demons. Something a half dozen of the best psychiatrists in Austin hadn't been able to do.

But this wasn't permanent.

She wasn't permanent.

Gelsey might gift me with a dozen sunrises, but in the end, she'd leave me in the dark.

A knock at the door saved me from having to witness her disappointment when I declined her invitation.

Shit. Someone who knew about our midnight journey must've sold us out.

"Stay here," I barked, throwing my legs over the side of the bed.

Gelsey hunkered down as I stepped into my jeans and shrugged on a T-shirt. Glimpsing her wounded expression, I sighed.

She rose up on her elbows when I dropped a knee to the mattress.

"Sorry." I swept a hand over her tangled locks. "You should get dressed. I don't know how bad this is."

"Bad?"

"Doesn't matter. There's a penthouse in one of the hotels on the other side of the island. If we have to, we'll go there." I tipped forward and kissed her lips. "Don't worry."

Another knock, and she jumped out of her skin. Grinding my teeth, I grabbed my phone so I could call Taryn and headed for the door.

Peering through the peephole, I groaned and let my head fall against the wood.

"What the fresh fuck, dude?" I growled as I pulled open the door.

Daryl scooped his duffel off the ground. "'Bout time."

"Oh, no. Fuck you," I said, my hand on his chest. "You ain't coming in here."

He glared at me over the top of his aviators. "I am."

"Says who?"

He held up his flip-phone. Who the hell still had a flip-phone?

"Tori Grayson and Taryn Ayers." I closed my eyes, and he chuckled. "You lose, brother."

"You're not my fucking brother, and—"

I pressed my lips into a firm line when a warm hand curved around my waist. Gelsey ducked under my arm wearing one of my T-shirts, which hit her around the knees.

"Morning, Daryl." She smiled wide. "I'm making coffee. Would you like some?"

"Love some."

The motherfucker smirked as he scooted past me.

"This ain't over, leaner," I hissed low enough for only him to hear.

He side-eyed me. "You got three women who say it is. My money's on them. So, shut up and drink some of your girl's god-awful coffee, and let me do my job, skippy. Oh, and," he lowered his voice as he dug his hand into his pocket, "I paid off the title loan. The guy at the shop remembered her. Asked if I was also here for this. I guess it was her mother's. I slipped him an extra grand and lost the paperwork."

Unfurling his fingers, he offered me a ring. Simple. Rubies and diamonds. And a vague memory tickled the back of my mind. Gelsey with the ring on her finger that first day at the Y. And then never again. *Fuck.*

"Thanks."

Dropping his duffel inside the door, Daryl headed for the kitchen while I looked out over the quiet street, wondering how the hell I'd gotten here. Or when I started caring so damn much.

"Where are we going?"

Backing Gelsey against the wall in the bedroom, I kissed her until her knees went weak.

"Quiet, baby," I whispered, hitching a thumb over my shoulder to the living room where my archenemy slept.

We'd spent the day on the deck, lazing in the sun. And then did a little shopping. Just the three of us.

Yeah, no. I was over it.

So I'd devised a plan.

Gelsey sank onto the side of the bed, watching as I added supplies to the growing pile.

Pup tent. Groceries. Flashlight.

In the bathroom, I ripped open the box of Trojans and stuffed an entire strip into my pocket. One could hope. They nudged against the ring I'd carried around all day, wondering just how bad the fallout would be when I gave it back to her.

As I returned, Gelsey scrutinized me with a narrowed gaze. Likely she'd figured out the scheme.

I didn't care. It was him or me time. Kill or be killed and all that stuff. The leaner wouldn't win.

Crouching in front of her, I slid my hand under the hem of her new sundress. "Follow me and grab the keys to Daryl's rental car from the bowl next to the door. Don't make a sound."

"Miles—"

I took her lips in a quick kiss. "We're not fooling around with him in the next room. You're a screamer, baby. Just sayin'."

Flushing crimson, she nodded jerkily as she pushed to her feet.

I grabbed my stuff, cringing at every creaking board as I tiptoed through the dark house. Somehow, we managed to make it to the porch undetected.

"Hit the button to unlock the doors. And grab that tiki torch by the tree."

I hauled ass for the curb while Gelsey fetched the lantern.

"Jesus Christ," I muttered as I popped the lift gate on the black four-wheel drive. "He rented a Jeep. How original."

Secretly, I was glad, since we were driving straight onto the beach. But dude needed some variety in his life.

"Let's go! Let's go!" Gelsey screeched, nearly spearing me with the torch as she tossed it into the back seat. "I saw a shadow! I think he's up!"

"Relax," I said, eyeing the house as I strode to the driver's side.

I almost wanted Daryl to appear at the window. Just so I could give him the finger.

Mess with me, leaner, and you're gonna lose.

Gelsey scrambled onto the passenger seat, her blue eyes wide as saucers. "What if he reports the car stolen?"

I snorted. "He wouldn't."

Would he?

My gaze cut to the house again as I fired up the engine.

Pushing the thought of a night in jail out of my mind, I grabbed Gelsey's hand, tossed her a confident wink, and sped off into the night.

I kept Gelsey in my sights as I tossed another log onto the fire. Waist deep in the water some twenty yards away, she stood perfectly still, except for her fingertips skimming over the ripples from the gentle waves. The glow from the torch I'd planted by the shore bathed her in a golden hue, highlighting every curve and every angle.

This side of the island was empty and mostly used for surf fishing. Our makeshift campsite was up against a small dune. Perfect for blocking the wind.

Reclining on my elbow on the blanket, I put together the ingredients for s'mores while I waited for the water to boil in the kettle for her hot chocolate.

This is what happiness feels like.

I paused as the notion dug itself into my gray matter. The lightness in my chest. And the stillness in my head. The peace in my soul.

I was happy.

"Brr...it's cold," Gelsey said, plopping down next to me on the beach towel. She held her hands in front of the flames, a small smile curving her lips.

Looping an arm around her waist, I settled her between my legs, and she melted against me.

"Are you happy, baby?"

She looked up at me with a brilliant smile. "Yes."

I pressed a soft kiss to her forehead. "Me too."

I gave Gelsey a little privacy, straightening up the campsite while she changed out of her bathing suit inside the tent.

After popping the last bite of chocolate into my mouth, I peeled apart the wrapper for the giant size Hershey bar and smoothed it against my thigh.

What do you want to make today, Miles? A bird, a butterfly, or a flower?

I pushed aside my father's voice, my hands working from rote, folding the paper this way and that until it took the shape of a five-sided flower. It was a simple design. Not nearly as intricate as the ones that had lined the shelves in my dad's office when I was a kid.

"It'll do," I muttered as I pushed to my feet.

Gelsey sat up when I slipped inside the tent. The flames from the fire provided just enough light to see the outline of bare shoulders. Reaching behind me, I tugged my T-shirt over my head with one move as I closed the small gap between us.

I tossed the flower onto her lap, then turned and busied myself with the button on my jeans.

"It's a flower," she said. And that voice. The same one my mom used to use when my dad would emerge from his pit of despair long enough to present her with one of his designs. A little piece of hope crafted from tissue or paper, as fragile as the promise that he'd get better someday.

I stepped out of my jeans and then dropped onto the sleeping bag, throwing an arm over my face. "It's folded paper. Made out of garbage."

Douchebag.

"No, it's not." She pressed a kiss to my chest. "It's beautiful, and you made it for me."

This girl. *Fuck.* It's like she had all the answers. The key to every door.

I tangled my fingers in her hair. "Easy to please. I like that."

Her hand dipped under my boxer briefs. "I'm not *that* easy to please."

My cock sprang to life, and I rolled her onto her back. "You're naked, baby." I kissed a trail to her breast. "Tell me what you want."

"You."

I sucked her nipple into my mouth, and she arched in a way that only a dancer could.

She gripped my shoulders as I shimmied lower. *"No.* I want you inside me."

I slipped a finger into her heat, and she groaned.

"This?"

She shook her head, even as she rocked against my hand. I continued to work her, adding another finger as I took her mouth in a kiss.

She was so fucking wet. So ready.

I swallowed her whimper when I pulled out to grab the condom I'd hidden beneath the pillow.

She watched with hooded eyes as I rolled the latex over my shaft. And fuck. The way her tongue darted out and her breath came in small pants. So hot.

She tilted her hips, and I was right there, my tip at her entrance.

"You ready, baby?"

She nodded, her eyes widening as I pushed in an inch.

"All of it, Miles…please."

Resting my forehead on hers, I thrusted with as much restraint as I could manage.

"Oh…God…" she moaned, fingernails digging into my shoulders. "A minute…" she panted, then blew out a slow, controlled breath, her gaze locked onto mine. "This…I never knew…" With a little shake of her head, she smiled. "More."

Reaching between us, I found her clit.

"You move," I roughed out, not sure I'd be able to keep from slamming into her.

Her hips glided forward, and my toes curled. She found her rhythm, wrapping her legs around my waist.

Slowly, I started to match her thrusts, whispering praises between fevered kisses. *You're beautiful. And…yes, fuck yes, just like that. And…take it, baby, take it all.*

She relaxed, giving in to the pleasure, my name on her lips and her eyes on mine when she flew apart moments later.

I brushed the hair off her brow as the waves took her, committing every sight and sound to memory. Wherever she went, and whatever she did, I'd always be her first. In some small way, we'd be tied together.

Forever.

Chapter Thirty-Four

Gelsey

RAIN.

I heard it in my dreams. Tiny droplets splattering against the tent and dying with a hiss in the dwindling fire outside. And it was so cold.

But, why?

Miles was here, wrapped around me. Like he had been all night.

Only he wasn't.

Sitting up with a start, I scrubbed the sleep out of my eyes. It was light. After dawn, for sure, but gray. Probably thanks to the rain.

And I was alone.

"Miles…?"

Heart pounding, I looked around for something to throw on over my panties. Finding my paper flower crushed on the ground, a wave of panic rose in my throat.

Miles wouldn't leave. Of course, he wouldn't.

Your own father left. Get a clue.

The rational side of my brain tried valiantly to seize control as I yanked my wrinkled sundress over my head. But the tiny part of me that had no faith whatsoever in humanity was clearly in charge.

Swallowing a sob, I crawled toward the open tent flap, nearly colliding with Miles when he ducked inside. I blinked up at him and tried to speak, but when I opened my mouth, nothing came out.

He dropped to his knees, hot chocolate breaching the rim of the cup in his hand. "Baby, what is it?"

Shaking my head, I flipped over onto my butt and pulled my knees to my chest. "N-Nothing. I j-just…"

Can't breathe.

Miles pulled me onto his lap and cradled my face in his hands. "Talk to me, sweetheart." His eyes locked onto mine. "Are you in pain?"

I fought to drag air into my lungs. "P-Panic attack."

Hopefully. Either that or my heart was going to explode. Tingling spread to my fingers and toes, and I squeezed my eyes shut.

"It's all right." He crushed me to his chest, long fingers digging into my hair. "You're all right. Just breathe."

Humiliation burned hot when the tears came. All the worse because I was relieved. Miles was here. He didn't sneak off in the middle of the night. Logically, I knew that. And even if he had, besides the obvious problem of getting back to Austin, I shouldn't have cared that much. People left. But the thought of Miles being one of those people…

Pushing the notion aside, I melted into familiar arms. "Sorry."

He kissed the top of my head. "I didn't know you had panic attacks."

"I don't. Usually. After my mom died, and we lost our house, I felt kind of—I don't know how to explain it—like I didn't belong anywhere. When my dad started driving a truck and leaving me alone in our new apartment, I had a couple of really bad attacks. But then I learned to handle it."

My thumb automatically moved to stroke the empty finger where my mama's ring used to sit. Why hadn't I gone back to the pawn shop this week? I had the money now.

I dashed the tears from my cheeks when Miles pulled back to look at me with an odd expression. Like…he couldn't decide what to do or what to say.

He dug his hand into the pocket of his jeans and sighed. "I know I should have said something. But I figured you'd refuse. I had Daryl pay off your title loan. And he came back with this."

The anger that had flared the second he'd uttered the words "title loan" melted away as his fingers unfurled, revealing the rubies and diamonds. My tears spilled over again as he pressed the ring against my palm.

Slipping the band back around my finger, I tried to speak through the sobs threatening to break free. "Thank you. It's all I have left of her."

The pattering against the tent forced me back into the moment, and I scrambled to my knees, scrutinizing him for any signs of…whatever.

"It's raining." I framed his face in my hands. "Miles, are you all right?"

He took my lips in a quick kiss. "I'm fine."

"Are you sure?"

Resting his forehead against mine, he lowered us to the ground.

This time he didn't ask permission. His hands were everywhere. On my breasts. Between my legs. Curved around my thighs when he pulled me against him. But his mouth never left mine. And when he whispered, "I want you," it was like he breathed it into my soul.

Chapter Thirty-Five

Miles

THE ONE THING GELSEY HAD ASKED ME TO DO, AND I SCREWED IT UP.

"Hold on," I said, and she nodded, sucking in a harsh breath when I gunned the engine and slid the Lightning into the fast lane.

I didn't speed. Almost dying in a fiery crash cured me of that habit. Still, I kept my foot on the gas. Since it was Sunday, the roads between the airport and downtown weren't their usual parking lot. But traffic wasn't the issue. It was a mechanical malfunction on the jet that had caused this bullshit. A light that had flickered once and went out, according to the pilot.

Per Tori's instructions, and far above and beyond FAA rules, the plane had stayed grounded until an exhaustive battery of tests were performed. Putting us three hours behind schedule. Since I'd planned to arrive with four hours to spare before Gelsey's rehearsal, we were barely late.

From the way she was abusing her bottom lip, that didn't matter, though.

"Almost there," I told her as if she couldn't read the street signs.

But I was on edge. Out of my comfort zone.

This Gelsey was a stranger to me. Quiet. Reserved. Even her hair was different—pulled back in a severe bun with no loose tendrils hanging for me to play with.

I took her hand instead, pressing a kiss to her palm. "Sorry, baby."

And just like that, my Gelsey appeared. Her shoulders relaxed, and she slotted her fingers through mine. "It's not your fault. And I had a great time. Thank you for everything."

She shifted in her seat, and her lashes fluttered. But not in a sexy way. More like: I'm in pain because I've been getting drilled on the hard ground by my temporary boyfriend for the last thirty hours.

Way to go, asshole.

I pulled into the parking lot at the dance company at four minutes past five. Not too bad.

I was actually quite proud of myself until Gelsey let out a little cry of distress.

"Miles, I have to go," she said as she grabbed her tote. "Thanks again. I'll see you later."

Hopping out of the truck, she beelined straight for some dude who'd just slipped out of the stage door.

"Micha! Wait," she called.

The guy barely spared her a glance, tearing up the asphalt like his hair was on fire.

"I'm sorry," she cried, stepping in front of him to block his path.

Douchebag glowered at her, and it took all my restraint not to throw the truck into gear and run him over for that sneer.

"Save it," he snapped. "If you're not early, you're late. Just because Ivan's not here doesn't mean you can show up whenever you want." He looked her up and down, and his lip curled even more. "You're not even dressed. Fuck this. I'm out."

He knocked her in the shoulder as he brushed past, and I shot out of my seat. Blood roared between my ears, drowning out their conversation as I strode toward them.

"Gelsey."

Her gaze snapped in my direction, and relief flashed across her features. It was brief, a second at most. But that was the only encouragement I needed. Closing the remaining distance, my hand caught skin when I rested my palm on the small of her back.

"You invited me to rehearsal. And since I'm already here…" I shrugged, then flicked a smile to the douchebag. "Aren't you going to introduce me to your friend?"

Gelsey let out a breath and lifted her chin to the arrogant prick with his arms crossed.

"Miles, this is Micha, my dance partner. Micha this is Miles."

Douchebag aimed his scowl at me. And it was like someone pressed pause. All the bravado melted away and he cocked his head. "Wait… Miles *Cooper*? From Damaged?"

For a second, I was stunned silent. Then muscle memory took over and I felt my face smooth despite my lingering anger. "Yeah…that's me."

Micha zeroed in on my hand still pressed to Gelsey's back.

That's right, buddy. Like glue.

"You two are…"

"Friends," Gelsey interjected.

Her coy little smile confirmed we were more. And I was all about it. But the way Micha's eyes raked her over, *he* was more too. Or he had been. Once.

He scratched his head, obviously confused. "You don't even like music." He released a huff of air. "Except for the Stones."

"Beatles," Gelsey and I replied in unison.

Whatever he'd been trying not to put together finally clicked, and suddenly Micha didn't seem so enamored with me. Good. That would make it easier to beat the shit out of him if he stepped out of line.

"Listen, man," I said through an easy smile. "Sorry Gelsey was late. My fault. I took her to lunch. *In South Padre.*" His nostrils flared, and my grin widened. "Private jet had a mechanical." I sighed. "What are you gonna do, right?"

No shame. None.

Micha's beady eyes homed in on Gelsey. "I guess we can get started. If you're here to work."

Challenge edged his tone, but my girl just smiled. "I'm ready whenever you are."

Undetectable poisons.

I typed the query into my phone as I stood outside Gelsey's dressing room waiting for her to change back into her street clothes. Given the pounding she'd taken at the hands of her dance partner, I wasn't sure how long she'd be. And that was fine. In the meantime, I could re-search the most effective way to end Micha's life. Because, after today, that was my new mission.

Grinding my teeth into dust, I pictured Gelsey on the ground with that prick hovering over her, his hand extended like he wasn't the one who put her there. And every fucking time, she took it, and the torture would resume. Three times he'd dropped her. Three times she'd gotten up.

The door swung open, and Gelsey emerged, a bag of ice strapped to her hip with some kind of plastic wrap. I stepped forward to take her arm, but she gave me an odd look, dodging my attempt.

"I'm fine," she said through a tight smile.

My brows went up, and she rolled her eyes.

"We were practicing a new sequence after a two-day break. Our timing was off."

Shoving my hands into my pockets as we walked toward the door, I kept my attention trained straight ahead. "Didn't see Micha on the ground much," I mumbled. "Or at all."

She stopped in her tracks. "What's that supposed to mean." I glanced over my shoulder and found her glaring. "Do you think I didn't try hard enough? Do you think—?"

Fuck. *What?*

"Gelsey, no." She took a step back as I advanced, but I caught her hand. "It was Micha, not you. He looked like…"

"What?" she bit out impatiently.

"Like he didn't care when you fell. Like it didn't bother him."

She inhaled a slow breath. "It's not his job to care. And you don't know what you're talking about."

"But—"

"He was executing the moves. It was me who was off balance. I was a little stiff." She shrugged, lips falling into a frown. "He could've adjusted. Who knows? Maybe he tried." Sighing, her eyes fluttered closed, and I could see the frustration in her furrowed brow. "We haven't found our groove. We might never find it. I wasn't his choice for a partner."

"So…he gets to toss you around because he didn't get his way?"

She offered a weak smile. "He can try. But those mistakes today, they really were on me. I couldn't react quick enough. It takes me longer to warm up. And I was late. Also, it wasn't as bad as it looked." My brows crashed together, but she remained steadfast. "Trust me, Micha doesn't want me out of commission."

Her fingers laced through mine as we continued our trek.

"Why's that?" I asked, thoroughly unconvinced and still plotting his death.

"I'm his ticket to the big show." She hit the tension bar on the door and stepped outside. "The only way Micha gets to New York is with me."

"So wouldn't that mean he'd do anything to keep you from hitting the ground?"

She took in a lungful of night air and gazed up at the stars. "Not if it means we don't hit the poses." Spinning around, she walked backward, a playful smile ghosting her lips. "What's the biggest venue you ever played? Like, your Mount Everest?"

Easy.

"Wembley Stadium. Ninety thousand fans."

"Okay… well, let's say you had to learn a new…whatever it's called for that show."

I smiled. "A riff."

"A riff. Right. So, you wouldn't want to half-ass it, would you? You'd learn that riff even if it meant your wrists were on fire and your legs felt like lead."

Rhenn's voice whispered from another time. A basement studio in London where we'd holed up, preparing for the most important gig of our career.

We're going to do it until it's right. All night long if we have to. We're not going on stage looking like a bunch of fucking amateurs.

Damaged was already on top. Coasting. But good was never good enough.

The cost of greatness.

Sweeping the memory aside, I pulled Gelsey into my arms. "So, what can I do to help you prepare for this big gig?" Dipping my head to the crook of her neck, I dragged my nose along the soft pillar of skin, up to her ear. "Warm baths? Massages? I'm down for massages. And you can be on top from now on."

She hummed as if contemplating, and I felt the vibration all the way to my balls.

Looping her arms around my waist, she peered up at me with hooded eyes.

"Massages are good. And I wouldn't mind being on top tonight."

Chapter Thirty-Six

Gelsey

I MANAGED TO PUSH ASIDE ALL THOUGHTS OF MY DISASTROUS REHEARSAL until I arrived at the dance company the following day. After years of obsessing over every misstep, I considered it progress. Maybe I could have a life outside dance as long as it didn't interfere with my routine.

That thought flew out the window when I pulled open the stage door and heard music floating from one of the studios. My music. *Dance of the Flower*.

Checking the time on my phone, I rushed down the hallway, nearly colliding with Olga when I rounded the corner.

"Whoa, sweetheart," she said, grabbing my arm to steady me. "Are you okay?"

"Fine. I just…" Glancing around, I forced a smile. "Where is everyone?"

"Studio A. Ivan called a companywide meeting."

I felt the blood drain from my face. "Nobody told me."

"Everyone was already here. Costume fittings for Swan Lake." She cupped my cheek. "Don't worry. If Ivan wanted you here early, he would've called. You know how he gets when an idea strikes. He was talking to Micha and—"

"Micha's here?"

"Yes, he came in early to discuss something with Ivan and Nadia."

Nadia. Ivan's right hand and assistant choreographer. Up until a few weeks ago, she'd worked exclusively with Sydney. But once upon a time, she'd been on my team. So far, though, Ivan had kept her out of the preparations for *Dance of the Flower*.

"I better go," I said, my shaky voice betraying the panic crawling up my throat. "We'll talk later."

I gave her hand a squeeze before speeding off to my dressing room to change. Once my leotard and leggings were in place, I grabbed the first pair of pointe shoes off the shelf. Usually, I spent hours tearing apart the seams and customizing them for my feet. But I was in such a hurry to get out of here yesterday, I'd forgotten to take this week's batch with me.

Slipping my feet into the satin, I winced when my toes hit the rigid box in the front. No way. I'd end up with blisters on my blisters if I danced in these.

Rifling through my bag, I found the pair I'd worn last week. The fabric was frayed at the toe, and the seams holding the sole in place were on their last legs. Just the way I liked them. Unfortunately, Ivan didn't feel the same. He insisted that worn shoes were a crutch.

Whatever.

I tied the ribbons as tightly as I could before grabbing a towel and heading for the studio.

My heart stuttered when I slipped inside the door and spotted Micha and Sydney in the front, running through a series of moves while the rest of the company watched. Ivan inhabited his usual spot by the piano, arms crossed, wearing an expression I couldn't read.

Swallowing hard, I skirted the crowd and took my place at the edge of the makeshift stage. When the music stopped, Ivan's icy blue eyes lingered on my shoes for a moment, and all the air seeped from my lungs. Suddenly, blisters didn't seem like such a big deal. Not when he could strip off my skin with just a glare.

Straightening my spine, I prepared to take whatever criticism he had to offer.

"Nice of you to join us, Gels," Micha said, throwing an arm over Sydney's shoulder.

Biting back an apology—because what the hell did I have to be sorry for?—I kept my gaze on our teacher. "I didn't know there was a meeting."

"Maybe you should check your messages," my partner quipped. "Group text."

Ivan slowly shifted his focus to Micha. "It is nice that you worry so much about your partner. But she is right on time. Early, in fact."

I didn't fail to notice the sarcasm in his tone. And neither did anyone else.

"Do you need time to warm up, *malysh?*" Ivan asked, ignoring the murmurs from the rest of the dancers.

Thanking my lucky stars for the hour I'd spent in the pool with Miles doing stretches, I shook my head. "No. I'm ready."

A broad smile broke on Ivan's lips as he closed the distance between us. "Good. Then we can begin." Resting a hand at the small of my back, he turned to our audience. "Gelsey and I will be dancing this sequence together. Nadia, you will videotape."

My blood pressure shot through the roof. "W-What?"

He smiled down at me. "You have a problem dancing with an old man?"

Old man?

Ivan was in better shape than most of the top male dancers in the world. For that reason alone, he rarely performed with anyone in the company. We simply weren't at his level.

"No problem."

"Good." He gave me a little pat before flicking his gaze to Micha, who looked as stunned as I was. "You will start the music on my mark."

My feet fumbled to find first position when Ivan's hands molded to my hips.

"You are nervous, *malysh?*" Hearing the smile in his voice, I shook my head. "Excellent."

He tipped his chin to Micha, and I closed my eyes, praying I wouldn't stumble as the first notes filled the air. Taking my hand, Ivan spun me around.

Unlike Micha, his touch was deft. A barely there whisper against my skin but commanding just the same. After our first lift, my toes found the ground with ease, sticking the landing. As the song reached a crescendo, I stretched toward the sky, reaching higher than I thought possible before dropping to my knees when the music ended.

The roar from our audience was deafening in the small space.

Forcing my attention to Micha as Ivan took my hand to help me up, I found him glaring at our teacher with murder in his eyes. At his side, Sydney gave me a begrudging smile.

"And that is how it is done," Ivan said, close to my ear. "You are in greater command than you think."

Pride bloomed in my chest, and I nodded. "Thank you, *uchitel.*"

He kissed the top of my head. "Now, you will come to my office. So we can discuss your new friend."

I finished rushing through my explanation about Miles, then reached for the bottle of water on the desk like I'd been deprived of fluids for a month.

"So, this musician is the man you told me about?" Ivan asked. "The one you are working for? Or do you have more than one job?"

Heat burned all the way to my hairline. Mostly because I'd need to spell it out for Ivan. I'd thrown around the word "friends" several times. Like every other sentence. But he didn't get the hint. And now that he'd mentioned money, I didn't know what to say to make it sound less like a business deal that included other benefits.

My mind wandered to Trinity and her arrangement with Miles, and my mouth went dry again.

Ivan quickly lost patience.

"Gelsey," he barked, sounding way more fatherly than usual. "Explain."

"Yes, I work for Miles. But j-just a few hours a week."

His eyes darkened to cobalt in the span of a second. "And you are also having sex?"

I felt my mouth drop open, and for the life of me, I couldn't force it closed. He did have a clue after all.

"I...uh..."

Before I could finish, he waved a dismissive hand. "This is not acceptable."

Not acceptable?

Every muscle in my body went rigid as his declaration sunk in. Even Sydney had a boyfriend. And so what if Miles and I were only temporary?

Chin jutting forward, I prepared to make an argument when Ivan inhaled a measured breath, interrupting my train of thought.

"I would prefer that you are not sleeping together *and* getting paid, *malysh*. That is all I meant."

My throat tightened around my response, and I took another drink to rethink my position.

"I *am* training Miles," I said eventually. "I negotiated a pretty large weekly amount before…well, before. And when he offered to let me move in, I insisted on paying rent." I looked Ivan in the eye, and pride stared back at me. "I'm only accepting five hundred dollars a week. One hundred dollars for each hour of training. I can't go to New York with no money."

He rubbed his fingers over his chin while I held my breath. I was old enough to make my own decisions, good or bad, but Ivan's opinion carried a lot of weight.

"When I found out your father was not supporting you any longer, I made some arrangements," he finally said, focusing on his laptop.

"Ivan. Please. You don't have to—"

I sealed my lips tight when he held up a finger. One finger. True, I'd never won a battle against this man. But I'd never given up so easily, either. In truth, I didn't want to ruin this moment. Whatever small gift he wanted to bestow, I'd take it.

He turned the laptop to face me, and I blinked when *Dance of the Flower* spilled from the speakers. A second later, a video flashed across the screen. *Me.* On stage at my first recital, my mother just inside the frame. On pointe when I was nine, holding Ivan's hand instead of the barre as I fought to balance on my tiptoes. Clutching a bouquet of roses at the curtain call for the company's performance of the *Nutcracker Suite* when I'd danced the lead at fourteen. A flurry of still photos of me in rehearsals spanning the years flickered one after another. Too many to count. And then it was over.

My throat burned as I touched the screen. "What is this?"

"It is you." He smiled. "I put together this video to present to our donors. Tatiana also directed some of her patrons to the site. So far we've collected just under twenty-four thousand dollars for your expenses."

My eyes filled with tears. "I don't understand. You did this? Where did all the clips come from?"

"They are mine. Little snapshots I have taken of you throughout the years." A crease formed between his brows. "I am sorry that I did not do this sooner. Sometimes we only see what we want to see. Maybe it is too late to offer, but you are always welcome in my home if you are not happy where you are. And the money, of course, is yours to spend as you see fit. Olga will give you access to the account."

Since there was nothing Ivan hated worse than tears, I tried furiously to keep the traitorous little drops from spilling onto my cheeks. "I don't know what to say. I always thought…"

He leaned forward, frowning now. "What?"

"With all my problems, I just assumed that you didn't think I was worth the effort."

As soon as the words left my mouth, I regretted them. Ivan's shoulders slumped, and for a long time, he didn't say anything. When he finally spoke, it was in a quiet voice.

"I did not push you because you pushed yourself so hard. After you were injured, I hoped…" His thought trailed off on another sigh. "I kept thinking you might choose another road. One that was not so difficult."

Staring down at my pointe shoes, I swallowed the lump of fear that always accompanied any talk of pursuing something besides dance. Ivan and I had never had the conversation. But the doctors and therapists had hinted.

Four good years.

That was the general consensus. If all the stars aligned.

"I don't even know what another life looks like," I said truthfully, and when I looked up, Ivan's gaze was liquid blue, not the frozen ponds I was used to.

"You have many undiscovered talents, *malysh*. But for now—*dance*. You will know when it is time to stop."

Chapter Thirty-Seven

Miles

H ours after Gelsey left for rehearsal, I finally shook myself awake. We'd had an early morning session in the pool, all business. Then a hot shower that included some pretty strenuous fucking up against the tile wall.

Gelsey hadn't even made it to the door before I'd crawled back into her bed.

The sheets smelled like us. Like the massage oil I'd used on her last night. And lavender. And sex. I wanted to drown in it. Then wait for Gelsey to come home so I could drown in her.

But since I didn't know when that would be, I forced myself upright and scrubbed a hand over my face. My attention strayed to my phone on the nightstand and the blinking light. Rather than get dressed, I slumped against the headboard and lazily scrolled my messages.

Deleting all but a few, I read Taryn's first.

Chase said to bring the kid by the studio anytime. There's usually someone jamming if you need some bodies to lay down tracks.

Blake in the studio? Was he even ready for that?

Blowing out a breath, I tapped out a reply.

I'll talk to his doctor. Not sure if it'll work. The kid is pretty damaged.

I massaged the muscle in my thigh out of habit. It didn't hurt as bad. Letting my hand wander, my fingers traced the ridges of my abs, and I considered working out.

Huh.

It didn't sound impossible.

Taryn's reply forced my thoughts back to the present.

We're all damaged, Miles. It's nice what you're doing for the kid. I love you.

Before I could talk myself out of it, I responded: *Love you too.*

Because I did. I'd never stopped. Even though I knew that letting Taryn back in meant dealing with all the shit from my old life. Friends that I'd left behind. And music.

My chest tightened, and I snagged my jeans off the floor. After digging the tiny silver case out of my pocket, I dropped the contents into my open palm. My daily dose of anti-depressants. Shaking the capsules in my hand, I considered what life would be like without them. The fist around my heart squeezed at the thought, and I popped the pills into my mouth.

They melted on my tongue, leaving a sour taste as I trudged to the bathroom for some water. Dipping my head to the faucet, I swallowed them down, along with a little of my pride.

Sheppard believed I'd always been depressed. That it was part of my DNA, like brown hair and the ability to strip any song down to a beat in seconds.

But I wasn't so sure. I'd managed to go twenty-four years without any chemical intervention. The best years.

Scrutinizing myself in the mirror, my fingers inched toward the ink over my heart. I brushed my thumb over Paige's name, and the *R* with the crown.

"Maybe twenty-four years is all you get."

The lifespan for happy.

A cloud peaked over the horizon, gunmetal gray and filled with rain. My future.

The walls started to close in—not tight—there was still plenty of room to breathe. But I backed out of the room, nonetheless.

My heart pounded as I searched for my T-shirt in the sheets. That's when I noticed a piece of paper on the pillow. Sinking onto the side of the mattress, I glanced over Gelsey's note.

Not a note. A poem.

Write me a song
Hold my hand
Find me when I'm lost
Even if I'm right beside you

The same lightness I'd felt in Padre filled my chest. And just as quickly, it evaporated.

What was worse? A moratorium on happiness, or a seventy-day stay of execution?

Rolling my shoulders, I folded the paper in half with intentions of leaving it where I found it. But instead, I folded it again. Before I knew it, a Kawasaki rose took shape in my hands. The most intricate design I'd crafted in years.

I placed the flower on Gelsey's pillow, grabbed my shirt, and headed for the door.

Emily was waiting for me when I strode through the kitchen door. She looked tan and rested and pissed off.

Hoping that she'd remember I was responsible for the former, I ignored the latter and brushed a kiss to her temple on my way to the fridge. "Hey, girl. Glad you're back. What's for lunch?"

Spinning to face me, she planted her butt against the counter, holding her phone in a death grip.

"Can you even pretend that you remembered our breakfast meeting?"

I paused with my hand wrapped around a bottle of Gelsey's pomegranate juice.

"Shit. I'm sorry. I just…"

Forgot wasn't even the right term. That would imply that I'd thought about it at some point. And I hadn't. Not even once.

"I saw you in the pool with Gelsey this morning. That little make-out session where you had her pinned against the wall was especially enlightening. I assume she's your new Trinity?"

Red painted the corners of my vision as I slowly closed the stainless-steel door.

"Gelsey is nothing like Trinity."

Regarding me with a cool glare, Em inclined her head. "So you're not paying her?"

I set the juice down on the island. "I'm not paying her for that."

Locking our gazes, I dared her to mention what "that" was, hoping she'd read the warning signs and back the fuck off.

Instead, she continued to look me over like I was a stranger.

"But you're still hedging your bets," she finally said, conceding her ground when she broke eye contact.

"I don't know what you're talking about." I snagged a glass from the shelf. "Stop speaking in riddles."

"Fine," she bit out. "You tripped out on Trinity when she dared to spend one night in your bed. I wasn't fond of the chick, but punishing her for falling asleep? That was cold. But now you've found a way around the rules, haven't you?" I scowled at her as the first taste of pomegranate burst on my tongue, and she huffed a breath in response. "You're sleeping in your own pool house! Way to commit! But I guess she's fine with it. As long as she gets to keep driving your cars and—"

Thick liquid went flying when I slammed the glass down on the granite with more force than I intended.

"Not that it's any of your business, but Gelsey moved back into the pool house after spending a night in my bed. A *full* night. She didn't want to make things awkward for either of us. She's considerate like that.

"Also, I took her to Padre Island while you were gone. I apologize if that doesn't constitute 'committing' in your eyes. But I'm a fucking grown-up. And Gelsey has a life waiting for her in New York that doesn't include me. So yeah, we're temporary. But while she's here, you need to mind your fucking manners. And keep your opinions to yourself."

Emily's face fell, and she opened her mouth to speak. But footsteps in the hallway caught my attention before she could say a word.

Gelsey.

From the speed at which she was retreating, she'd heard too much. Or not enough.

I shot Emily a glare on my way out of the room when she pushed off the counter to follow me. "Don't even think about it. This isn't a team sport."

She babbled something that may have been an apology, but I was already gone. Catching a glimpse of blond hair ducking around the corner one flight above, I raced up the stairs.

"Hey," I said breezily, skidding to a stop at the door to the guest room.

Gelsey stood at the window with her back to me, like she'd run out of space. "I guess I should've rethought my exit strategy."

I knew she wasn't talking about the day she'd leave for good, but that was the only thing that popped into my mind.

Our gazes met in the glass, and she watched me warily as I moved toward her.

"You have an exit strategy?" I asked as my hands landed on that spot on her hips that I loved.

"Don't you?"

"Nope. Guess I'm not much of a planner. Tell me why you ran off."

A little shrug. "Seemed like a private moment. And since we're only temporary…"

I spun her around. "See, that's what you get when you hear only half of a conversation."

Her hand found my cheek, thumb skating over my dimple. "There was more? I mean, before she jumped to the conclusion that you were paying me for something besides training."

"Gels—"

She shook her head. "No. It's a fair point. Which is the reason I was coming to find you."

Apprehension skittered up my spine, and I molded my forehead to hers to forge a connection. "That doesn't sound ominous at all."

She smiled, and some of the pressure in my chest dissipated.

"If I would've met you under different circumstances…" A light chuckle tripped from her lips. "Okay, I thought you were an asshole when we met so I shouldn't phrase it like that." She took a breath. "If I would've gotten to know you under different circumstances, and found out you needed help, I wouldn't have charged you. At least not thirteen hundred a week."

She pressed a finger to my lips when I tried to respond.

"But it turned out you weren't a jerk. And now I'm staying with you and living like a queen. Plus, you know, the sex."

I nipped her finger. "The sex is good, baby. I think we should keep having it."

From the way her cheeks pinked, she agreed. Which set my mind at ease a little. Until she slipped out of my arms.

"I do too. But…" My stomach dropped to my shoes when she turned her back to me again. "If we're going to keep doing that, then I can't accept this."

Whirling around, she shoved something in my direction. A check. My check.

I backed away like the thing had teeth. "Gelsey, that's yours. You were up at seven this morning training me—"

Grunting in frustration, she shook the slip of paper. "Didn't you hear Emily? We spent a good fifteen minutes making out. Take it. I'm not here for the money. And you're giving me a place to stay. We're even."

Snagging the check from her hand, I tucked it into my back pocket. I could always get her bank account information later.

"What about New York?" I guided her over to the bed and, when she took a seat on the edge of the mattress, I crouched in front of her. "You can't leave town penniless."

She took my face in her hands. "I'm not. Ivan took care of it."

I tipped back since I had the feeling she was trying to distract me. "How?"

Digging into her crossover bag, she took out her phone. "Press play."

Easing onto my butt, I did as she asked.

A video flickered to life over a hauntingly beautiful melody as Gelsey appeared on the screen. Dancing. Smiling. Lacing up the ribbons on her satin slippers.

Dropping down next to me, she pointed to a woman in one of the clips. "That's my mom." I tapped the glass to zoom in but didn't make it in time, and she frowned. "It's hard to tell from this angle, but she was really beautiful."

It wasn't though. Even from the brief glimpse, I saw the big eyes and golden hair. And that smile. Gelsey's smile.

I waited until the video started again to look up. "What is this?"

"It's a page where donors can go and support me. I guess it's like crowdfunding or something."

My mouth dropped open when I clicked a link at the bottom of the page. "You've raised over twenty-five grand."

She laughed, then playfully bit my shoulder. "A lot of rich people love ballet. Or pretend to, at least. Upside, I don't need your money anymore."

Making a mental note of the web address, I handed her back the phone. "So you're just going to train me for nothing? That doesn't seem fair."

Her lips curved into a smile as she nuzzled my ear. "Not for nothing. I'm staying in your pool house. And then there're the other things you're giving me."

Her hand slid to my crotch, and she palmed me through the denim. Catching her wrist, I flipped her onto her back, pinning her arm over her head.

"So you're just going to objectify me? Use me for the cool digs and the awesome sex."

She fluttered her lashes. "Please. I have twenty-five grand. I don't need your cool digs."

I tugged at the drawstring on her sweatpants. "So, just the sex then?"

Her grin widened. "If you insist."

A second later when I reached the warmth between her thighs, all the amusement faded from her expression. She jerked when my finger slid over damp cotton.

"Tell me you want me." I applied a little pressure to her clit, and she squirmed. "Say it, baby."

"I do. I want you," she panted.

I had our clothes off in record time. Scooting to the center of the bed, she watched me tear open the condom. I was about to hand it over and ask if she wanted to do the honors when she blurted, "I'm on the pill."

Clearing the surprise from my throat, I tried for something casual. "Why?"

"It keeps my periods regular. One accident in a light pink leotard and you learn your lesson." She swallowed hard when I didn't say anything. "I can show you the package if you don't believe me."

I blinked. Did she actually think my hesitation had something to do with her?

Even knowing that this conversation was going to put a serious damper on our afternoon playtime didn't keep me from easing on top of her.

"I'd like nothing more than to feel you skin to skin. But I need…" My throat closed, trapping the rest of the thought where it belonged. Away from Gelsey.

Cupping my cheek, she asked softly, "What do you need?" As if it were something she could give me.

"A test. To make sure I'm clean."

She flinched. "Oh…I…yeah…"

"I've never, ever had sex without protection," I was quick to add. "I mean, not in the last six years."

Why I'd chosen to reveal that little nugget was beyond me. Any hope that she'd let it slide faded away when she dropped her hand.

"So before, when you were on the road with your band, you weren't safe?"

A denial coiled around my tongue, but the truth was quicker, darting around the lump in my throat and flying past my lips. "I had a girlfriend."

The declaration stole the air from my lungs. In all the years Paige and I were together, I'd never described her in those terms.

Gelsey's expression softened, and she hooked her leg around mine, urging me to continue.

I managed a shallow breath. "Paige. My bandmate. She was my…"

Everything. Past tense. But I couldn't bring myself to say it. Whatever small flicker of us remained, in the music or in my memory, would always belong to her.

"The redhead?" Gelsey offered in a whisper, like she knew it was a secret.

"Uh-huh."

She pressed a kiss to my lips. "I'm so sorry, Miles."

I tried for a smile. "It was a long time ago. And it was complicated."

Her own smile was luminescent, if not a little sad. "All great loves are complicated. That's what makes them great."

Curving a hand around my nape, she guided me to her neck.

And for once, there was no crushing weight on my shoulders. No urge to run. And no need to hurry.

Gelsey's knees fell open to accommodate me when my mouth found its way back to hers.

"You're so beautiful," I said against her lips.

Soft thighs molded to my ribs. And she smiled.

"Show me."

Chapter Thirty-Eight

Gelsey

THE STUDIO CLEARED OUT QUICKLY AFTER OUR FIRST FOUR-HOUR rehearsal. The first of many.

There's a point in the preparations for every show where we all put petty differences aside to achieve a common goal. In this case a perfect performance. And we'd just hit it.

Dropping onto the floor with a groan, I began my abbreviated stretching routine.

"You feel like grabbing a late lunch?"

Pausing with my fingers curled around the toe of my pointe shoe, I looked up at Micha. Over the last week, we'd settled into an awkward alliance. He'd stopped trying to drop me on my head, and I'd refrained from muttering under my breath.

But sharing a meal? We hadn't done that in years.

"Me?" I asked warily.

Rolling his eyes, Micha held out his hand to help me up. "Yeah, you. Don't make it weird, Gels."

But it *was* weird. Why was he being so nice to me?

"I'm busy this afternoon," I said as I wobbled to my feet. "Raincheck?"

He shrugged, casual as can be. "Sure."

To my surprise, he followed me over to the bench. While I took a seat and stared down at my shoes, psyching myself up for what I needed to do, he plopped down in front of me and stripped off his shirt. After donning a hoodie he'd plucked from his bag, he let out a sigh.

"You're such a baby," he said with a smile. "Let's see what you got hiding in there."

Before I could say a word, he gently took my foot and rested it on his leg.

"I can get it," I said through gritted teeth as he untied the ribbon from my ankle.

Secretly I was grateful I didn't have to do the honors. And of course, he knew it. Because I'd never been good at this part.

"How bad is the pain?" he asked.

I lifted a shoulder. "Five."

He raised a brow. "That means eight."

Gripping the edge of the bench, I pressed my lips together as he peeled off the shoe. "See," he said. "That wasn't so bad."

With a weak nod, I crunched over to inspect the damage. But Micha beat me to it.

"You're not wrapping these piggies tight enough," he observed as he carefully unwound the bloody gauze from between my toes.

"Too restricting," I said through a labored breath. "And you should be wearing gloves."

He reached for the other foot. "Why, did Cooper give you a disease?"

It took me a beat to register the insult. By that time, he'd tightened his grip. "Sorry, Gels. That was out of line."

His tone hinted at true remorse. And since I was the bigger person, I wouldn't be the one to break our truce. Not over this.

"You don't even know him," I said wearily. "So keep your comments to yourself."

I braced for the witty retort. The one-off. Even if Micha was trying to be good, the last word always belonged to him.

After a moment of silence, my shoulders relaxed, but I kept my guard up.

Micha grabbed a plastic bag from his duffel and handed it over. While I fished out a couple of toe pads, he sprayed rose water on my fresh blisters.

"Is it serious with Cooper?" He flicked his gaze to mine as he dabbed the excess moisture off my skin with a cotton ball.

I couldn't help but smile. "Yeah. But since I'm leaving soon, we're only…"

Temporary.

Miles's conversation with Emily looped in my head. It wasn't even the word that tripped me up. But the look in his eyes when he'd said it.

Temporary.

I didn't realize I'd let my mind wander until I felt Micha scrutinizing me.

"We're good friends," I finished with a too bright smile. "He means a lot to me."

Nodding, Micha busied himself with the Band-Aids. "Do you ever think about us? What would've happened if…"

There was no way for him to finish the thought without looking like a total asshole. Because we both knew how it ended.

If you hadn't gotten hurt.

Like I'd had a choice.

"No."

My voice sounded too small for such a big truth. I *didn't* think about Micha anymore. Ever.

"Me neither." He sighed. "That's a good thing, though. Since we'll probably be sharing a room in New York."

I wiggled my toes, trying to break the new bandage in. "I'm sure we can spring for two hotel rooms."

He went to work on my other foot. "I'm talking about when we move there, not when we visit."

I froze. "What do you mean?"

"Seriously?" He snorted softly as he removed the tape binding my arch. "Haven't you listened when Ivan talks about how it is for the apprentices? They group us together by the Company of origination. At least for the first season."

I shook my head, my stomach a churning pit. "No. That's only in Europe."

It struck me now why he was being so nice. Conciliatory. We were going to be stuck together. Likely in a room the size of a postage stamp.

For a year.

"You can request a private room," he added as he ran his thumb over another blister. "For two grand extra a month. Since neither of us has that kind of *dinero*, I guess we'll have to make the best of it."

He looked up, hand still curved around my foot, and I nodded automatically, schooling my features into something that wouldn't give away the repulsion I felt.

A season? With Micha?

It would only take him a hot minute to charm the apprentice ballerinas. Then he'd give up the act of trying to be my friend and show me to the door anytime he had "company" in our joined room. Not that I cared who he hooked up with.

"Micha, are you sure—"

My words caught deep in my throat when the door creaked open. Expecting to find Ivan or maybe Olga, my heart stuttered when I met smoldering brown eyes.

Miles's focus shifted to Micha's hand, still locked around my foot.

Jerking out of my dance partner's grip, I offered a frozen smile.

"Miles. We were just…"

It didn't matter what I said, not right then, so I clamped my mouth shut. Miles's features smoothed into the mask he wore in public. But I could feel his irritation from across the room, little sparks dancing over my skin.

"Are you ready?" he asked.

When I nodded, he stalked over and grabbed my bag while I quickly shoved my feet into soccer sandals.

Miles waited until Micha stood up to crowd into his space.

"I know what your game is, dude. You missed your shot, and I get it. I'd be pissed too. So I'll give you one pass," he snarled, holding up a finger. "*One.* But touch her again, and I promise you won't be so lucky."

Chapter Thirty-Nine

Miles

H E TOUCHED HER.

And she let him.

Anger sizzled up my spine, propelling me out of the studio, down the hall, and into the early afternoon sunshine.

I didn't realize Gelsey wasn't behind me until I tossed her bag into the bed of my truck.

As I turned back to the building, I caught a glimpse of the empty parking lot. A perfect metaphor of what I had to look forward to.

Sinking onto the lift gate, a dry chuckle rumbled low in my chest. An existential crisis. Sheppard would be proud. He'd take it as a sign that my creativity was alive and well.

You're feeling. That's a good thing.

Fuck that.

I didn't want to feel. That's what medication was for. Only, nothing dulled my reaction to Gelsey. She was too bright. Too vivid. Color in a black-and-white world.

And I couldn't keep her.

Letting my head fall back, I gripped my thigh and pain shot down my leg.

Let it go, bud.

Why was it that whenever my fucked-up brain conjured a voice of reason it wasn't mine? Like I'd be more receptive if the good advice came courtesy of Rhenn's slow, southern drawl.

When I heard footsteps, I tore my attention from the sky and found Gelsey walking gingerly across the blacktop. Releasing the death grip on my thigh, I sat back, my weight on one palm. My leg continued to pulse in time with my erratic heartbeat as she hoisted herself onto the lift gate beside me.

"Warning Micha against touching me is kind of a waste of time since he's my dance partner." She smoothed her thumb over my brow and frowned. "Ask me, Miles."

Despite my lingering anger, I leaned into her touch. "Ask you what?"

"Anything you want."

Looping my arm around her upper thighs, I hauled her legs over mine with a sigh. My stomach twisted when I noticed the bandages on her toes and all the bruises marring her skin.

Slipping off her sandal, I found a spot on the ball of her foot with no blisters.

"Where's your family at?" I asked as I lightly massaged the area.

She blinked at me. "Why would you ask me about that?"

I chuckled. "You said anything. But I'm guessing you wanted the questions limited to that douchebag?" She followed my line of sight to Micha, striding to his BMW, phone pressed to his ear. "No thanks. I already know his story."

Her head swiveled back to me. "What do you know?"

"Well, the boy's got a thing for you. Probably wanted to swipe your cherry." I shrugged. "Probably tried. Anyway, I don't fucking care about him. He may have known you longer, but he doesn't know you better. He's never seen you smile in your sleep. Or felt you from the inside."

She caught me in those liquid blue eyes and held on tight but didn't say a word.

After a moment, I slid her sandal back on. "You ready to go?"

She nodded, and I helped her to her feet.

Once we were inside the truck, Gelsey let out a little gasp as she plucked the tissue paper flower from the dashboard. It was intricate, with leaves and a stem I'd fashioned from a cocktail straw. I smiled when she brought it to her nose.

"It's not real, baby."

She flushed pink, setting the bloom in her lap. "It's better. Because you made it. What kind of flower is it?"

"African violet."

Her finger whispered over the petals. "No one's ever given me flowers."

The girl was so easy to please. Shaking my head, I made a mental note to contact the florist as I fished my keys from my pocket.

"My grandma was a ballet coach in St. Petersburg," she said quietly. I turned to look at her, but she was focused on the flower. "She came here when my mom was five, after my grandfather passed away. She never accepted my mom's decision to quit dancing, and I think she blamed me and my dad. When I was nine, I overheard her tell my mom that I didn't have the talent to dance on the big stage." The column of her throat bobbed, and she squinted as if reliving a physical pain. "Even though I believed it, I tried harder. So I guess in some ways she's responsible for any of my future success."

Biting back a protest, I took her hand. "Where is she now?"

"She went back to Russia after my mom died. She said she had nothing keeping her here." Her eyes found mine for a second. "Ivan's the only one who has ever stuck around."

"Your coach?"

"*Uchitel.* My teacher." Her gaze wandered to the facade of the building, eyes tracing all the bricks and glass. "He built this place into what it is. I'm going to miss it."

Her lips bent into that smile she wore whenever she spoke about New York or her future. But for the first time I saw something besides excitement. Wishful thinking.

You can't keep her.

But I could. For two more months, she was mine. And we had better things to do with our time than visiting the past.

I brought her hand to my lips for a kiss.

"Let's get out of here. I'm starving."

Gelsey slanted her gaze to mine, pouting. "I don't get it. How do you remember all this stuff?"

Forlorn, she looked back at all the colored paper littering the bed.

I'd been trying for two hours to teach her how to make a basic origami flower, with little luck. But I didn't care. She was positioned between my legs, mostly naked, so I'd sit here all night if she wanted.

I took her hands and guided them, folding the paper into a triangle. "I've been doing this since I was five. So don't be so hard on yourself." I corrected a small error, and she fought me with stubborn fingers. "Stop. Let me show you."

She turned her face up to mine. "Who showed you?"

I narrowed my eyes and focused on the lines of the paper. The sharp creases. "My dad. He loved beautiful, worthless things."

Her fingers froze beneath mine. "Worthless? Why would you say that?"

I didn't. But my mother had. Right before she crumbled the iris he'd made her into a little ball.

Always in your head, Mick, with your beautiful, worthless things. It's paper, see?

Ignoring the question, I winked at Gelsey. "Hand me that tissue paper over there." She stared at me, frowning. "Come on. I think you'll like this."

Her fingertips skated over my jaw. "I like all of it."

One quick kiss and she crawled toward the box at the foot of the bed. I stared at her ass as she sifted through the contents. White cotton panties. When did that become my favorite thing?

"Miles."

Glancing up, I found her peering over her shoulder at me through strands of golden hair. "Yeah…sorry. What did you say?"

Her gaze dropped to my lap where the sheet was doing little to hide my erection. It took only a second for a smile to curve her mouth. A sweet invitation. And then she wiggled her ass.

"Stop with the 'fuck me' eyes," I warned, gripping my dick through the sheet. "Unless you actually want to fuck."

She thought about it for a moment before her hand slowly traveled down her belly and disappeared between her legs.

"Come here," I ordered, tossing the covers back.

She eased onto her forearm, her ass still in the air. And now I could see everything. The wet spot on her panties and her fingers buried deep in the fabric.

"No," she said huskily.

I rose to my knees, smiling. "No? You don't want to fuck? Or you want me to watch you fuck yourself first? Use your words, baby."

Her hand moved faster. But she didn't say anything.

I crawled toward her. "You're teasing me?" She shuddered as I pressed a kiss to her ass. "I bet I can get you to talk."

She shook her head, then gasped when I yanked her panties to her knees.

"Keep going," I cooed when her hand jerked to a stop. "I want to watch."

Sinking back onto my haunches, I stroked myself slowly as she found her rhythm again.

"Fuck, you're so wet. You like me watching you?"

Catching her bottom lip between her teeth, she nodded, then squeezed her eyes shut.

"Keep looking at me," I growled, thrusting a finger into her glistening pussy.

Her lids flew open. "Not... fair..." she whispered through a pant.

"Life's not fair."

The smile in my tone masked the tension through my body as I lazily stroked into her. When I felt her walls start to clench, I was on my knees again, my cock at her entrance.

And that's when she found her voice.

"Do it, Miles. *Please.*"

We both groaned as I slammed into her.

"Easy," I grunted, digging my fingers into her hips to keep her from moving. We'd only been skin on skin once before, about three hours ago after I got the email from the lab with the results of my test. So this was a new sensation, having all her warmth and wetness wrapped around my dick.

"Rub your clit," I instructed as I pressed a kiss to her spine. "I want to feel you come."

Gelsey was into it now, and the words were flowing. Along with the moans. I continued to whisper against her skin until she flew apart.

Teetering on the edge of my own release, I pulled out and flipped her over. She looked surprised. And flushed. And so fucking hot.

Bringing her fingers to my mouth, I entered her again while she watched me with wide eyes.

"Can you come again, baby?"

No sooner had I said the words then her back arched off the bed. Gelsey did everything gracefully. Even fuck. And for a moment, it was like a dance with no music. I lifted her to sitting without breaking our connection, and we were face-to-face, her legs wrapped around my waist.

You can't keep her.

This time the voice in my head was all mine. Which should've made it easier to ignore. But it didn't. As I opened my mouth to speak, she pressed her fingertips to my lips.

"Tell me something no one else knows," she breathed, gently rocking against me.

And when her hand fell away, it was right there, on the tip of my tongue.

I love you.

Maybe she knew it too, because one look into my eyes and she dropped her head back and came apart in my arms.

Gelsey

I woke in the middle of the night in my favorite spot—wrapped in Miles's arms. It didn't matter where. The pool house. Or his bed. Anywhere he was, that's where I wanted to be.

I shifted, and paper crunched under me.

The flowers.

Lifting onto my elbow, I looked around to see if any could be salvaged. But I gave up when I caught sight of Miles's profile. Moonlight kissed his skin, and I could just make out the angle of his jaw. And his strong nose. The furrow on his brow that never completely went away, even when he slept.

Smoothing the lines with my thumb, I felt my lips curve when he sighed. Who would be here to do this after I was gone?

Stomach twisting, I jerked my hand away and rolled onto my side.

Distance. I needed it.

But as I tried to will myself back to sleep, a paper figure on the nightstand caught my eye. I inched toward it, my heart crawling into my throat when I realized what it was. A ballerina made of tissue, arms stretched to the sky. I reached out and ran my finger over the pleats on the skirt, tears filling my eyes.

A beautiful, worthless thing. That wasn't worthless at all. Because Miles made it for me. And that meant it was worth everything.

Chapter Forty

Miles

TARYN CROSSED HER ARMS, SURVEYING BLAKE ON THE OTHER SIDE OF THE glass. We were at the Phoenix Souls Studios on Sixth, where I'd brought the kid so she could have a look see.

Sweat dampened both palms as I tried to gauge her reaction out of the corner of my eye. And what the fuck? Even if Taryn didn't like what she heard, what did I care? My name was gold in the industry. All the years out of the spotlight had only added to my mystique.

"Miles?" Blinking out of my trance, I noticed Taryn's scrunched up brow. "Is everything okay?"

I forced a smile. "Yeah, of course. I've got a lot on my mind." I re-focused on Blake. "You know, the kid's kind of fragile. So I don't want to put him through the wringer. If you're not interested, I can take him somewhere else."

Taryn turned to face me, a deep crease between her brows. "Hold the phone, cowboy. This is me. *Us.* If you like this guy, we'll offer him a deal. This studio…" She looked around with a soft smile. "This is the house that Damaged built. And you're Damaged." I raised a brow, and she rolled her eyes. "You know what I mean. None of this would be possible without…"

She swallowed hard, and I offered a nod, letting her off the hook. We'd fallen back into our easy friendship—texting and talking on the phone like we used to. But Taryn was still reticent about bringing up Paige and Rhenn, or even alluding to them. Like I might break down. That was the risk I ran when telling someone about my *condition.*

Taryn didn't understand that my depression didn't manifest with weepy tears. *Anger.* That was my jam. She'd seen the full measure of it when I told her to get the fuck out of my life. That was the last time I'd let that genie out of the bottle.

"I appreciate that, T-Rex. But I'd really like your honest opinion."

She tilted her head at me before shifting her attention to Blake. Assessing him with a shrewd gaze, she tapped her finger against her lips. And in that moment, I glimpsed what Taryn had become. A powerhouse. Brilliant as fuck with an unmatched eye for talent. Far removed from the eighteen-year-old girl who'd negotiated our first contract.

"I like him," she finally said. "He's got the IT factor, and he's easy on the eyes. I can sell him."

I smiled. "You can sell anyone."

She gave a self-deprecating shrug, but she knew it.

"Okay." I rubbed my hands together. "I guess the next step would be getting Tori in the loop? And Chase?"

They were the two other principals, but I wasn't sure who actually ran the studio.

Taryn pressed her lips into a firm line but didn't look at me.

"T-Rex. You don't have to go out on a limb for me. I'm not asking Phoenix Souls to front any money. I've got cash."

To burn.

Every time I looked at my bank balance it was bigger. And that was thanks to Taryn as well.

Tears shimmered in her blue eyes. "I've waited for this day, Miles. Hoped for it." She took her phone from her pocket. "Give me a second to call Chase. He'll finish up with Blake and you and I can talk."

I shifted my feet, wary. "We are talking."

"Upstairs. In the offices."

Taryn didn't say a word as the industrial elevator carried us to the top floor. The building had a rustic feel, since it was originally a warehouse. But the studios were state-of-the-art. I had a feeling this new venture would only add to what was already a thriving empire.

We stepped off the lift, and Taryn took off ahead of me down the long hallway. Slowing my steps when I came upon a wall of photos, I glanced over all the notable bands that were now with the new label.

"Wow, Taryn. This is really impressive."

A few yards away, she fumbled with some keys in front of a closed door. "Thanks." She smiled, but it didn't reach her eyes. "Let's talk in here."

And there was that word again. *Talk.* I managed a carefree smile as I took her up on the invitation.

"Why so formal?" I asked as I scooted past her and into the empty office.

A mahogany desk sat in front of the window facing Sixth. On the opposite end of the room, a leather couch and matching chair with the tags still attached cupped a sturdy round table. And that was it. Nothing on the walls. Even the carpet looked like no one had walked on it.

"This looks like the scene from a mob movie," I joked. "If you've brought me here to whack me, you should probably lay some plastic on the floor. You know, so you won't have to replace the carpets."

She smiled nervously. "Let's sit down."

But instead of taking her place behind the desk, she sidled to the sofa and eased onto the edge of the cushion. If this were ten years ago, she would've pulled out a smoke. I'd bet my life on it. Instead, she crossed her legs, and her foot began to bob.

Flopping down beside her, I ran a hand through my hair. "T-Rex, whatever it is—"

"This is your office," she blurted. "Please don't be mad. I know I've overstepped before. Just…hear me out."

Stunned, I jerked a nod, and she let out a relieved breath. Holding up a finger, she hopped to her feet and rushed over to the desk. When she reclaimed her seat, she had a file in her hand.

"When we formalized the plans for the label, Tori and I wanted to make you a part of it. But we didn't know how. She wasn't really talking to you and I…I was afraid you'd think I was trying to force myself back into your life."

Guilt swamped me, stealing my words. "Taryn…"

"Let me finish," she rushed out. "You own a fifteen percent share in the label and the studio. Tori, Chase, and I each own twenty-five percent shares. The other ten percent goes to Paige and Rhenn's endowment fund. Those shares can't be sold or revoked. And if we go public, they'll be converted to regular stock with a trustee." Smoothing her hands over the file, she looked up at me. "It's all in here. But I want you to know, it's not about the money. Or guilt. Or anything else. We—Tori and me—always dreamed that you'd come on board. Any way you wanted. As a producer. Or a studio musician. Or in talent acquisition."

I laughed when I heard the hitch in her voice. "Really, T-Rex? You know damn well the talent is your domain."

Her shoulders relaxed. "You're not mad?"

Taking her hand, I shook my head and sighed. "Of course, I'm not mad. Why would I be mad?"

I kept my gaze on our entwined digits, hoping she wouldn't answer. We both knew I didn't need a reason to be mad. I'd been mad for the better part of the last six years.

"I'm grateful…and not just for this." I chuckled, despite the burning in my throat. "You saved me, Taryn. And I never thanked you for it. But I'm thanking you now."

The file slid to the ground when she threw her arms around me. She mumbled something into my T-shirt about Rhenn and Paige and their legacy. And for once I didn't feel like crawling out of my skin.

After a long moment, she gathered her composure and pulled away.

Swiping a tear from her cheek with the pad of my thumb, I asked, "So what kinds of things can I do to help earn my keep around here?"

Taryn perked up. "Really?"

I sat back, my focus on the window where cotton candy clouds hung low in the sky.

"I'm thirty years old. Too young to retire. Music is the only thing I know. But I'm not sure what help I can be if it doesn't involve banging on the drums."

Taryn sank against the cushion, her head on my shoulder. "You can always travel around and show off that pretty mug. Get the girls all swoony." She grabbed my chin and gave it a squeeze. "Unless…" I felt her gaze burn into me when she leaned back. "You're off the market, aren't you? Kelsey? The ballerina?"

"It's Gelsey."

Denying the rest was pointless, so I didn't even try. Taryn's smile turned electric.

"Don't get excited, T-Rex. It's not like that. She's…" *Leaving.* Scrubbing my hands down my face, I shook my head. "Whatever. She'll be gone soon."

When Taryn's face swam into view, worry lines creased her brow. "When?"

"A little over a month. She's going to New York next week to shore things up." I craned my neck to the door. "We should probably head downstairs. I've got to get Blake back to Millwood."

Taryn nodded, taking out her phone. She tapped away while I took a last look around, wondering what it would be like to work here. My bio was filled with fluff about Grammys and platinum albums, but I'd never held a job in my life.

"Well, all righty then," Taryn crowed, slipping her phone back into her pocket as we headed toward the elevator.

Giving her a sidelong glance, I noticed her self-satisfied smile. "Something you'd like to share?"

"I just booked your first official appearance on behalf of Phoenix Souls Music."

Jesus, this girl. No moss growing under her feet. Or mine, apparently.

Resigned, I followed her onto the lift. "When and where?"

"Next week. You're doing the *Tonight Show with Jimmy Fallon.*" Smirking, she pressed the button for the third floor. "In New York City."

Chapter Forty-One

Gelsey

BLAKE SMILED AT ME FROM ACROSS THE SUV AS WE PULLED ONTO CONGRESS Avenue. "So, Gelsey. You're a ballet dancer?"

It wasn't really a question. And that made me stupidly happy. Obviously, Miles had told him about me.

Or maybe not.

They'd just picked me up at the dance company, and I was wearing a leotard under my sweats. It wouldn't take a genius to figure it out.

Miles laid a possessive hand on my leg, and Blake grinned at the gesture.

"Guilty," I replied a little too brightly, my words carving through the thick haze of testosterone. *Stupid boys.* "And you're a musician?"

Blake's smile faded, and he shifted his focus to the downtown traffic. "Remains to be seen." After a moment of awkward silence, he stretched and addressed Miles. "Do you mind if we stop at What-a-Burger? I probably missed dinner. And I gotta take a piss."

Miles relayed the request to the driver who swung the car into a shopping center parking lot a few minutes later.

"Be right back," said Blake, reaching for the door handle like he couldn't wait to escape.

"Hold up." Miles fished some money out of his pocket. "Can you pick us up a couple of number one meals?"

Pocketing the cash with a wry smile, Blake shook his head. "Seriously? You're not going to take your girl out for a nice meal?" Before Miles could reply, Blake tossed me a look of mock pity. "Your boyfriend's got no game." He waggled his brows. "Maybe we should—"

"Back off, you little shit," Miles interjected with only a hint of irritation. "Before I kick your ass to the curb and make you get your own ride home."

Blake's grin broadened as he threw open the door. "And how would you ever explain things to the good doctor?"

"I'm not afraid of Sheppard," Miles muttered. "Now get your damn food. I'm worn out."

"Because you're old," Blake shot back as he hopped to his feet. *"Really old,"* he mouthed to me before slamming the door.

I watched his broad shoulders curve inward as he sauntered across the blacktop. Despite his confident swagger, there was an air of defeat about him. And those eyes. Timeworn was the only way to describe them.

"I thought he'd be younger," I murmured as Blake ducked around a small group by the door.

Miles looped an arm around me. "He's barely twenty-one."

"So, my age, then."

My teeth sank into my bottom lip to hide my groan. Why did I say that? Our eight-year age gap really bothered Miles, and I wasn't sure why. Maybe Emily had brought it up. Or his manager.

"Yep. I'm surrounded by youngsters."

"Please. You're barely thirty."

"Which means I was in the third grade before you drew a breath."

His brow pinched as if the idea pained him, so I angled for a change of subject.

"How did you know when to pick me up?"

"Well, see, I'm a man of many talents. Mind-reading being one of them." I raised a dubious brow and he shrugged. "Fine. I called the car service and told them to check with me before they sent out a driver. We were in the neighborhood laying down tracks at Phoenix Souls, so I thought I'd surprise you." Sliding his hand between the seat and my ass, he gave me a squeeze. "So, are you?"

"Am I what?"

"Surprised."

He took my lips in a chaste kiss that quickly developed into something more.

"What about Blake?" I said, tipping back before he could dive in again.

"He can get his own girl." Groaning in frustration when I gave him a nudge, Miles flopped against the seat. "Okay, okay. I'll wait until we drop the little cock-blocker off."

I laced our fingers when he started to pout. "Tell me about the studio. What did you record?"

"Bits and pieces. Not quite a song yet. But if we manage to get it finished, you'll get a writing credit. And royalties if it sells."

"Me?" I spluttered. "Why?"

"The poem you wrote—the one you left me on the pillow? It's the hook for the track we're working on."

I waited a beat to see if he broke out in laughter. Because, surely this was a joke. My poem? It had taken all my courage just to show it to him.

Besides dancing, writing was my only passion, but I had no illusions. I'd only taken the minimum number of required classes to satisfy the school board so I could get my diploma. And that wasn't saying much. Texas was lenient.

I'd inquired about taking an English class at the junior college, only to be informed that I'd need to take a lengthy placement exam. Sure that they'd see right through my shoddy education and laugh me out of the building, I'd never pursued it.

"Where'd you go?" Miles asked, concern digging a crease between his brows. "Listen, if you don't want us to use your lyrics—"

A light chuckle parted my lips. "It's not that. I'm just surprised."

"Why?"

I hated explaining this stuff, but still, I kept my chin high. "I told you. With my dancing, there wasn't much time to study. I did the bare minimum to graduate."

Miles plucked a book from my tote and glanced over the cover. "Yet you read Dostoevsky for kicks?"

I reached for the paperback. "Don't make fun."

"I'm not. Why would you think that?"

My cheeks went up in flames. "Ivan…he said *The Brothers Karamazov* was required high school reading."

Shaking his head, Miles sighed long and hard. "I'm pretty sure they don't teach Russian literature until college. At least not around here. You're more advanced than you think, baby."

While I fingered the worn edge of my book, Miles looked out

the window to where Blake was chatting up some girls outside the restaurant,

"When does he complete his program?" I asked. "I mean, don't most rehabs only last thirty days?"

"It's a little more complicated than that."

Our eyes met, but his expression was one I'd never seen. Not just blank. But shuttered. Walled off. I was about to press the issue when the car door swung open.

Blake tossed the greasy bag onto the seat and followed it in.

"About time," Miles said, his gaze flicking to the window where the girls were eyeing the SUV. "I don't need you drawing that kind of attention. Have some respect."

Blake sank against the leather, while I made a grab for the burgers, aiming for a distraction. "I'm starving. Did you get fries?."

I could count on one hand how many times I'd eaten junk food in the last year, but still, I dove in like a woman possessed. When I looked up, Blake was fidgeting with the sleeves on his hoodie and scowling at Miles.

"Telling tales, bro?" he asked and then chuckled darkly. "We all fall down—remember that. You ain't special just 'cause you've got your shit together for the moment. We both know that could change."

My heart pounded against my ribs while I waited for Miles to defend himself. To tell Blake that his drinking days were behind him. But he didn't.

Instead, he shifted his focus to the passing scenery, ignoring everything else for the rest of the drive.

As soon as the car rolled to a stop in the driveway, Miles grabbed his backpack and the greasy bag of fast food and hopped out without a backward glance.

Meeting the driver's sympathetic gaze in the rearview mirror, I offered a tight-lipped smile.

"Thanks, Cody. See you next time."

Shouldering my gym bag, I got out of the SUV and started for the house. The front door was ajar, a sliver of light spilling onto the porch. Not really an invitation. More like an afterthought.

Is that what I was?

A screw tightened in my chest, preventing any forward progress. If Miles needed a night to himself, I'd let him have it. No questions asked.

Heaving a sigh, I changed my course and headed for the pool house. Fatigue set in as I pushed my way through the door. Dropping my bag onto the bed, I kicked off my sandals and shuffled to the bathroom.

After setting the water temperature in the shower, I peeled off my clothes and stepped inside. Closing my eyes, I took a deep breath as I tugged my hair free of the tight bun.

My heart slammed against my ribs when a rush of air whispered over my skin. Scrambling out from under the jets, I pressed my back against the stone wall.

Miles stood at the threshold where the marble met the tile, staring at me through the fine mist of steam.

"Miles!" I sucked in a surprised breath. "You scared me to—"

"Why didn't you come in the house?"

Swallowing hard, I blinked the water out of my eyes. "You stopped talking to me almost an hour ago. I thought you wanted to be alone."

He took a step, and one of the jets hit him square in the shoulder, but he didn't seem to notice. "No, baby. I don't want to be alone."

His brows crashed together, and he frowned like he'd just admitted to something awful.

"I didn't know what to think." Shifting my feet, I dug my fingers into the stone pebbles on the wall. "I didn't want to force my company on you."

My voice sounded as hollow as my excuse. And I wondered if he could see right through me.

Closing the small gap, Miles curved a hand around my hip, and warmth spread to every limb. "Why would you ever think that?"

"I don't know."

But I did.

People left. Checked out. Tossed you aside. As strong as I was, I couldn't face another rejection. Even a small one. Not from Miles.

His palm skimmed up my arm, coming to rest on my nape. Tilting my chin with his thumb, he coaxed my gaze to his. "I didn't mean to shut you out. It was a long day. And I had a lot going on."

I nodded, embarrassed. "Okay. I just...I don't know what we are, Miles. Or what this is. Where the boundaries are."

He touched his forehead to mine. "What do you want it to be?"

I watched the water trail down his cheeks and over his dimple.

"Enough," I finally admitted. "I want it to be enough."

Smiling, he reached behind his back and tugged the T-shirt over his head. "It's more than enough."

My eager fingers found the button on his jeans, but he stopped me before I reached the zipper. "I got an offer today," he said, pressing a little closer.

The crease between his brow gave me pause, but I managed a light smile. "What kind of offer?"

"Jimmy Fallon. The *Tonight Show*."

The butterflies in my stomach moved north on hopeful wings. "Isn't that in New York?" He nodded. "When?"

"Same time you're going to be there. We could go together if you want."

Our eyes met, and he smiled a shy smile that I knew I'd remember always. Framing his face with my hands, I traced the curve of his lips with my thumb. And then I kissed him. "I want."

Chapter Forty-Two

Miles

OVER THE NEXT WEEK, I TRIED TO PRETEND THINGS WERE OKAY. THAT Gelsey and I weren't heading off to the place that would tear us apart forever. I even managed to convince her—I think. But not myself. In the small moments between, like now, my mind went there.

From the second-floor gallery overlooking the studio, I watched Gelsey execute a flawless arabesque. And yes, I knew the names of all the moves. Because every morning when she went down to the gym to run through her routine, I tagged along.

It was the closest thing to perfection I'd ever seen—the way Gelsey moved.

Actual perfection?

Anytime she spoke. I wanted to spend the rest of my life in that conversation.

Gelsey's gaze found mine as she got back into position, and she graced me with a smile.

"She is lovely, yes?"

Whipping my head around to the voice, I met glacial blue eyes and sharp cheekbones. Ivan. We'd never been formally introduced, but his photos hung on the wall in every studio. In his sweats and basic black T-shirt with his blond hair curling over his collar, he looked far too young to be the founder and director. But there was an air of surety about him that was unmistakable.

"She is," I said, offering my hand as he took a seat beside me. "I'm Miles."

His fingers closed around mine in a vise-like grip. "Ivan Volkov."

Gelsey completed another series of moves, but this time when she looked up to the gallery, she froze. Ivan waited until he had her full attention to make a twirling motion with his finger, but she didn't budge.

After several seconds, he sighed and gave her a small nod. I wasn't sure exactly what that meant, or what silent promise she'd extracted, but she went back to work.

Once the music started again, Ivan turned to me and said bluntly, "She is very taken with you. Is the feeling mutual?"

The standard "we're just friends" fought its way to my lips. It wasn't a lie. And if Ivan were just her coach, I could probably get away with it. But, I didn't even try.

"Very mutual."

He searched my face for a long moment before turning back to Gelsey. And the adoration in his eyes. He masked it well when she happened to glance our way, but it was there.

When he didn't speak, I thought our chat might be over. But then he said quietly, "This life is not what I wanted for her. Too many sacrifices. I tried to…" A heavy sigh parted his lips. "I did not make things easy. Not because she does not have the talent. But because it takes more than that."

With every word, I felt the water rising, like a wave pulling me away from the shore. It'd be easier if he just told me to fuck off and stay away from her. Then I could ignore him. Stake a claim. But this…

"What do you mean?" I managed.

"Gelsey has worked hard. But the people holding the bar by which she is being judged do not understand that. They see only the advantages. She is the granddaughter of a renowned teacher and the daughter of a great dancer." His smiled turned wry. "Not to mention, the protégé of another. All Russian."

"And that makes a difference?"

He inhaled slowly and nodded. "All the difference. But even with that, she will face problems. She is an American who will be judged by Russian standards. We are the best. I say that not to be arrogant, but because it is true. She will need the support of the members of her dance corp. But she will not fit in easily. That is what I wanted to protect her from. Here, I can do that. But in New York, I would only make it worse."

"I don't understand."

"Gelsey must earn her way into the group. They will make or break her career. She will stand on their shoulders to achieve greatness. But only if they let her. She must eat with them and sleep with them, not in some penthouse apartment with her rich, rock star boyfriend."

His blue eyes turned knowing, like he could sense what I hadn't even admitted to myself. That I didn't want to give Gelsey up. And why should I? I could make a life with her in New York. And still keep a foothold here. Money gave me that option.

He smiled, but there was no joy in it. "I see the wheels turning. But I warn you now, do not push this. She will end up resenting you."

I didn't acknowledge him one way or the other. Whatever happened between Gelsey and me was between us. And I still wasn't convinced he was right. About any of it.

Ivan pushed to his feet, offering his hand again. Reluctantly, I took it. But I wasn't agreeing to shit. And maybe he knew that, because instead of releasing me, he tightened his grip. "A bird and fish can fall in love," he said with a shrug. "But where will they live? That is the question. Have a good trip, Miles."

His gaze flicked to the dance floor where Gelsey was just finishing her routine. Her eyes met his briefly before bouncing to mine. One look into those baby blues and my good intentions, if I'd had any, fell away.

"Ready?" I mouthed, not even sure what I was asking.

She smiled wide with no hesitation. "Yes."

Chapter Forty-Three

Miles

A T THIRTY THOUSAND FEET, IT ALL MADE SENSE. GELSEY AND ME. MY MUSIC. Her dancing. I could see our future written in the sky, the promise twinkling in a million tiny stars.

Nothing seemed impossible with her pressed to my side, her cheek resting on my arm.

She'd fallen asleep before we'd even reached our cruising altitude. I'd thought briefly about carrying her to the bed in the back of the Gulfstream. But she needed her rest. And I knew if I got her between the sheets I'd never be able to keep my hands to myself. Besides, if things worked out the way I wanted, we'd have plenty of time to join the mile-high club.

The phone vibrated with yet another text from Blake as I was putting the finishing touches on the origami Gerbera I wanted to present to Gelsey when she woke up.

The kid was getting on my nerves with his endless barrage of messages. Usually, he wasn't needy. More like fiercely independent. But not tonight.

Tipping forward, I read the latest.

Nothing feels right. I'm...off.

That sentence described every single musician at this stage of the game. Doubt always crept in right before it all came together.

The songs for Blake's debut EP were recorded. But by no means finished. I had the raw tracks with me, and once I got back, I'd do the whole spit and polish. He just needed to calm the fuck down and trust me.

I shot off a reply.

It's the middle of the night. Get some sleep. It's all good.

Maybe it sounded a little terse. Patronizing, even. But if I elaborated, the kid would just continue to spin. Read things into it that weren't there. Short and sweet was the way to go.

I stowed my phone in my backpack so I wouldn't get distracted again. One glance out the window at the rapidly approaching dawn, and I forced my fingers to move faster, folding and unfolding the sheet of paper. Normally I'd be more precise with the creases, but there was no need. Not for what I had in mind.

Gelsey stirred at the exact moment I laid the flower on the tray in front of her.

A faint glow had just begun to paint the horizon, and we were trapped in that magical place between night and day.

I feigned interest in the clouds as I watched Gelsey's reflection in the glass. The way her lips curved as she picked up the flower. She didn't care that we were on a private jet. And she hadn't even asked where we were staying once we arrived in New York. Those details didn't matter to her. She loved beautiful, worthless things.

The way I did.

The way my father had.

For a moment, I let the anger surrounding my memory of him fall away. A deep regret took its place when I imagined what he would've thought of Gelsey. Because I knew. He would've loved her.

"Open it," I said when she'd finished examining every fold.

Blue eyes met mine in the glass, and she smiled. "I don't want to ruin it."

I turned to face her, sinking a little lower in the seat. "You won't."

The look she gave me was priceless. Intrigued, but unsure. With a deft touch, she gently pried apart the paper, one fold at a time. I wanted to rip it out of her hands to speed things along. The suspense was killing me.

Once she'd finished, she smoothed the creases, her brows diving together as she studied the images.

Lifting her gaze to mine, she said quietly, "I don't understand."

That look told me she'd already jumped to the right conclusion, but she didn't want to put it out there.

So I did.

Taking the paper from her hand, I glanced over the photos of the

SoHo apartment I'd made arrangements to look at. "I think you do. My question is, what do you think of it?"

One beat turned into three, then five as she blinked at me. I'd vowed not to oversell this, but apparently some explanation was in order.

I took her hand, and she immediately laced our fingers. Good sign.

"Ivan told me that in order to make it at your new dance company, you couldn't live in your boyfriend's Fifth Avenue apartment." I sighed. "But there's only so much you can do if you're me. I can't exactly move into some place that doesn't have security. I could give a shit, but it would put *you* at risk. Do you understand?"

She nodded, but the knot twisting her brow told me she still didn't get it. Either that or she needed the words.

Of course, she needs the words, dumb fuck.

"I want to be with you, Gelsey. In Austin, or in New York. Or wherever you go."

Any other woman, and I'd know what kind of response to expect. Surprise, followed by elation. But with Gelsey I wasn't sure.

Her tongue peeked out, touching the corner of her lip as her focus returned to the page. "So you want us to live together? Here?"

Searching for a distraction of my own, I turned her hand over, running my thumb along the grooves on her palm. "I want you to live wherever you feel comfortable. If you need to live in the place the Company provides, I'm fine with that. Or if you want to split your time between both apartments, that's okay too. Or you can—"

I was so busy giving her all the options, I didn't see the sudden movement when Gelsey launched herself at me. Straddling my lap, her mouth crashed into mine.

"Yes," she breathed between feverish kisses. "Yes, yes, yes."

Burying my hand in her hair, I tipped back and looked her in the eyes. "Yes to what?"

"All of it. Any of it." Her lips found mine again. "I love you, Miles."

She froze. And so did I. But maybe not for the same reasons. I was kicking myself because I didn't say it first, and she looked like she wanted nothing more than to take it back.

Too fucking bad. It was out there.

Banding my arms around her waist, I pushed out of the chair. Her legs wrapped around my hips without hesitation.

"You don't have to say it back," she murmured, even though I could sense how badly she wanted to hear it.

Because I knew her. Every curve of her face. Every tilt of her lips. Every shadow in her eyes.

Pressing my mouth to hers, I shouldered my way through the door to the small bedroom in the back.

"I love you too, baby," I said as I eased her onto the white linen.

I hated the relief in her eyes. And the underlying astonishment. Didn't she know I was the lucky one?

She doesn't know a lot of things.

The inner voice brought me up short and left me cold as the truth sank in. There *were* things Gelsey didn't know. Things she deserved to know before she made a decision.

"Tell me again," I said as I kissed my way down her body.

Her fingers twined in my hair. "I love you. I love you. I…"

The declaration died on a moan when I reached the apex of her thighs.

She loved me.

And that was enough for now.

Chapter Forty-Four

Gelsey

THE CAR SERVICE TOOK US DIRECTLY TO THE SoHo APARTMENT AFTER WE landed.

Molly, the realtor, flipped out when she found out who her celebrity client was. And now she was in the other room, talking excitedly into her phone. The lack of furniture and high ceilings conspired, and I could hear every word she said. She mentioned Miles by name and identified me as "some ballerina."

Rather than taking it as an insult, her description made me stupidly happy. I wasn't just a girl on Miles's arm. I had my own identity.

"Doesn't that break some sort of client privilege?" I whispered as I gazed out the window at the bustling street below.

Miles slipped an arm around my waist, his lips ghosting over my shoulder. "I don't care about that. What do you think of the place? Ivan warned me off of Park Avenue. But if you want the Park…"

I spun around. "No. This is perfect. I love it."

He tucked a strand of loose hair behind my ear, an indulgent smile pinned to his lips. I felt my cheeks pink as I imagined what he was thinking. And he'd be right. I didn't know a Park Avenue view from a SoHo view from…well, anything.

I only knew that Miles had picked this place out. And it was beautiful. Hardwood floors. A stone fireplace. Exposed brick. An attended lobby.

And the best part?

It was small. Not tiny. But cozy. Only two bedrooms. I'd be able to hear Miles from anywhere in the apartment. Sometimes in the Austin house it felt like he was in another zip code.

"Why don't we reserve judgment until we explore the city a little more," he said, his hand moving under my shirt.

Swallowing my disappointment, I nodded. Because I didn't want to be *that* girl. Trying to lock Miles down before he changed his mind.

He wouldn't. He loved me.

Besides, there were a lot of moving parts. Things to consider.

"What about Austin?"

The question slipped out before I could reel it back in.

"What about it?" Miles kissed the tip of my nose, then ventured to the closet. He hissed when he pulled the door open. "Shit, we may need to do some remodeling."

I peered inside. Small, yes. By his standards. But I only had enough clothes to fill a quarter of the space. He could have the rest. "It's fine for me. I don't need much."

Or rather, I didn't *have* much.

His eyes flared with a hint of irritation. He'd offered on more than one occasion to take me on a shopping spree. Anywhere I wanted to go. But I'd declined.

If I ever had to appear with Miles at a fancy event, I might let him buy me a dress. *Maybe.* But other than that, I was good. Solid.

"What's the matter," I teased. "My Target leggings not doing it for you?"

And just like that, the sparkle returned. His palm found its way to my ass cheek, and he squeezed. *"You* do it for me. Every. Damn. Time."

He dipped his head, but I held him off, my fingertips brushing his chest. "You never answered my question. What about Austin? The studio? Your music with Blake?"

He leaned a hip against the doorjamb but kept his hand on my ass. "It's a three-and-a-half-hour flight. I can round trip it in one day." He shrugged. "Maybe I'll spend the night every now and then. You can come with me."

I chewed my lip, and he promptly freed the abused flesh with his thumb.

"What are you worried about, baby?" he asked.

Shifting my feet, I lifted a shoulder. "Won't Tori get tired of you using her jet?" His grin was back, the one that would make me feel dumb if it were anyone else aiming it at me. "What? It's a valid question."

"You didn't notice the difference between the jet we were on today and the one we took to Padre?"

Honestly, the only things I remembered about our flight were the cushy seats. And sunrise over Manhattan. And my flower.

"No. Why?"

"The jet we took out here was a Gulfstream 550. It has seven more seats than the one we took to Padre."

Confused, I crossed my arms. "Okay…so whose plane did we use?" Toying with the same fallen lock, he avoided my eyes. "Miles?"

"Technically, it belongs to Elite Aviation. But since I'd kind of like to defile you in that bed again, I think I should lease it."

My ears started to ring. Did he just…? No, he couldn't have.

"Unless you think I should buy it," he mused, clearly enjoying what I could only assume was my dumbstruck expression. "I'm down either way."

When my mouth dropped open, he took full advantage. His lips touched mine, curving into a grin when his tongue dipped inside.

Pulling back when I didn't respond, the humor faded, and he said, "I'm not trying to show off. It's just…flying commercial…it's difficult…"

I shook my head. "Wait. You'd do all this for me?"

His features softened. "I'd do anything for you."

Overwhelmed, I dropped my gaze to the floor. An apartment in SoHo. A private jet. I was confident of my own worth, but usually relationships were more evenly matched. What did I have to offer besides my love? Would Miles get tired of always being the one to give?

Long fingers threaded my hair, finding that spot on my nape that made everything less heavy. He tipped my chin up with his thumb.

"Talk to me, little mouse."

Miles rarely called me that anymore, and I felt the smile bloom in response. "It's a lot. Everything you're doing. I don't have…" I took in a deep breath. "I'll never be able to…"

He stroked my cheek as I tried to find the words. "I've told you how I feel about the money. It's just…there. I want you to have nice things, and I hope you let me treat you sometimes. But this—the apartment, the jet—it allows me to be with you without disrupting your life too much. Being with me won't always be a picnic. But New York, it's not a bad place for celebrities. Better than LA."

Miles dropped his hand when Molly called for him, her high heels tapping against the wood floors as she got closer. He slipped his arm around me, and we ventured back to the center of the room.

"So," she said, her smile bright and trained on my boyfriend. "What do you think? Do you want to sign some papers?"

I was about to wander off. Let them hash it out. But Miles held me in place.

"I like it," he said, looking around. "But it's really not up to me. My girl might need something bigger if she wants a practice space." His gaze found mine, and I jerked in surprise. "Or a view of Central Park?"

The realtor turned shocked eyes in my direction, and now they were both looking at me.

"I'm sorry," she said in a saccharine tone. "I'm terrible with names. You are…?"

Miles's palm skimmed up and down my back, and I drew strength from the touch.

"Gelsey."

Molly beamed. "What a lovely name. If you can give me a list of your requirements." Tipping forward, she lowered her voice. "And your price range. I'll be more than happy to help you find something."

"Don't worry about the price," Miles interjected, and I swear the woman nearly fainted.

Before she worked up a good head of steam again, I said, "I don't really want anything any bigger than this."

Molly's smile drooped. "So, two thousand square feet then?"

I inched a little closer to Miles. "Or smaller. I'm good with smaller."

Now she looked almost green. "You don't want anything smaller than this. How about if I compile a list of some other properties. If the price isn't an obstacle we have Tribeca and Chelsea. The Flat Iron District."

Miles took over when I started to fade. "We're simple folks," he drawled, his Texas accent peeking out. "So no penthouses. Nothing huge. I need an attended lobby. Security. Get a list together and send it to my email. We'll whittle it down and go from there." He squeezed my side. "Right, baby?"

I looked up into adoring brown eyes. And I knew right then, I could live with him anywhere. "Right."

Chapter Forty-Five

Miles

Gelsey's nose stayed pressed to the glass as the taxi inched down Broadway. I'd never been fond of New York, but seeing the city reflected in her eyes—it was magical.

As we approached Lincoln Center, her lips formed a little O, and if I didn't know any better, I'd think she was holding her breath.

"Change of plans," I said to the driver. "We'll walk from here."

Gelsey's head whipped around, blue eyes wide. "But...what about...?"

A part of me hated it that she felt this way. That it was necessary. But another part melted at the concern etched into her features. We were in this together.

"I'll be fine," I assured her as I handed the driver some cash. "Let's explore."

Her face lit up like I'd given her a present. So damned easy to make this girl happy.

Gelsey slid out first. And as I made to follow, the driver twisted around and said, "Miles Cooper, right? I love your music."

Meeting his smile, I offered one of my own. And for the first time, I understood why celebrities flocked here. The allure. Maybe I really could be anonymous. Just a face in the crowd.

"Thanks, man." His grin widened, surprise flashing over his features when I stuck out my hand for a shake.

I guess that wasn't done. But I was still a Texas boy. Raised with southern manners. My mama would slap the taste out of my mouth if I turned Yankee.

Hopping to my feet, I took Gelsey's elbow. But she hardly noticed. Her gaze was everywhere, bouncing from Lincoln Center to Julliard across the street and farther down Sixty-Fifth Street to where the tree-tops from Central Park were barely visible.

Pulling her into my arms, I dropped a kiss to her mouth. And right there on the busy sidewalk with all the people rushing by, her lips parted and welcomed me in. Welcomed me home. Because that's what she was. An anchor. My port in the storm.

Her lids fluttered open, those baby blues alive with excitement. A new adventure.

Lacing our fingers, I relaxed and gave in to it all. "Where do you want to go first, baby?"

After checking out the fountain at Lincoln Center and picking up cup-cakes at the Magnolia Bakery, we finally made it to Strawberry Fields, the two-acre preserve in the middle of Central Park dedicated to John Lennon. It was a serene place, purposefully so. No bikes or skateboards or music allowed.

My leg had started to throb, a stark reminder that I still had a ways to go in my fitness journey. I hardly limped any more, but the injury was ever present.

As I took a seat on one of the benches overlooking the stone mon-ument dedicated to a man who'd paid the ultimate price for his fame, I realized my own life hadn't turned out so bad.

Jesus. The guilt that accompanied that notion.

Letting my head fall back, I gazed up at the sky through the snarl of branches and thick leaves.

Time to lay it down, bro, came Rhenn's voice on a breeze.

But it was my thought.

Maybe it *was* time.

Gelsey eased down beside me and laced our fingers. Her warmth spread up my arm and took residence in my chest.

I looked down and found her smiling at me.

"I love you," I said, my free hand traveling the length of her golden locks. "And this hair."

She rolled her eyes. "It's kind of cliché, don't you think? A ballerina with hair to her waist?"

My heart clenched a little at the idea of her cutting it. Ever. Which was stupid. But I loved being trapped behind the silky curtain when she rode me. And feeling the strands soft against my face when I slept.

"I don't know, baby. I think it's beautiful."

Shrugging, she dipped into the pink box on her lap and pulled out a cupcake. Red velvet. A little piece of home. Though New Yorkers liked to claim it as theirs.

As if she could read my thoughts, she said, "Did you know it was a Texas company that first sold the red dye that made this cake famous?"

I did know, but I shook my head, urging her to continue. And she did, telling me all about the origin of the confection all the way back to the Victorian era.

When she finished, she tossed the silver wrapper in the box and hopped to her feet with her earbuds in her hand.

"Do you mind if…?" she pointed at the stones a few feet away, the mosaic with *Imagine* in the center.

"Go ahead, baby."

I watched as she plunked herself down in the middle of the monument and looked around. And her expression. Wonder and bliss. And peace. Love. I saw that too.

Taking out my phone, I snapped a dozen pictures. Maybe more. And then I reached into the box and retrieved the silver paper. The only thing I could fashion with a scrap so small was a rose the size of my thumb.

Once I'd finished, I hauled to my feet and walked over to my girl.

"For your collection," I said, dropping the flower into her open palm.

She examined the rose like it was a national treasure, then looked up with a wobbly smile.

"I feel bad. I don't have anything to give you," she said, looking truly bereft at the notion.

Taking her hand, I pulled her to standing and held her against me. "I'm sure I can think of something."

Chapter Forty-Six

Miles

WE STUMBLED THROUGH THE DOOR OF THE SUITE AT THE RITZ, OUR LIPS cemented in a hungry kiss. The air was electric, charged with passion hot enough to melt our clothes.

Gelsey's fingers worked furiously to unbutton my jeans, while I reached behind me, searching for the latch to flip the deadbolt. As soon as the locks snicked into place, she dropped to her knees, dragging my denim along with her. My erection sprang free, and for a moment, there was only heavy silence and wicked intentions.

My back met the door with a soft thud as I looked down at her. "What are you doing, baby?"

It was a valid question. I'd eaten her pussy from every angle, but Gelsey had never taken me in her mouth. And I'd never pushed. I figured we'd get around to it eventually. Sex with Gelsey was more about the journey than the destination. Maybe when I was younger and dumber, I wouldn't have appreciated it the way I did now.

Snagging her kiss-swollen lip between her teeth, she peered up at me, looking anything but sure.

I bit down my smile, my fingers sifting through her hair. "You don't have to do this, you know."

"I want to. But what if…?" On her knees, clearly lacking confidence, she couldn't finish the thought. Not if it meant revealing a perceived weakness. I loved that about her. The way she never backed away from a challenge. At the moment, with my cock no more than two inches from her sweet mouth, I thanked God for that particular trait.

"What if *what*?"

Her chin tipped up. "I don't want to do it wrong."

Fuck me. This girl.

"No way that could happen."

This was not a conversation we should be having in the foyer with Gelsey kneeling on the marble floor. She sank down, her bottom lip jutting out when I pulled up my jeans.

"Don't give me that look," I said with a smile. "Let's talk over there."

I motioned to the living area, and she reluctantly climbed to her feet.

"I hate that you have to talk me through everything," she said quietly as she eased onto the sofa, her gaze skittering to the Manhattan skyline.

Dropping down beside her, I hauled her into my lap, positioning her over my throbbing erection.

"Baby, I don't think there's anything you could do to me that I wouldn't like. But I want *you* to like it too. And giving me head with the marble biting into your knees doesn't sound like it would be that enjoyable."

She sighed. "That's how they do it in the movies."

I barked out a laugh. "What kind of movies are we talking about?" She squirmed, and I dipped my head to find her eyes. "Porn?"

She didn't blink. "Just because I never had sex before you doesn't mean I didn't think about it. I just didn't have the opportunity."

I'd seen the way men reacted to her, looked at her, including her douchebag dance partner. She could've had sex any time she wanted.

"Fair enough." Sliding my hand up her thigh, I let my lips graze her ear. "So about the movies. Sounds like they gave you a few ideas." Smiling when the column of her throat bobbed, I dragged my nose along the soft pillar of flesh. "I'm at your service, little mouse. What filthy thing do you want me to do to you?"

Gelsey

"Stay still."

Jerking my head in the direction of Miles's voice, my fingers balled into fists on my lap. I couldn't see anything with the T-shirt covering my eyes. But then, that's what I'd asked for. My fantasy.

Only now it seemed a little like torture. The best kind of torture if the tingling between my thighs were any indication.

I startled when his hand curved around my calf.

"Loosen up, baby."

His voice was pure sex. Commanding. And I loved it. Even if I wasn't sure what he had in store. So far, he hadn't done more than strip off my clothes and make me sit here.

Heat flooded my core when he draped my leg over the arm of the chair.

"Fuck..." he hissed. "You're so wet."

My cheeks went up in flames I could feel to my hairline. Because I knew he could see it all. Every part of me was open to him.

Squirming, I waited for him to do...*something*. "Miles..."

His breath fanned over my face, and I reached for him. But he caught my wrist before I made contact. Soft lips grazed my palm. "Don't move. Do you understand?"

"Uh-huh."

My stomach fluttered when his finger dipped between my folds. But I stayed still. Even as he teased my entrance.

"Your toes are curling, little mouse. You like this?" I nodded. "You want more?"

Did I?

"Yes."

The word flew out before I could think.

"You trust me?" I nodded again, and his dark chuckle made every-thing clench. "Open your mouth."

My mouth?

It dawned on me then, what he was going to do. Fifteen minutes ago I'd been ready to swallow him in the foyer.

But now...

His thumb brushed my bottom lip, and my reservations crumbled. My mouth fell open and his finger slid inside. I could taste myself on him. "Suck, baby."

And I did. Eagerly. I tipped forward when he retracted his hand. And I could imagine how I looked. Mouth open. Searching. I didn't have to wait long though, because something silky touched my lips. It was strange, the feel of it. In the back of my head, I knew it was his cock. Even before my tongue darted out and swirled around the salty tip. Maybe I should've felt embarrassed. And I probably would have without the blindfold. But the darkness was liberating.

Miles groaned when I took as much of him as I could. Not all of it. I didn't want to gag. Was I supposed to gag? I went a little farther and did just that.

"Oh, fuck yeah…" he muttered, fingers gripping my hair. "Take it, baby."

Breathing through my nose, I braced myself, expecting him to guide me farther down his shaft. But he didn't.

"Touch yourself," he bit out. "Finger yourself. Get yourself off while you're sucking my dick."

That old adage about walking and chewing gum sprang to my mind. And I wasn't sure I could do both successfully. But then I realized Miles just wanted a visual. My hand snaked between my legs, my hips tilting slightly to give him a better view. And all the while, I took him deeper and deeper, forcing my throat to relax.

It was always Miles guiding us when we had sex. He was the one in command. But even though he was giving the orders now, I felt the power. Pushing myself a little farther, I swallowed, and a groan ripped from his chest.

"*Fuuuck.*"

And then he was gone.

Disoriented, my hands flew up, searching for him.

One strong arm banded around my waist while the other looped under my leg as Miles plucked me from my spot. "What are you doing?"

His mouth crashed into mine as he eased me onto the bed. I reached for the T-shirt. "Don't take it off," he growled. "Spread your legs."

My knees fell open without hesitation, and I ached for the familiar heaviness of his body. The warmth. And the feel of his skin.

"Oh…God…" I cried when his tongue slid through my folds. He found my clit and went to work, sucking and laving. My orgasm hit me hard and fast, and I clenched. Before I'd even ridden out the wave, he was inside me, and I soared back to the top of the mountain.

He ripped the T-shirt off my head, and I blinked as intense brown eyes swam into focus.

"Tell me you love me," he demanded, stroking deeper.

Taking his face in my hands, I pressed a kiss to his mouth. And in that moment, everything slowed. The thrust of his hips. My breathing. Our heartbeats.

"I love you. Only you."

Always you...

Wrapping him in my arms, I held him tight as he whispered praises into my hair and shuddered through his release.

And I didn't think any more about what I couldn't give him.

Only what I could.

My body. My soul. My forever.

Chapter Forty-Seven

Gelsey

"Mmm."

Miles groaned, and I looked over my shoulder as I fastened the buckle on my strappy sandal.

Soft, eyes locked on me, and the smile followed melted my insides. Until he realized what I was doing.

"Where are you going, baby?"

Rising up on one elbow, he shook off the sleep and looked around. Morning light poured in from every angle, thanks to the windows that took up a large portion of the wall space in the corner suite. It felt like we were on top of the world, with the whole city spread out in the distance. I understood now about the allure of a Central Park view. Because there were also trees, a thick blanket of green laid out below us.

"Downstairs. Tatiana is meeting me in the restaurant."

I refocused on my sandals, because I didn't want Miles to see how frazzled I was.

Tatiana was *here*. At the Ritz.

We still had a full day before I was supposed to meet with her and the director at the dance company. More disturbing? I hadn't told her where I was staying. Because I knew how it sounded.

I was supposed to be in New York checking out the apartment that would serve as my home until I got on my feet. The tiny space crammed with other dancers. But here I was in a luxury suite at the finest hotel in the city. The place where my rich boyfriend took me after we arrived in a private jet.

Ivan's parting words pinged around in my head.

Try to fit in, dorogaya moya..

That was a monumental feat under the best of circumstances.

Because I'd never truly fit in here. I knew it. Russian, but not Russian enough. American, but not really.

In the real world, it didn't matter. The lines were fuzzy.

But in this world—the dance world—I didn't have a place to claim as my own. A home.

Except with Miles.

He was my home.

As if he could register my turmoil, he stroked a reassuring hand down my back. I felt better instantly.

"I thought you weren't meeting with her until tomorrow."

"She texted me," I replied brightly. Too brightly. And it didn't fool him.

"Why?"

There was worry in his tone now.

Shrugging, I tossed a smile over my shoulder. "Guess I'll find out."

Miles caught my hand as I wobbled to my feet on shaky legs.

We'd spent all night exploring my fantasies. And his. The sex was amazing. Transcending, even. And I'd lost track of how many times he'd been inside me. It was like he was trying to make good on his promise to live in my body. But now I was sore all over. And he noticed that too.

"How's your back?" he asked, brows drawn together in concern.

"Back's fine. I'm a little achy in some other places."

A smile formed on his beautiful lips. Like I knew it would. Miles was still a man. An alpha male no less. If he could slap a tattoo on my ass that read *Property of Miles Cooper,* he probably would.

He gave me a tug, and I gladly complied, crawling over the mattress until we were face-to-face, with me leaning over him. I hadn't bothered putting my hair up, and it fell around us in a golden curtain. Cupping my nape, he pulled me in for a kiss.

"I love you, baby."

A frustrated groan spilled from his lips when his phone buzzed on the nightstand. He'd been ignoring it since we got here, sending all his calls to voice mail.

I'd love to stay cocooned in this bubble we'd made. Tell Tatiana that I couldn't meet her. And toss Miles's phone out the window. But it was too late for that. Reality was calling. And it was time to answer.

I sat quietly with my hands folded in my lap while Tatiana perused the menu at the swanky bistro on the ground floor of the Ritz.

"You must eat," she said, without bothering to look up.

Her tone carried the same air of authority that Ivan had. And I found myself reaching for the leather-bound portfolio despite my queasy stomach.

Darting a gaze to the window, my breath caught in my throat when I noticed a gaggle of reporters milling around on the sidewalk. Waiting.

For me.

I still hadn't wrapped my head around the notion. It felt as if I'd walked into someone else's life. Miles's life, apparently. The one he managed by taking midnight flights on private jets and keeping a car service on standby. Not traipsing around Central Park like a tourist.

"Do not look at them, Gelsey," Tatiana said, as she picked up her cup of coffee. "You are only feeding the frenzy."

I nodded, my throat too tight to speak.

With a sigh, she pulled a copy of the *New York Post* from the front pocket of her Hermes tote and slid the paper in front of me. I felt the blood drain from my face as I glanced over the headline.

Miles Cooper Engaged to Pregnant Girlfriend. Iconic drummer leaving Austin and relocating to New York.

A picture of us in the SoHo apartment with Miles's hand splayed over my stomach took up the entire page.

It was one thing to be told about the articles—which Tatiana had done the moment she'd met me in the lobby—and quite another to see it in black and white.

"It isn't true," I blurted.

Her lips tilted up at the corners. But there was no joy in her smile. Only concern. But I wasn't sure it was for me.

Clasping her hands, she tipped forward, locking me in her icy blue orbs. "Which part? The pregnancy?" I nodded. "But you were looking at apartments, yes?"

I gripped my leg under the table to keep it from shaking. It wasn't that I'd planned on keeping my relationship with Miles a secret. But I'd hoped that I could at least prove myself before I had to make any announcements.

"My boyfriend was."

I held her gaze and even managed to keep my voice steady and true. Still, Tatiana wasn't buying it. Irritation flashed across her features for the first time.

"And you are not planning on living with him?"

My back stiffened in defense. "What would you like me to say, Tatiana? What is it that will set your mind at ease?"

The words flew from my lips with a velocity I didn't expect.

Taking a breath, I forced my muscles to relax, then continued in a softer tone, "Ballet is my dream, my life's work. I'm committed."

I left it at that, hoping it would be enough. It was true. All of it. And until Miles, there was no other dream. Nothing beyond the stage. But with him, I saw another path. A parallel lane on the same road. I could have both. Somehow, I'd make it happen.

This time when Tatiana smiled, I saw the affection in her eyes. Likely some lingering emotion she'd felt for my mother. But I'd take it.

"I fear you are not revealing the whole story, but I trust that you are telling the truth."

"I am."

Sliding her napkin out from under the silverware, she placed the linen on her lap. "Good, Then we will start by having a lovely breakfast." She looked around with admiration. "Your boyfriend has good taste."

My boyfriend has a lot of money. Which made it easy to have good taste.

I didn't say that though, just nodded my agreement.

My stomach had just started to settle when Tatiana added, "And after, I will take you to meet some members of the corps at the brownstone in Brooklyn."

When I didn't say anything, her attention shifted to my hand, balled into a fist next to my phone. Miles and I had plans today. Sightseeing and apartment hunting. A walk around the reservoir in Central Park. Lazy sex that went on for hours.

She picked up her coffee cup, gaze digging into mine. "You do not have a problem with that, do you?"

Forcing a smile to mask my disappointment, I shook my head. A small compromise. Not the end of the world. Miles would understand.

"Of course not. I'm ready whenever you are."

Miles

The minute Gelsey slipped out the door, I pulled out my laptop and took a seat on the couch. I had a feeling. More like a premonition. Things were about to get real.

And it was all my fault.

I'd been lulled into a false sense of security. Manhattan was ten times smaller than Austin, with twice as many people. And I was only one guy. Not even from here. Who'd notice me?

But I knew the answer to that.

Everyone.

Sure, it was easier to get lost in this city. But staying lost was another story.

My knee bobbed as I typed my name into the Google search box.

Please.

The one-word plea died on my lips when the screen populated with a dozen headlines.

Miles Cooper and ballerina girlfriend take a bite out of the Big Apple.

Miles Cooper relocating to New York after ballerina girlfriend snubbed by former bandmate Tori Grayson.

Click the link for the 411 on Gelsey Howard, Miles Cooper's hot new mystery girl.

I sank against the cushions, unable to catch my breath. The press had Gelsey's name. Which meant they had more. All the personal details that weren't personal at all. The bits and pieces of her life just floating around, waiting for someone to pluck them out of cyberspace.

Licking my dry lips, I tipped forward and hit the last link. A photo of Gelsey and me taken yesterday in Central Park flashed on the screen.

BALLET'S NEWEST IT GIRL, RUSSIAN BEAUTY GELSEY HOWARD, STEALS THE HEART OF FAMED DRUMMER MILES COOPER.

The article quoted "sources" who claimed that Gelsey and I were secretly married. Which, surprisingly, didn't bother me at all. The rest was just fluff. Some biographical information about Gelsey's mom. A link to the video of the Damaged reunion concert streaming on HBO. Stuff that anyone with an Internet connection and half a brain could dig up.

But then I scrolled down, and a photo of the SoHo apartment appeared. Not just one. Several. Including interior shots.

The fuzzy, off-center image of Gelsey and me gazing out the bedroom window proved who was responsible. Molly the realtor. Though I'm sure she'd never meant for that particular picture to be published. It was the bait she'd used to get the rag to buy the story. The proof that her claims were legit.

Blood boiling, I brought up my email program. Three messages from Molly. All with links to pricy apartments. The bitch had some nerve.

Firing off a reply, I made sure to c.c. the head of the brokerage firm, and Taryn, just because I knew my manager would make Molly's life a living hell.

Molly,

I hope you got a lot of money for selling me out. Because you won't be getting a commission. Next time you provide photos to a tabloid better make sure there's not one that incriminates you. Needless to say, I won't be requiring your services. You'll be hearing from my lawyer.

The last part was merely a threat. Bravado. Legally, there was nothing I could do.

I got some measure of satisfaction knowing she'd probably get fired. Taryn would demand Molly's head on a platter. And get it.

But that didn't do me any good. Or Gelsey. At this very moment, she was probably facing a shit ton of scrutiny from Tatiana.

Gelsey must earn her way into the group. They will make or break her career. She will stand on their shoulders to achieve greatness. But only if they let her.

This is what Ivan had warned me about. *And you didn't listen.*

After spending way too much time poring over the articles and ruminating on the best course of action, I decided to confront the situation head-on. My phone rang as I hauled to my feet, and I dove for it. Blake.

"Sorry, dude. No time," I mumbled under my breath as I pressed ignore.

Rushing to the bedroom, I quickly threw on some clothes. I wasn't sure if Gelsey wanted my help. But I had to do something. Explain the situation to Tatiana. She'd listen to me. I'd make her listen.

Stepping into the hallway, I fumbled trying to get the *Do Not Disturb* sign on the doorknob. Maybe if I weren't so distracted, I would've noticed the figure propping up the wall a few feet away.

"It's a mob scene down there," came the familiar voice. "You should probably go back inside."

When I spun around, Daryl assessed me with his usual bland expression, eyes hidden behind dark shades.

"What the fuck are you doing here?"

"Taryn sent me. Came straight here from the airport. And it's a good thing. It looks like you could use my help."

With every fiber of my being, I longed to send Daryl away.

His mere presence reminded me of everything I didn't want to be while I was in New York.

A rock star. Someone to gawk at. And worst of all—a distraction that Gelsey didn't need.

Gelsey.

Even if I could fend for myself, I wouldn't risk her safety. The press had her scent now. Which meant I needed Daryl.

Defeated, I felt my shoulders sag. "How bad is it?"

Sympathy flashed across Daryl's grizzled features and I knew I was fucked. Good and proper.

"Pretty damn bad." He pushed off the wall. "Now let's go inside and put our heads together so we can figure out how we're going to handle it."

Chapter Forty-Eight

Gelsey

Sipping my club soda, I glared at Micha like the traitor he was. Cozied up to Jelena and Sasha, the darlings of the New York City Ballet, he barely acknowledged me. But the Toxic Twins hadn't taken their eyes off me since I'd arrived at the Brooklyn brownstone.

Micha finally tore himself from their clutches, shaking his empty bottle of water at the pouting girls. As he strode toward the kitchen like he owned the place, I lightly touched his arm.

"It figures you'd befriend the only two female dancers whose last names end in vowels," I said.

He shrugged, not even bothering to deny it. Jelena and Sasha were the best, and Micha would shore up alliances to get ahead.

Seizing control of the conversation, he asked, "Where's your boyfriend?"

My tongue took residence on the roof of my mouth and I reached for my glass. Before I choked down even a sip, Tatiana took a seat beside me.

Micha took that as his cue to leave.

Coward.

Tatiana let her gaze follow him for a second before saying, "Jely and Sasha seem quite taken with your dance partner."

Out of the corner of my mouth, I replied snidely, "Is that the reason they're glaring at me? Are they jealous?"

She laughed lightly. "No."

"Then, why?"

"Not here," she said, a hint of warning in her tone. "Come with me and I will explain."

Jelena and Sasha sat up when Tatiana slid off her stool, but she turned icy blue eyes in their direction. *"Ne dvigajtes'."*

Don't move.

Smirking at me, they sank back down, safe in their assurance that I didn't understand the exchange. Normally, I'd let them think whatever they wanted. I'd done it for years. But instead, I gave them a demure smile. *"Izvinite."*

Their faces fell, but I kept walking. As soon as Tatiana and I stepped into the hallway the room exploded in spontaneous conversation behind us. I tried to block out the chatter. Unsuccessfully, since I clearly heard a couple of disparaging remarks about the shape of my nose and the set of my eyes. In heavily accented Russian. Lovely.

I side-eyed Tatiana as we headed for the stairs. "Please tell me I said 'excuse me' and not something else."

She patted my arm. "You did. And very well, I might add. How much of our language do you know?"

Your language. But I kept that to myself too.

"I understand everything." She raised a brow and I nodded. "But I don't speak it often. Only to Ivan."

Her smile grew, the way it always did when I said his name. It was a mix of admiration and something else. A crush? I scoffed inwardly at the thought. But then we topped the stairs and came upon the first photo on the wall, an image of Ivan performing on a stage I didn't recognize, and her features softened.

"Jelena and Sasha were raised on stories about Ivan. He is legendary in Russia…" Her gaze lovingly roamed the picture. "Of course, they know Baryshnikov and Nureyev, but Ivan's story is more…intriguing. Romantic."

I didn't think there was anything I didn't know about Ivan. But Tatiana's wistful smile told me I was mistaken. "Romantic?"

She shuffled to the right, where more photos lined the wall, and paused in front of one that took my breath away. My mother.

"There were a hundred companies where Ivan could have settled after his injury. Including this one. But he followed Katya to Texas of all places. Just to be near her. He wanted to win her back, you know?"

My stomach pitched. "Back?"

"Your mama was in much pain with her injuries. Your grandmother had worked her so hard since childhood. She wanted to retire. Start a family." Her shoulder lifted in a half-shrug. "With Ivan. But he had more to do. To accomplish. It was only after Katya married your father that he understood what he had lost. He was never the same after that. And he did not even try to rehabilitate his injury. He just…packed up and followed Katya." Tatiana sighed and refocused on the photo. "But he was too late. Katya was already pregnant with you."

"I don't understand," I said, swallowing past the lump in my throat. "Why wouldn't he just leave."

"Hope, I guess. He thought your mama would come to her senses. But Katya was not made that way. And she did love your father. And then you were born. And Ivan never once thought about leaving."

"Why? Because of me?" I squeaked.

"Oh, yes. He lavished you with all the love he felt for Katya. And she let him. She thought it might make up for you not having any family to speak of. Your grandmother was…distant. Bitter. But she did agree to work with Ivan at the studio. After Katya died, however, he severed those ties."

"Why?"

Tatiana hesitated, drawing in a deep breath before turning to me. "She had found two girls in Moscow whom she believed would be the next great dancers. Sisters, one year apart. She wanted them to train in Austin, with Ivan. They made a visit with their families. The mother said something disparaging about you. Something to the effect that you would never live up to Katya's potential. It was an offhanded remark. But Ivan refused to teach her daughters after that."

My lips parted in a gasp as I put the pieces together. "Jelena and Sasha?"

Tatiana smiled. "Yes. So you understand why they might feel animosity toward you even if it is not warranted?"

I nodded, then looked down at the phone buzzing in my hand. I'd called the car service that Miles had set up almost an hour ago, and they'd finally arrived.

"My car is here," I said, trying not to show how grateful I was for the reprieve. As bad as I thought it could be, moving in with a houseful of strangers, it was worse. My only saving grace was Miles. I'd come to the brownstone every night if I had to. But only to sleep. The rest of the time, I'd spend with him.

Tatiana chucked a knuckle under my chin. "You did good today. Get some rest, and I'll see you tomorrow at the theater."

Miles

I peered out the window of the limo, surveying the quiet, tree-lined street. The neighborhood was nicer than I expected. Cleaner.

Brooklyn. Who fucking knew?

Still, as my gaze slid up the facade of the brownstone, absently counting the windows, I surmised the whole building was about half the size of my house in Austin. And not much bigger than the SoHo apartment. I didn't have any clue how many dancers shared the space, but it was bound to be a tight fit.

The front door creaked open, and Daryl slid onto the seat next to the driver.

"It's a good neighborhood," he said as he twisted to face me.

Dubious, I lifted a brow. "And you can tell that from a five-minute stroll in the dark?

He glimpsed my hand, clasped tightly around my thigh. I'd been massaging the muscles for hours, the burn and subsequent pain keeping me focused on something besides Gelsey and what she was doing.

She'd sent me a text this morning informing me that she was leaving with Tatiana, but no further explanation. For all I knew, she'd spent the day defending our relationship. Or worse, listening intently while others enumerated all the reasons we shouldn't be together.

I knew she loved me. But I couldn't compete with the one thing she'd been working for her whole life. Her shot. And I wouldn't make any foolish demands. I'd tried that before with disastrous results.

Daryl took out his phone, spouting some crime statistics about the neighborhood to bolster his assertion. But my mind had wandered. Dark clouds pushed in, and I could smell the rain even though the skies were clear. It was always there; I realized. The impending storm. Ready to sweep me away.

Jerking to the present when the car door swung open, I met blue eyes that quieted the chaos.

Gelsey blinked in surprise. "Miles. You're here."

I wasn't sure where the lines were drawn. Which part of her life she was willing to share and what she wanted to keep to herself. Had I overstepped?

Before I could conjure a reply, she launched herself at me, arms looping around my neck. Her mouth crashed into mine, and I pulled her onto my lap.

"I missed you," I said truthfully, before darting my tongue between her lips.

Daryl cleared his throat, and Gelsey broke our connection with a start. Her head cocked to the side, brows drawn together in disbelief as her gaze shifted to the front seat.

"Daryl?"

He flashed her a rare smile, all teeth. Which, if I were honest, looked a little menacing. "Hey, pretty girl. Good to see you."

Genuine affection laced his Tennessee drawl, and I felt my own smile appear.

Biting it down quickly so he wouldn't get the idea I was happy about his presence, I said, "Yes, the leaner is here. We can all sleep better at night." Mock glaring at my bodyguard, I made a sweeping motion with my hands. "Now shoo. Be seen and not heard." I shook my head. "On second thought, I don't want to see you either."

I hit the button, and Daryl narrowed his eyes as the partition started to rise. His smile returned when my girl gave him a wave.

Pinning her back to the seat a minute later when the limo started to roll, I eased on top of her and dropped a kiss to her mouth. She tasted like lime and smelled like heaven.

Taking my face between small hands, she held me there in the moment, her expression serious. "I'm sorry."

Nothing good ever started with *sorry*. Sorry was a portent of disaster. The beginning of the end.

I turned solid, a stone in her arms, as every doubt found its way to the surface. "About?"

Her fingers moved up, gently pushing the hair out of my eyes. "Today. Disappearing on you like that. Ruining our plans."

Relief flooded me. But I tried not to show it. "It's just a day. We'll have plenty more." I rested my forehead against hers. "All the time in the world."

The phrase slipped from my lips and hung between us like a promise. I'd never actually said it before, but I'd thought it. Believed it. And fate had made a liar out of me.

This was different though. Because Gelsey and I were in it together. I'd give her all the days. And all the time. And she'd give me everything else.

Chapter Forty-Nine

Miles

"YOU REALIZE YOU'VE IGNORED LIKE FIVE OF MY CALLS," TARYN SAID FLATLY. "And now you're calling me at nine a.m. for a favor."

She wasn't wrong. And I should've been apologizing. But I was too busy trying to avoid the paparazzi outside Lincoln Center *and* find the side door to the theater.

"I'm ignoring everyone's calls, T-Rex."

And I had the voice mails to prove it. Thirty-six, the last time I checked.

"I'm not everyone." A little huff accompanied the declaration, and I smiled.

"You're right. I'm a dick," I admitted in my most sincere voice. "A terrible friend. Thoughtless." Hanging a sharp right when I noticed a couple of photographers congregating by the fountain, I double-timed it up the stairs. "Now will you just tell me the name of the security guard and where I can find him?"

Behind me, Daryl chuckled. He was enjoying this way too much.

When we'd left the hotel, I'd been prepared to ditch him, sure he was going to discourage me from my mission. But, surprisingly, he was all about it. I think he was too psyched to see Gelsey dance to worry about the logistics.

On the other hand, I was nervous as fuck.

Not that I was crashing the party. On the drive back to the hotel last night, she'd asked me to come and watch the rehearsal. But I'd figured the invitation had more to do with her riding the orgasmic high, since my face had been buried between her thighs at the time.

Once she was limp in my arms, I'd reminded her that my presence might be a distraction, and politely declined. She'd pouted in the most adorable way. But I was resolute. Steadfast.

Until this morning when I saw her standing in front of the window in her pale pink leotard, framed by the New York skyline.

No way I could miss this.

Taryn heaved a sigh, a sure sign she'd forgiven me. The girl was putty in my hands.

"Have to agree with you there. You are a dick."

Wait...*what?*

My steps faltered, and Daryl nearly crashed into my back. "Huh?"

"It's true. You are a dick sometimes." I grunted, and she laughed. "Promise to answer your phone from now on, and I'll turn over the info."

"Fine," I grumbled.

A triumphant little hum and I could almost picture Taryn's smug smile. And I didn't even care.

"The stage door is on the west side of the building. Salvadore, the head of security, is expecting you. I just texted him."

Resisting the urge to pump my fist in the air, I changed course yet again. "Thanks, T-Rex. I owe you one."

"You owe me more than one. And remember what you said about answering your phone!"

I rolled my eyes. "Yeah. Got it."

Ending the call before she could make any more demands, I gave Daryl the side eye.

"We're in." Surprise furrowed his brow, and I sighed, patting him on the back. "On days like this, it's good to be king."

We followed Salvadore up a flight of stairs to the balcony.

Peeling back a velvet curtain, he tipped his chin to the four seats inside the theater box. "Nobody will see you up here as long as you stay in the shadows. Try not to draw any attention to yourselves. Simon is really weird about privacy."

He darted a gaze to the stage, and I followed his line of sight to a man leaning against the piano. Dressed in dark jeans and a plain white T-shirt, he surveyed the dancers on the floor in various stages of stretching. He was young—late thirties—with sandy blond hair that grazed his chin.

"Choreographer?" I asked, my lips twitching when Simon's gaze lingered a little to long on Gelsey.

"Artistic director," Salvadore corrected, patting me on the back. "Better take a seat. I'll be waiting at the bottom of the stairs when you're finished."

I slipped him some cash as we shook hands. "Thanks, man."

Smiling, he trotted off, while I plopped into the seat beside Daryl. My spine went rail stiff when Simon glided over to Gelsey and crouched to eye level. She continued her preparation, her body moving in that way it did, like the performance had already begun. But she kept her gaze pinned to Simon's, nodding from time to time at whatever he had to say.

When he reached out and ran a hand down her arm, I couldn't hide my scowl any longer. "Why the fuck is he touching her?" I hissed under my breath.

The question was rhetorical, but for some reason Daryl thought I was talking to him. "It's her first day. Maybe he's trying to make her feel welcome."

Before I could banish him and his easygoing manner to the stairwell with Salvadore, voices floated up from below our box. Female voices. The odd shape of the theater and domed ceiling insured zero privacy. But with all the giggling, whoever was down there didn't seem interested in discretion.

"So, which one is she?" a nasally voice asked.

When someone answered in Russian, I went still. Because I knew she was talking about Gelsey. And her tone held no warmth whatsoever.

"English, Sasha," yet another girl piped up.

A snort. "You are the one forever claiming to understand, Mallory," came a fourth voice in heavily accented Russian.

The conversation lapsed between the two languages as the women traded friendly insults. I tried to keep up, but when I didn't hear Gelsey's name again, my focus returned to the stage. All the dancers were now on their feet, rushing to take their seats in the audience.

Except Gelsey.

Back straight, she stood next to Simon, her hands clasped in front of her.

"Where is Micha?" one of the Russian girls asked. Sasha, I think. "I do not see him."

"There," replied Mallory. "Front row. I wonder why he's not on stage."

Sure enough, Micha was slumped in the seat closest to the stairs, his head bowed.

Was he injured? Was Gelsey?

Conjuring up worst-case scenarios, I sat all the way up. Daryl lightly gripped my arm when I scooted forward. Instead of fighting his hold, I nodded and eased back while Simon grabbed a portable microphone.

"Settle down, everyone," he ordered, and the theater instantly fell silent. "One of our new apprentices is visiting today. Gelsey Howard."

He went on to list her accomplishments, but I didn't hear a word, all my attention on my girl as she tried to maintain a nervous smile. She looked so small up there under the lights. But so fucking beautiful.

"Before we get to our rehearsal," Simon continued. "Gelsey has agreed to perform a free form ballet of her own creation to show off her range."

The small crowd buzzed as Simon walked over to what looked like a soundboard. While he was busy fiddling with the knobs, Gelsey's gaze swept the theater. And I couldn't help it. I leaned all the way in, willing her to find me. To see me.

And she did.

For the briefest moment our eyes locked, and it was like an electric pulse. A beat I felt down to my toes.

I was so wrapped up, I didn't hear the music until Gelsey started to move.

"Blackbird."

The song that was playing the first time she'd ever danced for me. No longer constrained by a studio, she soared to new heights, using every inch of the stage to become the little bird.

When it was over, an eerie quiet consumed the theater.

One beat. Two.

Gelsey held her position, eyes locked on mine. But with every passing second, she wilted just a little under the oppressive silence.

"What did I tell you," came Sasha's voice from below. "Nothing special."

The comment jerked me to my feet, and I began to clap. The sound reverberated, knocking everyone out of their stupor. And soon the whole auditorium vibrated with applause.

Relief etched Gelsey's features as she slowly let her arms fall to her sides.

"I love you," I mouthed.

With a small bow of her head, my little mouse was no longer mine. She belonged to this world now. And I was the one along for the ride.

Chapter Fifty

Gelsey

"You're just being stubborn," I said as I reached over Miles to turn the small alarm clock in my direction.

I thought I was safe since he was half-dozing. But he grabbed me and flipped me onto my back before I could scurry away. One leg slotted between mine...and that smile. He was the best kind of trouble.

Linking our fingers, he brought our hands over my head. "I am stubborn," he said burying his face in my neck.

His distraction wouldn't work on me. Because I was stubborn too.

Looping my leg around his, I pulled him closer. "It's just one little party," I whispered as my fingers toyed with the soft strands at the nape of his neck. "I'd really like you to go with me."

He went solid in my arms, his lips frozen on my collarbone. I knew he was thinking. Contemplating. And probably wishing he hadn't stood up in the theater and made his presence known.

After that, things had gotten complicated. Simon had asked me to a party at the Plaza. An honor, considering that none of the other apprentices were invited. And I bet it had something to do with Miles.

Just stop by for drinks. No big deal. Bring your boyfriend.

Some of the Company's biggest donors were going to be there, according to Tatiana, who'd rushed over as soon as Simon had proffered the invitation.

"You must go," she'd said with a smile. "And convince your boyfriend to come as well."

Sealing her edict with a swift kiss to my cheek, she'd glided away before I could protest. Tatiana definitely had a softer touch than Ivan, but they both found a way to get their point across. To let me know what was expected.

I was going to the party, whether I liked it or not. Whether I wanted to or not.

But Miles was his own man. The only thing I could do was ask. Which I'd done while performing my version of a striptease to sweeten the pot.

All I'd gotten for my trouble was a polite "no thanks" when it came to the party and three orgasms after he'd pinned me to the mattress and pounded me into next week.

Apparently, I sucked at the seduction thing as a means of getting my way.

Propping up on his elbow, Miles looked down at me with a question pinching his brow. "Tell me why."

I pulled the sheets up to my chin to cover my bare breasts. "Why what?"

"Why you want me to go with you. Is it because Myron asked?"

I rolled my eyes. "Simon."

Something about my artistic director rubbed Miles the wrong way. But he wouldn't admit it.

Since I still hadn't answered the question, Miles's lips inched toward a frown, his eyes clouding with some impending storm.

Taking his face in my hands, I ran my thumbs over his stubble, then gently pressed a kiss to his mouth.

He leaned into my touch, the way he always did.

This was our thing. My thing. Maybe seduction wasn't my forte, but I knew how to chase the clouds away.

"I want you to come because I love you. And you're a part of my life. I know you think you're taking something away from me whenever you're around. Like, stealing my thunder. But I don't care. You're not my rock star boyfriend. You're…"

His gaze fell to my lips as I tried to find the words. But only two came to mine.

Coaxing those brown eyes back up, I smiled. "My everything."

The declaration took over all time and space and became a truth all its own. Miles *was* my everything. And I wanted to share everything with him. All the pieces of my life that paled in his presence but were still important.

Smiling, he eased his forehead against mine. "Then I guess we're going to a party."

Two hours later, I emerged from the bathroom after my shower, ready to brave the New York shopping scene to find a dress.

Miles was relaxing on the bed, mindlessly flipping through channels on the big screen.

Swallowing my disappointment that he wouldn't be joining me on my excursion, I set about to find my sandals. The room was kind of a mess. Not dirty, but cluttered.

We'd declined maid service for privacy reasons after Miles told me some horror stories about the lengths the tabloids would go to for a couple of pictures.

I thought he was being paranoid until he'd shown me a few online photos taken at the height of his fame. Whiskey bottles. Condom wrappers. White powder on the nightstand.

"All doctored," he'd said with a shrug. "I don't really give a shit about what people say about me. It's expected. But I don't want to drag you into anything."

Miles caught me around the waist when I popped up with one shoe in my hand, my gaze sweeping the room for its mate.

"Stop," I said, making a halfhearted attempt to break free when he pulled me onto the bed.

Prying the sandal from my hand, he tossed it to the floor. "There is no *stop*. Only *faster* and *harder*." His lips curved against my ear. "*Miles* is also an appropriate response. But only when I'm deep inside you."

My eyes rolled back when he wedged his muscular thigh against the apex of my thighs.

"I have to find a dress," I panted, my nipples tightening under my sheer bra.

Ignoring my plea, he dipped his head and clamped down on the stiff peak through my T-shirt. "Uh-huh."

I gripped his hair, but that only seemed to spur him on. "Miles…"

He finally rolled off me when the hotel phone rang. I took the opportunity to slide off the mattress and continue my quest for the lost footwear.

"Yep," he said, sounding a little annoyed as he threw his legs over the side of the bed. "Thanks."

After dropping the phone back in its cradle, he climbed to his feet while I continued to crawl around, peering under chairs and tables.

I blinked up at him when he stopped in front of me and offered his hand, the corners of his mouth curving into the heart-stopping smile I loved. "Let's go, baby."

Without hesitation, I let him help me to my feet. "Go where?"

"To find you a dress."

Miles eased back in the winged chair, his eyes meeting mine in the full-length mirror. We were in a suite one floor below ours at the Ritz with two personal shoppers from Saks. Violet, the younger of the duo, hovered behind me, making slight adjustments to the fabric of my latest choice, while her partner, Cynthia, stood next to one of the three wardrobe racks with her hands clasped in front of her.

"What do you think?" I asked Miles, running my hand nervously over the bodice. "Too much?"

The dress was beautiful. The most beautiful thing I'd ever worn. White with thin straps that tapered into a deep V at the back, the material merely a whisper against my skin. I'd never felt anything like it.

Miles smiled. "No. Not too much. But I thought you liked the black one?"

At that precise moment, Cynthia stepped forward with the dress in question draped over her arm.

Darting a gaze to Violet, scrutinizing my reflection with a most serious expression, I asked, "Which one do you like?"

Startled, her eyes met mine in the mirror. "You're asking me?"

Color rose in my cheeks. Wasn't that why she was here? I certainly didn't have any experience with cocktail attire. Or any attire that wasn't purchased at Target or Wal-Mart.

"Yes," I squeaked.

Cynthia, a few years older with maybe a little more experience, appeared behind me. "Both dresses are lovely." She tapped a finger to her lips. "And they fit you perfectly. It's just a matter of choice, really."

My shoulders sagged. How could I ever decide?

Miles cleared his throat, drawing everyone's attention. But he only had eyes for me. Soft eyes that held nothing but love. "We'll take them both."

Violet and Cynthia quickly rushed to the cart with the boxes of shoes stacked four deep while I gaped at my boyfriend.

"Both?" I hissed. "I don't need both."

When would I ever wear something like this again? At least if I found something at a discount store, I wouldn't feel so guilty if it just hung in my closet. And what did a dress like this even cost?

Miles pushed to his feet, closing the distance between us as I frantically searched for the tag.

Taking my hand, he brought it to his lips and pressed a kiss to my palm. "Yes, baby. Both."

Chapter Fifty-One

Miles

GELSEY SHIFTED HER FEET, A LITTLE UNSTEADY ON HER DESIGNER HEELS. She looked gorgeous, the extra four inches bringing the crown of her head to right about my chin level. Every time she moved, I got a delicious whiff of her shampoo.

Distracting, since I was trying to focus on my conversation with Kristof, the conductor from the New York Philharmonic. The hum of conversation in the Palm Court at the Plaza and his thick Austrian accent conspired against me, and I was only able to understand about half of what he said. But that was all right, because, in the end, we spoke the same language—music. It was universal.

Our discussion had run the gamut, shifting easily from the Beatles to Yo Yo Ma, and finally to the acoustics at the David Geffen Hall.

Kristof's wife, Astrid, a violinist in his orchestra, glided over. "You must come to a performance," she said, inquisitive gaze flicking from me to my girl.

I ran my fingers along Gelsey's spine to get her attention.

Clutching her untouched glass of champagne, she peered up with wide, blue eyes. "What?" As if she just realized that Kristof and Astrid were there, she jerked, and color rose in her cheeks. "Oh. I'm sorry. Did I miss something?"

Astrid touched Gelsey's hand, genuine warmth in her expression. "No worries, love. It is a bit overwhelming. Even an experienced performer would be nervous in this den of lions. I've never known Simon to invite an apprentice." Inclining her head, Astrid's eyes roamed over Gelsey's face with familiarity. "But then, you're not just any apprentice, are you?"

Gelsey licked her lips. "Sorry. I don't know what you mean."

"You are your mother's daughter," said Kristof jovially as he pulled his wife to his side. "We saw Katya perform at the Royal Ballet with Ivan Volkov before she retired. She was breathtaking. And the whole of New York is waiting to see her reborn in you."

Even I felt the pressure of his statement. The weight of the expectation.

But Gelsey merely lifted her chin, a practiced smile curving her lips. "I hope I won't disappoint you. But my mother was one of a kind. It'll be tough to fill even a fraction of her pointe shoes."

The couple laughed at the joke, but Gelsey's back was so stiff, it felt like granite beneath my touch.

Impulsively, I thrust my hand at the conductor. "It was nice to meet you, Kristof. But if you'll excuse us? I see someone trying to get Gelsey's attention by the bar."

A white lie. But I feared if I didn't get her alone for a moment, she might buckle under the stress.

Simon had definitely thrown Gelsey into the deep end. This party was overflowing with the crème de la crème of New York society. Patrons of the arts. And while there were probably a few genuine souls roaming around, like the conductor and his wife, most were busy showing off their jewelry and engaging in oh-so-serious conversations about their nannies and the price of real estate in the Hamptons.

"Thank God," Gelsey whispered as I led her to a quiet spot between two arched windows.

Once we were alone, her facade of calm crumbled around the edges, and worry lines creased her brow.

"What is it, baby?" I stepped in front of her, blocking her view of the party. "Not having a good time?"

Her lips fell into a frown. "I'm just…a little nervous."

When her gaze dropped to the floor, I threaded a hand in her hair, coaxing her attention to mine. "What else?"

She cringed. "Is it that obvious?"

For me, it was. Yes, Gelsey was her own woman. Strong. Capable. And so fucking beautiful. The confidence would come. One performance and she'd own any room she walked in to.

"Not at all. I just thought…you know…all the new faces."

Her eyes narrowed, and she tilted her head. "You don't seem to be having any problem with it."

I smiled.

Gelsey only saw the me I was now. One of the things I loved about her. I never bragged about meeting the Queen. Or doing a half-time show at the Super Bowl. Or even performing for the President. But then again, I had Tori and Paige and Rhenn by my side. Gelsey was all alone.

"I've had a little experience with this kind of crowd."

She blinked, gazing at me in that way she did sometimes. Like she was seeing me for the first time. I felt like a god when she looked at me that way.

Looping my arm around her waist, I pulled her close. "Have I told you how pretty you look tonight? And those heels." Dipping low, I smiled against the shell of her ear. "I can't wait to see you in them and nothing else."

"That can definitely be arranged." Clutching the lapels of my suit jacket, she dragged me in for a quick kiss. "Also—have I told *you* how pretty *you* look tonight?"

Easing back, I raised an eyebrow. "I'm not pretty, baby. Devastatingly handsome. Rugged. Well hung and totally fuckable. But—"

"Gelsey?"

The female voice was right behind me. Close enough to assure she might've overheard our conversation. Gelsey must've realized it too, because her eyes widened to double their size.

Winking, I gave her a little shrug before sliding out of the way.

"Tatiana." Gelsey leaned in for a hug, her smile melting when she noticed the two women standing behind the regal blonde.

After a tense moment, I gave her a nudge.

"Oh, yes," Gelsey squeaked, clearly flustered as she looked up at me. "Miles, this is Tatiana. She's the assistant choreographer for the Company." Her smile wobbled, and not in the adorable way I was used to. "And Jelena and Sasha. Two of the dancers from—"

"Principal dancers," one of the women spit out, pinning Gelsey with a disdainful glare. Two beats and she turned her frosty gaze on me, the ice melting the moment our eyes met.

"I'm Sasha." Her lips curved as she glanced at the other dancer. "And this is my sister, Jelena."

The accent combined with her bitter tone shook something loose.

Sasha.

The woman who'd insulted Gelsey at the rehearsal this afternoon.

What did I tell you? Nothing special.

Both sisters shrank from the scowl I couldn't hide.

Gathering my composure, I pointedly ignored the harpies and plastered on a semblance of a smile for Tatiana. Her lips twitched at the corners, like maybe she was aware of the vipers at her back.

"Pleased to meet you, ma'am."

"You as well." After offering me her hand, Tatiana shifted her focus to Gelsey. "Simon would like to see you. He has something important to discuss. Sasha and Jelena will show you to his table."

The sisters shot simultaneous looks of surprise at Tatiana. But she didn't spare them a glance.

Gelsey lingered like she wasn't quite sure. "I guess I should go then."

I gave her the slightest nod. Something just between us. But Tatiana noticed.

"Do not worry about Miles," she said, inching a little closer to me. "I will keep him company while you are gone."

Pressing a kiss to Gelsey's forehead, I kept my gaze on Sasha and Jelena. *Don't fuck with my girl.* I telegraphed the message with cold eyes. Not that Gelsey couldn't stand up for herself. But as an apprentice, I wasn't sure that she would.

"Have you ever seen a Lily of the Valley?" Tatiana asked as she watched the trio glide through the crowd, their golden hair shimmering like halos under the bright lights.

I frowned into my next sip of San Pellegrino. "No."

"It is a beautiful flower. Truly alluring. But extremely poisonous." A hint of a smile played on her lips. "That is Sasha and Jelena."

My stomach turned, but I didn't show it. "Does Gelsey know that?"

"She is aware. But enough about them. Do you have a moment to chat?"

Tatiana's affection for Gelsey seemed genuine, so I abandoned my plan to ditch her.

"Sure."

I followed her to a high table tucked in the corner and admired the view.

Though I'd been here before, the beauty of the place never ceased to amaze me. Stone pillars sat between arched windows, angels carved into the facades. Palm trees in ornate pots, their fronds dense and the lushest green, reached for the false light peeking through the stained-glass ceiling. But it was the round bar in the center of the room cupping a twelve-foot floral arrangement that really demanded attention.

A server scurried over, and Tatiana ordered a shot of chilled vodka. Waving him off, I held up my bottle of sparkling water.

"So, it is true?" she asked once we were alone. "Or are you just acting?"

Blunt. I liked it. And though I could guess what she was talking about from the way she eyed my water, I played dumb.

"Is what true?" I drawled, lifting the bottle to my lips.

She didn't back down. Not an inch. "That you do not drink?"

I raised both brows. "That's not what you want to ask, is it?"

Shrewd blue eyes locked on mine. "No. I suppose not."

"So ask," I said, tiring of the game.

She kept quiet until the server dropped off her drink.

"Are you an alcoholic, Miles?"

Rock, meet hard place. Most people didn't ask. Hell, Gelsey never even asked. Just accepted what was written in the tabloids and took her cues from my actions. She'd never seen me with a drink in my hand. Nobody had. Not in years.

"Something like that," I replied.

A barely there smile curved her lips as she tossed back her vodka. "You are equivocating."

It wasn't a question and therefore didn't require a response. But still, she waited, blue gaze digging into mine as she turned her glass round and round on her cocktail napkin.

"It's complicated."

What the fuck are you doing?

My closest friends didn't know my secret. *Gelsey* didn't know my secret. And here I was playing chicken with a woman I'd never met, daring her to excavate some long-buried truth.

"Everyone is entitled to their privacy, I guess." Her tone belied the point, but I nodded anyway. "And, truthfully, I do not care what bad habit you have. But I do care about Gelsey."

A bitter retort crawled up my throat. Did she think she was alone in that?

"I've already gotten the speech from Ivan," I said coolly. "And I'll tell you the same thing I told him. I love Gelsey. And I'm not planning on doing anything to hurt her career."

A chuckle parted her lips, and she shook her head, looking down into her empty glass. "Nobody ever 'plans' to hurt the people they love." When she lifted her gaze, her expression was soft. Almost mournful. "But sometimes, they cannot help themselves."

Her honeyed tone did little to mask the blunt force of her declaration. Coercion was still coercion, even wrapped in silk. And that's what this was.

Leave now, before you hurt her.

Like it was a certainty.

I could've told her to fuck right off. But something held me back.

Tatiana, like Ivan, had something rare. The courage of her convictions. She didn't see me as a prize. And I wasn't invited to this soiree so she could reach a hand into my pocket for a large donation. In fact, if I were reading her correctly, she'd just as soon never see me again.

Before I could make my case and tell her all the things I'd do to insure Gelsey's happiness, my phone buzzed in my pocket. It shouldn't have mattered, since I hadn't answered the damn thing in days. But I reached for it without thinking. A lifeline I'd gladly take.

"I have to get this," I said, already looking for a quiet spot.

Tatiana climbed to her feet with the same grace that Gelsey possessed. "You stay. I have to find Simon." She patted my arm. "It was nice to meet you, Miles."

A lie. The only one she'd let slip in the short time we'd been speaking. I let her have it and offered one of my own.

"You too."

Chapter Fifty-Two

Gelsey

LANCING OVER MY SHOULDER AS I WAITED FOR SIMON, I SEARCHED THE room for rich, brown hair. With his height, it was usually easy to spot Miles in a crowd. But he wasn't where I'd left him.

Sasha leaned close, her arm brushing mine. And to the outside observer it might have seemed like we were friends. But her touch was as icy as her tone.

"What is the matter? Afraid your boyfriend got distracted?"

Turning my head, I met pale blue eyes. An ocean of hatred. Even with everything Tatiana had revealed, I still couldn't understand Sasha's intense hostility.

A moment passed before her lips flatlined under my scrutiny. "What are you staring at?" she hissed, already retreating a little from my space.

Sasha was a bully. A mean girl who wasn't a girl at all anymore, but a grown woman. In the real world, she wouldn't be allowed to act like this. But she'd never lived in the real world.

For once I was grateful that Ivan had never let me believe the sun rose and set on my ass. If he had, this is what I might've become.

"Nothing," I replied in a light tone. "And I think that's what you're afraid of."

While Sasha blinked, no doubt dumbfounded by my boldness, Jelena took up the mantle, inching toward me with eyes blazing.

"Who do you think you are?" she growled. "We are the principal dancers in this Company. Not *you*."

I offered my blandest stare. "Is that what you're worried about? That I'm here to take your spot?"

A cold wind whipped around us. And I swear I saw the sisters shudder. I'd hit a nerve. Good. Best to disabuse them of the notion that I would stand by and let them berate me.

Before they could splutter a reply, I shrugged. "Well, you're right. That's exactly why I'm here."

It was true. But the same could be said for any apprentice. Every dancer dreamed of becoming a principal. For some reason, though, Sasha and Jelena believed it could happen. That I could ascend to that level. Even if I wasn't so sure.

Sasha finally managed to pull herself together, her eyebrows an angry pale slash over icy blue ponds. "Dream on. You are nothing more than a novelty. If you possessed true talent someone would have taken notice of you before."

"Someone did." A smile curved my lips. Sweet as honey. "Ivan Volkov."

She blanched, but not from disdain. Ivan was her hero. And he'd shunned her. Because of me. Digging the knife any deeper would be overkill.

Instead, I turned my attention over her shoulder to where Simon was wrapping up his conversation with the deputy mayor. He smiled and waved me over with a flick of two fingers.

"I'd really love to continue our chat," I said with a flutter of my lashes. "But Simon is calling me. *Do vstrechi.*"

Bony fingers wrapped around my arm as I made to slip between them. "As soon as the shine wears off you will be out," Sasha hissed. "Until then, do not cross me."

My gaze dipped to the rocks glass in Simon's hand, then up to his face. His cheeks were a rosy color, hazel eyes a bit glazed as he spoke to Kieran, his chief choreographer.

For the last half hour they'd been throwing names around, mine included, for some concept ballet they were planning.

Thanks to my dad, I was an expert when it came to deciphering that special brand of hyperbole that accompanied a few drinks. The alcohol-infused machinations that lost their luster in the morning light.

That's what this was.

No matter how much I'd impressed my new artistic director, apprentices didn't dance in principal roles.

But maybe someday.

Zoning out, I scanned the room for Miles, deflating a little when I didn't spot him in the crowd. I'd been stuck here for the better part of an hour and I was hoping to catch his eye, so he could rescue me. If my phone wasn't currently in the pocket of his suit jacket, I'd text him.

"Gelsey?"

Startled, my gaze whipped to Simon, eyeing me with an amused smile. The rest of the table was quiet as well, proving I'd missed something important.

Way to go, Gels.

Clearing my throat, I forced my lips to bend. "Sorry. I didn't catch that."

Kieran chuckled into his next sip of wine. "Most of the ballerinas hang on your every word," he said to Simon, his gaze roaming south from my face to my shoulders and beyond. "But I have a feeling this one is going to keep you on your toes."

I shifted uncomfortably under his intense stare as light peals of laughter rang out. Simon rolled his eyes, then lifted his glass to the server for another drink.

"Alexis Rowland has a stress fracture in her foot," he said once his order was squared away. "She's scheduled to perform a small part in the showcase we're doing next month. Nothing major. About seven minutes, total. I think you'd be perfect for it." A hush fell over the table and he clasped his hands in front of him, all his focus on me. "What do you say?"

I looked over at Tatiana, quietly scrutinizing me from her perch next to Kieran. She nodded, a slight tilt to her lips that was almost a smile. But not quite.

After a moment when I still hadn't answered, Simon added, "It would require you to begin rehearsals immediately. If that's not something you can do, feel free to decline. No one will judge you."

That wasn't exactly true, since I caught Sasha and Jelena's identical smirks when Simon offered me the out. *They* would judge me. Along with the other dancers in the corps.

Swallowing hard, I willed my voice not to crack.

"I'm honored that you'd give me the opportunity. And, of course, I'm ready."

Something was wrong. I felt it. The stiff set of Daryl's shoulders as his eyes dug into mine from the door confirmed it.

I stood behind Simon, my stomach twisting as his voice rocketed around the room. While he thanked all the patrons for their donations, my gaze combed every inch of the place searching for Miles.

But he was nowhere.

Only sheer force of will and Tatiana at my side kept me glued to my spot.

Hearing my name, I stepped forward on autopilot.

"For any of you who haven't met Gelsey Howard, the newest member of our tribe," Simon began, his hand finding mine, "she comes to us from Austin, Texas where she began her dance career under the tutelage of Ivan Volkov." He paused for dramatic effect. "And if Gelsey looks familiar, your eyes aren't playing tricks. She's the daughter of famed prima ballerina Katya Orlov."

Shifting my feet at the smattering of applause, I fought to keep my smile in place. I wanted to tell them I wasn't Katya. That I'd never be her.

What I really wanted was Miles.

He was the only one who made me feel adored for just being me. A queen in my own right. Not a pretender to the throne.

Another glimpse at Daryl only ratcheted up my concern. Because his eyes were on me, his attention solely focused on the patch of real estate where I stood.

Miles wasn't here.

It was only thing that made sense.

I took a blind step in Daryl's direction, but Simon squeezed my hand, snapping me out of my fog. I couldn't just leave. Not with everyone looking at me.

Smiling, I took the flute of champagne the server offered, praying that Simon would be quick.

After ten minutes that felt like ten thousand, he finally raised his glass. Kieran and Tatiana joined our circle while Jelena and Sasha lingered behind. Even though I felt their resentment like sharp blades against my spine, I wanted to step back. Out of the spotlight.

But Simon held firm, his fingers locked around mine. "Cheers to a great season."

As the crowd echoed his sentiment, he brushed a kiss to my cheek that I wasn't expecting.

"Welcome to your new home, Gelsey."

Chapter Fifty-Three

Gelsey

"GONE?" I REPEATED, BLINKING AT DARYL LIKE HE WAS SPEAKING A foreign language. "What do you mean he's gone?"

Fear stole my rational thoughts, a tight band around my chest squeezing until I couldn't breathe. Or talk.

Other people left. Disappeared. Disappointed.

But not Miles.

Taking me by the elbow, Daryl maneuvered us away from the small knot of people showing a keen interest in our conversation. "He's on his way back to Austin," he whispered. "Some kind of emergency."

Forcing myself to concentrate, I pushed aside the ramblings from the child inside my head who always feared the worst.

Daryl was here. If Miles had taken off for no reason, the bodyguard would be combing the streets looking for him. Not standing in the middle of a party trying to keep me from freaking out.

"What else?" I asked, sure that he knew more than he was letting on. "What aren't you telling me?"

Daryl scanned the crowd without really looking. "Not here."

Whatever he was hiding, it was bad. Bad enough he didn't want anyone to overhear.

"Let me go tell Tatiana I'm leaving." As I turned, the anxiety hit me full force, and I grabbed his arm. "Please. Don't go anywhere, okay?"

The crease between his brows disappeared for a moment, and he squeezed my fingers. "I'll be right here."

Infusing steel into my spine, I wove through the crowd, ignoring anyone who tried to get my attention. My stomach pitched when I spotted Tatiana, Simon, and Kieran schmoozing one of the bigger donors. An heiress with ties to Walton family.

Hovering right outside their circle, I tried to catch Tatiana's eye. But it was Kieran who saw me first.

"Gelsey." At his greeting, all eyes swung in my direction. "Join us. Tiffany has been dying to meet you."

The platinum blonde flashed a brilliant smile. But even as I stepped forward, offering my hand, her gaze was all over the place, like she was looking for someone. Miles. Women had flocked to him all evening. Flirting. Undressing him with their eyes. Not that I could blame them.

"Pleased to meet you, Tiffany," I said through a clenched smile before turning to Tatiana. "Can I speak to you for a moment, please?"

Her lips pinched with annoyance, but just as quickly it faded. "Certainly."

After a quick nod to the others, she fell into step beside me, grabbing a glass of champagne off one of the server's trays as we walked.

"Leaving so soon?" she asked as we tucked into a quiet corner.

The truth threatened to spill out, but at the last second, I thought of Ivan. All the lessons he'd drilled into me about discretion. And only telling someone as much as they needed to know.

"Yes. I'm heading back to Austin first thing in the morning, so I need to get some sleep." Suspicion shrouded her features, but before she could voice her concerns, I added, "Simon said I'd need to start rehearsals immediately, so I decided it would be best to go now before things get too busy. I'll be back in a couple of days."

Lifting the flute to her lips, she searched my face. "You are eager to begin, then?"

"Of course. I can't wait."

My response flew out too quickly, even though it was the truth.

"And Miles? He is on board with your sudden move?"

I nodded weakly, afraid my voice might betray the apprehension churning in my stomach.

Tatiana smiled, then folded me into a quick hug. "Safe travels, then." Just as I began to relax, she took me by the shoulders and looked me square in the eyes. "But know that if you are not back in three days to begin rehearsal, your spot will be forfeited."

Daryl remained tightlipped, scanning for threats as we trekked the quarter mile from the Plaza to the Ritz. I knew better than to distract him, so I kept my eyes glued to the sidewalk, counting the cracks in the concrete.

Miles was gone.

Even though I knew it was true, my knees threatened to buckle when I entered the suite and surveyed the devastation. It looked like a tornado had ripped through the place. Every drawer was open, clothes on the bed and the floor.

Sinking onto the mattress, my heart slammed against my ribs when I spotted two empty mini-bottles of Jack on the nightstand next to a paper flower. A cherry blossom, fashioned from a scrap of the New York Times, perched atop a note on the hotel stationary.

The bloom all but fell apart in my hand, the folds coming undone as I ran my thumb over the uneven petals and read Miles's note.

Gelsey,

I'll explain everything later. Please, do what Daryl says.

I love you.

Daryl.

I'd almost forgotten he was there until I found him staring at me from his spot next to the door.

Dashing a tear from my cheek, I wobbled to my feet.

"Tell me everything you know. And don't you dare leave anything out."

Chapter Fifty-Four

Miles

THE PLANE BANKED RIGHT, HEADING WEST. AWAY FROM GELSEY. AND the life I thought was within my reach.

Outside the tiny window, the lights of the city grew fainter as we gained altitude, until all that was left was a shimmering pool of gold in a sea of black.

Snatching up the mini bottles of Jack I'd pilfered from the cart before takeoff, I pushed out of the plush seat. Years of sobriety and the three shots I'd sucked down in the hotel room made me a little unsteady on my feet.

"Mr. Cooper." The lone flight attendant curved a hand around my bicep. "The captain said we should stay in our seats. There's a storm over West Virginia, and it might get a little bumpy."

Spinning around, a bitter laugh rumbled low in my chest. "Well, if God is intent on finishing the job he started, I don't think a seat belt is going to save me."

Her eyes widened to the size of saucers, alarm etching her features as she took a step back.

One thing I knew from years of travel, it didn't matter if I was paying for the private jet. Or the fucking crew. The pilot's word was law up here. If he decided to ground this baby, I was fucked. One word from the nervous flight attendant and he just might do it.

Darting a gaze to her name tag, I plastered on an Oscar-worthy smile. "Sorry, Ella. My sense of humor takes a bad turn when I'm tired. I'm going to splash some water on my face, then I'll be right back in my seat."

Concern I didn't deserve creased her brow. But she didn't know me. Or what I'd done. Why I was flying to Austin in the middle of the night.

She only saw the smile and the aura of celebrity.

And I wasn't above using it.

A ding rocketed around the cabin, followed by the captain's announcement about cruising altitude and the turbulence in our path.

Ella stepped out of the way. "Guess you'd better hurry, then."

With a nod, I brushed past her, my smile melting as I thundered toward the bedroom at the back of the plane. Once the door was locked behind me, I flopped onto the mattress and turned my face into the pillow. It still smelled like Gelsey. Like lavender and promise.

Blowing out a breath, I rolled onto my stomach, my phone in my hand. A string of Blake's messages littered the screen. Long rambling notes that I'd never opened because I was too busy. But it was the last one from Dr. Sheppard that pierced me like a sharp blade.

Call me.

My eyes stung as I tapped out a reply.

I'm in the air. Any news?

I stared at the screen without blinking, like maybe it would make a difference. One minute. Three. I heard Ella outside the door, but still, I didn't move.

Finally, Sheppard answered. *He's still unresponsive. Brain function looks good.*

There was more. Some nonsense about it "not being my fault" and "taking care of myself" and whatever else he needed to say to make sure I wouldn't do anything stupid. Like pop the razor out of my shaver and run it over my wrist. Or down the whole bottle of painkillers in my backpack.

But I wouldn't do that to Ella. I knew too well how that scene would play out. The blood. The shock. The guilt.

And Gelsey...

I didn't deserve her comfort, but I'd damn well take it. Swiping a finger over her picture, I closed my eyes and flipped onto my back, the phone at my ear.

I jerked when something vibrated against my chest. And then a song floated up from the inner pocket of my suit jacket. "In My Life," by the Beatles. It took me a moment to realize it was Gelsey's phone. That I still had it tucked against my heart.

Lyrics formed on my lips, and I sang along until the melody faded. And even though she wouldn't get the message, I left her one anyway.

"Blake's in the hospital." Digging the heel of my palm into my eyes, I willed my voice not to crack. "Suicide attempt. They don't know if he's going to make it."

And it's my fault.

I left that part out, along with the rest of the details. But I could picture it all. A small bathroom with blood on the floor. Pale skin and lifeless eyes. Only it wasn't Blake's face behind my lids. It was my father's. The way I'd always remember him.

Pushing the image aside, I cleared my throat. "Anyway, I just...I just wanted to hear your voice." I ended the call without telling her I loved her. I did. With every breath. But love like mine could only bring heartache. I knew that now.

Chapter Fifty-Five

Miles

SHIELDING MY EYES FROM THE NEWLY MINTED SUN, I TRUDGED DOWN THE metal stairs and onto the tarmac.

My leg hurt like a bitch, a searing pain that felt as if someone had buried a hot poker in my thigh. I'd passed out less than an hour ago, falling into the fitful kind of sleep that wasn't exhaustion, but the first sign of something else. Something more. I'd lost days to that kind of sleep, too bogged down by my own dark thoughts to leave my bed.

Shaking off the gloom, I headed for the limo where Cody, the driver, waited, looking wide-awake considering it wasn't even six in the morning.

"Mr. Cooper." He reached for my backpack with a smile, but I waved him off, ducking into the back seat without so much as a hello.

My heart lurched in surprise when I nearly fell across Taryn's lap. She surveyed me with a frown, from my red-rimmed eyes to my rumpled suit to my defeated posture.

"Taryn. What are you doing here?"

My voice was gravel, reed thin with a desperate quality that she picked up on immediately.

Instead of answering, she folded me into her arms where I melted like an ice cream cone in the sun. I was vaguely aware of the door closing behind me as she whispered words of reassurance.

We'd been here before, and I'd pushed her away. But not this time.

"I fucked up, T-Rex," I breathed, my chest so heavy I could barely get the words out.

I felt her exhale slowly before breaking away to look me in the eyes. "It's not your fault. You couldn't have known."

Obviously, Daryl had called her. Told her what was going on. Just the broad strokes, though. I'd need to paint her the full picture.

Flopping against the seat, I let my head fall back and stared out the moonroof. Clouds rolled by, white ribbons lazily drifting on a breeze.

"He called me, Taryn."

Blake. I couldn't even say his name.

My confession hung between us, heavy with implications. I was self-ish. I'd always been selfish.

You're just like your father. Tragic. And weak.

That's what my mother had said the one and only time she'd visited me at Millwood. She knew it wasn't an accident, my mishap with the pills. More like a family tradition.

And she was right. I was selfish. Consumed by my grief. I'd bought her a house in Florida. Inked the deal before my meds even kicked in. That way she'd never have to be forced to visit me again.

Taryn's hand found mine, and she linked our fingers. "The night that you tried to… That you…"

Turning my head when her thought trailed off, I watched her struggle to find the words.

"You called me," she finally blurted, wincing as the admission tumbled from her lips.

I sat up straighter. "What?"

With a heavy sigh, she pulled her phone out and began to scroll, her finger swiping the screen over and over. Her lip disappeared between her teeth when she got to where she was going.

Holding the phone between us with a shaky hand, she stared down at her lap as a barely intelligible voice spilled from the speaker.

"T-Taryn…I n-need you. P-Please come."

It was me, all right. Though I didn't remember calling.

Sniffling, a tear spilled onto her cheek. "I was out," she admitted, her tone flat. "At a business dinner trying to finalize the plans for…" She shook her head. "It doesn't matter. The point is, I ignored the call. When I finally listened to the message, I…I rushed over to your place. And you know the rest."

"Taryn—"

She sucked in a breath and continued like I wasn't even there. "They didn't know if you were going to make it. Or if you would have brain damage. They told me in the ambulance that I'd saved your life." Her watery gaze finally found mine. "It didn't feel like it, though. You didn't wake up for seventeen hours and thirty-two minutes."

My heart shattered behind my ribs as I pulled her against me, pressing my lips to the top of her head. "Fuck. I'm sorry. I'm so sorry."

She peered up at me, and I wiped her tears. And even through her smile, I saw the pain I'd put there, etched into tiny lines around her eyes. An unwanted gift she couldn't give back.

"Don't be," she said. "I'm just glad you're here. And that it's all behind you now."

Was it?

She looked so hopeful; I didn't voice my reservations. The niggling thoughts at the corners of my mind where the rain clouds lived.

I merely nodded and forced my lips to bend.

The day nurse guarding the locked door in front of the psych ward at St. David's looked me up and down like she couldn't decide if I were a patient or a visitor.

I'd managed to choke down a cup of coffee and a breakfast burrito, leaving me somewhat revived. But I'd decided against going home to change my clothes.

No time.

According to Sheppard, Blake had regained consciousness. While that should've eased the heavy mantle of guilt, it didn't. I still needed to see him. To explain. Maybe then the dark clouds would evaporate. And the heaviness in my chest would go away.

But the nurse seemed hell-bent on keeping me from my mission. The woman had no clue who I was. None. More proof that my luck had taken a hard left into shit town.

I couldn't take a piss in a public restroom without someone loitering behind me waiting to shake my hand or get my autograph. Yet, here I was, standing in front of the one person in the whole damn city under the age of fifty who didn't recognize me.

A little cajoling and she finally picked up the phone, her gaze set-tling on the tattoos peeking from the rolled-up sleeves of my dress shirt. The way her nose wrinkled, I got the feeling she wasn't a fan of ink.

"I've got a Mr. Conner here to see Blake Peterson," she said, giving me her back as she swiveled in her chair.

"Cooper," I corrected in a voice loud enough to be heard by anyone in the vicinity. "Miles Cooper."

If I weren't dead on my feet, I might've gotten some measure of satisfaction when she turned around and blinked at me with wide eyes. "Yes. He's tall. Uh-huh…brown hair." The column of her throat bobbed as she continued to describe me in great detail. Right down to my dim-ple. Which I proudly displayed when the smile spread wide on my lips.

She definitely knew who I was now.

After stammering her thanks to whoever was on the other end of the line, she set the phone in the cradle and addressed me with a tight smile. "You can go right in, Mr. Cooper. Room 415."

The double doors swung open, and a cacophony of sounds traveled from the busy ward. Mostly patients' voices. The discordant mix of an-ger and confusion in their tones froze me in my spot.

The sound of madness.

I'd recognize it anywhere.

Clenching my fingers into tight fists, I forced my feet to move. My throat tightened when the doors *whooshed* closed behind me, the lock engaging with a loud *thwack*.

Was it possible to experience claustrophobia in a space this large?

My racing heart responded with a resounding *hell yes* as I ventured further down the long hallway. Room numbers swam into view, but nothing clicked until I saw the 415 next to the closed door.

I grabbed the handle, and the metal slipped under my sweaty palm.

You can do this, said the voice in my head. Rhenn's voice. The irony didn't escape me, my dead best friend popping up to cheer me on during a visit to the psych ward.

Blowing out a breath, I let my mind go blank and stepped inside. The room was quiet, just the steady beep from the heart monitor echo-ing off the pale green walls. And Blake. So still, his gaze cemented to a shaft of light spilling from a split in the heavy curtains.

As if he could sense my presence, he turned his head in my direction. Washed out eyes wandered over my face but there was barely a hint of recognition.

I could only guess what kind of cocktail was flowing through his veins. Sedatives. Anti-psychotics. Anti-depressants.

Shifting my focus to the IV in his arm, I shuddered at the restraints anchoring him to the bed. Right above the bandages covering his wrists.

A chuckle parted his pale lips, a tiny spark returning to his gaze. "We all fall down. Right?"

I grappled for a reply. Something profound enough to pull him from his pit of despair. But I wasn't the guy to wax poetic about the beauty of life. And we both knew it.

I took a seat in the chair beside the bed as Blake's attention returned to the window.

Rather than offer meaningless platitudes, I pulled out my phone and scrolled to the playlist with the tracks from his EP.

Blake closed his eyes, a tear rolling down his cheek as the first song began to play.

This was what I had to offer.

Music. Another beautiful, worthless thing. Like paper flowers. And promises.

The door swung open, meeting the wall with a loud crack a second before a booming female voice rocketed around the room.

"Get out!"

I jerked my gaze over my shoulder, not particularly concerned. This was the psych ward, after all. And not all the patients were restrained. Didn't mean they weren't crazy, though. Or delusional.

The woman glaring daggers at me with her hair standing up in every direction like she'd been pulling on it all day appeared to be both.

I shoved to my feet, a halting smile curving my lips.

Just play along. Find an orderly.

Those were my only goals as I inched toward her. But as I got closer, one dip into her gray eyes stayed my progress.

I knew those eyes.

My attention floated to Blake, still staring at the shaft of light peeking through the curtain. But I didn't need his confirmation.

"You must be Blake's mom," I said, holding out my hand as I closed the gap between us. "I'm Miles. A friend of your—"

"I know who you are," she spat, brushing past me to stand at the foot of her son's bed. "You're the man who put all those ideas in my boy's head. Told him he could be normal. Make music. And look at him now!" Her voice rose an octave as she pointed at Blake. "He almost died because of you! I've already lost one son! I won't lose another!"

At the mention of his brother, Blake clenched his eyes shut. The machine monitoring his heart rate began to beep louder as his agitation increased.

"I'm sorry," I said holding up my hands in surrender. "I'll go. Just… let me grab my phone."

She folded her arms over her chest, watching me like a hawk as I walked to the bed. Risking her wrath probably wasn't the best idea, but I didn't care.

Leaning in close, I curved a hand around the back of Blake's neck and rested my forehead against his temple. "I got to go, bud. But I'll be back soon."

His fingers flexed, mildly rebelling against the restraints. "Promise?"

The hope in his voice made my throat burn. I didn't deserve his trust. But here he was, offering it.

I gave his neck a squeeze. "You have my word."

Slipping my phone into my pocket, I started for the door with Blake's mother on my heels.

"Don't come back," she snapped as I stepped into the hallway. "You're not welcome here."

Over her shoulder, I locked eyes with her son. And I nodded, letting her think she had my agreement. But the small smile curving his lips told me that he understood.

I would be back.

Whether she liked it or not.

Chapter Fifty-Six

Gelsey

EMILY SHOT TO HER FEET, THE MAGAZINE SLIDING OFF HER LAP AS DARYL and I dropped our bags on the kitchen floor.

"Hey." She ran a nervous hand through her messy hair. "I wasn't expecting y'all tonight."

Obviously. Since it was nearly midnight and she was still here, in my boyfriend's kitchen. Not that I was jealous. The opposite in fact. Emily cared about Miles, and I was glad he wasn't alone.

"The jet wasn't due to arrive back in New York until tomorrow," I replied, letting Daryl ease the backpack off my sore shoulder. "So we took the first flight we could get. We would've been here sooner, but we got stuck in Chicago for six hours because of a weather delay."

I clamped my mouth shut to keep from spilling any more details. I'd never been Emily's favorite person, so it wasn't like she cared about my twelve-hour trip from hell.

To my surprise, her features softened. "You poor thing. That sounds awful. Miles is in the studio. Went straight there after he got home from the hospital. I haven't seen him since."

Apprehension twisted a cold hand around my heart. "How long ago was that?"

Her brows pinched together over troubled eyes. "Going on ten hours."

The horror must've shone on my face because she wrung her hands. "I went down there two of three times, but he told me to leave him alone. I didn't know what to do, so I just stayed here. In case he needed something when he came up. Food or...I don't know...someone to talk to."

Her gaze found Daryl's, and something passed between them. But I didn't have time to figure out what it was. I needed to get to Miles. Only my feet wouldn't move.

What if Miles blamed me for dragging him to New York? The only reason he'd set up that appearance on the *Tonight Show* was because of me.

Daryl's comforting hand curved around my arm. "Do you want me to go down there with you?"

Ignoring the mounting feeling of dread, I peered up at him. "No. I'm sure everything's fine."

Since I had no idea what frame of mind Miles was in, the reassurance sounded halfhearted at best.

I shifted my attention to Emily. "It's really late. Why don't you stay over, so you don't have to drive across town at this time of night?"

She blinked at me, and for a moment I thought I might've overstepped. It wasn't my house, and she certainly didn't need my permission to be here.

Before I could backtrack and rearrange the invitation in a way that wouldn't offend her, Emily sprang forward and threw her arms around me.

"Thank you. I'm so glad you're here."

Taken aback by the spontaneous show of affection, I awkwardly returned the embrace. "Don't worry. I'm sure Miles just fell asleep downstairs."

Easing back, she offered a watery smile. "You're probably right. Are you hungry? I could run to What a Burger?" She wrinkled her nose. "Shit. You don't eat junk food. Why don't I make you—"

"No. That's okay. I'm not hungry." The mere thought of food turned my stomach. "I'm just going to go find Miles."

I started for the door, then paused and looked back. Emily and Daryl already had their heads together. And again, I got the feeling there was something I didn't know.

"Any news on Blake?" I asked.

She lifted a slender shoulder in a half shrug. "He's alive. That's all I know."

Alive.

I guess that was something.

I rapped lightly on the door to the studio and got no answer.

More than likely, Miles was asleep, and the tightness in my chest was an overreaction. But still, I had to check. Just in case the pang was his heart talking to mine.

We were joined that way, whether I liked it or not. Whether I wanted it or not. Whether it was *convenient* or not.

I tried the doorknob, and it turned easily in my hand.

Shaking off the feeling that I was invading his privacy, I stepped inside; the air squeezing from my lungs as I took in the scene.

Miles was slumped on the couch, a thick cloud of smoke hanging over his head. There was no shock on his face as he looked me over with bloodshot eyes, slowly raising the cigarette to his lips.

"Hey, little mouse."

Drawn by the anguish etching his features, I moved toward him, my throat too tight to speak. It wasn't until I was on my knees in front of him that I noticed the half empty bottle of Jack clutched in his free hand.

"You're d-drinking?"

The question sounded hollow. Unnecessary.

Obviously, he was drinking.

Still, I wanted to hear the words. Feel his remorse when he said them.

But he just stared at me without an ounce of contrition.

"Miles...please..." My voice wobbled as I tried to pry the bottle from his hold. "I know you're upset. But you can't drink."

He tightened his grip; the warmth seeping from his gaze. "That's where you're wrong. It's my house. And I can do whatever I want."

The words stung like a slap across the cheek, and I jerked back. "M-Miles..."

Jaw clenched, he tipped forward, so close I could smell the whiskey on his breath.

"You don't know me, Gelsey. Not really. So stop trying to *fix* me. I can't *be* fixed."

Shaking my head, I laid my palm flat over his heart. "No."

It was all I had. One tiny little word.

He blinked at me. And when his hand covered mine, I thought maybe I'd gotten through. But then he released me like my touch was something he couldn't abide.

Hauling to his feet, he stumbled over to the sound system, and after a moment of fiddling, a Damaged song floated over the air.

Alter Ego.

"This is me, baby. Like it or not. And if not…well…" Gesturing to the door with the neck of the bottle, he shrugged. "You can always get the fuck out."

Tears burned my eyes, and everything turned soft and shiny. But I wouldn't let him see me cry.

"Is that what you want?" On my feet now, I pulled my shoulders back. "Say it."

He stared at the floor, the only sign that he was bothered at all. "Yeah. That's exactly what I want."

"Drink this."

I wiped my nose on the sleeve of my T-shirt, then reached for the glass Shannon offered with trembling fingers. "What is it?"

She flopped down next to me on her couch—my bed for the night—and propped her feet on the coffee table. "Merlot." Shaking my head, I tried to hand it back. But she was having none of it. "Drink."

If she knew what I'd just witnessed in Miles's studio, she wouldn't be trying to ply me with alcohol. But I couldn't tell her.

I trusted Shannon with my life, but there's no way I'd risk outing Miles like that.

If she told anyone. Even in passing.

Shuddering at the thought, I choked down a sip of the wine. "Ugh. This is awful."

Rolling her eyes, she confiscated my glass. "How would you know? You don't even drink."

I *didn't* drink. But my boyfriend did. To excess, apparently. And why was I surprised? Miles's history of substance abuse wasn't a secret. Nor was his time in rehab. Or his overdose.

You don't know me, Gelsey.

The words stung even more because they were true. I didn't know *that* Miles. We'd never been introduced.

Until tonight.

Fresh tears welled, and my heart sank into greater despair.

Stupid girl.

Shannon took a large gulp, then pressed the goblet back into my hand. Resigned, I took another sip. I'd drink battery acid if it meant I could take a breath without hurting.

"Can I say something without you thinking I'm not being support-ive?" she asked, curling a strand of my hair around her finger.

I nodded into my next swig of Merlot. It wasn't quite as bitter, and the warmth was starting to make everything a bit more bearable.

"You've never had a relationship, Gels."

My narrowed gaze shot to hers. "Your point?"

Looping an arm around my shoulder, she pulled me close. "People fight. Say horrible things to each other. Just last week I told Brian that I hoped a colony of fire ants would attack his balls."

Horrified, I tipped back and peered up at her.

"What?" she asked, like she couldn't understand the alarm that was surely etched on my features. "I didn't mean it. I like his balls. But not at the time. And he's said some nasty shit to me too. It doesn't mean we don't love each other."

Love wasn't the problem between Miles and me. The fact that he couldn't look me in the eye when he told me to leave proved that.

He loved me. In a place way down deep.

Just like my father.

But that didn't mean that either of them wanted me around.

Shannon let out a little gasp when I dissolved into tears. "Aww...

sweetie." She swiped at my cheeks. "Just forget I said anything. I didn't mean to upset you any more than you already are."

I shook my head. "You didn't. I just...I don't understand why people..."

Leave. I couldn't bring myself to say it. Because then it would be true.

Miles was gone. Out of my life. And tomorrow after I picked up my stuff, I might never see him again.

He'd be here, and I'd be in New York. Someday, he might get married. And I'd have to read about it in the papers.

Doubling over, I clutched my stomach, unable to hold back the sobs.

"It's all right," Shannon soothed, rubbing small circles on my back.

Only it wasn't. And from the way it felt right now, it might never be again.

Chapter Fifty-Seven

Miles

MY BEDROOM DOOR SWUNG OPEN, AND IN WALKED EMILY, CARRYING A CUP of coffee and a bottle of pain relievers. I was too engrossed with the scene playing out on my iPad to acknowledge her with more than a nod. Which didn't go over well.

Whatever.

Ignoring the little huff she let out when she placed the goodies on my nightstand, I hoped she'd get the point and just go.

No such luck.

"So, you're spying now?" she asked, her tone as sardonic as her smile.

I darted my coldest glare in her direction, the one that said: *tread lightly, the life you save could be your own*, but didn't answer.

She responded with an equally scathing *fuck you very much; I'll take my chances* kind of glare and parked a hand on her hip.

"It's my house," I bit out, my stomach twisting when I realized I'd used the same line on Gelsey yesterday. "So I'm not spying."

I was totally spying.

Returning my attention to the screen, I ground my back teeth into dust as I watched Daryl help Gelsey load the last of her belongings into the ancient Honda Civic.

I'd specifically told the leaner to get rid of that piece of shit. It wasn't safe.

But somehow, between last night when Gelsey had stormed out and this afternoon when she'd shown up at the front door, ringing the bell like she was a guest, the car had ended up back in my garage.

I knew it was Daryl's way of trying to get me to come downstairs. To deal with the mess I'd made.

But I couldn't.

If I got within five feet of Gelsey, I'd cave. And all my good intentions would fly right out the window.

So I'd told Emily to give her the note I'd penned early this morning, fashioned into an origami camellia. Another pretty, worthless thing to add to her collection. This time with words.

And then I'd watched as Gelsey laid the paper flower on the passenger seat of her car. So gently. Like it was priceless.

She'd made no move to unfold the design and read the note. Maybe she never would. And my apology would stay locked within the creases. My last *I love you.*

And I did love her. So fucking much I'd set her free.

Emily shifted her feet, her gaze slicing into me like a sharp blade.

"You're just going to let her go?"

Let her go…

That was the plan. But it seemed impossible when she carried the biggest piece of me in her pocket. The one I'd thought had died so many years ago.

But I couldn't risk Gelsey getting caught up in the storm when it made landfall again. And it would. Someday. Just like it had for Blake.

He and I lived under the same sky. Filled with ominous clouds just waiting to destroy. While Gelsey existed in pillows of white fluff and endless blue.

"Yep."

My finger hovered over the button on my screen to cut the video feed as Daryl loaded the last bag into Gelsey's trunk. She hugged him, then slid behind the wheel.

Look at me, baby. One last time.

I sent the plea out into the cosmos. Calling on whatever magic still existed between us. As if she could hear me, Gelsey lifted her big blue eyes to the camera.

I love you.

She must've heard that too, because she smiled. A sad little smile full of regret.

Squeezing my eyes shut, I didn't care that Emily could see the tears leaking from the corners. Drowning me. And when my lids fluttered open a moment later, Gelsey was gone.

Chapter Fifty-Eight

Gelsey

I STOOD JUST OUTSIDE THE SECURITY GATE AT AUSTIN BERGSTROM, chewing nervously on my lip while I fingered the edge of my freshly minted passport.

"Ticket to Ride" floated through the tiny speakers in my earbuds, drowning out the last sounds of home.

The Beatles. Miles had even ruined that for me. I couldn't listen to the songs I loved without thinking of him.

But he didn't deserve my thoughts. Or even one minute of my time.

I wanted to kick myself for holding out even the tiniest bit of hope that he hadn't turned his back on us. I'd kept that sprig alive, drowning the seedling with tears and praying it would grow.

But Miles hadn't even cared enough to say goodbye when I went to his house yesterday to pick up my stuff.

Instead, he'd sent Emily with a paper flower. A note. Rejection scribbled across pretty petals.

My heart rate spiked as I gripped the body of my tote bag where his offering was now encased in a small piece of Tupperware.

I might not be able to read it. But I wanted it with me. Preserved and uncrushed.

And I hated myself for that weakness. Also, for the panic attack I was barely holding at bay. Everything inside me screamed to turn back. To hide out at Shannon's instead of getting on the plane.

My throat burned from swallowing tears. Better than my eyes, though. I couldn't let Ivan know what I was thinking. He'd be so disappointed.

Slanting my gaze up to his, I smiled. But he was distracted, shifting his feet and looking anywhere but at me.

Maybe I was keeping him from something?

I turned off the music and tugged his sleeve. Our eyes met, and I made an awkward gesture to the terminal. "I can wait inside if you need to go."

His brow creased with something I couldn't name. "We still have…" He glanced at his watch and frowned. "Twenty-two minutes."

His face fell, causing my heart to clench.

"What's wrong?" I choked out, sure that it had to be monumental.

My gaze was everywhere at once, only coming to rest on his when he stroked a hand down my hair. The arctic blue calmed me, and I could breathe again when he smiled.

"I will miss you, *dorogaya moya*. That is all. I am so proud of you."

The sob clawed its way north and I fought to keep it in. But lost the battle when he kissed my forehead.

"I don't…k-know if I can do it," I said to the ground, since I couldn't look at him. "What if I want…t-to stay…h-here?"

Strong arms wrapped around me, holding me up when my knees went weak.

"I would love nothing more than for you to never leave," he said softly.

Shocked, I tipped back and blinked up at him. "Wh-what?"

He brushed a lock of hair behind my ear. "You think this is easy for me?" He shook his head. "I have dreaded the thought of this day since you were this big."

He held his hand to his waist.

"But you must go," he continued, his eyes shining faintly. "If you do not like it, you come home. But you must try."

My stomach sank. Because he was right. Like always. I had to get on the plane. And start a new life. The one I was born to lead. Though, nothing sounded worse.

Sniffling, I nodded. "Okay."

An announcement boomed, directing all passengers for my flight to the gate for boarding. I squared my shoulders, but before I could pull away, Ivan framed my face with his large hands.

"I love you, *dorogaya moya.*"

Tears spilled onto my cheeks, and he swiped them away with his thumbs. After placing one final kiss on my forehead, he rested a palm on the small of my back and urged me into the security line.

And when his hand fell away, taking all the warmth and safety with it, I was more alone than I'd ever been in my life.

Chapter Fifty-Nine

Miles

D R. SHEPPARD STOOD NEXT TO THE OPEN DOOR OF THE MEETING ROOM where group therapy was about to commence.

"Miles," he said with a placid smile, dipping his head to catch my eyes under the baseball cap pulled low on my brow.

"Satan," I grunted as I slid past, denying him my gaze.

The doc had me over a barrel with this therapy bullshit, but that didn't mean I'd be playing along. I was here for Blake. And that was it.

After the kid had gotten out of the hospital, his parents had put him back under Sheppard's care at Millwood for the foreseeable future. But Blake had decided to take a stand. Refusing to participate in the communal gut-dumping sessions unless I was here.

Which made things really tense, since I was pissed as hell at Sheppard.

The dark clouds had rolled in after Gelsey had left town a week and a half ago, like I knew they would. Murky and gray and unwelcome, they blanketed the sky with despair.

Everything was darker without her. She not only took the sun, but all the color, leaving me to ponder life in a black-and-white world.

It sounded so fucking poetic. But it wasn't. Just lonely and empty. And tragic.

And Sheppard, that fuck, had refused to increase my dosage of antidepressants. Even after I'd sat in his office, soaked to the bone from the rain that wouldn't stop following me.

We need to talk this through.

Fuck that and fuck him.

When I'd been a resident in his nut house, I'd never shared. I'd kept all the fractured bits to myself. Since I'd earned them.

Pills. That's what I needed. Something to make everything less.

But the asshole was unmoved and underwhelmed by my plight.

He didn't even budge after I'd told him I was drinking. *Self-medicating.*

Blake fell into the chair beside me, his extra-large coffee in hand.

"Hey," he said breathlessly, his leg bobbing up and down like a piston.

Caffeine was the only drug he was allowed given the situation. But his current hyperactivity and good mood might've had more to do with the meds they were trying to regulate.

I mumbled a quick good morning, then pressed my lips together, ashamed to my core that I was jealous of his energy. His mania.

All I'd wanted to do for the past week was sleep. Or stalk Gelsey's social media. Her ballet company had set up accounts for her on Instagram and Facebook, publishing short videos of her in rehearsal or at the brownstone to up her visibility.

She looked as miserable as I felt. Never smiling. But I knew someday she would.

It was like torture, watching and waiting for the moment in time when she'd move on.

A small part of me hoped that someone would catch it on film, so I could see it. But the bigger part of me prayed it would never happen. Proving I was an asshole. Unworthy of her love.

Good thing you turned her loose, then.

Rhenn's voice pinged around in my head. Maybe I'd get the good stuff if I told Sheppard my dead best friend was talking to me on the regular now. Doubtful. Because I knew it wasn't really Rhenn.

The doc called the meeting to order while I surreptitiously slid a single earbud in place. I tapped the tiny unit, and the first song on my Beatles playlist drowned him out. Paul McCartney singing about daybreak and heartache. And tears cried for no one.

My gut twisted into a knot, and I shifted my focus to the window. Trees swayed in time to the beat, gnarled limbs reaching for the sun I couldn't see.

Dancing.

Always dancing.

Chapter Sixty

Gelsey

SASHA RAN A GREEDY HAND OVER THE BUTTERY LEATHER UPHOLSTERY IN the back of the Town Car, her eyes locked on mine.

"So, Gelsey…" As soon as the queen bee opened her mouth, her stupid sister and their two stupider friends stopped talking. When she was sure all the attention was on her, Sasha smiled sweetly. "I have not seen your boyfriend since you have been here. Will he be joining you soon?"

From the way her gaze dug into mine, then slowly dipped to inspect the dark circles under my eyes, it was like she knew my secret. My truth.

But of course, she didn't.

Nobody did.

As callous as Miles had been when he'd kicked me to the curb, he'd gone out of his way to ensure I wouldn't be humiliated in public. He'd set up a car service to take me to and from the brownstone. And I had a bodyguard who shadowed my every move. To the outside world, Miles appeared to be every inch the doting boyfriend. Even though we hadn't spoken since the night I walked out of his basement.

Almost two weeks had passed, and it still hurt to breathe. My shattered heart rattled around my chest so loudly, I was sure everyone could hear it.

Including Sasha and her gang.

They didn't like me. Would never like me. But they made sure they were on my heels every time I left the stage door at Lincoln Center, just so they wouldn't have to take the subway back to Brooklyn.

When I realized Sasha was still waiting for an answer, I forced a smile. "Miles is busy in Austin. So I'm not really sure when he'll make it out."

Sasha tilted her head, her lips parted with another question, but her sister beat her to it. "Surely he will be here for your debut?"

All four women leaned in, eager for my response. If I would've fallen in love with anyone but Miles, this humiliation would be mine to keep. Private. But soon enough the truth would come out.

Not tonight, though.

"I hope so."

The car glided to a stop in the quiet Brooklyn neighborhood, and the gang of four grabbed their stuff. Like the entitled little divas they were, they waited until Lenny, my new bodyguard, opened the door, then poured out onto the sidewalk. Their flats padded softly against the concrete as they laughed their way up the steps and to the door without giving me a backward glance. Or a thank you.

Lenny shook his head as he offered me a hand. "You're too nice, Ms. Gelsey. If you don't mind me saying so."

I didn't. But I couldn't publicly disparage my fellow dancers—even if they deserved it—so I just smiled.

"See you tomorrow, Lenny."

Shouldering my bag, I dodged cracks in the uneven sidewalk as I headed for the stairs.

Tammy, the house manager who handled the business for the two brownstones the Company owned, waved to me from next door. "Gelsey? Can you come here, please?"

I bit down a scowl when I thought about walking the extra thirty steps. My back was killing me. Another secret I had to keep.

Fastening on a tight-lipped smile, I trudged over. "What's up, Tammy?"

"You are *so* cute with that accent. My parents used to take us to Myrtle Beach in the summer on vacation and you sound just like that."

I didn't. In fact, my Texas twang was barely there. And South Carolinians sounded much different. But I just shrugged demurely, having heard the same comment a dozen times since I'd moved here.

"All your stuff is in your new place," Tammy said cheerily. "Do you have time to do a walk-through?"

I looked down at the key she'd pressed in my hand. "Walk-through?"

"Yeah." She tilted her head. "You did know it was today, right?"

"I think you have me confused with someone else." I tried to hand her back the key. "I'm sharing a room with Layla and April next door."

"You were," she said slowly in that way some New Yorkers did when encountering someone from another state. Like there was a language barrier. "But I got an order when you moved in to clean up a single unit with a private bathroom. A year's lease paid in advance."

My heart swelled as I blinked at her. *Ivan.* It had to be him.

"I didn't know," I said, unable to hide my excitement. "My coach must've set it up."

I was already reaching for my phone to call Ivan when Tammy hooked her arm through mine. "Not your coach, silly. That rock star boyfriend of yours. Miles Cooper." She pulled me toward the door. "You have to see the furniture. And the bed. Oh my God. I've never felt a mattress like that. He must be planning on visiting often."

My stomach turned as she waggled her eyebrows and yanked me over the threshold.

"I don't think so."

The confession slipped out before I could reel it back in. But Tammy didn't notice. And once we were inside, it didn't matter anyway, since my tongue was stuck to the roof of my mouth.

The brownstones were identical. But not. This one was more elegant, with higher end furnishings in rich shades of cream and scarlet. And no clutter.

"That's the living room," Tammy said as she dragged me out of the foyer. "Mira doesn't like to figure out what belongs to whom, so make sure you don't leave your stuff in the common area."

I grabbed the polished banister for balance as we ascended the stairs. "Who...who is Mira?"

"The maid. It's included with your lease. The paperwork is in your room. You can eat next door if you want, but most of the dancers in this building use a service for meals. That's an add-on too. But your boyfriend paid for the full package."

I licked my dry lips. "F-Full package?"

"Maid service. Special meals and grocery delivery. I'll take care of that for you if you give me a list. Laundry and dry cleaning..."

Tammy continued to tick off items as we made our way to the bedroom tucked in the corner on the second floor. She chuckled when I just stared at her.

"It's locked," she said as she pried the key from my hand. "Your man has good taste. I'll give him that."

She threw the door open, and my jaw came unhinged.

The room was bigger than the one I shared with April and Layla and painted a sunny shade of pale yellow. And the bed. Four posters with a massive headboard fashioned from dark wood. It was Miles's taste. Expensive and on the masculine side. But the comforter was snow white—down—and incredibly fluffy. Just like his.

With a lump the size of a baseball lodged in my throat, I ran my fingers over the matching dresser. All my stuff was here. Including the pictures of my mother and Ivan in the pewter frames I'd kept on my small nightstand next door.

"How many dancers live here?" I asked, meeting Tammy's gaze in the mirror.

"Four. Plus Kieran." She pointed to the ceiling. "His room is right above yours."

I nodded, still too shocked to piece together my thoughts.

Why would Miles do this? It went far beyond keeping up appearances.

A parting gift.

And one I wouldn't be sending back. Even if I could. The hardest thing about the move so far was the living arrangements. Sasha and her minions had the run of the other brownstone, and even in my room, I felt unwelcome. I'd get some shit for this. But it would be worth it.

"Oh!" Tammy clapped her hands. "I almost forgot!"

She went to the closet—a walk-in that looked empty with my sparse wardrobe hanging from the dowels—and retrieved a box from the shelf.

"This came for you today. I had to sign for it." She lowered her voice to a whisper. "It was insured for forty thousand bucks. From Sotheby's. In London."

Taking a step back like she was offering me a live grenade, I shook my head. "I...uh...."

"Take it," she urged and, when I did, she produced a small box cutter from the pocket of her hoodie. She smiled sheepishly when I raised a brow. "I've been waiting all day to find out what's inside."

From the look on her face, she wouldn't leave until I opened it. Taking a seat in the wing-backed chair next to the window, I proceeded to slice open the tape securing the flaps.

After digging through layers of bubble wrap and tissue, I pulled out a polished cherry wood box. It looked old. Finely crafted. An antique. With a rose inlaid on the lid fashioned from lighter woods. Birch and ash, maybe.

Tears misted my eyes as I ran my hand over the flower.

"Oh my God," Tammy breathed, ducking her head to get a better look. "It's gorgeous. Aren't you going to look inside?"

I wanted to save that for when I was alone. But Tammy didn't get the hint. And I didn't want to be rude, so I carefully lifted the lid.

There was a card on heavy stock. Some kind of authentication from Sotheby's. I handed it to my nosy house manager and then plucked the little envelope taped to one of the sides. A tiny brass key fell out.

"It's a music box," Tammy said, reading the card. "Seventy notes. Crafted in 1890." Her breath caught, and my gaze shot to hers. "For Pyotr Tchaikovsky. It was part of his private collection."

She continued to babble while I searched for a place to fit the key. What was left of my heart squeezed painfully when *Swan Lake* filled the air. I had no words. But one. *Why?*

Tammy clasped my hand, smiling. "Miles must really love you."

As if to protest the lie, the tear dancing on my lash broke free and spilled the truth onto my cheek. But I just nodded and swiped it away.

For a little while longer, I wanted to pretend.

Miles

Bringing the bottle of beer to my lips, I read the text from Gelsey for the millionth time.

One word: *Why?*

I'd received the email from the property manager with a receipt for the lease payment on Gelsey's new apartment. It had taken all my resolve to respond "no" when she'd asked if I wanted to be listed as a tenant.

I did.

Hell, I'd live in Gelsey's closet if it were an option.

But it wasn't. So fuck me.

Dropping onto the bed in the pool house with the sheets that still smelled like lavender, I stared at the screen while I tried to think up a viable response to her question.

Because I love you.

Because I need you.

Because I can't fucking think without you.

All true. But none of them appropriate.

Shaking my head, I downed the rest of my Shiner Bock. No whiskey tonight. I had an appointment tomorrow at the studio on Sixth. Taryn wanted me to consult on something. And I couldn't show up with liquor seeping from my pores. She'd have me back at Millwood before sunset.

Maybe that's what you need.

"Fuck off," I said to the voice in my head as I flopped onto my back, throwing an arm over my eyes.

God, I was tired. Surprising, since I'd slept all day. Weary. That was a better word.

Semantics.

"I said: *fuck off!*"

As if to punish me, the voice went eerily quiet. And that was worse. The only other time that had happened was right before the overdose. Hell, it was the reason for the overdose. When there was no one to talk you out of it, not even yourself, suicide didn't sound that bad.

Is that what Blake had felt when I didn't answer his calls?

Stop.

I rolled my eyes. "Easy for you to say, bro. You're already dead."

And I wondered then, if I was talking to Rhenn, or to the part of me that had downed the pills. Was he still lurking inside with dark thoughts and darker intentions?

I shuddered, then forced myself upright, my phone falling to the floor with a thud.

I still needed to respond to Gelsey. Or did I? If I just ignored her, she'd go away. Pride. The girl had it in spades. She wouldn't message me again.

With a sigh, I reached down to grab my phone. I wasn't ready to break our tenuous connection just yet.

Pathetic.

Ignoring the jab, I patted the hardwood, but came up with nothing. Maybe that was the universe's way of saying I shouldn't drunk text.

Fuck the universe.

Sliding to the floor, I ducked my head and peered around under the bed. I spotted my phone, but also a small black notebook. Tattered. Gelsey's book of poems.

I don't keep a diary. I'm not that interesting. Just this.

Recalling her smile and the look in her eyes when she'd shown me the little book, I ran my fingers over the handwritten G on the cover, right under the sketch of the ballerina. And I laughed. Gelsey had said she had no talent beyond dancing, but the drawing was beautiful. Simple but elegant. Like her.

After crawling back onto the bed, I rested against the lavender-scented pillow and opened the book. Thumbing to the first page, I glanced at the date in the corner. August, 2013.

Each day when I look in the mirror
I fight the ghost inside the glass
Dressed in pink
She wears my smile
And it isn't her whispered lies I fear
But her veiled truth
"You're not good enough, and you never will be"

Tossing the book aside, I scrubbed a hand over my face and tried to erase the mental picture of a sixteen-year-old Gelsey, alone in a shitty apartment.

At least I'd changed that much for her. Her room in the brownstone was everything. Top-end furnishings. A six-thousand-dollar mattress. And the music box.

But she's still alone.

"For now."

Flipping onto my stomach, I buried my nose in the pillow. And like the fucking masochist I was, I reached for the notebook again.

This time, I flipped to the end. The final entry, dated the last night Gelsey was here.

Lightning on my skin
Thunder in my soul
Heavy on my heart
You were my perfect storm

And she was mine.

Chapter Sixty-One

Miles

I HAD IT COMING, SO I TRIED NOT TO WINCE AS TARYN READ ME THE RIOT act in her office at the studio. "Don't even try to tell me you're not hung over," she accused as she paced in a tight circle behind me.

I spun my chair around and shrugged into my cup of coffee, which seemed to enrage her even more.

She tossed me a withering glare, and my balls shrank up, making a valiant attempt to crawl back inside my body.

"I had a few beers last night," I finally said when it was apparent she wouldn't let it go. "I'm dealing with some shit, okay? Not a big deal. I'm ready to work."

Taryn eased onto the couch, stunned by my admission. And I got it. A few years ago, I was all about the denial. But not now.

"Is it Gelsey?" Tipping forward, she tried to catch my eyes, which were currently glued to the contents of my coffee cup. "Or Blake?"

I met her gaze with a heavy sigh. "Both," I admitted in a solemn tone. "I'm trying to get a handle on things, T-Rex. But I don't know if I ever will."

Fear ravaged her features. Pure and unadulterated. She wanted an assurance. Something she could tuck away that proved I was all better. Like one of those chips her boyfriend carried from Narcotics Anonymous.

Thirty days clean. One year clean. A hundred years clean.

But I'd never be clean. Because what I had was in my mind. My broken, damaged, splintered soul. Passed down from my father.

"Have you talked to Dr. Sheppard?"

Did begging for more anti-depressants count? Probably not. "No."

She was out of her seat in a flash, determination replacing the fear when she looked down at me. "You have to. You can't just give up."

Anger seeped from the hollow place in my chest, spreading to my limbs. "Does it look like I'm giving up? I'm here, aren't I?"

Crouching so we were almost at eye level, she took my hands. "You're here because I'm safe. I'll never walk away from you. Tori will never walk away from you. Blake? He idolizes you. But Gelsey...you're afraid of her. What she's going to do if you tell her the truth."

I shook my head, a chuckle bubbling from my lips. Bitter and ironic. "I'm not afraid of what she's going to do, Taryn. I already know. She'll stick."

Confusion darkened her already stormy blue eyes. "Then why?"

"Do you remember what it was like to find me on the bathroom floor?" She flinched as if I'd slapped her, then nodded jerkily. "Would you ever wish that on anyone else?" Her lips parted, but I squeezed her fingers before she could speak. "Don't. You can't tell me it won't happen again when even I don't know that."

"But...your meds."

She looked so lost, blinking up at me for answers. I had them, but not the ones she wanted to hear.

"What if they stop working?"

"They won't." The determination in her voice was so convincing, I almost believed it myself.

"I'm sure Blake thought the same thing. And look at how that turned out."

"You're not him."

Easing back, I kept our fingers twined. "No. I'm not. But I can't risk it. I love her so much, Taryn. So fucking much. More than..."

I didn't mean to say it. Or even think it. But it was true. I'd loved Paige with all my heart. But what I felt for Gelsey was different. *More.* She wasn't just the sun. She was the whole sky.

Taryn blinked at me, her shoulders curving inward the way they always did when she thought of Paige. It was her tell. Like she had to protect herself from the memories. The loss and the pain.

She swallowed hard and took a shuddering breath. "Even more reason you should talk to Sheppard. *Please.* Just talk to him."

Suddenly we were back in that room at Breckenridge Hospital. She'd saved me then by begging me to save myself. I'd done it. But she'd paid the freight when I'd pushed her away. So I owed her now. One final gesture and we'd be even.

I let my head fall back. "All right, Taryn. You win. I'll talk to him."

She rested her cheek on my knee, and my hand found her sable locks.

"When?" she asked softly.

Always pushing, this girl. I wish I had half her strength. And a fraction of her belief.

"Soon."

Chapter Sixty-Two

Gelsey

I PULLED MY FEET FROM THE BUCKET OF ICE AND PATTED THEM DRY WITH a soft towel. Calluses had begun to form in a couple of spots since I hadn't had a pedicure in three weeks. A few of the dancers had a salon they went to in the city, but I'd put off making an appointment. I was still pondering the idea of getting a tech to come to the brownstone. It was one of the extras I was afforded, thanks to Miles. An add-on.

He'd given me everything on the list. And according to Tammy, he'd pre-paid, in case I got it in my head that I wanted to decline any of the services.

I hadn't gotten up the courage to ask how much it cost. Thousands, I would imagine.

And after the appearance I'd made at the Plaza, I now had donors coming out of my ears, filling my bank account with more money than I could spend.

I'd set up a meeting with Tatiana to discuss spreading the wealth to some of the other apprentices. She wasn't pleased.

"Reeks of communism," was her observation when I'd brought up the plan.

I didn't see it that way, though. The only reason my coffers were so full was because I was Katya's daughter. A shiny new penny for the patrons to pin their hopes on.

For years, Ivan had shielded me. What I thought was indifference was really protection.

But now, there was so much riding on my first performance. I felt it—the heavy blanket of expectation—every time I set foot on the dance floor.

Jerking my head up when I heard a rap on the door, I quickly covered my feet with the towel.

"Come in!"

Expecting to find Mira with my dinner, I blinked in surprise when Kieran strolled in with my tray. His gaze coasted over the pumice stone, cuticle scissors, and other tools of the trade.

"Don't you have someone who takes care of all that?" he said, sliding my dinner onto the table between the two chairs by the window. "A princess like you?"

I hobbled to my feet. "I'm not a princess," I called over my shoulder on the way to the bathroom to wash my hands.

Glancing over the French milled soap and two-hundred-and-seventy-five-dollar bottle of Le Mer moisturizer on my sink, I scowled. The upscale toiletries had shown up in a gift basket a couple of days ago.

Another gift from Miles, I assumed. But there was no card. And since he'd never responded to my first text, I didn't bother to send another. The man had more money than God. But all I'd ever wanted was his heart.

I took a seat across from Kieran, who was digging into his own prepared meal. He snickered when I peeled the foil off my plate.

"You're right. You're not a princess." He waved his fork over my pan seared ahi tuna, fingerling potatoes, and broccolini. "Because that's a meal fit for a queen."

I looked at my food. "It was on the list," I said quietly.

"I'm sure it is. But you do know that *your* list is a different list than the rest of ours." Chuckling, he reached across and snagged a fingerling potato. He groaned loudly as he chewed, his eyes rolling back in his head.

Sipping from my bottle of mineral water, I waited for the last shudders of his foodgasm to subside. "What do you mean?"

Incredulity painted his features. "You don't know?" I shook my head. "The items on your 'list,'" he used air quotes around the word, "are comprised from the best restaurants in town. Whatever you're doing to make your boyfriend jump through those kind of hoops, you better keep it up."

He speared a piece of my broccolini while I did my best to melt into my chair.

"I left," I blurted, tossing my linen napkin over the plate.

His brows drew together. "Come again?"

Fighting the burn in my throat, I lifted my chin. "I left. That's what I did. Miles and I aren't together anymore."

Easing back, he studied me intently before looking around the room. "If all this is any indication, he really wants you back."

Pain lanced through me as I stared out the window. In the distance, the lights of the city cast a yellow halo over the skyline. "Not likely, since he was the one who broke up with me."

I jumped when Kieran's foot nudged mine under the table. Expecting to find pity, I swallowed hard when I noticed the heat in his hazel eyes. His hand covered mine, full lips tilting into a seductive smile.

"Does that mean you're available? Because I'd really like to take you out sometime."

Later that night, I snuggled under my comforter with my phone, gazing at my last text to Miles.

Why?

Maybe he couldn't bring himself to answer because he felt guilty for not loving me. And all the gifts were a way to make up for it. It's not like money meant anything to him.

But maybe friendship did.

I'd lost enough people in my life. And so had he. If we started talking again, even sporadically, maybe then he'd see that he didn't owe me anything. And we could be friends. My heart would heal, and I could move on. Maybe even with Kieran. Not anytime soon. But someday.

Blowing out a breath, I opened my camera app and snapped a picture of the skyline in the distance. He couldn't see Central Park. But it was there. Along with the memories of our perfect day.

Before I could think better of it, I hit the send button.

And then, as I'd done every other night since the music box had arrived, I opened the lid and let Tchaikovsky lull me to sleep.

Chapter Sixty-Three

Miles

FOLLOWED SHEPPARD TO HIS OFFICE AFTER GROUP. HE DIDN'T SEEM surprised when I said I wanted to talk.

Maybe Taryn had called him. She couldn't get any information, but she might tell him about her concerns.

"Have a seat," the doc said. But instead of motioning in front of his desk where I usually sat during my med check, he tipped his chin to the couch.

"Really?" I muttered when he punctuated the request by dropping into the matching chair.

"I just thought we'd be more comfortable over here."

He shot me a smile as he picked up his notebook.

"Do people really fall for this cliché bullshit?" I grumbled, easing onto the cushion. "I'm warning you right now—you tell me to lie down and I'm outta here."

Chuckling, he shook his head. "You can do whatever you'd like Miles. It's your session."

I dug my fingers into the muscle on my leg, which, coincidentally, had started to throb the moment I'd sat down. "Don't you think we're going backward? I haven't had a fucking *session* since the day I got sprung from this place."

He held his hands out and looked around. "Yet, here you are. Returning to the fold."

"Are you making a joke?" The goofy smile told me he was, but I had to be sure. Because this shit wasn't funny.

He shrugged. "Just trying to lighten the mood."

I searched his face. "Seriously, man. You're freaking me out."

He jotted something down on his notepad. "Why?"

"Why what?"

"Why does my good mood 'freak you out'?"

"First off," I tipped forward, "air quotes are for douches. Second, I think the reason you didn't prescribe me any more pills is that you're saving them all for yourself. Either that or you just smoked a joint."

Amused, he fished around in the bowl on the table for some M&M's. "Do you realize that you've never come here without an agenda? Med checks or mandatory monthly sessions. That's the only time you ever come around."

Irritated, I waved off the candy when he offered me the dish. "So what?"

"Well," he drawled. "You said you wanted to *talk*. I've never heard those words from you before. As your doctor of over five years, that pleases me." He caught my gaze and held it. "Tell me. What do you want to talk about, Miles?"

As I searched for an answer, my blood pumping so hard I could feel the rhythm in my toes, I absently typed the passcode into my phone resting on my knee. Glancing down at the screen saver, a photo Gelsey had sent two days ago of our bench in Central Park, my stomach unwound.

"I'm afraid."

Sheppard nodded, canting his head like he wanted me to elaborate. So I did.

"I don't want to be afraid anymore."

I hated the plea in my voice. Why was I even here? This was never going to work. I'd always been uptight. High-strung. Waiting for the world to end.

Just relax, bro.

That's what Rhenn used to say. Always with that knowing look. Like he could read me.

"Do you know what you're afraid of?" Sheppard asked, pulling me back into the conversation.

"No."

He scribbled something in his notebook. "Are you afraid of dying?"

"No."

His eyes shot to mine. Wrong answer, I guess.

"So death doesn't scare you?"

I shrugged. "Not really."

He tossed his notes on the table, along with his pen. Guess that was that.

After a moment, he leaned forward, bracing his elbows on his knees. "I need to ask some questions, Miles. And I need honest answers."

My throat tightened. "Okay."

"Do you ever think about suicide?"

Was he fucking serious? Welding my back teeth together, I focused on the window behind his desk.

"Yeah," I finally replied.

Sheppard didn't react. But why would he? After all these years he could probably smell the crazy on me.

Relaxing a bit, because I had nothing to lose, I smirked. "Not surprised?"

His lips curved. "That's what you call a 'baseline question,'" he explained. "Like asking if you've got brown hair. Or if you live in Austin. Basically, it lets me know if you're telling me the truth."

I pinched the bridge of my nose. "So, you ask all the nutcases that question? Good to know."

He took a deep breath and let it out slowly while he shook his head. "I could ask anyone that question, and if they said 'no' they'd probably be lying."

Dubious, I lifted a brow. "Whatever you say."

Dipping into his stash of chocolate again, he popped a piece in his mouth and chewed slowly.

"Do you think about killing yourself, Miles?"

I blinked at him. One beat. Two. Ten. Then I thought about it. Really thought about it. And I felt like I was free falling.

"No."

It was the truth. And that was what surprised me the most.

Sheppard's shoulders relaxed, and he eased back in his chair.

"Thinking about suicide, especially given Blake's recent attempt, is not surprising. It's when you internalize those thoughts, when they become ideations specifically related to yourself, that you have to worry."

I buried my head in my hands, my ears ringing as I tried to process what he'd said.

"Then what's my problem?"

Sheppard nudged the candy dish toward me, and when I relented, snagging a couple pieces from the bowl, he picked up his notepad and pen from the table.

"That's what we're here to find out."

Chapter Sixty-Four

Miles

M Y PHONE BUZZED WHILE BLAKE AND I WERE EATING LUNCH ON THE BACK lawn at Millwood.

Swiping my finger over the screen, I smiled at the photo of a crack in the sidewalk, Gelsey's pink Converse peeking from the bottom of the frame.

Flipping to my camera app, I eased onto my back on the lush bed of St. Augustine grass and snapped a picture of the sky.

"And they say I'm crazy." Blake snorted as he reached for his Dr. Pepper. "At least I don't take pictures of nothing."

I propped up on my elbow. "Not nothing."

Every day, Gelsey sent me photographs. Her pointe shoes. The fountain at Lincoln Center as the sun was rising. Times Square at night.

The pictures were a chronicle of her life in New York. And for every image she sent, I returned one of the sky. Wherever I happened to be when I got her message, I walked outside and turned the camera to the heavens.

We hadn't progressed to actual words. And that was fine. I did enough talking to Sheppard and in group therapy.

For now, I was content to save all my thoughts for the day I'd see her in the flesh. Hoping that maybe it would be enough. But prepared if it wasn't. She could very well tell me that friendship was all she had to give.

Not that I'd leave it at that. Some things were worth fighting for. Even if it took months. Or years.

Gelsey Howard was one of them.

After sending the photo, I sat up and grabbed what was left of my burger.

"How are things going with your parents?" I asked Blake as I polished off the last bite.

His nose wrinkled. But there was no scowl. Progress. "Okay."

"Just okay?"

His eyes unfocused. Whatever he was picturing, it wasn't part of this landscape. And when he answered his tone was flat. Faraway. "I killed their son. So, you know, as good as can be expected, I guess."

I inhaled a sharp breath, gaze drawn to the maze of scars on his flesh. Not the ones on his wrists. But the others that trailed up his arms. He'd carved his pain on his skin for years so the outside would match the inside.

It took his parents a long time to acknowledge the wounds. Not because they didn't see them. But denial was a complicated thing.

"You're their son too."

Blake nodded, lips pressed together to keep the self-recrimination from spilling out.

After a long moment, he cleared his throat and looked over at me. "So you're leaving, huh?"

Guilt lanced through me. I took it in, then let it go. "I have a plane, dude. So I'll be back once a week."

I stopped short of telling Blake it was so I could check on him. While that was partly true, he wasn't ready to hear it. He'd filled all his empty spaces with self-loathing. Love wasn't something he could abide. Yet. But like Gelsey, he was worth fighting for. So I wouldn't give up.

"What makes you think things are going to be better there?" he asked, picking at a few blades of grass and releasing them on the wind.

"I didn't say they'd be better."

"Then why?"

I shifted, and the skin on my ribs where my new tattoo resided burned from the effort. "Because it's time."

Chapter Sixty-Five

Gelsey

"What's so interesting?" Kieran asked, his palm sliding to my hip as he peered over my shoulder at the phone in my hand.

My body went rigid as he inched a little closer, his chest molding to my back. Not that I minded the contact. I was a touchy-feely girl. But it was the intent behind it. Kieran had a thing for me. He'd been angling for a date ever since I told him that Miles and I were over.

But I wasn't ready to start anything up. And I didn't want him to think I was leading him on.

Peering up at him, I forced cheer into my tone. "Nothing."

At least that much was true. Miles hadn't responded to my last picture message. Normally, I sent him scenery. But tonight, it was a full-length shot of me in front of the mirror, dressed in my costume for the performance.

I guess I'd overstepped. Lesson learned.

Tomorrow or the next day I'd go back to sending him images of the city. Maybe. I really needed to wean myself off of my Miles addiction.

Plastering on a smile, I turned to face Kieran, trying not to make it too obvious when I brushed his hand away.

"You look beautiful, Gels."

Don't ask. Don't ask. Don't ask.

"How about you and I go out for a drink after the show? To celebrate."

My gaze coasted over his handsome face. Kieran was perfect for me. We shared the same interests. He understood dancing, and the hours I spent at rehearsal. We even ate the same foods. But he wasn't Miles.

"We'll see."

His eyes lit up, and guilt flooded me.

"I told you I wasn't ready for anything serious," I added, shifting my feet. "But, maybe…"

He pressed a finger to my lips. "That's okay. I can wait." He leaned in and I could smell his aftershave. "You're worth the wait."

Right words. Wrong man.

I took a step back, and his smile evaporated.

"I'll let you finish getting ready," he said in a slightly broody tone.

He couldn't pull it off. Because there was no darkness in Kieran. He was all light, and very little shadow. Unlike Miles.

Catching his arm as he turned to leave, I blurted, "Do you like the Beatles?"

His lip curled and, seeing my reaction, he tried for a smile. It was forced, though. Fake. "They're a little before my time."

I nodded, letting my hand fall to my side. "Yeah. I guess. See you after the show."

Spinning for the dressing room, I dodged dancers and a few patrons who'd bought their way backstage with large donations.

My phone buzzed, and I skidded to a stop in the crowded hallway.

Miles.

Tucking into a quiet corner, I swiped my finger over the screen. My stomach dropped to my toes as I read the message from the unknown number.

Thinking about you on your big night. Your mama would be proud. Love, Dad.

A million responses floated up. I was still pondering, my thumbs hovering over the keyboard, when a familiar voice caught my attention.

Lifting my watery gaze, I spotted Ivan a few yards away, talking to Simon. My heart swelled when he threw his head back and laughed.

This was his night as much as mine. Without him, I wouldn't be here.

As if he could sense me watching, Ivan looked around and, spying me in the shadows, he held out his hand. "Come," he mouthed, lips curved in a wide smile.

Nodding, I held up a finger, then dashed off a quick reply to my father.

Thank you.

It was all I could spare and more than he deserved. I pressed send and then lingered a moment, waiting for a response.

When none came, I pinned on a smile and glided to the man who'd raised me.

Ivan pulled me to his side and pressed a kiss to the top of my head. "Are you nervous, *dorogaya moya?*"

I beamed up at him. "Why would I be nervous? You're here."

Miles

The usher led me to my box seat in the performance hall at the last possible moment. In order to escape detection, I'd loitered in the lobby, tucked behind a potted plant and shielded by my bodyguard until the lights flickered, indicating the ballet was about to begin.

If the ball gowns, evening gloves, and expensive jewelry were any indication, I didn't have to worry about being recognized. I did get a couple of curious glances on my way in.

Probably because of the suit. All black. Including the button-down shirt. It looked like I was going to a funeral. And maybe I was. It all depended on Gelsey.

My bodyguard for the evening—a rent-a-cop I'd hired at the last minute—took his post in front of the curtain. Taryn had squawked up a storm when she'd found out I was in New York without a member of her security team. I wasn't planning on telling her at all, but apparently, the ballet was more popular than I'd anticipated, with every ticket sold out.

I couldn't exactly go nosing around for myself, unless I wanted people to know I was in town.

Which, I didn't.

Sliding the usher—a kid in his early twenties—a hundred dollar tip when we shook hands, I whispered, "Do you know who I am?"

He swallowed hard, bobbing his head. "Miles Cooper."

Hooking an arm around his shoulder, I leaned in close. "There's an extra two hundred in it for you if you *don't* text any of your friends and tell them I'm here."

Damage control. All I needed was a mob to show up in front of Lincoln Center before the ballet ended.

"You don't have to pay me. But…can I get a picture?"

After a quick inspection of the darkened hallway to make sure no one was around, I nodded. "Let's make it quick."

I smiled for a couple of selfies with the kid before reiterating my request for privacy.

"Not a soul," he vowed with a huge smile as he held open the curtain.

I ducked inside, my feet growing roots when I noticed the large figure occupying one of the four seats. I was about to back out when the giant looked over his shoulder at me.

"About time," Daryl drawled, glancing me over with a smirk. "The show is about to start."

We hadn't seen each other since the day Gelsey had picked up her stuff at my house. As soon as she was gone, he'd left too. And he'd never come back.

Shaking my head, I dropped into the seat beside him. "Fancy meeting you here."

He grunted. "Not here for you. I'm here for Gelsey."

A lump formed in my throat as I pulled out my phone and pointed it to the ceiling.

"Me too, brother. Me too."

Nerves had my leg bouncing as I waited through five different acts to see the only dancer I cared about. According to the program, Gelsey was to perform a short piece entitled *Emerald*, from Balanchine's *Jewels* ballet.

Butterflies exploded in my stomach when a pale green spotlight engulfed the stage.

Daryl leaned forward in his seat. The first spark of interest he'd shown all night.

And then, she was there. So still, like an angel, with her gaze cast to the heavens.

Soft, romantic music drifted from the orchestra pit, lifting her to her toes, and I held my breath. Or...maybe she'd stolen all the air. Captured it, and let it carry her across the stage, as if she weighed nothing at all.

Breathe, you idiot.

I did, but only so I wouldn't have to stop watching.

The tempo changed, and she soared like a bird, her feet barely skimming the ground as she floated from one move to the next.

To my eyes, Gelsey was flawless. But it was more than that. She *became* the music.

That was her gift. Not a perfect arabesque, or even the extraordinary strength she needed to be able to do all of this with a broken back.

Frozen in time, I remained transfixed as she commanded the stage.

The final notes swelled to a crescendo, then tapered away, leaving her alone with the green spotlight trained on her perfectly still form.

Thunderous applause filled the theater, and before Gelsey took her curtsey, the joy in her eyes shone brighter than the sun.

My sun. In my sky.

Forever.

Chapter Sixty-Six

Gelsey

ASHA TOOK ONE LOOK AT ME WHEN I SLIPPED FROM THE RESTROOM AND burst out laughing. I glanced down at my skinny jeans and silk blouse, then back to her shimmery gold mini dress that barely covered her ass.

Spinning for the mirror, she proceeded to apply another coat of red lipstick. Not that she needed it. "You were not invited to any of the after-parties?" she gloated.

I was. All of them, in fact. But even though I'd just danced the performance of my life, I was still a little sad. Miles wasn't here. And that cut my joy in half.

Eventually, the ache would subside. I'd survived the loss of my mother. The abandonment of my father. But right now, there was a hole in my heart that no amount of applause could fill.

Answering Sasha's question with a little shrug, I took a seat in front of the lighted mirror where all her cosmetics were laid out. Pausing with the lipstick an inch from her pouty lips, she glared at me for having the temerity to sit next to her. Even though I'd left a stool between us.

Foolishly, I thought after tonight, I'd earn her respect. Because I understood Sasha. And I knew how fragile the mind of a dancer was. Regardless of the hard shell, doubt and fear and lies whispered louder than applause.

She'd been cast as the ruby to my emerald in tonight's performance. Both of us with solos. Simon had misstepped by making us equals. Upped the ante on our rivalry.

Maybe he thought it would bring out the best in us. And who knows? If I were in Sasha's shoes, I might react the same way. Doubtful. Since I had a soul and she was a hell hound with pretty bones, good hair, and a beguiling smile.

Sasha dropped her lipstick tube and straightened her spine. "You may have stolen that piece from my sister tonight." She smoothed a hand over the shiny fabric on her dress. "But know this—" Cold blue eyes met mine in the mirror. "It takes more than minor talent to make it in this city. Personality. Je ne sais quoi." She flipped her wrist as if to dismiss me. Not just my presence. My entire being. "You have none of those things. You are merely trading on the name and resemblance of your dead mother."

That was it. I was done. Fire leaped from the pit of my stomach, my fingers clenching in my lap to keep from jumping up and wringing her pretty neck. "Don't you ever, *ever* speak about my mother. Or I will end you, Sasha. I'm not kidding."

Her eyes twinkled. But before she could say a word, someone cleared their throat from the doorway.

In tandem, our heads whipped in that direction.

Ivan was there, leaning against the frame, frozen arctic ponds leveled on Sasha. The temperature dropped by ten degrees, and I swear I saw her shiver.

"Still a spoiled child," he mused, then inhaled deeply, shaking his head. "I saw it in you from the first day." He stepped inside, still a good distance away, but Sasha backed up as if pushed by an invisible hand. "Your sister?" he shrugged. "There was still hope for her. But in the end, you corrupted her too."

Sasha's throat bobbed, the blood draining from her face, but when she opened her mouth, nothing came out.

Ivan laughed. "You have nothing to say? A pity. *Vy talantlivy s chernym serdtsem, i poetomu ne stoit moyego vremeni. Togda ili seychas.*"

I winced, and Sasha's gaze shot to mine. I had understood every word. And somehow that made it worse.

You are talented with a black heart, and therefore not worth my time. Then or now.

"Do not look at her," Ivan snapped, his tone low and lethal, as serious as I'd ever heard. "She is not here for you to ridicule. She is here to dance. And if I find out that you are speaking ill to her, I will have this same talk with Simon." His smile was cold enough to cause frostbite. "*Vy ponimayete?*"

He waited for her jerky nod to shift his attention to me. "I will meet you outside by the fountain, *dorogaya moya*. We are having dinner with Tatiana to discuss your future."

He threw that last part in to drive his point home. He had power here.

No, Ivan was not a part of this company. But he could've been. He could've been anything. Instead, he moved to Texas. Out of love for a woman he'd never have. And he stayed there because of me.

My throat burned as I swallowed tears of gratitude. And love. But all I could manage was a nod.

Once he was gone, I met Sasha's gaze in the mirror. Her eyes skittered away, fear replacing all her bravado.

It is better to show mercy than to gloat when you have the upper hand.

Ivan had taught me that too.

"I'm not going anywhere, Sasha. So you'd better get used to it." She nodded as she stuffed her cosmetics in the bag, her hand going still as I scooted closer. "But we don't have to be enemies. We don't have to be friends either. We can simply *be. Peredyshka?*"

It was too soon for me to offer her a hand. She might bite it off.

After a moment of contemplation, she lifted her chin. Still proud and fierce.

"Truce."

Smiling, I pushed to my feet and applied a light coat of lip gloss before heading out the door.

Ivan and Tatiana were waiting by the fountain when I arrived. They didn't notice me at first, their heads together. He wore a smile I'd never seen, and she was practically glowing. My gaze fell to their joined hands, and a little twinge of something pinched in my chest.

Not jealousy. Well, maybe a little. Ivan was the only father figure I'd ever had. And I didn't want anyone taking him away from me. But seeing him like this—relaxed and smiling—brought more joy than any-thing else. In all these years, Ivan had never dated. And I desperately wanted him to find happiness.

Selfishly, I also knew if he were seeing Tatiana, he'd probably spend more time in New York.

Separating as soon as they spotted me, their hands fell to their sides.

Tatiana, who'd never projected anything but total confidence, looked down at her shoes. Was she blushing?

"Hey," I said, stepping into their little half circle.

"'Hay' is for horses, *dorogaya moya*," Ivan said, his tone playful. "Did you escape Sasha's clutches unscathed?"

Tatiana's head snapped up, her gaze clouding with apprehension

"We've come to an understanding." I smiled. "A *peredyshka*." Ivan pressed his lips in a thin line. He may have preached discretion, but he abhorred weakness. It was a fine line with him.

"She's going to leave me alone," I clarified, my tone jovial. "And I'll do the same. No bloodshed."

Tatiana's shoulders curved in what I could only describe as relief.

After an awkward moment of silence, I faked a yawn.

"I'm really tired," I said with a weary smile. "Do y'all mind if I take a rain check on dinner."

Disappointment flashed over Ivan's features. But it didn't linger. "Are you sure?" he asked.

"Positive. It's been a long night."

Ivan nodded, pulling me in for a hug. Over his shoulder, Tatiana smiled at me and I smiled back.

"I am so proud of you," he whispered, running a hand over my hair, now free from the bun and hanging to my waist.

Closing my eyes, I melted against him. "I love you, Ivan."

We rarely spoke those words to each other. It was a line we didn't often cross. Teacher. Student. Parent. Child. Our roles were ever changing.

"I love you, too," he whispered back with no hesitation.

And a little piece of my broken heart mended right there on the spot.

I ducked inside the Town Car and flopped onto the seat, exhausted. But happy. Mostly. I'd managed to push Miles to the back of my head for the majority of the evening. I thought his absence might tarnish my triumph, but it hadn't. Strangely enough, I'd felt him with me in every pirouette and arabesque. The piece of him I still carried in my heart.

The partition slid down, and Lenny twisted to offer me a smile. "Congratulations, Ms. Gelsey."

I smiled back. "Just Gelsey. And thank you."

"Where to? One of those after-parties in mid-town? Or—?"

"The brownstone."

His lips fell into a frown. Great. Now I was getting pity from the man getting paid to guard me from no one. He must've been bored to tears since I never went anywhere. Tomorrow, I'd contact Daryl and tell him to convince Miles to let this go. Nobody was following me. Or harassing me. Except Sasha.

I smiled because maybe that was over now too.

"Whatever you say, Ms., er, Gelsey," he said. "It might be a few minutes. The traffic is terrible, what with the performance tonight."

I nodded. Where did I have to be anyway? *Nowhere.*

I reached into my bag for my phone as the partition slid into place. Blinking at the screen, my heart stalled when I saw the text from Miles. A photo of the ceiling of the performance hall.

Was this some kind of joke?

With shaky fingers, I opened the app and tapped furiously on the glass to enlarge the picture.

There was no message attached. No words.

The car made a right turn, slipping into traffic, just as the phone buzzed in my hand. Another photo. This one of the sky. Leaves encroached on the corners of the frame. I'd spent enough time staring at those leaves over the past month to recognize them. Or maybe that was just wishful thinking.

The air left my body in a rush when a message flashed across the screen, along with another picture. This one left no doubt where he was.

Waiting for you.

"Stop!" I croaked, my finger jamming the button for the intercom in rapid succession.

The partition went down, and Lenny peered into the back seat, alarm etching his features. "What is it, Miss Gelsey?"

I whipped my head to the window and scanned the street, trying to figure out where we were. Sixty-Fifth Street.

"Let me out!" I said, sliding to the door. I tried the handle, but it wouldn't work. "I said: *let me out!*"

Lenny continued to pepper me with questions I didn't hear as the car coasted to a stop. The locks clicked, and I jumped out, assaulted by exhaust fumes and the sounds of the bustling city.

But none of that mattered. My only focus was the cluster of trees a block away.

Central Park. And Miles.

Chapter Sixty-Seven

Miles

Lightning crashed, illuminating a piece of sky in the distance as I waited on our bench in Central Park

Ten yards away, Daryl leaned against a tree, arms crossed over his chest, scanning the area for threats.

With the rain starting to fall lightly, people scattered like ants. Likely trying to find a place to take cover before the inevitable downpour.

Letting my head fall back, I took a deep breath. There was no smoke. No burning sky. No voices. Just the soft patter of droplets against my skin.

My phone was lifeless in my hand; no response from Gelsey to my messages.

Maybe she wasn't coming.

And that was all right.

Tomorrow, I'd visit her at the brownstone. If she wouldn't see me then, I'd wait for her by the stage door at Lincoln Center.

Stalker.

Possibly. But I wasn't going anywhere until she told me to fuck off. In words. Maybe not *those* words. But if she told me we were through, I'd let her go. It wouldn't be the end of the world. Though, it might feel like it.

Pushing the thought aside, I picked up the bouquet of paper flowers. Beautiful, but not worthless, since each of the blooms were crafted from one of Gelsey's poems. Copies. I had the originals tucked safely in my suitcase. They were hers, and I'd give them back. But for now, I'd guard her thoughts and dreams. The good ones and the bad.

I felt her before I saw her, a prickle of awareness drawing my attention to the tree-lined course. She stopped at the entrance to the memorial, the invisible boundary where the benches formed a circle.

Rain clung to her hair, the droplets shimmering like tiny diamonds under the street lamp. When it was clear she wasn't going to budge, I pushed to my feet, fist clutched tightly around the stems of her roses.

"You're here," she said when I stopped two feet in front of her.

I wanted to take her in my arms. Lick the rain from her skin. And tell her how much I'd missed her. How much I loved her. But I was getting way ahead of myself.

Friendship.

That was all she'd offered in those pictures she'd sent. But her poems told a different story.

I held out the bouquet. "Where else would I be?"

A smile ghosted her lips as she reached for the offering. "You brought me flowers."

This girl. So easy to please.

"Actually, they're poems." I inched toward her as her fingertips glided over one of the blooms.

The ink was beginning to run now, blurring the words. But that didn't matter. I knew them all by heart.

"Poems?" Her brows pinched together as she examined one of the petals. "You are my…"

When she tilted her head, turning the flower to get a better look, I placed a finger under her chin, coaxing her gaze to mine. "You are my mirror. And through your eyes, I see the me I wish I was."

Her lips parted, shock painting her features.

I smiled, thumb skating over the curve of her jaw. "It's one of my favorites. If I had to choose."

She blinked at me. "But…how?"

"I found your book of poetry in the pool house." Flinching at the clap of thunder, I let my gaze snap to the sky.

"That was close," I joked, hoping she couldn't hear the anxiety in my voice.

Sheppard was helping me work through my bullshit. But I might never be completely at ease in a storm.

Gelsey's hands framed my face, coaxing my eyes to hers, where there were no clouds. Just endless blue.

Levering up on her toes, she pressed a kiss to my lips.

"You're okay."

And for the first time since she walked out of my life, I actually believed it.

Chapter Sixty-Eight

Miles

SOAKED TO THE SKIN, WE STUMBLED INTO THE SUITE AT THE RITZ. GELSEY paused in the foyer, dripping water onto the marble floor as her gaze crawled over every inch of the room. When she came full circle and those baby blues landed on me, a smile curved her lips.

"You got the same room."

I could play it off. Tell her that every suite at the Ritz looked the same. But why bother? I was trying to win her back.

"Yep."

Fighting desperately to hide the heat creeping up my cheeks, I looked down and shook the water out of my hair.

I went solid when I felt her at my back. She wasn't touching me. But her warmth. And that scent. Lavender and rain and…her.

My carefree smile melted like cherry ice cream when I turned and she frowned up at me.

"What are you doing here, Miles?"

No easing into it with this girl. Her eyes fluttered closed of their own accord when I ran my hands from her elbows to her shoulders. Good. I still affected her. "You're cold. Why don't you jump in the shower and—"

She tilted her head. "So you want to fuck? I guess I should be flattered that you flew all this way to get me into bed."

Her bottom lip disappeared between her teeth as she waited for me to speak. But I was too stunned. Shocked stupid.

Fuck her?

Is that what she thought?

When I didn't answer, she sighed as she fiddled with the button on her blouse.

My hands closed over hers. "No." The word flew out with more force than I intended, ricocheting around the room. "That's not...I didn't..."

"Then what, Miles?"

Her voice was small. Hesitant. But those eyes. Like blue steel. Battle lines were drawn, her on one side and me on the other. Words were our weapons. And they cut deeper than any sword.

What Gelsey didn't know was that I was prepared to surrender.

This was her fight to win or lose.

"I have a lot to tell you," I said softly. "To explain. But you're shaking like a leaf. If you don't want to take a shower, at least put on a robe so you don't freeze to death."

She thought about it for a moment. "Fine."

I watched her trot to the bedroom, staring at her ass the whole time.

Yeah, I loved her. I was *in* love with her. But my body had decided it was the perfect time to show her in other ways. Lay her down and spread her legs. Taste that sweet honey between her thighs. Make her scream my name.

Not yet.

Maybe not ever. And wouldn't that be a shame?

Sheppard called it life. The human condition.

"We never know when the last time will be *the last time. Final goodbyes. A glancing touch. It's the nature of being human. And you* are *human, Miles."*

I pushed thoughts of Sheppard aside. They didn't belong in the same head space as Gelsey right now. Especially since I was picturing her peeling off her clothes one room away.

When I heard the shower, I took it as a good sign. She wasn't exactly going to run out of here in just a robe. Which meant I had a little time.

My leg bobbed as I flipped through the room service menu. Soup, that was always good when you were cold. Comforting.

What are you, her grandma?

"Fuck you," I muttered, snatching the phone to place the order.

Since I was also dripping water all over the place, I slipped into the bedroom to change into some sweats and a T-shirt.

Only I couldn't find my favorite pair. And I needed them. Since they were good luck. And luck was something I desperately wanted on my side.

Wearing just my boxers, I dumped my suitcase, sorting through my clothes like a man possessed.

I snapped my head around when Gelsey gasped.

Framed by the bathroom door, my elusive sweats hung loosely on her slim hips, held in place by the drawstring. The T-shirt was also mine, but she'd knotted it at the waist showing just a little bit of her belly.

Sexy as fuck.

But the look on her face.

"What is it, baby?" The endearment slipped out, a tiny infraction, or a strategic move. I wasn't sure. We were still at war, after all. And I was taking no prisoners.

She rushed toward me and I froze as she dropped onto her knees.

Resisting the urge to tangle my fingers in her hair and make this something it wasn't, I stayed still.

Flinching when her fingertips traveled over my ribs, I watched as she lovingly traced the ink on my side.

"It's...a ballerina..." She peered up at me. "*My* ballerina."

The one from the cover of her book of poems. I'd taken the sketch to the best artist in Austin, and he'd worked his magic, bringing the rendition to life on my skin.

Taking her by the shoulders, I lifted her up. She weighed nothing, even less than the last time I saw her.

Tinted gloss clung to her lips and mascara trailed down her cheeks. She looked wrecked. And beautiful. And mine.

"Not your ballerina, baby." I ran a hand over her tangled locks. "It's you."

Her small hand curved over the tattoo as she swayed. "Why?"

So many ways to answer that question. But the best way out was always through. At least according to Robert Frost.

I'd become quite an expert on poetry in the last month. Because I knew if I got the chance, I wanted to speak to her in sonnets. All the beautiful words that she deserved.

But these words were all mine. Spoken straight from the heart she carried in her pocket. My heart.

"Because I love you." I stole a kiss. A tiny piece of ground. "Now come sit down. There're some things I want to tell you."

Chapter Sixty-Nine

Gelsey

I watched Miles as I stirred my soup. His hands never stopped moving. Nervous fingers coasting through his hair. Tugging the frayed hem of his flannel pajama bottoms.

His eyes found mine often, but never stuck, darting to the window like there were answers written in the sky.

I wanted to help him. To crawl into his lap and comfort him. But our last conversation played on repeat in my head, keeping me rooted to my spot.

You can't fix me, Gelsey.

Oh, how I wanted to try. I believed in Miles. The man he was. And more importantly, the man he could be.

But he was right. I couldn't help him if he didn't want to be helped. It was a losing battle. Me against the bottle. My father had taught me that.

"How's Blake?" I asked, bringing the spoon to my lips.

He blinked at me, and I smiled. That look. Like he couldn't believe I was here. I knew the feeling.

"Oh…uh…fine." Clearing his throat, his hand went to the back of his neck, brows drawn together like he was struggling to form a thought. "He's getting better, I think. His parents are in the picture now. So that'll help."

I placed my bowl on the table, the heavy soup not sitting well in my nervous stomach.

"Do you want something else?" Miles hopped to his feet like he was on springs. "I can get you anything you want."

He blinked at me, chewing his lip. Waiting. Whatever I asked for, he'd give me. His eyes, sincere and stripped free of guile, told me that.

Taking his hand, I gave his arm a gentle tug. He dropped down beside me, his gaze on our entwined digits.

"What I want is the truth," I said quietly. "You owe me that."

He owed me nothing. And I was prepared for him to tell me so.

Instead, he nodded. When it became apparent he wasn't going to volunteer any information, I took a deep breath.

"Were you drinking the whole time we were together?"

His eyes shot to mine. "No. It wasn't like that. My drinking... drinking in general..."

Pressing his lips together, he shook his head, a bitter laugh rumbling low in his throat. "Fucking hell," he muttered. So defeated.

Scooting closer, I pushed the hair out of his face. Beautiful and tortured.

He leaned into my touch, and my heart squeezed, tears burning my throat. So many times over the last month, I'd replayed our moments together. Even convinced myself that I'd only imagined our connection. But this was real. We were real. And wrecked. And damaged.

Pressing my lips to his forehead, I whispered, "You can tell me, Miles."

Please tell me. I needed to know.

He blew out a shuddering breath, then eased back against the cushions, our fingers still loosely threaded.

"You might not feel the same way if I do."

Doubtful. Impossible, really.

I'd love Miles regardless of any dark truths he spilled.

But I loved myself more. So I couldn't—*wouldn't*—sit by and watch him destroy himself. It's the reason I'd left in the first place. If he wanted to drown in the bottom of a bottle, he'd have to do it alone.

"I guess we won't know until you tell me."

He swallowed hard. "I'm not an alcoholic, Gelsey. My problem isn't booze."

I tried not to scoff. Or roll my eyes. Because I'd heard it before from my father.

"So your stint in rehab?" I shrugged. "Just a way to pass the time?"

His attention strayed to the window again, and I lost my patience.

"Look, Miles—"

"I didn't go to rehab. Millwood isn't…I mean it is…" He pressed the back of his head against the cushion and closed his eyes. "Millwood is a mental health facility. They treat addiction. Bi-polar. Eating disorders… and in my case, clinical depression."

His lids fluttered open, but his gaze stayed glued to the ceiling.

"That 'episode' you read about in the tabloids? My 'accidental overdose'? Not an accident. You don't *accidentally* chase a hundred pills with a fifth of whiskey." Our eyes finally met, and he smiled. Sad. Tragic. And so beautiful. "That's called an 'on purpose.' Or a suicide attempt. Take your pick."

I blinked at him, waiting for the punchline. Because this was a joke, right? It had to be. Only I knew it wasn't. Somewhere deep inside, it all made sense.

"You tried to k-kill yourself?"

He nodded, a kind of resolve washing over his features. "Yes."

"Because of the accident. Losing Rhenn and…" Her name coiled around my tongue. But it took a moment to force out. "Paige."

I didn't realize we were still holding hands until his fingers moved north, grasping my wrist. He tugged. Not enough force to pull me on top of him. More like an invitation.

I scrambled onto his lap, and he let out a breath, his whole body relaxing.

"Not just that," he finally said, looping his arms around my waist. "I'm sure it had something to do with it. The straw that broke the camel's back. But it goes deeper than that."

Nestling closer, I drew my knees up and spoke into his neck. "How deep?"

When he didn't answer, I curved my hand around the fresh ink on his side. To remind him. I was part of him now. Under his skin. Just like his secrets.

"My dad had it too. Depression. I was about five when I figured out he wasn't like other dads. He stayed in his room a lot. Or in his office. He used to make all these pretty things."

"Like the flowers?"

He nodded, his voice a little lighter when he said, "And other things too. Birds. And animals. Anything you could think of. He sculpted. And painted. My mom told me that's the reason he was like he was. That he had an 'artistic temperament.'" He chuckled. "I thought that meant he liked to sleep a lot. Because he did that too."

I traced a finger over his heart. "Was he mean to you?"

"No. Just the opposite. He never raised his voice. When he wasn't…when things were good…he paid a lot of attention to me. He showed me how to make things. Not just origami. Kites. And things with wood. That's what he did for a living. He made furniture."

Something clicked, and my breath caught in my throat. I jerked back, blinking at him. "Furniture? Wait…Was he—?"

"Mick Cooper. I take it you've heard of him?"

I nodded, dumbfounded. Mick Cooper Creations were known throughout the world. More like art than furniture or decor. Mostly because they were so scarce. And after he'd died…

"He killed himself." Horrified, my hand flew to my mouth when I realized I'd said it aloud. "Miles…I didn't mean to…I'm so sorry…I…"

"It's okay." Smoothing a hand over my hair, he silenced my stammered apology. "It's not a secret."

"Then why didn't you ever tell me?"

"I never told anyone. Rhenn was the only one who knew." He twirled a lock of my hair around his finger, seemingly entranced by the golden strands. "My mom said people would look at me funny if they found out. That they'd think I was crazy like him."

"But…he wasn't crazy…" I propped up on my elbow, searching his face. "Was he?"

"No. Just depressed. Chemically imbalanced or whatever." He sighed. "But she was right. I was like him. I think she always knew it. I was the one who found him."

He said the last part so casually, I almost missed it.

"Wh-what?"

"That morning, he told me to come straight home after school. He was going through one of his productive periods. He'd spent all winter storing pieces for some collection…" He shook his head, frowning. "Doesn't matter. The point is, I was the only one he let into his studio. So he knew it would be me. That I'd be the one…"

A shudder wracked his body, and he threw an arm over his face.

"He left me a note. Told me he loved me. It was attached to a print-out of all the inventory in the storage unit. Neat little rows of prices and names of people to contact to sell off his life's work."

"What did you do?"

Peeking at me from under his arm, he shrugged. "What I was told. I called everyone on the list and sold everything. Then I crawled into bed and didn't get up for about a month. It was the first time I'd ever thought about killing myself."

He rolled onto his side and took me along with him. We were face-to-face now, and I cupped his cheek. He smiled. Odd considering his confession.

"What stopped you?"

"My mom found out I was ditching school. It was easier to go than listen to her bitch. People grieve in their own ways, I guess. My mom was just...pissed. Anyway, a friend of mine had decided he wanted to start a band. I was the only person he knew with a drum kit. So he asked me to join."

A tear leaked out of the corner of his eye and rolled down his cheek.

I kissed the droplet away. "Rhenn?"

"And Paige. Tori. It's not that they cured me. That's not how it works. But I had music and my friends. And then the fame. Fans. I was happy. I really was."

"And then..."

"It ended. I don't remember much about the time right after the accident. I just know I wanted everything to stop. It wasn't until the overdose that they diagnosed me with depression." He laughed. "I thought it was bullshit. But the pills worked. Took the edge off. I stopped thinking about killing myself, and just got on with it. The life I had left. I wasn't happy. Or sad. I just...*was*."

"What about your mom?"

His eyes rolled to the ceiling, a bitter chuckle parting his lips. "My mom told me I was weak like my father. And that she couldn't handle going through it again. She didn't want to be around when I finally fulfilled my destiny."

I struggled to sit up so I could look into his eyes. "You're joking?"

"Nope."

"What did you do?"

"Bought her a house in Florida." He shrugged like it was no big deal. "Now she pretends like I don't exist. And I pretend not to care. She leaves me alone as long as the checks keep rolling in. I pay for everything. Her shiny new life. But I've only seen her twice since I was released from Millwood."

Miles held tight to my waist as I struggled to get to my feet, possibly to find the woman's phone number so I could call her and tell her exactly what I thought of her.

"Easy, killer," he said, settling me on top of him like I weighed nothing. "I only told you so you'd understand."

"Understand what?" I spat. "That your mother's a heartless bitch?"

I pressed my lips together, fearing I'd overstepped. Miles just laughed. When he got himself under control, he said, "The reason I didn't tell you, or anyone else, is that I believed it. I really thought that someday I might wake up and just…end it."

"And you don't think that anymore?"

He pulled me flush against him, so close I could hear his heartbeat and feel his breath. If I had a safe place, this was it. And nothing he'd told me would change that.

"I can't guarantee that the clouds won't come for me again," he said solemnly. "You don't *cure* depression. But it's not a death sentence." He kissed the top of my head. "I don't want to die, baby. I want to live. The choice is mine. I'm stable. I was just afraid. That's why I pushed you away."

"Afraid of what?"

"Feeling. I haven't felt anything in years. Sheppard—that's my doctor—he said that was the clearest indication that I was in remission. If I was afraid to feel it meant that I had something to lose."

Fear gripped me. I loved Miles. But I couldn't be anyone's reason for living.

"Me?" I croaked.

He tipped my chin with his finger and looked deep in my eyes. "No, baby. *Me*."

Miles

I stood in front of the window facing the park and looked out at the city. Even at four in the morning, people strolled the sidewalks, darting in and out of the taxis idling at the curb.

Could I really live here?

My gaze found Gelsey's reflection in the glass. Curled on her side on the king-size bed, she hugged her pillow, still wearing my sweats and over-sized T-shirt. Moonbeams shimmered over flaxen locks fanning the pillow like a river of spun gold.

Yeah, I could live here. Or anywhere, as long as Gelsey was with me. Home wasn't a place on the map.

Not anymore.

Home was lavender-scented linen and blue eyes and promise. And joy. So much joy.

In the living room, I dug the poem from my backpack. Not one of Gelsey's. This one was mine. Amateur at best. But she'd never read it. Maybe someday. But for now she'd tuck it away with the rest of my creations, unaware of the declaration hidden between the creases.

And on my journey from here to there
I learned that happiness is more than not being sad
It is a smile in the dark when no one can see
A glow from the inside in the absence of light
And a voice above the chaos that speaks of a promise yet to be revealed
You are my dark and my light
My sun from another sky
My everything

I let my mind wander as my fingers worked the folds. Back to a place I rarely visited.

You can make anything beautiful, Miles. Even scraps of paper people throw away.

My father's voice guided me as the flower took shape. It didn't have a name, this bloom. It only existed in his mind. And mine.

I finished right as the sky turned from inky black to gunmetal gray.

Tiptoeing back into the bedroom, I placed the offering on Gelsey's nightstand, jerking when her fingertips grazed the ink on my ribs.

"Morning, baby," I said.

She gave me a sleepy smile and made room. So I eased down beside her. Face-to-face.

"What time is it?" she whispered, tucking a strand of hair behind my ear.

"Early."

Her leg slotted mine as she scooted closer, her hand cupping the back of my neck. "Sorry I fell asleep last night. Before...you know..."

She pressed a kiss to my mouth, her lips curving when my tongue darted out.

"Let me brush my teeth," she said, tipping away. I shook my head. "But...morning breath."

"It's not morning yet." I rolled her onto her back, and she stopped squirming, a little moan escaping when my hand slipped under her shirt.

Her legs wrapped around me as I toyed with her nipple, the taut peak now standing at attention.

"You want me, baby?" I asked, lightly pinching the hard nub between my thumb and forefinger.

"Always."

I rose to my knees and slid the loose fitting sweatpants over her hips. No panties.

Fuck.

My cock, already rock-hard and ready, threatened to punch a hole in the thin flannel of my pajama pants as my eyes skimmed over her milky skin.

"No," she rasped, grabbing my arm when I settled her leg over my shoulder and dipped to press a kiss to her belly. "I want you inside me."

I smiled as I moved lower. "Are you sure?"

She blinked at me, suddenly serious. "Yes."

Confused by the sudden change, I eased on top of her, touching my forehead to hers. "What's wrong, baby?"

"Nothing. I just want…I want you to love me. Like this."

Love her. Not fuck her. Didn't she understand that I'd stopped fucking her long ago? This—*us*—we were more than tangled limbs. More than pleasure. We were magic.

"I do, little mouse. I will."

Small hands framed my face as I slipped deep inside her warmth.

Locked in her gaze, I began to move. Slowly. Because I wanted this to last.

I kissed my way to that spot on her neck where I'd whispered all my promises. Too faintly for her to hear. But they were there, shadows on her skin, waiting to be fulfilled.

The story of us.

Chapter Seventy

Gelsey
One year later

SEVENTEEN DEADBOLTS. KIDDING. IT JUST FELT LIKE THAT WHEN I WAS unlocking the door to our Fifth Avenue apartment.

Miles was still getting used to living in New York. And even though we resided in a safe building with a doorman and special key-cards to get to our floor, he wasn't taking any chances when it came to security.

We still had a bodyguard.

Sadly, it wasn't Daryl. He was back in Austin. Not that we had a chance to miss him, or anyone else, since we jetted home at least a couple of times a month.

Before I'd even pushed the door open, the sound of claws tapping against the hardwood coaxed a smile to my lips. Mac, our tiny chihuahua, careened around the corner, with Lennon, our bulldog, close on his heels.

Mac danced around on his hind legs, yapping his head off while Lennon waited patiently, milky eyes trained in my direction. At times, I swear he saw me. But that was impossible. Lennon had been born blind.

Miles had read a story about him online, chronicling Lennon's friendship with the chihuahua who'd taken him under his wing.

A week later we got a visit from the woman who ran the pet rescue where the boys were living.

Mrs. Clauson was a hard nut to crack, but crack she did.

After it became clear I'd fallen in love with the mutts, Miles had donated an ungodly sum to the Bulldog Rescue Society and agreed to let Mrs. Clauson drop by for "wellness checks" to assure we were fit parents.

Miles rounded the corner, shaking his head when he found me on the floor being licked to death.

"Leave your mother alone." Scooping Mac up with one hand, he tucked the squirming fur ball under his arm and offered me the other. I climbed to my feet and levered up on my toes to give him a kiss, but at the last second, he turned his head, offering his scruffy cheek instead.

"You smell like anchovies," he said, wrinkling his nose and casting a hard gaze at Lennon. "He got into the pizza. Again."

I groaned and followed Miles to the living room, glancing over the mangled box on the coffee table. "Please tell me that wasn't the only pizza. I'm starving."

A devilish smile curved his lips as he sauntered to the bookshelf where another box sat too high for anyone but a human to reach.

I parked a hand on my hip. "Why don't you just admit that you always order one for the boys."

He dropped the box onto the table. "That would make me a bad parent. Since dogs aren't supposed to eat people food."

I flipped open the shredded box. No cheese. All meat. And from the looks of it, a gluten-free crust. "That's not people food."

Just like the cookies in the jar in the kitchen. I found that out the hard way when I went searching for a midnight snack.

Apparently, Miles had the dog treats specially made at a bakery on the other side of the park. Pretty as the little cookies were, they tasted faintly of bacon and something else I couldn't identify.

Gross. But endearing.

Someday, Miles would make a wonderful father.

I was still daydreaming about a raven-haired little boy with my eyes and his father's smile, when Miles stretched out on the couch.

"So…" he drawled, running a hand over his bare chest. "Netflix and chill?"

He was wearing his favorite sweats. The ones that hung indecently low on his hips. And that smile.

Netflix, my ass.

Fiddling with the button on my blouse, I watched as his chocolate gaze turned molten. *Me.* I did that to him. "What kind of movie are you in the mood for?"

His eyes snapped to mine. "Huh?"

"Action? Rom-com?" Tugging my hair free from the bun, I closed the gap between us. "Drama?"

I squealed when he hooked an arm around my waist, pulling me down on top of him.

"Definitely action," he growled, his fingers inching toward the waistband of my yoga pants

My lids fluttered closed when our lips met in a soft kiss, only to fly open a second later when Mac muscled his way between us, dragging his leash behind him.

"Jesus," Miles groaned, throwing an arm over his face. "Not now, boy."

But it was too late. I was on my feet, hooking Lennon's leash to his collar.

This was our life. They one I'd dreamed of. Chaotic and messy and everything in between.

With a sigh, Miles hauled to his feet with Mac in his arms. Looping an arm around my shoulder, we headed to the door. To our bench in the park. And our sky.

Epilogue

Three years later.

GELSEY DROPPED ONTO HER SEAT ON THE JET, HER GAZE ON THE WINDOW. I tossed the tattered doggie bed in the usual spot, and Lennon and Mac quickly climbed on top, making themselves comfortable. Our pups were seasoned travelers, having visited almost every continent.

But now, we were going home. To Austin. For good.

Gelsey's final performance at the New York City Ballet had taken place last night. A standing-room-only crowd filled the theater, giving her a sendoff fit for a queen. Because she was. In three short years, she'd become ballet royalty.

Then, out of the blue six months ago, she'd announced her retirement.

I want to go home, Miles. Please, take me home.

The look on her face when she'd said it had sent chills down my spine. And a fear I'd never known.

I'd always kept my distance when it had come to Gelsey's career. Supporting her. But never encroaching.

But this time, I'd insisted on accompanying her to the specialist who'd kept a close watch on her condition since she'd moved here.

Gelsey had sat stoically while Dr. Thatcher had explained about the narrowing in her spine. The deterioration of the bones. The arthritis that had increasingly made it more painful to dance.

"Stop now, and you can lead a perfectly normal life. Teach. Have kids. But if you keep going…"

He'd let the threat dangle. But I knew what he'd tried not to put into words. Nerve damage. Partial paralysis. Or worse.

I didn't want to think about the *worse.*

Surprisingly, Gelsey had been upbeat about her decision. Until last night. She'd cried herself to sleep in the guest room, sobs wracking her body that she thought I couldn't hear.

But I had.

And now she was quiet, so fucking quiet, her gaze fixed out the window as the plane taxied down the runway.

The flight attendant rose from her seat when we reached our cruising altitude. But I caught her eye and shook my head. Her attention flicked to Gelsey, who hadn't moved a muscle, and she nodded, then closed the flimsy curtain.

Looping an arm around my girl, I pulled her to my side. "I'm sorry, baby."

Sniffling, she blinked up at me. "Why?"

Searching her face, I struggled to find the right words. I kissed her forehead. "Because you're sad, I guess."

She straightened, then let out a shuddering breath. "I'm not sad. It was time. I'm just going to miss it, that's all." Her lips fell into a frown as she glanced around the plane. "I'm going to miss this too."

Her tone held an edge of guilt. Even though she complained often about the carbon footprint, I knew she loved the jet. Which is the reason I'd agreed to purchase it when the lease was up. We still had plenty of places to see. Adventures to embark upon. And flying commercial was worse now than ever. Between Gelsey's fame and mine we couldn't go anywhere without being recognized. Even Mac and Lennon had Instagram profiles and Facebook pages with followers in the thousands.

Crazy.

"Come on," Gelsey said, climbing to her feet.

"Where are we going? I asked, already out of my seat. Because I knew. Gelsey confirmed it with a raised brow.

Mac and Lennon hopped up, trotting down the aisle toward the bedroom.

I grabbed their doggy bed and followed my girl, my dick already straining within the confines of my jeans.

"I'll be right back," Gelsey said as she levered up to press a kiss to my mouth. "Don't start without me."

"Not likely," I growled, pinching her pert little ass as she spun for the bathroom.

While she was gone, I set the doggie bed in its spot by the chair. It was the only place in the cabin where the boys wouldn't have a clear view of me defiling their mother. And defile her I would.

Lennon dropped onto the cushion, while Mac defiantly held his ground.

I pointed at the bulldog, ready to square off with the chihuahua. "Get into your bed with your brother."

Nothing.

"Mac," I warned, taking a menacing step. "I'm not kidding."

Still nothing.

Scratching my head, the bargaining phase of the process began. In reality, I was begging. Promising. Pleading.

The bathroom door swung open, and Mac's furry little mug swiveled in Gelsey's direction.

"Bed," she said firmly. "Now."

With what I swear was a nod, Mac jumped right onto the cushion and snuggled up next to his brother.

Shaking my head, I tugged off my T-shirt. "I have no idea how you do that," I grumbled, reaching for the button on my jeans.

Obstinate dogs aside, I was ready for some action. But Gelsey hadn't budged.

"What?" I asked, looking her up and down.

"I want to show you something."

Since that sounded promising, my grin widened.

"Just sit down," she said, rolling her eyes. And like Mac, I did as I was told. "Close your eyes."

I raised a brow, causing her to huff in frustration. For a moment, I considered resisting a while longer. "Frustrated Gelsey" was a wildcat in bed. But the look on her face told me it was a bad idea.

I closed my eyes.

"Now, hold out your hand."

Smirking, I offered her my palm.

"You can look now," she said.

Pressing my lips together, I examined the paper animal perched on my hand. Despite her best efforts, Gelsey had never gotten the hang of origami. I'd tried. Really, I had.

"It's...beautiful."

She narrowed her baby blues to slits. "Do you even know what it is?"

I took a closer look. *Fuck*. No idea. It sort of resembled a platypus. If the platypus had mated with a giraffe. "Uh..."

Sighing in defeat, she dropped down next to me with a thud. "Not even a guess?"

Regretfully, I shook my head. "Sorry, baby." I hooked my arm around her and pulled her in for a hug.

"I should've just given you the pee stick," she grumbled against my neck.

I went still, examining her creation for the third time. Long legs. And a beak.

"It's a stork?"

She smiled shyly, nodding.

"But I thought the doctor said it could take a while."

Gelsey had only gone off her birth control pills two months ago. And for a month after that, we'd used condoms to make sure the hormones were out of her system. Even though the doctor had said Gelsey's chances of getting pregnant off the bat were slim.

"Guess doctors don't know everything," she said with a shrug.

I took her mouth in a kiss, grateful and happy. So fucking happy.

"Wait. Is that why you said you were going to miss this?" I asked, sweeping my hand around at the cabin.

Pink bloomed in her cheeks as she nodded.

I bit back my laugh as I aimed a glance at the boys, both snoring quietly in their bed. "Any baby of ours, little mouse, is going to have their passport before they get their first tooth." Sliding my arms around her, I eased her back onto the mattress. "You'll never even have a *chance* to miss this."

As she slanted her lips over mine, I slid my hand to her belly. A baby. A life.

Outside the small window, a cloudless sky. Our sky. Fucking perfect. In every way.

Jayne Said

Thank you so much for reading ANOTHER SKY. Technically, this isn't a part of the Sixth Street Bands Series, but I couldn't help but sprinkle a few characters into some of the scenes.

Since I always get personal at the end of every book, here goes.

Depression.

Where to start?

I've always been a little bit depressive. Not like Miles. Or, maybe, since we never know what someone else is feeling. Let's just say, I've never thought of ending my life. I love my life. My family. My daughter. But that's not to say that people who love their families don't commit suicide.

My husband's best friend loved his family. He loved his wife. And his parents. His friends.

That didn't stop him from blowing his head off one sunny, summer morning. While his wife was on the phone with him.

This happened a long time ago. I was twenty-one, my husband twenty-three. And we'd just seen Billy two days prior. He came by and asked to borrow a hundred dollars to take his wife to a fancy dinner. They were having marital problems. That happens in every marriage, but I guess he didn't see that. He thought the dinner would fix everything. It didn't.

So, he went home to his parent's house that night, while she stayed in their apartment. And the next morning he *did it*. The big "IT" that you can't take back. The permanent solution to a temporary problem.

His wife, my very good friend, called that morning after it happened. Minutes after. In shock. My husband answered and mouthed "Vicky," (that is her name) when I asked who it was.

Being my smart-ass self, I replied, "Tell her to make sure Billy pays us back that hundred bucks!"

That's what I said. I said that. Because I didn't know.

My husband's face fell a second later. Slid right off and dropped to the floor. And then he told me. And nothing was ever the same.

It was one of those watershed moments. Those stitches in time that scar and shape you forever. Billy was gone. I would never hear him laugh again. Feel his hug. Listen to his stupid stories. Billy would never have children or know my daughter.

Because he wasn't here anymore.

I wanted to give Miles a better ending to his story than Billy had. The happily ever after that Billy didn't get. Because there is hope. There is a sunny sky...somewhere. You just have to get help. To believe. And that belief has to be stronger than any fleeting thought whispering promises of oblivion.

If you know someone suffering from depression, please help them. In any way you can. Listen to them. Be with them. Find them when they're lost. Even if they're right beside you.

National Suicide Prevention Lifeline: 1-800-273-8255

Acknowledgments

Jeff … Words and music, baby.

Maria … There are too many things to thank you for. You are so much more than the best designer in the business. You're my greatest champion. Best friend. Reader of all my words, when they're merely thoughts. Love you from the bottom of my heart.

Patricia … You're the best editor on the planet. I'm not just saying that. I couldn't do any of this without you. Love you.

Marla Esposito … Thank you for accommodating my crazy schedule. I keep saying I'm going to get better. Spoiler alert: I probably won't.

My Beta Readers … Christy, Megan, Jenny. Y'all rock! Thank you so much!

Astrid … Thank you for all the late night talks and support. You are truly dear to me. Love you.

Heather … Thank you for devouring all my words. Your support means everything.

Candi Kane … You're the best. Thank you for putting up with me. Someday I'll make a schedule…and stick to it. Maybe

Alyson Santos … You make me jealous with your pretty words. Can I be you when I grow up? All the love.

Jill Bengtsson … I couldn't think of a better partner in crime. You're a wonderful storyteller. Love you!

Frost's Faves … I cherish each and every one of you. Thank you for all your support. The posts and the pictures keep me going. Y'all are the best of the best!

And to all my readers…. Thank you isn't a strong enough word. You've made all my dreams come true. And I couldn't be more grateful or humbled by your support.

SIXTH STREET BANDS SERIES

The Sixth Street Bands is a series of **standalone** rock star romances with recurring characters. While it is not necessary to read the books in order, I hope that you do. You won't regret the time you spend in the Sixth Street world

GONE FOR YOU | BOOK 1
FALL WITH ME | BOOK 2
MISSING FROM ME | BOOK 3

Audiobook available at Audible
Narrated by Jacob Morgan and Elena Wolfe

LOST FOR YOU | BOOK 4
Audiobook available on Audible
Narrated by Jacob Morgan and Elena Wolfe

DOWN TO YOU | BOOK 5
Audiobook available at Audible
Narrated by Jacob Morgan and Ava Erickson

BOX SET
The CAGED BOX SET | Books 1-5 in the Sixth Street Bands Series

About the Author

Jayne Frost, author of the Sixth Street Bands Romance Series, grew up in California with a dream of moving to Seattle to become a rock star. When the grunge thing didn't work out (she never even made it to the Washington border) Jayne set her sights on Austin, Texas. After quickly becoming immersed in the Sixth Street Music scene … and discovering she couldn't actually sing, Jayne decided to do the next best thing—write kick ass romances about hot rock stars and the women who steal their hearts.

Made in the USA
San Bernardino,
CA

MY WORLD STOPPED TURNING SIX YEARS AGO.

MY BEST FRIEND. MY BEST GIRL.

A BURNING FIELD IN THE POURING RAIN.

I SURVIVED, BUT I LEFT THE BIGGEST PART OF ME WITH THE

AND NOW I SIFT THROUGH THE RUBBLE OF MY BROKEN LIFE

I DIDN'T WANT A SECOND CHANCE.

REDEMPTION. CLOSURE.

NOT FOR ME.

UNTIL GELSEY.

A DANCER. A DREAMER. EVERYTHING I'M NOT.

SHE'S THE LIGHT TO MY DARK.

THE SUN FROM ANOTHER SKY.

BUT SUNNY DAYS NEVER LAST.

THE STORM IS COMING.

AND THIS TIME WHEN DARKNESS FALLS,

I MIGHT SURRENDER.

ISBN 9781075338182